THE
SISTER
IN LAW

BOOKS BY SUE WATSON

Love, Lies and Lemon Cake
Snow Angels, Secrets and Christmas Cake
Summer Flings and Dancing Dreams
Fat Girls and Fairy Cakes
Younger Thinner Blonder
Bella's Christmas Bake Off
We'll Always have Paris
The Christmas Cake Café
Ella's Ice Cream Summer
Curves, Kisses and Chocolate Ice Cream
Snowflakes, Iced Cakes and Second Chances
Love, Lies and Wedding Cake
Our Little Lies
The Woman Next Door
The Empty Nest

THE
SISTER
IN LAW

SUE WATSON

Bookouture

Published by Bookouture in 2020

An imprint of Storyfire Ltd.
Carmelite House
50 Victoria Embankment
London EC4Y 0DZ

www.bookouture.com

ISBN: 978-1-83888-508-3
eBook ISBN: 978-1-83888-268-6

To Sharon Beswick, my friend and fellow Northerner,
who lives too far away under a hotter sun.

PROLOGUE

I looked down onto the pool, trying to make sense of what I thought I could see in the water. Long hair billowing out, opening and closing slowly like a golden parachute, her body floating on the bright, bright blue.

I sometimes wonder – if I'd known what was going to happen last summer, would I have gone? Would I have taken my family to that whitewashed villa on the Amalfi Coast where secrets were spilled and lives imploded in the beautiful, dreadful heat? But then – how could I have known what malevolent thing would fly in on the citrus-scented breeze and transform all our lives forever?

A year on and I remember the details so clearly. The way she smelled like salt and lemons. The way her skin shone gold, and the way she laughed, throwing back her head, white teeth bared, lost in the moment. I sometimes hear her voice: honeyed, and sickly-sweet, even when she said the cruellest things. I think I see her sometimes, disappearing around a corner in the supermarket, ahead of me in the queue at the post office, walking with me through the park on cold autumn mornings. Slipping through the dark trees, she's suddenly there, shrouding me in guilt and fear – reminding me of what happened. She finds me, she always finds me.

And no matter where I go, I know she'll always be there, my sister for a season, my nemesis, the woman who changed everything.

CHAPTER ONE

It was only a year ago, yet it seems like a lifetime since we drove along the spectacular Italian coast road, and I felt my stress unfurling behind me like a long, floaty scarf. Danger was the last thing on my mind as I abandoned my angst to the pristine white clouds gobbling up the debris of daily life. Even the fringe of fear that had recently been edging around my stomach was slowly being nibbled away.

Dan was with me, the children were on the back seat all fast asleep, and I remember thinking, *I have everything I need now, here in this car, and no one can take it from me.* We needed this break, I was excited at the prospect of spending time together as a family – two whole weeks of fun and no worries. I couldn't wait to play with the children, eat tonnes of pasta and lie under that hot sun. Most of all, I looked forward to me and Dan just spending time together, talking about everything and nothing, enjoying each other's company, remembering why we were together.

I turned away and gazed out of the passenger window. 'You have to work at a marriage; the best marriages don't just happen,' my mother-in-law had said. And she was right. Joy was always right.

Dan was driving too fast again. I clutched the passenger seat with one hand and my seat belt with the other, but didn't comment. I didn't want to spoil the mood so tried to focus on the shimmer of heat rising from the road ahead. My inner voice was begging him to slow down, our children were sleeping on the back seat, this was precious cargo. The winding roads were too narrow for more than one car, and I held my breath as we swept along, climbing up into the hillside rising above the glittering sea now. I stopped myself from saying anything about his speed. I would feel like a killjoy – the nagging wife as opposed to the sexy carefree one I wanted to be.

But, after fifteen years of marriage, we sometimes communicated without words, and when he glanced over, Dan must have caught the panic on my face.

'So, you don't like doing 100 miles an hour on high coastal roads?' he said, with a smile. 'Weird.'

'No, I bloody don't,' I laughed, 'and I'm not *weird*,' I added, slapping his arm affectionately. 'We might be in Italy, but you're not part of the Ferrari team and this isn't a race track.'

'A boy can dream.' He glanced over at me and smiled, squeezing my knee affectionately.

'Eyes on the road and both hands on the wheel please,' I said in mock indignation, leaving his hand on my knee, enjoying his attention. With three children under ten, a hand on my knee was as close to foreplay as it got for us, but I was sure this holiday would put everything right.

I turned around again to check the three perfect, sleeping faces on the back seat and was, as always, filled with a rush of love.

'Can't believe they're being so considerate and sleeping in sync,' I said. 'Such delicious peace, but it's almost *too* quiet.'

'Not for long. We'll be there soon, and then they'll wake up. Let's enjoy the peace,' he said, his eyes on the road. 'I can't wait, big pool, loads of vino, big blue sky – chasing them round the pool,' he said, gesturing to the back seat with his head, and finally slamming on the brakes. I felt sick.

'You're still going quite fast, Dan,' I said in an attempt at a light-hearted voice, sheathed in panic. Dan wasn't usually a fast driver, it felt dangerous – *he* felt dangerous. Was he becoming a middle-aged thrill seeker? My thoughts flickered briefly to my friend Jackie's husband, who bought a sports car and left her for a teenager.

Eventually, Dan slowed down and I relaxed slightly, enjoying the gorgeous view, as we climbed higher up the mountain road.

We were spending our annual holiday, as always, with Dan's family, his parents and brother. This year was something of a watershed as Dan's parents, Joy and Bob, had decided to retire from the family business and wouldn't be returning to work after our two weeks away. Dan had been part of the company for twenty years, but now as their parents stepped down, his younger brother Jamie had suddenly decided to come home and join 'the firm'.

Now thirty-two, Jamie never been involved in the family business, a small property company on the outskirts of Manchester. He was too busy seeing the world and on visits home would enthral everyone with colourful and probably exaggerated stories from Nepal, Thailand, Africa, the coasts of Australia, the killing fields of Cambodia. It was all a far cry from Dan, who'd gone straight into the family business that recently he'd worked hard to keep afloat. Meanwhile, their parents indulged their youngest son, allowing him such freedom, tempered only with an affectionate eye roll whenever his latest 'adventure' was mentioned.

'My free-spirited son won't be pinned down,' Joy would say, feigning frustration but glowing with pride. She missed him dearly when he was away but was delighted when he FaceTimed her from some exotic destination, always brandishing his Instagram photos for anyone who cared to look – and even those who didn't.

'I just don't get the complete turnaround. Why on earth has our Jamie suddenly decided to give it all up to work at Taylor's with me? It won't last,' Dan was saying as we headed for the villa.

'Mmm, no beaches, no exotic food, no gorgeous women in bikinis – what on earth will he do?' I sighed, thinking of the photos of Jamie, a montage of blue skies, beaches and beautiful people.

I understood Dan's slight resentment; his little brother's lifestyle seemed rather selfish, not least because his parents often had to help him financially. The Taylors were what Joy described as 'comfortable'. They weren't rich and, understandably, Dan resented the way his parents gave his brother handouts. But Jamie was still Joy's 'baby', and she and Bob would do anything for their two sons. Joy missed Jamie terribly when he was travelling, and when he didn't call or text for a while she'd pore over his social media, hungry for titbits. 'I can always find my Jamie on his Instagram,' she'd say, like he'd set up his photographic account for her personal use. She'd delight in some photo of Jamie on a beach in Cambodia and be amazed when he turned up on the doorstep. 'But your photo says you're here,' she'd exclaim, holding up her phone, and he'd point out that it was posted days ago and she'd laugh and shake her head in wonder at 'my Jamie' and his online 'magic'. I reckon she knew exactly what was going on, it was all part of the game she played with her 'boys': a way of making them feel special, superior even. I was never sure with Joy who was playing who – though I think it's safe to say that despite appearing as the ingenue, Joy was usually in the driving seat.

'I spoke to your mum yesterday before we left, she says the villa's lovely. They got here about eight last night,' I said, as we continued along the Italian coastline. 'I just hope they take time to relax and kick back a bit,' I said wistfully. This was an impossible dream for me. As well as being a full-time nurse and mum, I also maintained Taylor's website, which sometimes felt like another job. Consequently, relaxing was sadly not on my daily agenda while at home, but for the next fortnight I wasn't going to do a thing, and the website could wait.

'Imagine Dad being with Mum all day when they retire, she'll never let him rest.' Dan smiled, shaking his head slightly at the thought.

'He'll be being dispatched to Sainsbury's for sun-dried tomatoes or pickled figs or whatever it is she's giving the ladies who lunch that day,' I added.

He glanced over and we smiled knowingly at each other.

'They don't have much in common, do they? I sometimes wonder what they actually talk to each other about, your mum and dad.'

Dan shrugged. 'What do *any* couple talk to each other about?'

My heart stung a little at this. Is that how he saw us too, as *any* couple? Did he see us like his parents, an old married couple with little in common? I didn't have time to hurt for too long, as he negotiated a tight corner. Too fast.

'Dan, please slow down,' I said. 'The kids are in the back. What's wrong with you?'

I saw his jaw tighten, but he did slow down.

The drive from the airport at Naples to our villa was, according to the satnav, just over an hour. We'd gone from the bustling city to glimpses of calm, glittery ocean and now we were climbing up the steep hillside past vineyards. Canopies of feathery green leaves in every shade of green played hide-and-seek with the sun.

Between the trees, the sea appeared now and again below us, shimmering in the dusk – how beautiful it was. I remember feeling a rush of excitement for the fortnight ahead. I couldn't wait to swim with Dan and the children, cook lovely food with Joy, and spend long afternoons all together in the sunshine. Our lives were so busy that this would be a rare chance to talk, spend time with the children, and Dan's parents too. It was going to be wonderful, just what we all needed. My real priority this holiday was getting Freddie used to water and teaching Alfie to swim.

My dad had taught me to swim in the local baths. We'd go every Saturday afternoon and, one Saturday, on my ninth summer, I swam a whole length. I remember feeling like an Olympian, my feet off the ground, my arms splashing and heaving me forward,

Dad cheering me on. The following winter he was killed when his lorry took the wrong turning on an icy road.

Mum never got over my Dad's death and our lives changed overnight. At nine my childhood ended and I spent the following ten years mopping up her grief, until she died herself. It was cancer, but I knew really it was a broken heart, and at the age of nineteen I was an orphan, alone with no family. Until I met Dan, and the Taylors.

CHAPTER TWO

A little voice from the back of the car suddenly punctured my thoughts. It was Violet, my nine-year-old, who, as the oldest child, was responsible, sensible and slightly anxious. 'Are we there yet?' The sunlight caught her long, golden hair as we drove through the trees, and I took a moment to look at her, my little girl was growing up.

'Not far now, darling,' Dan said soothingly.

'Are Granny and Granddad already at the villa?'

'Yes.' I turned to smile at her, her fretful little face pale from waking somewhere strange. 'They arrived yesterday, sweetie. Granny says it's a lovely villa. Boys, boys.' I touched Alfie's leg. 'Try to wake up, we're almost there.'

Four-year-old Alfie stirred, still half-asleep, but, at two, Freddie was unable to process waking up in the back of a strange car and started to cry. Alfie told him to 'Shut up!' Then Violet told Alfie to 'Leave him alone,' and as they began an argument, Freddie's cries just got louder and louder. Oh, the joy of having three children. When they were excited and happy, it was an overload of wonderful bubbling happiness, but when they were grumpy or tired, they just endlessly ricocheted off each other.

I dreamed of just five minutes' peace, and the luxury of reading an uninterrupted chapter of a book or the heady prospect of a lone toilet visit, which could make me dizzy with desire.

I turned around to offer calming words to the passengers on the back seat. 'Not long now! Tell me what you see out of the window?' I asked, hopefully, and the boys started shouting about trees and rocks. Then Alfie said he'd seen a dinosaur and Violet said he was stupid and another vigorous argument ensued.

'Good job, Clare,' Dan laughed.

'I'd like to see you do better,' I said and stuck out my tongue, which he caught a glimpse of and smiled at. 'Come on now, kids, calm down,' I said gently and, going against all the parenting bloggers' advice, made vague promises of a swim and ice cream on arrival if everyone behaved. The bickering immediately melted as Violet excitedly told the boys she'd be having 'strawberry ice cream with sprinkles'. Alfie suggested 'mashed frog flavour' and collapsed into fits of laughter, before Violet informed him, 'That isn't a flavour, stupid.'

Smiling, I turned back to look through the window, just as we drove past a gaggle of young women in shorts and realised with a jolt that, at forty-one, I was probably old enough to be their mother. I envied their relaxed, youthful beauty, and all that 'me time' we don't appreciate until we have kids. I was once like them, but now I didn't even get chance to shave my legs. Long gone were the days of a pre-holiday bikini wax, whole body exfoliation, followed by fake tan and a glam new summer wardrobe. I really should have made time to shave my legs though. I could almost hear Joy's voice. 'Good grooming is the best gift a woman can give to herself – and her husband,' she'd once told me. She'd meant it as a piece of motherly advice, and I loved her for it, but Joy's advice on marriage was decades out of date. I hoped these days we were evolved enough for our partner's feelings not to be altered by the state of one's leg hair growth. I wondered if Dan would even notice my hairy legs. I doubted it, and they weren't exactly a priority for me either. Whatever Joy's Stepford advice on a wife's good grooming, no one died because they didn't shave their legs or wear lipstick. For the next two weeks, I was going to slob around as much as I wanted, and not waste precious time applying make-up or de-fuzzing my body.

Finally, we pulled onto the steep gravel driveway of the villa that would be our holiday home for the next two weeks. Tucked between the sea and the mountains, the large three-storey villa looked like it had once been rather grand, but the crumbling white paintwork showed the ravages of sea air.

Dan had barely put the handbrake on when I leapt out of the car door and walked towards the trees for a better look around. The air was still bubbling with the day's heat, especially after the cool air con of the car, but there was a faint breeze coming from the coast below, and it tasted of salt, tinged with pine. The garden was framed by cypress trees, and beyond was a bright turquoise mosaic tiled pool and, further still, a spectacular ocean view that in the dusk had opened up into a million shades of blue, melting into golds.

I wanted those first moments alone, just me taking it all in, breathing in the clean, quiet air in anticipation of what was to come. While Dan helped the kids to disembark, I took this moment for myself and held it, like a butterfly in the palm of my hand, until it flew away, disappearing into the last fragments of the day's sun.

After about ninety seconds of peace – a long time for me – the children began their vigorous campaign. 'Mummy, Mummy…'; 'Mummy, can I have…?'; 'You said we could…'; You *promised…*' And so it began.

Alerted by the children's eager voices, Joy suddenly appeared, freshly lipsticked and powdered, Bob ambling behind, smiling in anticipation.

'Hello! Welcome! Oh, I'm glad you're all here safe and sound,' Joy said, as she hugged us all. She smelled of damp roses.

Bob was his typical warm self. His usual refrain of 'lovely, lovely' could be heard as he hugged us all, visibly delighted to have his family around him again.

'Come on, Clare, let's leave the men to carry those heavy cases. Let me show you the garden,' Joy urged, grabbing me by the elbow and guiding me through an archway of green while Bob helped Dan with the luggage.

The kids danced around and the men's talk of roads and journey comparisons faded as Joy and I headed towards the large garden, now sinking into twilight. Always aware, I carried Freddie, while calling for Violet to keep an eye on Alfie near the pool, while Joy pointed at the bougainvillea smothering the Italian tiled doorway. 'The colour!' she gasped loudly. I marvelled at it and, as the kids screeched excitedly around the pool, she talked about what we'd eat and the wonderful recipes she'd discovered since our last holiday the previous year. We both enjoyed discussing and dissecting recipes and loved cooking. It was something that bonded us, something I'd once shared with my own mum, and in her own way, Joy had been there for me. 'I'll never be your mum, but I'll be the closest I can,' she'd said to me at our wedding. Her kindness had made me cry, but she was there with a tissue to save my make-up. Just like a mother. In the years since, she'd kept to her promise, and times when I'd been desperate for support, she'd stepped in and been the mother I needed.

'I'm preparing risotto for tonight,' she said as we admired the garden together. She said risotto in an Italian voice. She'd never said it like that before, had probably heard a waiter in the previous evening's restaurant. Joy was a chameleon. Having grown up in a working-class family with no money, aspiration was in her DNA and she sometimes sat rather awkwardly between two worlds. Her life seemed divided into past and present. Bob was her penniless teenage sweetheart who'd eventually been able to provide her with the life she felt she deserved and given her access to a different world. And though they weren't hugely wealthy, she'd certainly moved up in the world – a detached house with the same postcode as Manchester United footballers in Cheshire is considered royalty when you're from a backstreet terrace.

Over the years, Joy had transformed herself, hiding her roots under good tailoring and listening to the other ladies who lunched, emulating their voices, mannerisms and old-fashioned ideals. Men were meant for two things in Joy's world: making money and lifting heavy stuff. Everything else was left to 'us girls'. Meanwhile, Bob had been too busy making money to put on a tie or lose his northern vowels, but somehow they rubbed along.

'Muuum, can we swim now?' Violet was calling me from the other side of the large pool.

'Oh darling, I'm not sure…'

'Pleeeeeeease,' she started, which set the other two off.

I was too tired from travelling to argue, and wanted an easy transition into the villa that night, so within seconds I'd given in.

'Okay,' I sighed, with a roll of my eyes. 'I have to go and supervise,' I said to Joy. I was wearing jeans and a T-shirt – if I rolled up my jeans and kept the children in the shallow end, I could paddle with them.

'Oh, darling, don't you think it's a little late for them to swim?' Joy said pointedly. This was a rhetorical question as if I was expected to agree with her and simply announce my change of mind to the children. It was a long time since Joy had had children, and she sometimes seemed to forget that a broken promise could mean the start of World War Three. As indomitable as Joy could be in the face of disobedience, three frustrated kids on the verge of tears was far more daunting to me.

I could see this was an inconvenience for Joy who was no doubt ready for her gin and tonic. 'It's never too early for a drink, the sun is always over the yardarm somewhere in the world,' was her holiday mantra most afternoons. And as hard as she tried to hide her feelings now, she couldn't. Her lips locked together like she'd sucked a tart lemon. She'd had in her mind the perfect image of her grandchildren, like a photograph, sun shining through their blonde hair like halos. She expected them to be sweet and biddable, have supper, go to bed and fit into her plans without a quibble. But, sadly for her, the kids didn't get the memo.

As lovely as she was, there were times when none of us quite came up to Joy's expectations, even her precious grandchildren, and this wasn't how she'd planned our arrival. She held her hands together tightly over her stomach like if she didn't anchor them down she might be forced to swim too. Poor Joy looked in pain. She loved our girlie get-togethers on holiday, as did I, but with the men busy unloading the car, we were on children duty until Dan appeared or the kids were safely inside. As much as I wanted to, I couldn't be her gin-drinking companion yet. On the other side of the pool, Alfie was already stripping off.

'No, Alfie, not at that end,' I said, 'it's deep. Come over here.' I headed off in his direction, looking back at Joy apologetically, while she smiled but raised her eyebrows in vague disapproval. 'Alfie wait... stop!' I shouted, as he continued to take off his clothes, throwing them in the air like he was bloody Magic Mike. 'Alfie, if you don't come to the shallow end NOW, you will *have* to come inside,' I said, in an attempt to show him who was boss.

'NO!' he shouted, following up with a slight change of tack. '*Muuum...*' He began an elongated whine.

'You *promised* we could swim,' said Violet, finishing off her sibling's sentence from the other side of the garden.

'You haven't even looked around yet. Wouldn't you like to see inside first?' Joy called to Violet, who wasn't buying the blatant attempt at distraction and didn't answer. 'Mum and I are going inside,' Joy then threatened, presumably hoping they'd abandon the pool in favour of viewing the interior decorations – she had no clue.

I looked from her to Alfie, now standing precariously on the edge of the pool, totally naked, while Violet stood in the shallow end waiting for me. Maybe part of me *would* have liked to follow Joy in and see inside, to wander into the beautiful villa, drinking an ice-cold G and T with a bright wedge of lemon while she gave me the tour. But, damn it, my four-year-old was standing precariously close to 6 feet of water.

'It's a little late, Clare, are you really allowing them to swim *now*?' she asked through perfectly painted lips.

'I promised,' I offered apologetically, but before she could respond, there was a loud smack followed by a terrifying silence.

CHAPTER THREE

A terrifying deathly silence as Alfie disappeared was followed by the equally terrifying rush of loud, intermittent screaming, as he desperately tried to get his breath in 6 feet of water. Everything felt like it was in slow motion. I was focussed only on one thing and barely saw or heard anything else. I was vaguely aware of Joy open-mouthed watching him, as I instinctively dumped Freddie in her arms. I powered across the ground to the side of the pool to reach my drowning four-year-old, jumping in fully clothed and gathering every ounce of strength I had I grabbed my little boy, lifted him from the depths and dragged him up to the surface. I held his sobbing face above the water as he tried to breathe and cry and call 'Mummy!' all at the same time, and I thought I might have a heart attack, but that didn't matter, I just had to get him to safety.

Eventually, with a little help from Joy, we both climbed out. She was still holding Freddie and had already instructed Violet to run inside and get towels.

I hugged him close. I wanted to cry, to hold him forever and just sob with relief, but I also had to stop him from doing this ever again and so channelled my tears into stern words once he'd recovered slightly.

'Alfie, that was *so* naughty,' I said, removing my wet T shirt and jeans and taking a towel from Joy. 'You could have really hurt yourself, and Mummy's very cross.' I frowned to make my feelings clear.

'Told you we should have gone inside for gin,' Joy said under her breath. She was white with shock as I'm sure I was too.

'Yep, you were right, Joy,' I murmured back.

'So, Alfie, what have we just learned?' Joy asked gently.

'Not to get wet?' His little chin was trembling – it had scared him.

'I think what Granny means is you just learned that you must never jump into the water like that without a grown-up there, or your armbands on. It's too deep. You won't ever do that again, will you, Alfie?' I added.

He shook his head vigorously. I just hoped it had scared him enough to be careful, but not so much he wouldn't want to go near water ever again.

'I think we should all go inside, so you can choose your beds,' Joy said to the kids, once Alfie and I had taken off our clothes and were wrapped in towels. In that moment, I was grateful to have Joy around, even if she did take over a little. Within minutes, the children were racing up the stairs, Alfie's near-death experience forgotten. By him at least.

'Hold Freddie's hand tight on them stairs,' Bob called to Violet from the landing where he and Dan were still sorting the luggage.

'*Those* stairs, darling,' Joy corrected, as Violet negotiated Freddie up the steps, Alfie following on, as my mother-in-law and I watched from the bottom of the stairs.

Bob rolled his eyes at me and I smiled. 'You and Alfie been for a swim already?' Bob asked, looking from me to Alfie. Joy and I watched on from the hallway and glanced at each other.

'Don't ask, Bob.' I smiled.

'Yes, let's put it this way, it's gin time for Clare and Daddy time for our Dan,' Joy laughed, leading me into the sitting room.

I just hoped Dan would supervise the chaos and arguments that were bound to happen when the kids reached the top of the stairs and one wanted the other one's chosen bed. Bob didn't have the speed or stamina to handle that, but Joy wasn't fretting, she'd handed our charges to 'the men' and was now settling in an armchair with her glass. She'd put mine on a coaster on a little tray table next to the chair nearest to her, and I plonked myself down, still wrapped in a big grey towel, taking the ice-cold gin gratefully.

'How is *everything*?' she asked, conspiratorially.

'Good,' I answered quickly. I wanted to embrace the holiday feeling and forget about our recent troubles. Joy liked to poke her nose in, but really it was only because she worried about us all.

'You and Dan just ask us if you want to escape to a bar or something,' she said, nodding slowly. 'And Jamie's arriving tomorrow,' she added. 'I can't wait to see him, we haven't spoken for weeks.'

'But you're keeping up with his Instagram?' I said. I also followed Jamie and knew he'd recently been in India. I sometimes messaged him, but not for a while. Life was too busy.

'Yes, looks like he's having a whale of a time,' she said, smiling at the thought of her youngest son. 'You haven't seen him since Christmas have you; the three of you have lots to catch up on. Bob and I can keep an eye on the children if you three would like a night out one evening?'

'Yes, that would be nice,' I said. It was nice to get together, just the three of us without Joy or Bob. We could talk about anything and everything and we always had a laugh.

One year when we were in Spain and I'd just had Violet, the three of us went to a nightclub and left her with Joy and Bob. We enjoyed each other's company and made a point of getting together on these family holidays and family Christmases. Despite some brotherly competition and 'banter', as they called it, Dan and his brother got along, and I enjoyed spending time with them both. Jamie could be lazy, staying in bed until noon and never helping with meals or washing up, but he was good with the kids, and when he did eventually get up, he had lots of energy – something poor old Bob didn't have too much of any more.

I always worried the kids were a bit much for Bob. The previous summer, we'd gone to the South of France and when Violet asked to see the sunflowers in a nearby field, Bob had offered to take her and Alfie. I was more than a bit concerned Alfie might run off and Bob would be so distracted by what they were looking at that he'd not realise he was a child down. My only hope was that Violet, then eight, would keep an eye on her three-year-old brother. I remember I couldn't relax until they were back and found myself actually surprised when they all wandered up the hill to the villa, Alfie on Bob's shoulders, Violet chatting away, all three of them smiling.

I'd been sitting with Joy in the garden and I recall her looking over at me. 'Bob is fine,' she'd said. 'I know he can seem like he's another child, and God knows I sometimes wonder how he gets through the day, but he adores those kids. He'd never let them come to any harm, Clare.'

I remember feeling embarrassed that Joy had picked up on my concern, like I didn't trust him with his own grandchildren. Mind you she picked up on most things. I sometimes felt like she could read my mind – so I wasn't surprised.

This year I hoped Dan would be more involved and this would free me up more to relax – so I could be a bit more like the laid-back woman he once married. I knew this was his holiday too but I sometimes felt he expected his parents to take on the childcare when we were away. I'd pointed out to him that we couldn't expect that of them, they were getting older and Alfie and Freddie were exhausting.

'I have discovered a book of fabulous recipes,' Joy said, as we sat in the living room while the kids chose their beds upstairs. I'd heard some raised little voices, but they sounded more excited than angry, so I concentrated on the nice clinking sound Joy's drink made as she sloshed her gin and ice around the glass.

'Ooh a new recipe book? I'm up for that, chef,' I joked. We'd always cooked together on holiday, Joy and I. She was a great cook and I'd learned a lot from her, but it was more than that, it was ritualistic: the women of the house coming together. It was as we sliced meat, prepared vegetables, talked about recipes, the food we'd cooked before, the food we'd cook again, that we were closest. We had a shared culinary history, something I'd never had with my own mother, and I relished it. In the cosy warmth of Christmas in Joy's kitchen we'd ponder over the temperature of the turkey, debate the quantity of herbs in the stuffing. And now, in the midsummer heat of a Mediterranean kitchen, we'd fill the air with talk and steam and garlic. And later, when the food was in the oven, the children with the men, Joy would reach into the fridge, loosen some ice cubes, grab two glasses and we'd find a little spot to drink gin together. Like clockwork. 'Come on, let's have a livener before everyone comes back,' she'd say, and we'd clink our glasses and share our stories. She was at her absolute best then, in those golden moments. Here was a woman who loved my husband and my kids as much as I did. We were fighting the same battle, facing the same problems – we were united.

Food always played a central part in the family holidays and get-togethers, an opportunity for us all to sit round the table while Joy reigned at the head.

Every Christmas Eve we'd arrive at Joy and Bob's big house for a sparkly Christmas with all the trimmings. One year, Violet had a terrible cold, but Joy wouldn't hear of us staying home. 'Wrap her up warm and dose her up with Calpol, Clare,' she'd said. 'You can't miss the family Christmas.' But I didn't want to take her out into the cold and unsettle Alfie, and I pointed this out to Dan, who said, 'It wouldn't be Christmas if we weren't with Mum and Dad.' Then he'd added, 'It would break Mum's heart if we didn't spend it with them.' I'd given in, and within a couple of hours Violet had been revived. It was as if Joy had the power to will the perfect Christmas. Nothing got in her way – and she was always right.

The holidays were the same, family occasions organised, paid for and enthusiastically booked by Joy. And here we were on the Amalfi Coast in Italy, somewhere I'd always longed to visit, and so far it was just as beautiful as I'd imagined it would be.

Sitting drinking gin with my mother-in-law was a pleasure, not least because she always drank the best, and was good company. Daughters-in-law often have strained relationships with their husband's mothers, and it wasn't plain sailing, but apart from a slightly bossy nature, Joy was okay. On that first evening in Italy it was hot and the I was exhausted, emotionally and physically, and as Joy talked, I put my head back in the leather armchair. It felt good to be here, and the villa was lovely. The thick, high walls of the living room were painted white, and filled with big velvet sofas, built-in cabinets in beautiful dark wood, huge lamps and pictures all over the walls. But there were darker touches too – a birdcage filled with a stuffed bird whose dead, black beady eyes seemed to reproach me every time I caught its glance. It made me slightly uncomfortable, but was a small thing and the vaulted ceilings, wooden shutters and cool, marble floors more than compensated.

'There's a lovely boutique Margaret told me about, just off the—' Joy was saying.

'Great!' I said, not convinced the kids would enjoy a day's boutique shopping, but I didn't like to say no to her. I just didn't want to disappoint her. It was the same with Dan and Bob, even Jamie – we all wanted to make Joy happy, she was just that kind of person.

I remember the first time Dan took me home to meet his mother, I'd felt that I'd seen disappointment in her eyes. I'd met Dan one Saturday afternoon when he came into A & E where I worked as a nurse. He'd brought his friend in who'd been injured after a particularly vigorous game of rugby and our eyes met over a plaster cast. I was young, single, just out of college and Dan was good-looking, with dark hair, huge brown eyes and his concern for his friend was really quite endearing. So having sat in the waiting room on a plastic chair for several hours for his friend, he asked for my phone number, and I gave it to him. He called me the next day and asked me out. I liked his sense of humour, the way he held himself, and, on our first date, the way he held me. I first met Joy and Bob for drinks at their home; it was summer and we were in their huge garden. A diminutive blonde with pearly pink lips, Joy shook my hand, and pulled her soft grey pashmina around her, as if to keep out the non-existent chill.

According to Dan, his mother had hoped to matchmake him with one of her friend's daughters who had a horse and a private education. I felt like I had to work hard if I wanted her approval, which I did, because I wanted Dan, and I knew even then that Joy had a ladylike, but nevertheless strong, hold on both her sons. She wasn't an easy challenge, and I doubt I charmed her in the early days with my mousy hair and lack of glamour. I was almost on a par with poor old Bob, who even at that first dinner was being told not to lick his knife. But after a few more get-togethers, she began to thaw and perhaps realise I was good for Dan, and most importantly, had no plans to leave the area and take him away from her. Why would I? I longed for stability and family, and in the absence of my own mother was glad to take Joy's advice on anything and everything – even my wedding dress.

But what I didn't know back then, as we considered white or ivory against my skin and pondered the toppings for the wedding breakfast profiteroles, was that there'd be spikes along the road ahead. And if someone had warned me, I wouldn't have listened. I truly believed that my happiness was complete as I walked down the aisle, greeted by my handsome groom, and welcomed into his loving family. But now I know that my happiness was as fragile as the lace veil covering my face, and the future held far more tears than laughter.

CHAPTER FOUR

That first night at the villa was magical, the heat didn't abate and by 7 p.m. the evening was bare-arm warm. We all sat around the big oak table on the patio, eating Joy's sublime wild mushroom risotto, and one of my child-friendly salads with orange segments and pomegranate, to encourage the kids to eat leaves. We'd also filled a platter with Italian meats and cheeses, and as Joy and I set the table with cutlery and food, Violet lit the tea lights I'd brought from home – they were scattered across the table like stars.

'We should start our own catering business, Clare,' Joy said, standing back, admiring our work, acknowledging our partnership. I smiled. This was fun on holiday but Joy was quite a taskmaster, and liked to be in charge. I doubted the fun would last if this were a permanent arrangement.

Once everything was on the table, we ate hungrily, and later let the evening wash over us, talking and drinking coffee. Freddie slept on a nearby sun lounger, while Violet and Alfie played hide-and-seek, mostly under the table. Joy asked me if I felt it might be the children's bedtime.

'Another five minutes,' I said. 'They're enjoying themselves.' Sometimes I needed to dig my heels in where my mother-in-law was concerned, but I'd learned how to handle her.

'Oh these children must be tired,' she sighed, reminding me again that she thought they should be in bed. I glanced at my watch. It was after 8 p.m. so I was ready to give in, but just as I was about to stand up and announce it was bedtime, Joy screamed.

Then started laughing, as she looked under the table, from where Alfie had apparently tickled her legs. 'I thought that was you for a minute, Bob,' she laughed, and Bob almost choked on his beer. Dan and I joined in and, seeing the adults laugh, the children joined in too, and I looked round at all the Taylors laughing and I realised it was one of those rare times when I felt like I belonged. All the struggles, the heartaches, the daily grind, the little squabbles were suddenly turned into gold by the pure alchemy in the air. And I thought, *This is what life is about – family*. No worries, just warmth and laughter, easy conversation with people you love, your children close by, everyone safe and sated and happy.

Encouraged by the adult laughter, Alfie continued to tickle Granny's legs under the table and I looked at Dan, who told him, 'Enough,' and gathered him up onto his knee.

'He's *definitely* tired,' Joy warned, and not wanting to spoil the bonhomie, I agreed with her.

'Bedtime,' I said, and she smiled, a hint of triumph in the curl of her pearlised lip. But for me, nothing could cast a shadow on the evening. The air was warm and filled with promise, and when I looked into Dan's eyes across the table, as he cuddled Alfie on his knee, I felt blessed.

Later, after putting the children to bed, Dan and I retired to our own big double room, and I flopped down, lying like a starfish. It was perfect: a huge bed, right in the middle of the room, clothed in thick, cool white cotton, floaty white curtains at a picture window that looked out onto the garden and, beyond, to the coast in the distance.

Dan turned out the light, opened the curtains fully, and joined me on the bed, where we lay in the warm, silent darkness looking out at the stars. 'I know it's not been an easy time for you recently,' he said quietly. 'I'm sorry.'

He took me in his arms and we made love like two strangers, like we were starting out all over again. And, in a way, we were.

This was going to be a good holiday, the intense heat was thawing my bones, mending my heart – and later, as I lay in his arms, I had this wonderful feeling that we were going to be okay. I hadn't had that feeling for a very long time.

Jamie didn't arrive the following day; he didn't arrive the day after. He turned up a day, and several hours, late, on the Wednesday. No one was surprised. Even Joy admitted 'My Jamie's always late,' with a shake of the head and an indulgent smile. Apparently Jamie had texted Joy to say he'd be there in the morning, and Joy had been like a cat on hot bricks popping out to the front of the villa to see if she could see him. But it was after lunch when he finally arrived.

Joy and I were clearing up in the kitchen. It was small and cosy and the external door led out onto the patio, so it was perfect to serve from when we were eating al fresco – which we always did on holiday. It was only our third day in Italy, but I knew from previous holiday experience how the routine would go.

'It's almost twelve,' Joy would say to me, wherever we were. She didn't have to utter another word, my response was Pavlovian and I was immediately ready for the delicious ritual of preparing lunch. We would basically empty the fridge of cured meats, cheeses and salads and put them all in the baskets and crockery we found in the cupboards – it was like a treasure hunt. As Joy said, 'Lunchtime is less about cooking and more about compilation.' Then we'd call our 'staff' – the children – to help us take the food onto the terrace, where we'd eat at the wooden table set under a thicket of shady vine leaves. It was the same with all our holidays, and I realise now I took great comfort in the security of this routine, like it would always be like this, that it would go on and on forever. And when you're nine years old and the police knock on your door to say your father isn't coming home again – you don't take forever for granted. Our lives were changed in an instant, we weren't a family any more, we were me and my mum and as an only child, I had to mop up my mother's grief. She couldn't let it go, and I spent the next ten years caring for her, until she died from cancer… at least that's what they said, but I knew once your heart had broken you could never really fix it.

I was putting the leftover cheese into the fridge (and enjoying the chill) when I heard a car pull up on the gravel outside. I knew it was him. Jamie.

I pushed the platter firmly into the fridge and, removing myself from the delicious coolness, peeped through the window. 'A taxi,' I said. 'It's a taxi, Joy…'

She almost dropped the bowl she was holding in her rush to look out of the window, her face flushed with heat and pleasure, her eyes darting around the drive to get the first glimpse of him as he arrived.

Within seconds, the passenger door of the taxi opened and he climbed out – tall, slim, like Dan, but not like Dan. His hair was lighter, his smile quicker, handsome, but in a different way. The second son, the one who didn't have to carry the weight of the family on his shoulders, who took risks, thumbed lifts and had never paid a household bill in his life.

'Jamie,' Joy sighed, ripping off her 'Queen of the Kitchen' apron – a birthday gift from the kids – and throwing it on the kitchen worktop, before scuttling off.

I stood watching at the window as he paid the taxi driver then went to the back of the car to get his luggage.

Joy was outside now. I heard her calling for Bob and didn't have to wait long to see him ambling through the garden towards Jamie's taxi. Joy was rushing past Bob, almost colliding with him in her eagerness to get there first. And when she did, she hurled herself at Jamie and, as slight as she was, almost knocked him down in her excitement.

After taking a few seconds to recover, he laughed and lifted her in the air while she screamed like a teenage girl for him to put her down. I was smiling at this scene – it was good to see him. We were already having a lovely time, the last few days had gone perfectly, spent laughing, eating and playing with the children, and we were all beginning to relax – but Jamie always brought that extra special something. As I watched him hug Bob, my eyes were suddenly drawn to the back seat passenger-side door. It was slowly opening, and after a few seconds, one, then two, long, tanned legs appeared in high-heeled designer sandals. And then the rest of her stepped out onto the powdery white, hot gravel. Another beautiful twenty-something Jamie had collected on his travels, slim, stunning, deep golden hair, even deeper tan, anointed with that faraway glamour you couldn't buy at a make-up counter. Cool as a cucumber, she stood a few feet away from Jamie and his mother. Joy, still unaware of the extra guest, was immersed in Jamie, giggling and hugging.

Another of Jamie's girlfriends? He sometimes brought them along on these family get-togethers. They were usually nice enough, but, as Joy always said, it wasn't the same as having him to ourselves on holiday.

I watched as he gestured for the girl to come closer, and the introductions began. Joy as always was warm and effusive, though I reckoned she would have preferred Jamie there by himself. 'I've never particularly liked any of Jamie's girlfriends,' she once told me, 'but none of them have ever guessed. I'm always nice to them, for Jamie – and let's face it, we know they are only ever fleeting,' she'd giggled. This latest one was wearing a white maxi dress, which set off her deep tan perfectly. I looked down for a moment at my own pale, freckly arms and wished I'd bought some fake tan. Finding it hard not to watch, I looked back through the window. She was smiling serenely, perfect features, perfect figure, and I noted that long honey-coloured hair had been caught by the sun, or a good hairdresser. She was probably in her twenties, and even though

I couldn't see her that closely, it was clear that, unlike me, this woman had definitely de-fuzzed.

Now Dan and the kids had joined the welcoming throng, and suddenly aware that I was the only family member not present, I knew I should go out there and say hello, be part of the welcoming committee. So I smoothed my pool-straggled hair and grabbed a kitchen towel to wipe the sweat from my face, wishing Jamie had at least mentioned he wasn't coming alone, so I could have been prepared and looked a little less wild.

Walking out of the stone villa, the heat hit me like bricks; now even more sultry, the sky was turning dark, like a shadow had crossed the sun. The air was heavy, and it occurred to me that we might be in for a thunderstorm as I approached the tight little group gathered around this new stranger.

Violet was jumping up and down excitedly, which was what the kids all did when Uncle Jamie was around. But it wasn't just general excitement and a family welcome, they were all focussing on something in the girl's hand. When Violet saw me, she broke free from the group and grabbed me by the elbow, urging me to 'Come and see Uncle Jamie!'

I fixed my smile and, suddenly feeling shy, allowed Violet to pull me between Dan and Bob into the circle. I felt a bit like the odd one out, everyone already knew her name and why she was here – except me.

Jamie was looking at me with a stupid grin, clearly proud to have snagged an even younger, even more beautiful woman than usual. So proud in fact, he had his arm around her shoulder, which I felt was rather territorial for him, and thought he must be quite keen on this one. But then he was always keen on them to begin with.

'Hello,' I said, smiling at her, waiting to be introduced.

She gave me a little wave with just her fingers.

'This is Clare… Dan's wife,' Jamie said as I got closer. They were both so tall, like models, making me feel very short.

'Clare,' she said, white teeth, dazzling, open smile.

She really was stunning and unless that maxi dress hid the secret of unshaved legs, I suspected this woman was completely without physical flaws.

'This is Ella,' I heard someone say. I think it was Jamie, or Dan.

'*Ella*, how lovely to meet you,' I said, and before I could add anything she came in, with firm, gym-honed arms open wide, for a hug. This took me by surprise; she was confident for someone so young, and among all these strangers too.

I opened my arms clumsily and we did an awkward hug – the awkward was all me.

'So, welcome to the family, Ella,' Dan said, and I wished he wouldn't come on all son-and-heir – we weren't bloody royalty. I found it a little cringey the way Dan sometimes took on his mother's delusions of grandeur.

Ella smiled sweetly – gosh, she was so pretty.

'I just wish you'd *told* us,' Joy said, unable to hide her irritation, the initial warmth fading slightly. Her lips were slightly locked, and the stance was pure self-protection. 'We'd have loved to be at our son's wedding, wouldn't we, Bob?' she said pointedly.

Bob nodded, and looked slightly confused, but not as confused as me. In a couple of seconds, I managed to process what Joy had just said, looking from Jamie to Ella, to her left hand.

And there it was – a platinum ring. That's what they'd all been admiring as I'd watched from the window. The others hadn't been looking at something *in* her hand, it was something *on* her hand.

'Wedding?' was all I managed to say. This wasn't Jamie's latest pretty girlfriend, to be replaced by someone prettier next time. This was his wife.

'Yes, these two ran off and got married – yesterday! They were in Italy already and didn't even tell us,' Joy said, accusingly. She masked this in faux annoyance, but it was real. I could only imagine how she felt having been robbed of one of her son's weddings. Not only was she not present on the big day, but she hadn't had the chance to stage-manage the event – and worse still, no opportunity to vet her new daughter-in-law.

'Sorry, Mum, but when you know, you know. I also *knew* if I didn't grab her, someone else would.' He looked at Ella and she positively cooed. 'I mean look at her.' There was an awkward silence as the two of them stared at each other like no one else was there.

'So where did you meet? We need to hear all about it,' Joy said, linking her arm through her son's and walking him slowly across the gravel, away from Ella – taking ownership back. The past shimmered through me. I was remembering how Joy had done the same with me and Dan.

'We met a while ago, in Manchester actually,' I heard him say. 'We bumped into each other in a bar. I fell in love in the first five seconds. It took her a little longer.'

'An hour!' Ella laughed from behind them, a reminder to him that she was still there.

Jamie gently pulled away from Joy and turned back to his new bride. 'Anyway, we were both planning to head off to India, and I suggested we go together.'

'Not like you,' Joy said pointedly. I detected a flash of anger in her eyes at his abandonment of her. 'Jamie usually likes to travel alone, don't you, darling?' she continued, addressing them both.

'Not any more.' Ella beamed, and I wondered if perhaps Joy might have met her match.

'Yeah, I knew I couldn't live without her so I asked her to marry me and when she said yes we headed for Italy to get married… and also to meet up with you guys,' he said, like his family were an afterthought.

'I always wanted to get married in Positano.' Ella glanced dreamily at her new husband.

'Oh, I wish you'd waited so we could all be there, Jamie,' Joy sighed, with a sad, loving look at her son.

'Sorry, Mum, we just wanted to get it done.'

Ella nodded enthusiastically at his side.

'So how did you sort it all so quickly?' Dan asked, as he man-handled Alfie, who'd suddenly gone shy and was swinging from his dad's leg. 'Must have been one hell of a rush to get it all done in time,' he continued, always the practical one. Dan didn't see the mad urgency of love, just the problems of planning a wedding in a short time in a different country.

'Easier than you'd think,' Jamie said. 'Just a case of getting the right papers and knowing what to do. Turns out my new wife isn't just a pretty face, and within a few days we'd signed the forms and booked the wedding.'

'We wanted to have a quiet wedding, just us...' Ella added, looking at Joy, who raised an eyebrow before softening this with a smile. A rather stiff one.

'I didn't want to hang around and let this one get away,' Jamie said, for once oblivious to his mother's disapproval. He didn't see anyone but his new wife. He was smiling at her, lost in her eyes.

'Of course, of course.' Joy was rallying in the face of all this. 'We can always do something for family and friends when we're back home, perhaps the golf club?' She looked at Bob, who shrugged.

I was sure the very reason Jamie and Ella had eloped was to avoid places like 'the golf club'. With its wooden tables and beige buffets, it wasn't exactly Instagrammable. No, these two were made to marry in the glamour and beauty of the Italian Coast.

'Oh Jamie,' Joy sighed again. She seemed flustered, no doubt torn between delight at her son's arrival and panic at the fact he'd just introduced a complete stranger as his wife. 'I just wish you'd *mentioned* it. I didn't even know you would be bringing... anyone.'

'It doesn't matter, we're all together now, and you've got ten days to get to know Ella and for her to get to know you.' Everything was always so simple and straightforward to Jamie, he just saw what he wanted and took it without ever having to consider anyone else.

'I'm looking forward to it,' Joy said. She clearly wasn't. I could see by her face this had blindsided her – well, it had all of us. 'And now I feel awful because I put you in the small single room, Jamie.'

'No worries,' he said, picking up his rucksack and grabbing Ella's Gucci holdall. 'We can sleep anywhere, we've slept outside… under the stars, haven't we, babe?'

'Yes, babe.' Ella nodded, smiling at the memory and looking up at him, gently pushing her arm through his, reclaiming him once more from his mother.

I put my arm around Violet, who was now staring at Ella as if she was in the presence of a real-life Disney princess.

'No, no, you can't sleep *outside*. I mean, technically this is your honeymoon,' Joy said, with a sideways glance at me, knowing I would share her discomfort at all this. I looked at Bob to see if I could gauge his reaction to the news, but he was on autopilot and was now picking up Jamie and Ella's other bags.

'Oh, there's still stuff in the boot too,' Jamie said, which caused the kids to dash around the back of the car and scramble in the open boot. I think they were expecting their usual gifts from Uncle Jamie. As he only saw them several times a year and he'd usually just returned from somewhere, he'd buy them a souvenir from wherever he'd been. But maybe this time Ella was the only souvenir he'd brought back.

CHAPTER FIVE

'OMG! This is SO heavy,' I heard Violet say, as she dragged a huge Versace shopping bag along the gravel.

'Is it a present for me?' Alfie asked, in his adorable lisp, looking up at Jamie big-eyed and questioning as Jamie looked down at him. Then I saw it register on his face — in his loved up, newly married bliss, he'd totally forgotten to bring the children something.

'Sorry, mate,' he said, with a smile. 'I was going to pick you something up this morning, but your Auntie Ella took too long in all the dress stores.' Then he bent down, ruffled Alfie's hair, and lifted Freddie onto his shoulders, much to my younger boy's delight.

'Go horsey, go!' Freddie yelled, pulling on Jamie's ears like they were reins. For the children, Uncle Jamie didn't really need to bring gifts, his attention was more than enough.

Joy's eyes followed Dan, Bob and Violet trailing past carrying an array of Italian designer shopping bags. 'Ooh, you've been busy,' she said to Ella, a vague hint of disapproval in her voice.

'Oh yes, we went into town earlier,' Ella replied. 'I needed a few bits and pieces.'

'A few bits and pieces?' Bob started, laughing. 'All this must have cost an arm and a leg.'

'Now, now, Bob, don't embarrass Ella,' Joy said, backtracking. She preferred a more subtle approach when showing her distaste. 'If a bride can't buy nice things on her honeymoon, then it's a poor show, isn't it, love?' she said to Ella, in an attempt to compensate for Bob's rather vulgar comment about the cost.

Ella smiled indulgently at Bob. 'Men never understand shopping,' she sighed, turning to Joy, who rolled her eyes in agreement. Had I just witnessed a bonding moment? Was everything going to be okay? Perhaps Ella would fit in and it would all be great? As an only child, I'd always wanted a sister. Who knew, Ella might be the younger sister I never had.

The men and the kids went inside laden with luggage and shopping, while Ella watched the taxi drive off, and Joy called instructions to Bob about which room to take the stuff. He didn't turn around, just put his hand in the air to acknowledge that he'd heard her.

'Bob! BOB!' Joy was shouting, presumably needing confirmation he'd got this. She tutted, and turned back, watching the taxi make puffs of white dust from the gravel as it disappeared into the distance. 'He never listens,' she muttered, 'just does his own sweet thing and, before you know it, he'll have taken everything up to the wrong room and we'll have to move it all again.'

The three of us were now alone, standing on the gravel. I glanced at the two other women, who made no attempt to move, and wasn't quite sure what to do. Should I go and help the others with the bags and leave Joy alone with her new daughter-in-law, or did she want me there for backup? More likely, did *Ella* want me there for backup? After all, meeting a whole family of new in-laws would be intimidating to anyone.

The young woman sighed and lifted her huge shawl of sun-kissed hair from her neck. 'It's so hot!' she murmured.

In the strappy dress, I could see even her shoulder blades were perfect, like a sculpture – I'd never considered my own, but I bet they weren't like that. Who has shoulder blade envy? Was that even a thing?

Ella kept her hands behind her head, holding up the tresses, golden tendrils escaping into the back of her neck, damp from the heat. She looked like a model in a magazine, the showpiece in an article about summer skincare or how to get that perfect tan – her back arched, her breasts pert, and those shoulder blades. My eyes wandered back to her hands, and that sparkly diamond that made her one of us.

'Oh, let me show you around,' Joy said, taking Ella's arm, and escorting her through the garden. I heard her promising 'G and T on the patio later,' just as she had with me.

I toddled along behind, carrying the last of Ella's bags, abandoned in the heat and dust. I don't think she realised I had them, and by the time I caught up, she was too busy gasping in awe at the view of the pool and beyond.

'We are going to have such fun,' Ella murmured, almost to herself.

Joy nodded at this as they walked towards the door of the villa, and turning, she smiled rather pityingly when she saw me sweating and struggling inelegantly with Ella's final bag. 'Are you okay there?' she asked, and the younger woman immediately walked towards me, away from Joy.

'Oh Clare, let me,' she said, carrying only a Prada handbag on her delicate, Tiffany-glinting arm. She made a rather weak gesture to take the bag from me. Just one look told me the weight of it might break her wrist, so I shook my head.

'I'm fine, no problem.' I smiled.

'Are you sure?' she said, then under her breath added, 'I mean, at your age, it's not too heavy for you, is it?'

I stood still, unsure if I'd heard her correctly. 'What...?' I asked, half-smiling, assuming this was some kind of joke.

'Nothing. Just be careful on the stairs,' she said leaning towards me, now in a more audible voice. 'I'd never forgive myself if something happened to you.'

She wandered back to where Joy was standing, oblivious to what Ella had just said to me.

'Come inside Ella,' she was saying, 'the air con isn't great, but it is a little bit cooler than out here; we're having a heatwave.' Joy then swept her into the villa. I didn't go inside after them, but stood for a moment, feeling like the wind had been punched from my stomach. Had I completely misheard her? Did she really say 'at your age'? And that comment about being careful on the stairs, it felt weirdly less like a health and safety observation, more like a veiled threat.

Eventually, I walked into the villa, still carrying Ella's stuff, hoping Dan would appear and relieve me of my burden before we reached the stairs, but there was no sign of him. Ella was now at the top of the curving staircase chatting animatedly to Joy, and I followed, convincing myself I'd misheard, while panting upstairs with her bag like the bloody bellboy, determined to prove I wasn't past it.

On arrival in the single room allotted for single Jamie, I sat on the bed. Perhaps the comment about me being old had been a joke? Some people had that kind of humour, like Dan and Jamie when they bantered. Yes, if she did say that, it's all it was – banter.

I watched her move elegantly around the room while Joy fussed with the bags.

'I'm literally Italian,' she was saying. 'My father was Italian – Sorrento, born and bred – it's in my blood.'

'Oh, Sorrento's just down the road,' Joy replied, like she was referring to the nearest convenience store, when Sorrento was at least ten miles from where we were staying. 'Do you speak any Italian?' Joy asked hopefully.

'A little,' Ella said, lifting wisps of white lace underwear from one of her shopping bags and laying them out on the bed. I looked away. It felt like a rather intimate thing to do in front of your new husband's family.

'I'd love you to teach *me* some Italian,' Joy said, always eager to impress, and a whole Italian sentence taught by her new daughter-in-law would certainly impress 'the girls' (all in their seventies) back home.

I was smiling to myself at this when Dan appeared in the doorway. He too saw the underwear, and I instantly wondered if he wished she was wearing it for him? It was an unwanted, irrational thought, and I pushed it to the back of my mind as he beckoned me with his head to go to him outside the room, as though if he walked over the threshold he might be cursed.

I reluctantly stood up and followed him out of the room and down the hall. 'What, Dan?' I said, slightly irritated, like Violet when she was told it was time to come off her tablet.

'I feel bad that they're on their honeymoon and they're sharing a single bed,' he said in an earnest whisper.

'Jamie said they were fine,' I responded.

'Yes, but I don't think *she* will be – imagine if you'd been told we'd be crammed into a tiny bed on our honeymoon?' he added.

'It's not the same. There was no chance we'd be crammed in a single bed because we *planned* our holiday, like normal people do,' I said, unable to risk a dig at the spontaneous lovebirds now in our midst. I'll admit I was also a little disappointed; I'd hoped Jamie would spend time with me and Dan on the holiday. Now Jamie was going to be working with Dan I'd assumed we would get back to being the three musketeers, playing cards and drinking too much together. As Joy had offered to watch the kids while we were there, I'd looked forward to us all venturing out one evening. But now Jamie was married, it seemed like things had changed already.

'I just think…' Dan was saying, then took a breath. 'I just think that perhaps we might offer them our room?'

'That'd be a nice gesture, Dan, but where would *we* sleep?'

'I thought… perhaps *we* could sleep in the single room? Or one of us could sleep with the kids, and the other could sleep in the single room?'

I couldn't believe what he was suggesting. 'But we don't get any time as it is to relax together at home, this is our holiday, *our* marriage… What about us healing, Dan?'

'We can still have our holiday, spend time together, but I just feel like we should be the grown-ups, and offer them the double room.'

At that point, Joy popped her head out of the bedroom doorway. 'You two okay?' she asked.

'Yeah, yeah, we're fine,' Dan said, uncertainly, which Joy must have picked up on.

But by now I could feel myself tearing up: it wasn't just about a room, it was about the way Dan always put everything before me, before us. Jamie had just turned up and announced he was married and now Dan was suggesting we vacate our lovely room for them, like it was too late for us, we were a lost cause. I was hurt that he could dismiss us like this. Giving our room away to his brother was giving away our only chance to reconnect.

I turned and walked quickly down the hall to our room leaving Dan and his mother in the hallway. I didn't want Joy to see me upset, she'd want to know why and then she'd try to fix it. But for once I wanted Dan to understand how important this was to me and not leave it to Joy to sort out our problems.

I lay on the bed for some time, hoping he might come in and we could at least talk about it, on our own, but I could hear Dan's voice as he headed downstairs. He was laughing about something and clearly had no intention of coming to see me, and I wondered, not for the first time, how much he really cared. A few minutes later, I heard Violet asking where Mummy was. She was just outside the room, and I was about to get up and open the door, but Joy's soothing voice coerced her away with the promise of a swim and a story.

'Mummy's tired, darling,' she said.

I wanted to go to Violet, but my face was puffy from crying, so I didn't call out. I continued to lie on the king-sized bed with the beautiful cool bed linen where Dan and I had cautiously begun to rebuild a marriage which needed intensive care. How could he even suggest we give up the loveliness of the big white bed to sleep in a single bed or even separate rooms?

It was Jamie and Ella's honeymoon, and it was kind of Dan to think of them, I just wished he'd think of me sometimes. Like Ella, I'd always wanted a honeymoon in Italy. I remember discussing it excitedly with Dan and leaving the travel agents with a clutch of Italian brochures. We'd found a wonderful hotel among the primrose yellow and terracotta buildings stacked high on the hillside above Positano. A sea of bright buildings, rampant purple bougainvillea and that view – I could imagine the two of us on a balcony sipping wine, planning our future. We took the brochures back to Dan's parents' house, me fully expecting Joy to clap her hands and join in with the excitement, but she'd been slightly subdued, said it seemed expensive, and perhaps we should stay in the UK? I later teased Dan, saying that 'Mummy didn't want her little boy to go on honeymoon'.

Now, looking back, I don't think I was too far wrong. I know, in the first few years, Joy found it hard to accept Dan had another woman in his life apart from her. I guess it was to be expected. Until I came along, she'd been used to having her two sons to herself.

Anyway, our Italian honeymoon wasn't meant to be, because just before we were due to book it, one of Joy's friends offered us her cottage in Devon for a week, as a wedding gift. As Joy pointed out, it would be rude to say no, and the money we'd have spent on Italy could buy us a lovely three-piece sofa. Dan agreed, and promised we'd go to Italy another year, so I accepted the kind offer from Joy's friend graciously, while hiding my disappointment. As Dan's parents had paid for our wedding at the golf club, I was grateful and didn't want Joy to think I was behaving like a brat.

The wedding was lovely –200 guests, a three-course meal, flowers from floor to ceiling and a dress to die for. I'd wanted a smaller, less expensive, more intimate occasion, but, as Joy said, 'You only get married once, Clare – and we have a big family and a lot of friends, we want to do this for you.'

They even helped with the deposit on our first house, not too far from theirs – Joy liked to keep her boys close, and I think Dan being nearby paid for Jamie being away so much. We paid the price in a different way with regular, impromptu visits at the weekend or evenings, which rather curtailed those stolen moments of intimacy in the early years of marriage. Having Joy peer through the glass squares of the front door saying to Bob loudly, 'I know they're in,' as we lay on the sofa together was enough to stop anyone mid-passion. 'We just stopped by, we were going to the supermarket and wondered if you needed anything,' she'd usually say as we opened the door. I think Joy needed the company, Bob was never really enough for her, so we would invite them in and make a cup of tea and talk to them. I did this out of politeness, but mostly to keep Joy happy – because that's what we all liked to do.

And she was happy now. Even if Jamie had surprised her, the globetrotting, rebellious son had come back into the fold: both sons were back in her orbit – the family together at last.

I could hear them all now, the Taylors, their muffled laughter downstairs, as I lay on that king-sized bed, alone. A little later, the laughter was punctuated by clinking glasses, the awakening chorus of early evening. Joy would be starting on dinner and expect me to join her in the kitchen, so I brushed my hair and washed my face. I thought of Ella's beautiful dress, her tanned legs, the way she lifted her hair to cool her neck, and looked through the clothes hanging in the wardrobe. What had seemed fine when I took them out of my case now looked frumpy, but I alighted on a pink cotton dress that I'd bought specially for the holiday. I'd loved it in the shop and imagined myself wearing it with a tan, which hadn't happened yet because I'd been too busy with kids to sunbathe. I pulled it on over my head, remembering how slimming it had been when I tried it on. I wandered over to the mirror, and instead of a golden, slimline version of me, a hot, chunky, middle-aged woman in pink looked back at me. It hadn't mattered yesterday, or the day before, but now Ella was here, I worried we'd be compared and I'd come out badly. I told myself I was being silly, and digging out an old silk scarf, I wrapped it around my head and tied it in a lose bow at the top. I could carry this off, I was sure. I'd seen one of my younger colleagues wearing her hair like this, and perhaps it was time I did something a little different with my look.

Whatever I told myself, the presence of this beautiful woman was putting me under pressure. She was bound to turn up for dinner in something fabulous with a full face of make-up. A scarf tied in a bow might be edgy, but it wasn't enough, and coupled with my face, red from the heat and this morning's sitting by the pool, I wasn't at my best.

I suddenly heard someone coming up the stairs, not frantic little children's feet, or the heavy landing of men's squeaky sandals, but dainty heels tapping lightly on the wood. It was so quiet in my room, I soon worked out that the footsteps were heading into Joy and Bob's room. Joy had probably popped upstairs to freshen up before cooking the evening meal.

I wondered if perhaps she had some miracle foundation I could use. She loved to offer a solution, always had a tissue in her handbag for wet-nosed children and weeping daughters-in-law. Joy had the medicine for any occasion: the ointment to eradicate a nasty rash, the plasters for a grazed marriage… the script for the phone call to remove the other woman.

I'd go and ask if she had any calming cream, and see if she was okay – support her through this shock news about Jamie's wedding.

So, I spritzed some water on my face to cool down and went to see her in her room. The door was almost closed, and I didn't want to walk in on her getting dressed, so I just peeped through. But, to my amazement, instead of Joy, I saw Ella, standing at Joy's dressing table. I moved closer to the crack in the door so I could see what she was doing. Was she alone? Like an answer to my question, I heard Joy shout at Bob for helping himself to something in the fridge. 'That's for supper,' she yelled from downstairs.

I continued to lean in as close as I could and saw Ella pick up Joy's jewellery wrap, then take out a pair of diamond earrings. I knew which ones they were and even from that distance I caught the sparkle as the sun from the window hit them. I watched, fascinated, as she put them to her lobes, like she was seeing how they'd look on her. I was confused – what was she doing? Who would go into someone else's room when they weren't there and go through their jewellery? Perhaps Joy had asked her to fetch them for her? But why would she do that? No, this was very dodgy, and became even dodgier when I saw her look around and then slip the earrings into the pocket of her sundress. I was open-mouthed in shock. Had she just stolen her husband's mother's jewellery?

I didn't know what to do; I tried to rationalise what I'd just seen. Had Ella really taken the earrings and put them in her pocket? I couldn't take in what I thought I'd just seen as I continued to peer through the crack in the door. I watched her look around again, like she was checking no one had seen. I stepped back from the door slightly, causing a floorboard to creak, and through the mirror I could see her swing round and glare at the door. I kept flat against it, really still, not breathing, but sure she could hear my heart beating. Through the mirror I saw her continue to stare at the door, and then, apparently satisfied no one was there, she folded up the jewellery roll and put it back exactly where she'd found it. When she turned to leave, I quickly ran back to my room, trying not to make a noise, cursing the creaking floorboard and the sound of my flip-flops on the landing. Once safely inside, I locked the door so I could think. I had to say something, didn't I? Ella may be Jamie's wife, but they'd talked vaguely in terms of 'weeks' when describing their romance earlier. How well did he know this woman?

CHAPTER SIX

I couldn't stop thinking about what I'd seen and kept trying to work it out. Eventually, I had to go downstairs and join everyone, but seeing Ella made me feel rather strange. I felt like I was watching the others through glass. I didn't feel like one of them, I was like an observer trying to analyse everything Ella said, the way she behaved.

'And the flowers… did you have a bouquet Ella?' Joy was asking questions about their wedding, clearly still stung by the exclusion.

'This explains why you suddenly want to join the family firm,' Bob said, lifting his glass in a 'cheers' gesture. 'You've finally settled down, our Jamie.'

'Yes. I expect you'll want to buy a house…' Joy added brightly. Jamie may have a wife, but the silver lining for Joy would be the prodigal's return, no more travelling.

'You'll probably want a few of these too?' Dan pointed in the direction of Freddie and Alfie, now rolling along the rug and shouting at each other.

Jamie laughed and, I noticed, squeezed Ella's knee. It was subtle, but I wondered if she was already pregnant.

I sat on the arm of Dan's chair, feeling like a spectator watching a love story unfold. Ella permanently had her hand on Jamie's arm and he had his on her knee. And if one shifted in their seat or moved an inch away from the other, they'd move closer again. It was like a game of twister, where at least one of their respective body parts had to touch the other. Their eyes were always meeting, dancing, their own private conversation happening underneath the public one. I remembered feeling like this once upon a time.

I glanced at Dan, but he didn't see me. He was looking at Jamie and Ella, nodding at their words, smiling at their stories. But Dan and I weren't touching at all.

'This place is, like, so cute,' Ella said, an upward inflection on the word cute, like it was a question. 'Joy, is it nineteenth century?'

'I… Do you know, I'm not sure.' I could tell Joy was mortified that she didn't know, she liked to be an authority on everything. 'It's original, but some of the building has been extended,' she offered, desperately trying to be informative. Her face suddenly lit up as she remembered something, had a fact to impart: 'Oh, and the marble is Carrara.'

'Yes, it's exquisite,' Ella said, 'just gorgeous. The soft veining is almost white… so much more subtle than the brighter white Calacatta marble.'

'Sounds like you know your marble!' Dan said, clearly impressed. And all the time, I kept thinking *Why, why have you taken Joy's earrings?*

Meanwhile, Joy smiled and nodded in agreement at Ella's marble analysis.

'Ella knows all about architecture too, she's been in palaces all over the world,' Jamie said proudly.

'Wow, palaces? I'm envious,' I said, and she smiled at me.

'She's into photography, aren't you, darling?' Jamie added, looking down at her with such love, it stung me slightly. I wanted that kind of love too.

Ella nodded eagerly and crossed her legs. Her bare toes were small, compact, the toenails like silver jewels. I wasn't sure if I was jealous of her or wanted to *be* her, but looking at Violet's face, my daughter definitely wanted to be Ella when she grew up.

'So did you say you went to India together? How romantic – had you known each other… long?' I asked.

'Long enough,' Ella replied, looking at Jamie, not at me.

'Oh, what do you do?' I asked, undeterred.

'She's a model,' Jamie said proudly.

Violet's eyes widened at this.

'I've done swimwear for designer friends, that kind of thing – but I'm not like a *serious* model. I want to move into stuff that matters – photography, vlogging, blogging – saving the planet and all that.'

'Wow! You would be an amazing YouTuber,' Violet suggested, awe shining in her eyes.

'Maybe,' she said, like she could be anything she wanted to be. I envied her confidence… or was it arrogance?

'Ella's selling herself short,' Jamie added proudly. 'She's modelled all over the world, all the catwalks on fashion week, fashion photography, lingerie. Designers and photographers are always messaging her, asking her to fly off—'

'Gosh,' I said. Catwalk and photographic fashion, plus lingerie, were, I thought, quite different kinds of modelling. Didn't models usually stick to one kind? I wasn't sure, and after what I'd seen earlier I was now questioning everything that she said. There was no denying Ella could model anything. She'd make a bin liner look like high fashion but then again perhaps Jamie was just exaggerating, bigging up his new wife for the family? Sometimes Jamie did that. All the Taylors had a slightly irritating tendency to embellish sometimes, but Jamie was the worst.

'Ella's wasted in modelling. She's not a clothes horse, she's so creative,' Jamie said.

'You're sweet,' she said, kissing him on the cheek.

'She has twenty-five thousand followers on Instagram.' He beamed.

'I just do what feels right, and hope people like it,' she said.

I found her hard to read. I thought maybe if I looked at her Instagram, I could try and work out who she was? Then again,

Instagram could sometimes be more confusing – it was often more about who we *wanted* to be. When I started the Instagram account for Taylor's, I'd also made one for myself and wasn't above posting the odd family photo at Pizza Express styled to look look more like dinner in Milan.

'So, are you one of those Instagram influencers?' I asked. 'Do you have lovely things sent to you for your Instagram page?'

'Page… it's called a *profile*, Clare.' She gave a little giggle and looked at Jamie, who looked down. I wasn't sure how to take it; was she making fun of me?

'It's all far too technical for me,' Joy said, coming out in sympathy with me.

'Oh yes, I meant *profile*,' I said, giving her the benefit of the doubt. 'So what happens, do you model the stuff you're sent?' I asked again, like a dog with a bone.

'Yeah, yeah, yeah,' she said dismissively, without looking at me. She clearly didn't want to discuss it. But I did.

'How wonderful,' I said, smiling. 'What a great job to have.'

She didn't respond. I hoped I hadn't been too probing; she seemed confident, yet at the same time quite shy about her career. I wondered if perhaps she wasn't quite as successful as Jamie was making out. I knew it must have been important for him that Ella was accepted into the family, but he didn't need to sell her to us. But again, I think it was mostly about pleasing Joy – if Mum was happy, then *everyone* was happy. And right now, the fixed smile on her face as she clutched her glass of gin was quite hard to read.

'Ella's got so much' to offer – I always say she should be on TV, you know, a reality show or something?' he was now saying.

'Oh my God, I'd LOVE to, that's the dream,' she sighed.

'Ooh no, not one of those awful programmes,' Joy piped up. 'Anyway, most of the people on those are single. You're a married woman now, Ella.'

'Oh, it's only a job,' Ella said, with a shimmer of irritation. 'And the money they pay, I mean – some of them are millionaires.'

'Mum's right, they might want you to have relationships on screen,' Jamie said. 'I don't mind if you make a million, but not if you have to be with someone else.' He laughed nervously.

'Oh goodness no,' Joy chorused, horrified at the prospect of her daughter-in-law involved in some tawdry sexual encounter on TV. What would the neighbours say?

Ella didn't really respond to either of them, and I have to admit, I wondered just how far she'd go for that million pounds. It looked like she'd already started with the diamond earrings.

'I just can't wait to photograph this place,' she said, moving on from reality TV and running one hand along the back of the sofa, the other up and down Jamie's arm.

'The pool is stunning,' Joy offered. 'Mosaic tiles in every shade of blue.'

'Yes, I spotted that. I'll be using the pool as a backdrop.' She smiled, then suddenly sat forward. 'If that's okay... I mean that's okay with you guys, isn't it – for me to take photos of the place?' She looked from Joy to Bob and back to Joy again. She'd clearly worked out in her first few hours where the power lay.

'Of course, my darling, shoot away.' Joy smiled, but I was sure I noticed a flicker of uncertainty on her face – she didn't really know how to take this young woman, this stranger who'd turned up on our holiday. No one had asked Joy's permission, and until that afternoon she hadn't even been aware her son had a girlfriend, let alone a wife.

'Do you have any wedding pictures?' I asked. This was mostly out of politeness, but I was intrigued to see Ella's dress, Jamie all suited up, the gorgeous Italian setting.

'One or two,' she said, and started to look through her phone to find them, then offered it to me.

I got up from the arm of Dan's chair to take the phone, but she kept hold of it. She patted the arm of her chair, for me to perch there. Was this power play, or did she not want to surrender her phone to me for some reason?

I sat down close to her on the arm of the chair; she smelled of salt and lemons, of places I'd never been, a hint of floral spice, a waft of jasmine. She smelled how she looked – fragrant, exotic, like nothing else.

As she scrolled through the photos, I noted the designer watch, the sparkle of that huge diamond on her ring finger. I wondered how she'd 'acquired' it – Jamie didn't have that kind of money, perhaps he'd borrowed it? Perhaps Ella had money? But why, if she had money, would she steal someone's jewellery? I tried not to think about the earrings and focussed my eyes on the photos of their breathtaking wedding on an Italian clifftop. I confess I had to swallow down little pangs of envy.

'This was the ceremony,' she said, long nude nails touching the screen, to reveal the bride and groom, her in a long, silk blush-pink dress, tight around her slim body and full breasts, ending with a swirling fishtail. Jamie in a designer suit, open-necked shirt, several people standing around them, probably witnesses. But they were of no consequence; the bride and groom looked like film stars smiling with their perfect teeth, sun-brushed skin, the Amalfi Coast glittering behind them. They looked so happy, and young, and sexy and rich and I could only imagine the life they'd go on to have. It would be so different to ours.

Despite claiming to want to join the family firm, I couldn't imagine either of them living the nine-to-five in rainy Manchester. Jamie had never settled into a job, or a home, and looking at Ella, I didn't see her destiny in a life of work and kids in a new build on a suburban estate. No, they were so different to us – I imagined their Instagram, black and white photos of a large, shuttered town house in Paris or Milan. In this stylish European love nest they'd make beautiful, bilingual children and she'd never get fat and he'd never lose interest.

'Lovely,' I murmured, trying to reconcile this beautiful bride with the woman I'd seen only hours before stealing earrings from her mother-in-law's room.

'I'll get some of the photos printed off,' Ella said, 'so the family can have some to frame.'

'Great.' I smiled and went back to the arm of the other chair, wishing Dan would offer me his seat and show everyone that he loved me as much as Jamie loved Ella. He didn't.

'So, are you ready for some *real* work?' he asked Jamie.

'I was born ready,' Jamie responded, sticking his chest out, his prowess clearly threatened by the older lion in the jungle.

'Good. Just hope you know what you're in for,' Dan added, no doubt glad that Jamie was finally having to face up to real life. He might have hidden his glee slightly.

'If you mean – do I know I'm in for showing you how it's done, bro, then yes, I am,' Jamie said, his smile hinting at banter.

'We'll see,' Dan said, unsmiling.

I'd never experienced this before between Dan and Jamie – the sibling rivalry had always been cheeky but affectionate, but this had an edge. Now Jamie had a wife to impress, it seemed he wasn't happy playing the little brother role any more.

'Actually, Ella and I have been talking a lot about the business,' he said. So he *was* still planning to join the company? I'd thought it was all talk, I just couldn't see it working and it would be so stressful for Dan having to 'manage' his younger brother. 'Ella's got some great ideas for Taylor's.'

I quickly turned to look at her. She couldn't possibly be interested in our little property company; surely Ella had much bigger fish to fry? What about her photography, her modelling, the reality TV show?

'*Lovely,*' said Joy. I could see by her rictus smile that she definitely didn't mean it. Joy and Bob would never really let go. They probably didn't even trust their sons to do things right in their retirement, let alone the new daughter-in-law they hardly knew.

'Ideas?' Dan repeated, not even attempting to hide his doubts. 'Okay, let's hear them Ella.' He said this with a teasing in his voice, his eyes twinkling – was this because he found her amusing, or fascinating? I couldn't tell, but he leaned forward to hear what she had to say.

Ella looked up from caressing Jamie's ear. 'Well, Jamie's told me all about Taylor's, and it sounds like it just needs a little push on the marketing side.' She sat up a little, like she was being interviewed by Dan, like she wanted to impress him, show him she was serious about this. 'Thing is, you need a new website, you need to be on Instagram and all social media platforms… These days, you *have* to be interactive, you have to ask questions… like "Look at our new penthouse for sale, can you guess who the architect is—"'

'*Penthouse?*' I said, smiling, looking around the room for the other incredulous faces, but everyone was looking at Ella.

'Clare, you just interrupted my train of thought,' she said, holding her head with both hands quite dramatically.

'Sorry,' I muttered, then shut up, while everyone else waited politely for her to continue. Even the boys were quiet, though that had more to do with them being engrossed in some game on the iPad.

Violet meanwhile was waiting with bated breath to hear what her new heroine had to say. 'You were talking about an architect… in a penthouse,' she said, giving Ella her prompt.

'So… yeah, that's it, thanks Vee.'

I bristled slightly. Her name was Violet, but perhaps I was being petty?

'Yeah… so,' she continued. 'The penthouse, so I'd get involved with a paint company, do a giveaway – something like, "What colour palette would *you* use if this was your new home? Tell us and win all the paint you want for a year." You know?' she looked around, nodding for affirmation. 'So, like, you're asking questions to your followers and if they want the free shit they have to respond?'

Violet shot a look at me and smirked slightly at the mention of shit. I didn't flinch, but Joy did. 'Taylor's has based itself on old-fashioned values, Ella, so Instagram and Twitter hasn't really been its thing,' she said.

'We do need to get a grip of social media though,' Dan said. I agreed, it would be up to Dan and Jamie to modernise the company in order to compete with the biggest and best. And the most effective weapon could be social media.

Ella smiled at Dan. 'You are so right.' She smiled, and I caught a glance between them that made my stomach dip.

'Yes, we do need to get a grip of it,' I echoed, wanting to interrupt, to come between them. 'I'll look into it when—' I started, but she spoke over me.

'I do the same with *my* followers, I get them to interact with me by asking them which bikini I should wear, what bra fits me best.' She brushed her hands across her breasts, as Dan listened intently. 'I ask them what they think I should wear for a party, or a date... That was before Jamie of course.' She suddenly remembered him and squeezed his knee, which seemed to be enough for him – he smiled lovingly back.

'Wow, that sounds brilliant,' Dan said, gazing at her like everything she uttered was vital to his existence. I knew this, because he once looked at me like that, but in the madness of marriage and children, I'd forgotten. Women found my husband irresistible. 'We might not be able to afford to pay you *and* Jamie to work at Taylor's, so let's just have you, Ella,' he laughed.

Ella positively glowed.

'We already have an Instagram account,' I said defensively, 'not as many followers as you, but we do okay. And I ask questions...

interact,' I offered, a lone voice in the wilderness. 'I just don't have the time to do it every day – I've been running the social media on my days off.'

'Yeah – I've seen your social media. And, er, no offence, Clare, but… well, days *off*? I mean, this isn't something a company should be doing part-time in between the washing and cooking.'

I flushed slightly at this. 'I work actually – I'm a nurse,' I added defensively. 'I work full-time in long shifts. I couldn't possibly do any more on the website than I already do.' I was trying to stay calm and not allow my voice to give away my irritation and upset at her remark.

'Exactly, you're busy doing other stuff… and sounds to me like you're doing enough as it is,' she said, in what I felt was a slightly patronising way. 'No, Clare, you're making a real effort, and gosh… all while working as a nurse? All those beds to make… you must be exhausted. But really guys, the website needs to be professionally managed, it isn't a hobby. No offence, Clare.'

No offence? I took *deep* offence, but stopped myself from saying anything.

'… polished, more interactive, Taylor's needs to be attracting bigger clients.' She was still talking. 'And those clients who want bigger buildings… beautiful buildings.'

'I agree in essence Ella,' I said, still perched on the arm of Dan's chair. 'But we're a small company, we do need someone but we can't afford to pay them ,' I explained, waiting for Dan to agree with me; after all I was only repeating what he'd always said.

'You can't afford to pay someone because your social media's so bad you aren't getting enough customers,' she sighed, like she'd told me this so many times she was bored.

'Yeah, but we don't have a huge following because most of our clients don't use Instagram. They probably don't even know what it *is*,' I added, knowing I should just be quiet and leave it, but feeling rather bruised by her criticism. I looked around for some kind of confirmation of what I'd just said, but again no one said a word, and Dan was staring so intently at Ella, I don't even think he heard me.

'Oh Clare,' she said, like I'd just made the most ludicrous statement. 'If most of our clients don't know what Instagram is – might I suggest we start looking for some new ones?'

'I'm sorry but—' I started.

'Just hear Ella out,' Jamie said, and no one argued. I glanced around at my family, trying to gauge their reaction to this. Dan was enthralled, Joy's face was a blank mask and Bob just looked confused.

Ella gave Jamie a 'thank you' smile and turned to me. 'Look, Clare, I don't blame you for the fact the social media isn't working, but a company like Taylor's needs a... younger, more fresh approach. We need new ideas, faster thinking.' She spoke softly, like she was explaining something complicated to a child. 'You don't want to be the one that's left *behind*, do you?' There was something in the way she said this that felt like she wasn't just talking about the importance of social media.

Jamie was nodding in agreement as she flicked her hair. I'd done my best helping out with the family business, but perhaps my best hadn't been good enough? Neither Dan, Bob nor Joy were sticking up for me. Maybe they all thought Ella was right, they needed someone younger, with fresh ideas, someone like Ella. Maybe Ella was right and maybe, just maybe I was taking all this too personally. Ella was trying to help, and who was I to say what would work and what didn't? She was the expert.

'Okay.' I smiled, getting up from the arm of Dan's chair. 'I think we all want a work-free, carefree holiday, so can we just talk sun cream and gin?' I asked. 'And, talking of which, who wants another drink?'

'What a lovely idea,' Joy said, relief flooding her voice as Ella glanced at Jamie who put a steadying hand on her arm.

Everyone wanted another drink, and as I poured and passed them round, I tried not to show any signs of the bashing I'd just been given in front of everyone. I hoped this was just early teething problems, people getting to know and understand each other. I hoped that maybe there was some simple explanation for what I'd seen with Joy's earrings. Maybe once I'd got to know Ella better, we could think back to this first meeting and laugh about it? I hoped that we could be friends, sisters even. I had no family of my own, that's why the Taylor's were so precious to me.

After my father was killed, any semblance of family was obliterated. I was old enough to remember my father, and I knew my life would have been richer if he'd been around longer. Even as a little girl, he'd tell me stories and share ideas I was perhaps too young to grasp the full meaning of, but later I appreciated his life lessons. One of my favourite 'stories' was the one about the butterfly. 'Tell me about the butterfly, Dad,' I'd ask. And he'd smile and tell me how a butterfly flapping its wings in New Mexico could eventually cause a hurricane in China. I loved this idea and we played this game where we added our own theories of what might happen all over the world. I know now it was more than a game: My dad was also teaching me – telling me to be responsible for my actions, and be aware of the impact of what I did. 'Life is about consequences, Clare. Everything you do will have an effect on someone, somewhere, just like that butterfly,' he'd say. I didn't understand what he was telling me then, but as I grew older, it made sense to me. And last summer, after everything that happened, I was made even more aware of the consequences of our actions, how the faintest flutter of a butterfly's wings can lead to unimaginable things.

CHAPTER SEVEN

In the few days before Ella and Jamie had arrived, I'd enjoyed going down onto the terrace each morning at about six thirty, before anyone else was up. It was perfect, so quiet, the pool and the trees so still, the birds slowly awakening, everything new and fresh and untouched. I'd make a pot of real Italian coffee on the stove, grab my book and a chair and just sit there enjoying the quiet. It was a part of the day that felt precious to me, so on the morning after Ella and Jamie arrived, I couldn't help but be a little disappointed to step outside with my coffee to see Ella already on the terrace. She looked stunning in coral pink Lycra and, what's more, she was bending over touching her toes – something I hadn't been able to do since about 1998.

'Oh, I didn't expect anyone to be here,' I said, and Ella immediately shot up.

'You made me jump, Clare,' she laughed.

'Sorry,' I said, sitting down at the table, putting my coffee down, my book already waiting.

She looked great, no bags under her eyes, and even without make-up, her skin was flawless, not a line or crease. Her nails were now shiny cappuccino, and I couldn't help it, my eyes strayed down to mine, what could only be described as an angry coral. The colour had looked lovely and summery when I bought it from Boots and painted it on a couple of nights ago, but her sophisticated, shiny cappuccino polish put mine to shame.

'Lovely here, isn't it?' she said, standing in front of me, taut tummy, hands on small hips.

'Yes, we're so lucky. Joy and Bob book a holiday every year and always invite us along.' I smiled.

'That's nice,' she said. Then she bent her head down and said in a low voice, 'Are they okay, Joy and Bob? They seem nice but…'

'Yes, they're lovely, really kind.'

'Joy can be a bit overwhelming, can't she?'

'Yes, but once you get to know her—'

'Is she a bit bossy?' She smiled.

I had to laugh; Ella had spotted that straight away. 'Yes, I suppose she is just a bit bossy, and she *can* take over if you let her – but she's kind, and really supportive. She's fun too and there are a lot worse mothers-in-law than Joy. My friend's mother-in-law, she—' But before I could finish, Ella had walked away, to the other side of the patio and, when she got there, closed her eyes and stood with her arms out. It seemed a bit rude, but clearly she didn't want a gossipy chat about my friend's mother-in-law. Oh well, I thought, at least I could get on with reading.

'You doing yoga?' I asked, as I turned a page in my book.

'No, I'm baking a bloody cake.'

I looked up, surprised.

She opened her eyes. 'Yeah, I'm doing yoga, Clare.' She smiled, rolling her eyes. I nodded and smiled back – it was just her sense of humour, again. 'What's that you're reading?' she asked, now reaching forward, stretching her whole body.

'Oh, it's actually a book I found in the villa, about the history of the place.'

'It looks good. I wonder if I could nick it for my bookshelf at home? Joy wouldn't mind, would she?' She was standing now, arms behind her head, tight little bronze tummy pushed out.

'You don't need to take it with you,' I said. 'You can read it while you're here, I've nearly finished.'

'Oh, I don't want to *read* it,' she laughed. 'No, I love the cover. It's a gorgeous colour, be great on my rainbow bookshelves – they look incredible on social media.'

'Oh, I see,' I said, watching her start to manoeuvre her amazing limbs into all kinds of contortions. I thought of Jamie and her making love on that single bed. So much for Dan's campaign to give them our king size (which I hoped he'd forgotten about). It was clear with her flexible joints Ella could probably be creative even in a tiny bed. 'I guess the owners do an inventory,' I said, a warning shot in case she was thinking of taking the book. I thought again about the earrings, but pushed it away. The more I thought about it the more uncertain I was that she'd stolen them – I may have been mistaken.

'The owners do an inventory? Isn't that Joy and Bob?' She stopped stretching for a moment to look at me.

I laughed. 'No, they don't *own* it, they're just renting it.'

At this she turned her back to me to perform some kind of thigh stretch, so I couldn't gauge her reaction.

'Where are your rainbow bookshelves at the moment?' I asked, changing the subject.

'What?'

'Your bookshelves. Are they at home... in storage, where do you live?'

She stopped for a moment then began to lift her leg around her head in a way I didn't think possible, and eventually she said, 'Storage.'

'Oh, so you're not living anywhere then?'

She didn't respond.

'Where do you come from?' I tried the more direct approach.

'I used to live in Manchester, I have a place in London... A small apartment in New York...'

'Wow, really? I didn't know.'

'Why should you?'

Her sharpness caught me slightly; she was probably trying to concentrate. I wasn't going to say anything else, but I was so intrigued.

'I'm just surprised, two properties? Seems like a lot for someone your age.'

'Does it? I'm a different generation than you – we're go-getters Clare. I'd made my money before I was twenty-five. I wanted an apartment in New York because my dad's a lawyer there.'

'Oh, he's a New Yorker?'

'Born and bred.'

'So you and Jamie don't have any plans to move to London then… to your flat?'

'So many questions, Clare…'

'Sorry, I'm not prying. It's just that if you have two properties, why aren't you living in either of them?' She made me feel like I was asking too much, but I was only trying to get to know her better. I wondered why a woman like Ella, with a jet-setting lifestyle, would want to settle into a suburban corner of Manchester and a small family business, when she could be living in two of the most exciting cities on the planet.

She didn't answer me, just kept winding her legs around herself. I can come over as a bit nosey, and it was up to her if she didn't want to tell me everything about herself straight away. I decided to just keep the conversation light for now, and who knew, in time I might be able to gain her trust, even perhaps her friendship? It would make life a lot easier if the two of us could get along.

'I suppose it's the yoga that keeps you trim?'

'Yeah, that and the *amazing* sex,' she said, staring at me, while slowly opening her legs wide.

'I wonder if I should do yoga,' I said, trying hard to ignore her rather defiant crotch. 'It… it might be good for me?'

'Possibly?' She finally pulled her knees together. 'Older people do have to be careful though, Clare. I'd suggest you do lots of warm-ups to start those muscles, especially as you're menopausal.'

'I'm not,' I snapped.

'Oh, sorry, I just thought you must be.'

Was she being bitchy or just tactless?

'I'm only forty-one, Ella,' I said discreetly wiping the sweat off the back of my neck, lest she thought I was having a hot flush.

'Sorry, Clare, would you mind not talking?'

'I understand,' I said, still giving her the benefit of the doubt. 'That's why I sit here on my own each morning, so I can concentrate. No kids, and no patients.' I smiled.

'Exactly. I feel you,' she said, still twisting her limbs. 'I need to concentrate – and talking about how well your kids are doing at school, or how many beds you made in hospital last week, is distracting. Thanks for understanding.'

I couldn't quite believe what she'd just said. Was she joking?

I looked back at her, and for a few moments there was no expression on her face. She meant it, and I wasn't going to sit and take it.

'Wow,' I exclaimed.

'What?'

'That was a bit rude.'

She looked at me for a moment, like she was going to say something but then seemed to think better of it and instead her face went all wide-eyed. 'OMG, Clare, I was just having a laugh with you. I didn't offend you, did I?' she said, putting her hand to her mouth in horror.

Was she really horrified at the thought of offending me or was she making fun of me? I would give her the benefit of the doubt and assume she didn't mean to be nasty. 'I just think sometimes perhaps you say things, and people don't always get your meaning,'

I said gently. 'What might seem funny to you doesn't sound funny to everyone else – it just sounds rude.'

'To you it does,' she snapped, without looking at me. Perhaps I'd embarrassed her. I hadn't meant to. But then she seemed to think better of it, and looking up, gave me a half-smile. 'Hey, I'm sorry.' She walked over to me, touching my shoulder.

I still wasn't sure if she'd been joking, but Dan always said I took things to heart too much. Perhaps he was right. I needed to 'woman up'.

'I guess I just don't have the same sense of humour as you,' I conceded.

'Yeah, you'll need to get used to it, Clare.' She went back to what she was doing, and standing with her back to me, said, 'Because that's who I am.' Before I could respond, she called, 'Joking!'

'Not funny,' I said, echoing her sing-song tone and returning to my book.

'Hey Clare,' she said, after a few minutes. 'You can join me if you like, as long as you warm up first and don't talk. I could help you do something about that tummy?'

I knew then Ella wasn't suffering from a lack of tact, or a strange sense of humour, it was deliberate. 'Thanks,' I smiled through gritted teeth, 'but I'm okay.'

'Okay, I need quiet now,' she said, and started making humming noises.

'I need quiet too,' I murmured, and went back to my book, but she didn't respond. She appeared to be totally engrossed as she started waving her arms around, then threw her body into all kinds of positions. By now I was so distracted I abandoned my book and watched her.

'I haven't seen yoga like that before,' I said, unable to resist commenting.

'I don't suppose you have, it's only for the very flexible. I learned it when I lived in LA.'

'LA. You lived in LA?' I said, ignoring the implication that I wasn't flexible. Well, I could hardly argue about that. 'Gosh, you've fitted a lot into your life.'

She didn't respond.

'Sorry Ella… I know I keep asking questions.' I forced a smile. 'It's just that… Well, you said your dad is a New Yorker, but I could have sworn you said he was Italian – from Sorrento?'

'*What* did you say?' she asked, staring right at me in what I felt was a threatening way.

'I'm just saying, how can he be a New Yorker "born and bred", and an Italian "born and bred" too, all at the same time?' I stared back at her.

'Are you saying I'm a liar, Clare?' She stopped what she was doing, stood up and walked towards me, hands on her hips in a rather confrontational stance.

'No… I'm not saying that.' I was slightly shaken by her response; suddenly everything had changed.

'You need to be very careful, Clare.' Her tone was suddenly threatening as she came even closer. She was standing over me now, blocking out the sun. In moments this had changed from verbal sparring to something far darker.

I caught my breath. Her beautiful face was close enough for me to see the smooth, botoxed forehead sloping down to perfect brows. But something had turned ugly in her – those sparkly eyes were now cold and dark, the perfect skin now creased as jagged, angry lines escaped across the top of her nose.

Then she leaned down towards me, her nose almost touching mine. She slowly put two fingers to her eyes, and then to mine, like she might gouge them out. 'I see you,' she said, and held herself there, in my face for far too long. Eventually she stood up straight again. 'I bet you can barely sleep at night,' she spat.

My eyes were now locked with hers. I daren't move, my heart was beating in my chest. I wanted to push her over, run away, escape from this – but I couldn't. I was there, in her shadow. Still on my chair. Clutching my book.

'You don't think Jamie and I have secrets, do you? No, we tell each other *everything*.' She smiled. 'Including *your* dirty little secret. So, thinking about it, maybe it's time to start being nice to me?'

CHAPTER EIGHT

Later Dan took the children to the nearby village for breakfast. There was apparently an amazing café that did pancakes and the children were excited to try it out. Normally I would have gone with them, but I was so distraught I needed time alone to think. I spent the next couple of hours worrying and washing the kids' clothes in the little kitchen, mindlessly scrubbing, terrified that Ella knew what I'd been hiding all this time. Did she know *everything*? She was bluffing surely. What on Earth had Jamie said to her? Even if she knew some of it I was in trouble. If I upset her, she'd likely tell everyone – it would ruin my life, and my family. She was mean and I knew I couldn't trust her, but now had to try and keep the peace, at least until the end of the holiday. Perhaps if I really made the effort to be friends with her, she wouldn't say anything? But just remembering the hate on her face, the jabbing fingers near my eyes – it felt impossible, because despite barely knowing me, she already hated me.

I decided not to tell anyone about the earring theft yet. I'd just keep it to myself, and use it if and when I had to. For now, I'd bide my time, watch her, try to find out more about who Ella really was – and keep myself and my secret safe.

A little later, when the washing was done, I saw only Joy by the pool, and felt it was safe to go out there. But within minutes of me settling down, Ella appeared, like an apparition.

'Hey,' she said sweetly, as she approached.

'Hi. It's still so hot,' I said, miming wiping my brow, trying hard to show her there were no hard feelings.

'Yeah, love the heat though,' she murmured, her flip-flops heading towards us and stopping a few feet away. She turned and looked back at the villa. In the few seconds silence I was scared she might say something in front of Joy, so I leapt in with some vague talk about the weather to keep the atmosphere light.

'The villa looks gorgeous in this bright sunshine, doesn't it?' I said. No response, so I tried again. 'Have you posted any photos of the villa?' I asked brightly, then realised she wasn't looking at the villa, she'd turned around to take a selfie.

She looked at me, a frisson of irritation crossing her face.

'Do you mind if I follow you on Instagram so I can see the photos of the villa?' I was trying to keep her on side, but in truth there was a part of me that wanted to know more. After all, she claimed to know *my* secrets.

She shrugged. 'Yeah, sure. Didn't realise you had an account, Clare.' She sat down on the other side of Joy and pouted into her phone screen.

'Yeah, even boring mothers are allowed on Instagram,' I said, with a smile.

'Oh Clare, I'm sorry. I upset you last night, didn't I? I can be so tactless sometimes, please forget I said that – about you being a part-time housewife, or whatever it was.'

'Already forgotten,' I said. I wondered if perhaps she'd also forgotten the way she'd spoken to me only hours before?

'Thing is, you seem to take offence so easily,' she added. 'I had no idea you were so touchy, but I promise from now on I won't joke with you about how you spend your time washing and cooking… oh, and making beds for a living.'

'Thanks.' I wasn't rising to her.

'Hey, I just thought of something really cool,' she said, positioning herself onto the sunlounger.

I looked at her over my sunglasses. 'What?'

'You should take photos of your kids and start your own mummy Instagram. Stay-at-home suburban mummy with pretty kids trying to lose weight... or something?'

I pushed my glasses back up. 'Yeah, fat, middle-aged mum who makes beds for a living,' I said, sarcastically.

'You could have something there, Clare. Let me know if you need any help,' she said with a smile.

I didn't answer her. It seemed any hopes I'd had of ever being friends had vanished. I couldn't figure out why she seemed to have taken against me so much. It wasn't like I was a threat to her.

'Oh no, I haven't upset you again, have I?' She sighed theatrically. 'Honestly, she's so sensitive, isn't she, Joy?'

Joy was engrossed in her book and briefly looked up and smiled, which I'm sure Ella took as an affirmative.

'Not sensitive at all,' I said, and closed my eyes so she'd know the conversation was over.

What was her game?

Later, when we all sat together to eat the meal that Joy and I had spent all afternoon preparing, Ella asked Joy what was in the sauce and how we'd cooked the vegetables.

'Clare cooked the vegetables,' Joy said.

'Nothing special, just steamed over slightly salted water, a knob of butter and seasoning and they were done.' I smiled.

'Oh wow, so much salt – and butter, Clare?' she gasped, and looked at Jamie.

'There isn't that much,' I said. 'Anyway, a little butter and a sprinkle of salt doesn't do anyone any harm.'

'*Clare*. Human beings weren't meant to eat salt – and yeah, a *little* butter is fine, but, honey, you've *drenched* these carrots.' She smiled sweetly at me.

'Oh, sorry.' I continued to eat. I wasn't going to rise to this.

'No, I'm sorry, that was rude of me – I mean, I can't expect everyone to understand clean eating.'

'You mean you have nothing processed?' I asked, doubtfully.

'Absolutely, and I try to eat wholefoods, often raw. And I'm vegan – I eat nothing with a face.' She stared pointedly at the juicy lamb I was biting into – I almost heard the 'baa' – and the look she passed at me across the table made me feel like a cannibal. For a moment I considered putting down the next forkful of lamb, but then told myself I wasn't going to allow a woman who'd arrived only the day before to make me feel guilty about eating. This was a dinner I'd helped to cook in a very hot kitchen on a hot afternoon which she'd spent on a sunlounger, photographing herself.

I continued to chew slowly and smiled at her. I liked my family to eat well and was an animal lover too. But I *enjoyed* eating meat and I resented how she made me feel about that. I was about to say something, then remembered our conversation earlier that day – her veiled threat – so I smiled through it, and continued to eat and chat and pretend she wasn't there. I was beginning to feel uncomfortable in her company. I felt so defensive, but I couldn't respond because I wasn't sure what she might say, in front of everyone. If this was just another of Jamie's girlfriends, I would politely avoid her. But Ella was *married* to Jamie, she was family. Not only was she now a Taylor, she was coming back home with us, like an unwanted souvenir. We wouldn't be saying goodbye at the airport – this was for life.

After the lamb dinner, Dan and I put the children to bed and he suggested we go for a walk together, and thinking perhaps it would be romantic, I jumped at it. But, apparently, he hadn't been driven by desire to take me into the garden at ten o'clock at night to kiss under the stars.

'Clare, I brought you out here because… I have something to confess and you're not going to like it,' he started.

'You're not seeing… *her* again, are you?' I heard myself ask. The breath had been taken from me.

'No, no, it isn't anything like that. It's just that… well, I was feeling bad for Jamie and Mum asked if we minded them having our bedroom, as it's their honeymoon.'

I just looked at him; he knew as much as I did how important it was for us to be together on this holiday. However persuasive Joy had been, surely after everything, he wasn't going to just give up our room, our chance to get our marriage back on track? It made me wonder if he'd meant what he said about wanting to stay in the marriage.

Our relationship hadn't always been smooth, of course, but, really, it was discovering he'd cheated on me with a woman half his age less than three months before that had really made things fall apart between us.

CHAPTER NINE

'I'm sorry, but what else could I say?' Dan sighed, when I didn't speak. 'It's only a bedroom, and it's only for another nine days.'

My dismay and disappointment turned to anger and resentment. 'It's not *only* a bedroom. It is so much more, after everything that's happened.'

'I know, I know. But you know what Mum's like, she wants something and she just keeps on until she gets it. She feels bad because they didn't have the big wedding like we did.'

'That was *their* choice.'

'Ssshhh, they'll *hear* you,' he said, turning to look back at the villa. Through the window, I could see them all sitting at the table, could hear the faint laughter, the chink of glasses, and here we were outside in the unbearable heat, both pulling in opposite directions.

'What's this *really* about, Dan?' I asked. 'Is it about appeasing your mother, or your brother? Or is it just that our marriage isn't important to you? Do you want to sleep alone so you can think about *her*?'

'Stop it, Clare. I've told you it was a mistake,' he said, irritated.

'A mistake that went on for months.'

'I gave her up, didn't I?' He said this like he'd done me a bloody favour.

'You gave her up because you didn't want the inconvenience of leaving me. And upsetting your mother and the kids.'

'Please, Clare, not again. This isn't about us, about what happened. It's about me and you doing something nice for my brother and his new wife. Mum put me under pressure, yes – but at the same time I agree with what she said. Jamie and Ella, they're newly-weds and they *should* have a double room. It's their honeymoon!'

I didn't respond. I was in that no man's land of wanting to push him away, and hold him tight. He'd hurt me so much, I couldn't tell the difference between love and pain any more.

'Look, it could be just as romantic as the double if you and I shared the small bed?' he tried, with a smile. Dan said a lot of nice things, he had the same charm as his brother, he just used it more sparingly, probably saving it for the twenty-somethings. I wasn't buying it this time. I'd known Dan for too long to be swept away by his flirting and flattering. I just wanted a husband who was honest, who I could trust.

'They don't need our big bed, the way they were pawing at each other over supper, that was evident,' I snapped. 'Jesus, she was practically mounting him at the table!'

'Oh, don't be so dramatic. I know you said you didn't want to give up our room, but you're always the kind one, Clare. I'm sorry, I just assumed you'd say yes. But if you really don't want to, then we won't.'

'I don't.'

'Okay, that's fine, I'll explain that to them.'

'*Them?*'

'Mum… and Ella. She was there when Mum suggested we swap.'

'Great, how tactful of your mother to ask in her presence,' I said. I understood why Joy had suggested this, she genuinely felt she owed them a wedding, a honeymoon of sorts, but I wished she hadn't put us on the spot. She didn't seem to be aware of the friction between Ella and I, but I wonder now if she was perhaps being a little mischievous? Did she guess I'd be wholly against a room change and wanted Ella to be aware of this too?

'You and I can still spend time together,' Dan was saying, his forehead shimmering with sweat and exasperation.

'I know, but can't you see that by agreeing to it you're suggesting their marriage is more important than ours? And if I then *don't* agree to it, I look like a terrible, selfish person?'

'You won't look terrible,' he sighed. 'I just thought it was kind of Mum to suggest it. And who cares who was there when it was discussed?' He said it in that classic way men see something hugely significant as irrelevant. It was too late for me to even begin to describe the female complexities, the betrayal of the girl code around this. 'Clare, what do you want me to do? Mum's asking me if I'll give up my room to a worthy cause, you're telling me not to. As always I'm trying to please everyone and end up pleasing no one.'

'*Your* room?' I said.

'*Our* room… you know what I mean, stop tying me up in knots.'

We continued to walk slowly through the garden, and looking at the beautiful view, remembering that we were here in this lovely place thanks to Joy and Bob, I felt bad. Perhaps I should offer them the room; it might make Ella a little more pleasant towards me. After all, she was now in our family. For good.

It was all just such bad timing for us, and to be honest, being in the presence of a honeymooning couple was not what we needed right now. While we were attempting to heal wounds and work through the past, Jamie and Ella were looking towards a bright future. And Ella had landed on her feet with Jamie. He was more demonstrative and openly affectionate than Dan, and always seemed to put his girlfriends on a pedestal, hugging and kissing them in front of anyone and everyone. Dan was far more reserved.

Jamie and Ella were a constant reminder of what Dan and I once had, what I now missed. Walking through that beautiful garden in the dark, I realised this wasn't a conversation about bedrooms – it was about me trying to make everything better again, to go back to how it had been before. Before Dan's bombshell.

'I've met someone,' he'd said one evening, three months before, as I grilled fish fingers for the children's tea. I'd guessed something was going on before then; he'd been short-tempered, not engaging with the kids, distant with me. I had told myself it was because he was tired, overworked, worried about the business – but in my heart I knew.

'I didn't mean for any of it to happen... it just...' he'd said.

I'd stood by the grill, watching the bread-crumbed fingers turn from golden, to brown, to black. I thought I might die. He told me it started after Taylor's Christmas party the previous year; she was the accountant. I recalled seeing her once in the offices, a keen, pretty, twenty-something in a navy-blue trouser suit, with shiny auburn hair. I remembered she wore glasses, she suited them, and I'd said to Dan, 'It's funny how names don't fit people sometimes. I mean, bless her, she's hardly a Marilyn Monroe, is she?' He'd laughed and said people weren't always what they seemed. I should have known then, but I didn't. I was too busy working late shifts, giving patients their dinner and bed baths before coming home to three children who needed much of the same.

He never actually threatened to leave, but that's essentially what an affair is – it's implicit, it's a *let's try this on to see how it fits*. The threat was always there – it lay between us under the sheets, it waved across the restaurant at me when we tried to have what we optimistically called 'date night'. That was Joy's idea. 'I think the youngsters call it date night,' she'd said. 'A nice dinner in a good restaurant, that's all you need, a chance to talk through things,' like it was a mark that needed to be wiped with a damp cloth.

I hadn't meant to tell her. She'd popped round one afternoon – I was getting ready for a night shift, she was sitting with the kids until Dan got home. I was upset, she asked me if everything was okay and before I knew it, I was telling her all about Dan's affair. I just needed someone on my side, and as she'd guided me through problems in the past, I trusted her. Joy was of course horrified, and particularly furious that it was with one of their employees.

'Never trusted her,' she murmured, a faraway look on her face.

'It's not just her – I don't trust *him*,' I said.

'Look, she's nothing, I promise you, she won't be a problem,' she'd said, brightening. 'Get your hair done, buy a nice new dress and tomorrow night you're off – I'll babysit.' As sweet as this was, I couldn't help but hear the implication that had my hair looked better in the first place my husband might have kept his trousers on.

The following night she'd swept into the house like bloody Joan Collins, all bright lips and clipped tones. 'Come on, you two, sort yourselves out, go to that new French restaurant in the village,' she'd suggested, convinced that a good filet mignon would cure her son's roving eye.

By the last of three date nights, we hadn't actually 'talked through' anything, just bickered, Dan told me one of 'our' problems was that I wasn't 'spontaneous' and that he needed more in his life 'than just work and sleep'.

And I, who was exhausted from work and children and little sleep, had said, 'Everyone wants more sometimes, Dan, even me.'

His response? 'Why do you always have to make it about *you*, Clare?'

We didn't stay for dessert, or coffee. We headed back early, telling Joy we were tired and wanted to go to bed. She gave me a sly wink at the front door, like she was the marriage fairy, assuming we couldn't wait to rip each other's clothes off. And when she left, we went upstairs together, as she'd hoped – but Dan slept in the spare room, and he'd been sleeping there since.

I wonder even now if he's ever really been in love with me. I'm the mother of his children, I play my part in his life, I fit in with his family, his commitments. I'm his wife, the accepted and appropriate daughter-in-law on the cast list of the Taylors' drama. But is that all I am to him?

I recalled Jamie saying earlier that his heart beat faster every time he saw Ella. It made me think, had Dan's heart *ever* beat faster when he saw me?

I knew I loved him, it's why I didn't leave when he told me he'd fallen in love with someone else. It seemed this wasn't just a casual fling like before, this was apparently something deeper, more intense. This had been a shock, but was also painful proof to me that Dan was capable of real, passionate love. I saw by the way he looked when he talked about her that she meant more than anyone – more than me. I never told him how I felt, I found it too raw to see the faraway look in his eyes when he told me he'd finished it with her.

But I had to forgive him because I loved him, and that night in the garden of the villa I still believed that, in forgiving him, he'd finally come to love me. It's why I took the time to understand his dilemma – he was completely torn between his mother's wishes and my happiness. In the moonlit darkness, I saw panic in his eyes and knew only I could release him from this awful tug of war. So I reached out my hand, which he took gratefully, and murmured, 'Okay, they can have our room, but you owe me one.'

The relief made him laugh. His whole body seemed to relax, and he instinctively hugged me. 'Thank you. I knew you'd agree. I know how much it meant to you, to us – but I just felt bad saying no in front of Ella.'

'I understand, your mum shouldn't have put you in that position, but she was probably only being thoughtful,' I sighed, catching his hand as we continued to walk through the garden, both drawn to the pool, still lit, a bright turquoise rectangle in the darkness. We stood together, by the edge, mesmerised by the blue glow and, still holding his hand, I sat on the edge. He sat down too and I slipped off my sandals, lowering both feet in. It was cool and so refreshing and, in the airless heat, I had this urge to slip into the water, fully clothed, and let the blue cold wash over me.

'I want to get in,' I said to Dan.

He smiled. 'You can't.'

'Why not?'

'Because… you'll get all your clothes wet.'

'I could take them off first?' I suggested, and looked into his eyes. 'We could get in together?'

For a moment, I could see he was thinking about it; he had that cautious smile I'd fallen in love with a long time ago. Was it too late to start again and get it right this time?

'Go on,' I muttered, waggling my toes under the water, longing to slip into the glinting turquoise, for it to swallow our heat.

He didn't answer me, just looked out over the massive blue, contemplating the prospect. The wine from dinner was making me carefree, less inhibited, and I slowly unwrapped and removed my dress. I sat in my underwear, glad of the semi-darkness. Joy used to joke that moonlight was flattering for a woman over forty. I liked that theory. 'Why don't you buy some good-fitting underwear and turn down the lights?' she'd suggested after Dan's affair, convinced a push-up bra and a pair of lace knickers would bring him to heel. I was sure she had a checklist of 'things a wife should do to stop her man straying' and it seemed I hadn't done a single one. So it was, in essence, all my fault.

I remember laughing to a friend of mine, 'Jesus, it will take more than good underwear and bad lighting for me to look like the twenty-five-year-old he's been sleeping with.' And here I was, sitting in my underwear by moonlight, straight out of Joy's 'Ten Ways to Get Your Man Back' series.

'Are you coming in?' I asked, trying to sound flirtatious and mysterious, which wasn't easy after fifteen years of marriage and three kids. I took his silence as a sign that he was considering it and, encouraged by this, I stood up and jumped in.

The thrill of the cold water was a wonderful antidote to the intense heat, but as I emerged, all I could see in the watery moonlight was Dan's irritated face. 'Oh Clare, no!' he was saying. 'Get out. The children's room's over there.' He pointed to the side of the house. 'If they hear you…'

'They won't. They're exhausted, and fast asleep. If they call out, Joy'll go to them. I thought you were coming in with me?' I said, now feeling a little foolish that I'd gone into the water.

'Sssh!' Another shushing. 'No, I'm not. It's late, and you're drunk. It's dangerous.'

'I've only had two glasses of wine,' I said, too loudly.

'Come on.' He was holding out his hand to help me out, but I was damned if he was ruining my fun.

'You asked me to be spontaneous, Dan.'

'Yes, but not now, not here…'

'But that's what being spontaneous is.' I was hurt, disappointed.

'It's… not… it's stupid. Get out, take my hand,' he said, angry now.

'No, sod off, I don't need your help.'

'Oh, do what you like,' he said and stepped away from me.

I was trying to be what he wanted, and still he was rejecting me.

'You're the one who isn't spontaneous,' I yelled. 'You're so bloody scared of your mother you can't do anything without permission,' I added, my throat now tight with tears. I was goading him, desperately wishing he'd turn around and come back, even to have the last word, but he didn't, he just kept walking until he'd disappeared into the blackness.

Okay, I'd had a drink, so perhaps I shouldn't have been swimming, but even then, in my tipsy anger, I couldn't help but wonder, *if he thinks it's so dangerous, why is leaving me here, alone, slightly drunk in deep, dark water?*

CHAPTER TEN

I swam to the shallow end of the pool, and pulled myself out. It felt dark and lonely, the slightly frivolous excitement I'd felt only minutes earlier now smashed. I felt foolish. I'd wanted Dan to be so carried away by passion that we made love in the pool, or outside. I'd tried to be who I thought he'd wanted me to be, and I hated myself for it, for trying to be who I wasn't.

Until Marilyn I'd been happy, I'd even learned to quite like myself. I wondered, as I had for months now, how I compared to her. Did Dan look at me and wish I was her, did he scroll through his memories of Marilyn, and use them like porn to turbocharge his desire when with me? And did I come up short?

I don't know why I'd been so surprised that he'd fallen for her. They were together twenty-four/seven; she worked on the money side, and he on the business. She was important to the growth of Taylor's and had ways and means of making their money go further. She also happened to be pretty, seventeen years younger and three children lighter. It might have been predictable to anyone on the outside (anyone, apparently, except me) that they were falling into each other's arms. But then I've never been good at guessing surprises – from Dan's marriage proposal fifteen years before, to the surprise party he threw for my fortieth birthday. But the fortieth fireworks and Tiffany bracelet paled into insignificance when he said he'd been having a six-month affair with the accountant. Yes, Dan always had the ability to take my breath away.

But this wasn't the first time. About three years before, he'd had a fling with a stewardess he'd met on a business flight to Dublin to look at some properties – apparently her name was Carmel. I'd heard him on the phone to her, when we were on holiday in Greece that summer. It was horrible, I'd been so hurt, so disillusioned. And later, much later, he told me about her, said she'd been a fling, nothing more, and he'd had to say he was leaving me because she was threatening to kill herself. But eventually he finished it, and that's when all the trouble started.

'She won't accept it was nothing,' he'd told me. 'She's been calling me at work, making things difficult – texting me at all hours.' Dan explained that she was a fantasist, virtually a stalker, she couldn't leave him alone and he was genuinely worried about me and the kids being caught in the crossfire.

I was devastated. I'd ranted and raved and cried and beat his chest with my fists, leaving bruises and hating myself for becoming that woman. But as Joy, who'd been aware of the calls to work, pointed out, we had two young children, were both exhausted from sleepless nights, so it was no wonder he'd strayed – we weren't connecting. Dan said it was a terrible mistake, he'd learned his lesson and it would never happen again.

So I bought it, deciding it wasn't worth losing a marriage, splitting a family, for a silly mistake. Besides, I had my own problems by then, and I didn't want anyone discovering what I'd been hiding, so accepted what had happened and tried to make my marriage work.

But it wasn't plain sailing. There'd been some calls to our landline at home, and when I picked up, nothing, just silence, it was really creepy. I couldn't be sure, but I assumed it was Carmel trying to make contact with Dan; he said to ignore it but I found it quite distressing. One day when Joy had popped round to see the children the phone rang and again I was greeted with silence. By now I was so freaked out by this, I wanted to cry.

Joy saw the way I was. 'Is it her?' she asked quietly.

I nodded.

'Tell her you know about her, he's told you she's nothing – and you're pregnant.'

'I know everything,' I repeated, trying not to let her hear the tears in my voice, while my heart beat out of my chest. 'Dan's told me you meant nothing.'

Joy was silently urging me on, smiling, her hand on my arm.

'I'm pregnant with our third child,' I added, trying to compose myself.

There was a slight noise on the other end, it sounded like crying. I put the phone on speaker so Joy could hear.

'He told me he was single… I didn't know he was married,' she said then through tears.

'Tell her she's a stupid little girl… tell her to go away and he doesn't care, never has,' Joy was whispering at my side. 'Threaten her with the police.'

'Go away, you stupid little girl,' I repeated. 'And if you don't stop this now, we'll go to the police and report you for harassment,' I added, then slammed down the phone.

God bless Joy. She was on my side and wanted my marriage to work as much as I did and, what's more, was prepared to get rid of anything that might endanger that. After that incident with the first girl, Joy had said, 'Don't let Dan's midlife blip ruin everything.' She was right, of course, so in the same spirit of onward and upward, I was now here, trying to make good out of the second, more recent affair. But, in truth, it had been agony, and in the weeks after I found out, I became very anxious. I imagined them together in the office, having secret trysts over lunch, and if he was late home, my anxiety was through the roof.

After the failed date nights, the anxiety and dealing with my own issues, I felt like there was nothing else for it but to give up. Surely life didn't have to be this hard? I told Dan I wanted a divorce,

I couldn't do this any more. Dan told his parents – there were times when I felt like he couldn't do anything without his mother's support or approval – and Joy was round in a matter of minutes.

'Don't try to talk me out of this, Joy,' I'd said. 'I'm taking the kids – that's it, I've had enough, I can't live like this. He may have finished with her, but she's still in our marriage.'

'Sweetie, that's nonsense,' she'd sighed. I remember she was holding both my hands in hers, while desperately trying to down-play my husband's treachery. 'I know you're hurt, but this isn't just about you, and how it makes you feel – think of the children. Family is what's important, Clare,' she'd said. I remember seeing tears in her eyes, and it occurred to me that in the ten years I'd known her, I'd never seen Joy cry. Even on our wedding day. 'If you left this family… Well.' She'd sniffed and turned her face away. 'For me and Bob, you're the daughter we never had. It would be terrible, for all of us. We'd be ripped apart. Children need their mother.' At the time, I'd felt so lost, so alone since finding out about Dan's affair, my friends told me I was stupid for staying, that I should get out, but here was Joy telling me I had a family, and I was so *bloody* grateful. But since then I've wondered, was this a threat of excommunication from the Taylors' inner sanctum? Was Joy suggesting that by leaving Dan I'd be saying goodbye to everyone… even my children?

'I can't forgive him while Marilyn's still in his orbit,' I'd said to Joy, who nodded and poured more gin.

'Don't worry about Marilyn,' she said.

I don't know exactly what happened, but the next day Marilyn left Taylor's. Even in my anger, I felt guilty that someone might have lost their job, but I didn't want details of Marilyn's departure. I was just happy at the speed with which she was dispatched. It reminded me how fiercely loyal Joy could be – especially when it concerned one of her family. I remember thinking, I wouldn't want to ever make an enemy of my mother-in-law.

And now, months later, under a starry Italian sky, I was coming some way to accepting what happened. And with Marilyn out of the way, I was beginning to believe Dan and I had a chance. I was trying with all my might to help the tiny seed of hope inside me grow, to remind myself of his promise that this wouldn't happen again. This was naïve on my part I know, but I loved him and didn't want to throw our marriage away if there was the glimmer of a chance for us. This wasn't just about me, it was about my family, and there was too much at stake for me to give up… and yet at the same time I was also seeing things slightly differently, and it was causing me to question my faith.

Now, in the dark by the pool, I sat alone, still damp, remembering how earlier that evening he'd kissed the back of my hand when I'd said something funny. We'd posed for photos, and smiled at each other, almost flirtatiously. If I'd been watching us, I'd have envied this blissfully happy couple who couldn't wait to be alone together. But the reality was quite different, and I wondered if it was all for show – was Dan trying to convince himself and his family – mainly Joy – that the wheels hadn't come off?

He'd never been demonstrative, or passionate with me, and I assumed that was just how Dan was. He'd been kind and loving to me, but I'd seen something different in his eyes when he'd talked about Marilyn. I'd seen a glimpse of what he could be, and I wanted all of him, I wanted what the air stewardess and Marilyn had seen, not the Dan he chose to show to me and his family. What I failed to realise last summer was that our marriage hadn't healed, it was a façade of meaningless smiles captured in framed photographs on Joy's mantlepiece.

CHAPTER ELEVEN

That night, after Dan left me in the pool, I felt abandoned. I really thought he'd have come back, if only to check I was okay. But he didn't and it made me angry and defiant, so I jumped back into the cool, dark water. I wanted to swim, to hide, to forget about everything and everyone and be alone without any worries, just me and the water.

The moon was high, sending only a spotlight onto the pool, leaving the rest inky black, and deep. I propelled my body through the dark, waiting for the release, the sweet freedom that came with swimming, but it never came. After a few more minutes, I saw the silver handrail glinting faintly in the dimness and I grabbed for it, but my hands were slippery and I fell back into the water. The drink allowed me to relax, to let the water take my weight, and I just sank into it. The sensation was lovely: a magic feeling of drifting but at the same time being held; it was like a freedom I'd never experienced before.

A noise suddenly pierced the watery silence – a rustling in the trees. It was probably just the late-evening breeze wiping some of the heat from the earth's surface, but I suddenly felt vulnerable. My dress, a pool of silk, lay where I'd left it, when I'd tried to entice my husband into the water. He'd made me feel foolish, but, as much as I wanted to, I couldn't stay out here all night. I had to go inside that villa and play my part, pretend that everything was okay. I grabbed the handrail and levered myself out of the water.

I picked up my dress and sandals from the side, and like a child who'd been left behind after swimming, made my way back to the house.

I was saddened to see that Dan hadn't even left the front door ajar for my return. It made me realise how alone I'd been out there, how even if I had yelled, no one would have heard me with the door closed. The windows had also been closed tight in the vain hope that the rickety old air con might be seduced into bringing some coolness to the incessant, overbearing August heat. The family were cool and safe on the inside, while I'd been left on the outside.

I turned the big, brass handle. This was an ancient, heavy door that creaked and moaned, and was not easy to open quietly, but I tried and, putting my weight behind it, finally managed to move it and get inside. Walking into more darkness, the silence was even thicker, no rustling trees, no lonely owl hooting in the distance, just velvet quiet. Lamplight from the living room was creeping under the door, providing a sliver of much-needed guidance in the dark while I tried to find a switch for the hall light. I didn't want to disturb whoever was in there. I was wet through and not in the mood to explain why, though it was probably Bob; he often stayed up late. I imagined him relishing a cheeky cigar, a rare moment of peace, with Joy safely upstairs, blinded by the pink silk eye mask, her face bound in Crème de la Mer.

I ran both hands along the wall like a mime artist, when the silence was suddenly broken by voices, women's voices coming from inside the room. It must be Joy and Ella, and I guessed they might be drinking gin and tonic and it occurred to me that even half-dressed and damp I could knock and go in. Instead of being embarrassed about what had happened, I could make it work for me. I could tell them I had fancied a moonlight swim, but Dan was too tired. Joy and I would laugh about the lack of romance in our men and Ella might thaw slightly and see I wasn't a boring mother of three, that I could be a little wild when I wanted to be. I might even be the glue in our new relationship. I could help Ella be accepted into the fold more easily and she might soften towards me, and I wouldn't have to endure her spiky comments and rather intimidating threats.

So I walked down the hall, barefoot and dripping, knowing that towels were kept in a linen basket just outside the living room. I moved towards the door and, I don't know why, hesitated before knocking, and just as I lifted my hand to do so, I heard my name mentioned. My instinct naturally was to hang on, to try and hear what came next – looking back, I suppose I didn't completely trust Joy, and I certainly didn't trust Ella.

'—But she's a good mother,' Joy was saying. It was the 'but' that preceded the comment that bothered me. What could possibly have been said before that? And by whom?

'Oh, I'm sure she is. I'm sure she's a wonderful mum. Your grandchildren are super adorable,' Ella oozed. 'And Dan, he's a *great* dad,' Ella's cutesy little voice added. 'Alfie's so like his dad, isn't he?' She continued with the small talk, the flattery.

'Oh, he's the spitting image,' Joy gloated. 'Dan was just like Alfie at his age too. I'm a proud mother *and* grandmother.'

The conversation then moved on to Ella's travels, and how she knew Jamie was *the One* – 'As soon as I saw him, I knew, I just *knew*. He has the most amazing eyes, like blue pools.'

Christ, I almost puked. She went on about how wonderful he was and I could almost imagine Joy's chest rising in pride, and when she asked if Ella would like another gin, I realised my new sister-in-law didn't need any help from me in being welcomed into the family, and right on cue she said, 'Joy, I feel so lucky, not just to have met Jamie, but to be part of this family.'

'And we're delighted to have you,' Joy answered. A clink of ice, a thank you from Ella, another gin.

Unable to take any more of Ella's creeping, I was just about to leave, when I heard her say, 'And you're not bossy at all.'

'Bossy, dear?'

'Yeah, Clare said you were super bossy and not to let you take over, but I just don't see that, Joy.'

I almost died on the spot. I had said this but only when cajoled into it by Ella. To me it had been a bonding thing between two sisters-in-law, but repeated to Joy it sounded so mean.

'Oh, I'm sorry she feels that way,' Joy said, and I could imagine her pinched lips; this would have hurt her. 'I try to help – in fact I think I've helped her quite a bit. She's obviously misinterpreting my help as being bossy. But I have never tried to take over…'

'Of course not. I can see that, Joy. Clare's lovely – but so insecure, it must be like walking on eggshells for you, and for Dan too.'

I couldn't believe what I was hearing. I had this urge to rush in and explain myself. I knew Joy and I knew how this would make her feel about me; our relationship had been built on years of me being careful not to upset her, only to be smashed in one sentence.

'I do worry about Clare and Dan,' Joy conceded, and I held my breath, hoping she wasn't going to tell this new girl all about my mess of a marriage. 'Clare especially. She's a little fragile… on the defensive at the moment, especially with someone as attractive as you.'

'Oh gosh, I'm not a threat to anyone.'

'No, of course not.' There was a pause, and then she said, 'I hope *you* don't think I'm bossy, Ella?' she asked, returning to the subject. The comment had clearly hit a nerve.

'Not for a minute. In fact, I think you might be the best mother-in-law a girl could have… especially as my own mother isn't here any more.'

'Oh love, Jamie mentioned that you had no family. You're young to be without a mother, when did you lose her?'

There was a silence, and then Ella said in a broken voice, 'Years ago.'

'Oh no. And your father?'

'The same…' This was followed by silence, until eventually Joy spoke.

'Well, darling, I'm glad I can be here for you – I'm glad we all can.'

I imagined Joy putting down her glass, walking over to hug her, a new daughter, another motherless girl she could take under her wing and shape into the daughter she'd never had. Slowly, and quietly, I moved away from the door and tiptoed upstairs, leaving pools of water on the wooden floor. I didn't even go back to wipe it up. Terrible of me really, even though it crossed my mind that it was dangerous and someone might slip on their way upstairs after too many gins. I felt so upset and frustrated, crushed to think that Ella had almost forced me to agree Joy was bossy and was now using it as a complete quote from me.

No one did fall down the stairs that night, but I surprised myself at my own dark thoughts – at the way I felt about Ella and Joy. I was like a jealous child whose mummy had a new favourite. I felt betrayed, not only by Ella, for making me look bad, but by Joy, for being taken in so easily by her. Was she that desperate to trade me in for the new daughter-in-law model? I just wished I didn't care so much, but that's how you are when you lose your real family young, you spend your life looking for another one to belong to. But that's the problem, you never completely belong, and your pseudo-family relationship is always hanging by a thread: so easily breakable.

Reaching our beautiful bedroom, I opened the door and was disappointed, but not surprised, to see the light was out. Dan often went to bed early and alone. The room was stuffy, the heat unbearable, and I took off my wet underwear and lay on the bed; it was too hot for a cover. But Dan was all wrapped up, no flesh bared. He didn't want to be touched by anything – the stuffy heat or me. This holiday could have been so good for us, it could have been the beginning of the end of his betrayal, the start of my forgiveness, but tonight would be the last night together in this room with its huge bed and window looking out onto the moon-splattered pool. And he hadn't even waited for me to come to bed, nor had he been to find me in the dangerous dark.

His lack of attention, desire, whatever you want to call it, had unnerved me. I'd had this rather naïve idea that the minute we reached Italy, the heat, the surroundings, the freedom from day-to-day pressure would somehow unleash us both, but it seemed we'd brought our baggage with us. The idea of him loving someone else had lain heavily on me for too long and wasn't going to melt away under the Italian sun. As he slept, I lay on top of the bed, still wounded in the thick, dark silence. I wanted him to wake up, or stir and just turn around and say something, or nothing, just to look me. He didn't *look* at me any more.

After about half an hour, I heard Ella and Joy staggering up the stairs, all whispers and giggles. It blew my mind how quickly those two had bonded. Did Ella have something I didn't? Was my mother-in-law playing games? Or had Joy Taylor given in to this confident young woman who seemed to know exactly what she wanted from life – and probably from the Taylors?

It was hard to sleep in the heat, but eventually I drifted off, to be woken soon after by a gentle thudding. I dreamed it was Joy knocking on our door and, caught between sleep and reality, I climbed out of bed, finding myself halfway across the room. I glanced over at Dan; he was quiet, sleeping soundly. The thudding was coming from the room next door and within seconds I realised what it was. Jamie and Ella – the cries, the groans, the longing.

I remembered how it used to be and tears rolled down my cheeks as her cries became louder and Jamie's groans deeper. I wondered if they knew I could hear them – the sounds of her pleasure mocking me, mocking my messy, faithless marriage.

CHAPTER TWELVE

Next morning, I was woken by Dan, reminding me that we had to move our stuff from the room. My stomach dipped as I then recalled the conversation I'd overheard, and I knew I had some making up to do with Joy. I was still hurt and angry that Ella had told her what I'd said. What a nasty thing to do. But then again, I suppose I shouldn't have said it, and now I *knew* I couldn't trust her. I resented giving up our room for her even more now and threw my clothes into a suitcase, snapping at Dan over everything. The bed was rumpled, the sheets creased; how ironic that an onlooker might think we'd had a night of passion, but of course we hadn't. The bed was now waiting for Jamie and Ella to mess it up, rolling around in their brand new love.

I finished packing and took my suitcase across the hall to the children's room which is where I'd decided to sleep.

'We can stay together if you like,' Dan said, when he popped his head around the door. 'The bed's too small for two of us, we'd never get any sleep – but I could sleep on the floor?' I was reading to Freddie, who said he had a headache 'like Mummy does'. It bothered me that my headaches were now being adopted by my kids. In truth, they were my euphemism for 'I'm going to lie down because I'm desperately unhappy and fear for the future'. Anyway, it seemed my children had picked up on my use of the headache, as something one wore like a hat, putting it on when one needed quiet time. I wished I could use that excuse now. I didn't want to have this conversation with Dan, the bed hadn't been too small for Jamie and Ella the previous night, but apparently was too small for the two of us.

'It's fine, Dan, I'll sleep here, with the kids,' I said, looking up from Peppa Pig, much to Freddie's annoyance. 'No need for anyone to sleep on the floor,' I added. If he was going to offer to swap our room, then he could sleep alone.

I went back to the book sulkily and continued to read while he stood in the doorway for a few seconds, until Joy called for him downstairs and off he went. And there was the rub – he was torn between his wife and his mother. He'd been used to being told what to do all his life, but with two of us, he had to choose, and he always chose the stronger.

Eventually, Freddie confirmed that his 'headache' didn't actually hurt, as I'd suspected.

'It isn't a headache then,' I said.

'It IS, Mummy!'

'It has to hurt to be a headache, silly billy.' I ruffled his hair.

'I'm not Billy, I'm Freddie,' he giggled.

'Oh, I thought you were Billy, where's Billy then?' I said, and started calling for Billy, which made him giggle, and when I looked under the pillow, he collapsed in mirth. He really didn't have a headache, so I suggested we join the others by the pool. He was delighted at this prospect, and I helped him on with his swimming trunks and stepped into my own black one-piece. I'd cut down on wine and sugar a few weeks before the holiday and hoped my old costume – I hadn't had time to buy a new one – would look better on me than previous years. I'd worn my costume the first couple of days, but after Ella's arrival, I couldn't face having to stand near her while she was wearing some fabulous fluorescent thong. Just the thought of Ella's swimwear made me feel insecure as I stared in the full-length mirror.

No two ways about it – I needed a sarong for my dimpled thighs, something I hadn't really thought about until I saw how smooth Ella's thighs were. I dug out a big black one and wrapped it around me and, clutching a huge bottle of sun cream like a shield, I carried Freddie down the huge staircase and set off for the pool.

As we approached, I could see Ella standing at the side, stretching and holding her thick blanket of hair up to the sun in worship. I was shocked how tiny her bikini was –the bottoms didn't even cover her backside! Was it a bit much in front of her new in-laws, or was I showing my age?

I couldn't help but notice the S bend of her spine as she leaned back to stretch, her breasts pointing to the sun in a way that was either magical or surgical. Even as I walked around the far side of the pool, I could see her tummy was taut, hips enviably svelte, her body confidence through the roof. At seventeen years younger than me, she wasn't just from another generation, she was from another planet. Waddling by the pool, a child on one hip, scars from childbirth and baby weight still clinging on from my two-year-old, I felt like the resident brood mare. I watched her from behind my sunglasses – she was perfect. Even bending over into the bushes to pick up Alfie's beach ball didn't cause a ripple or a dimple, just golden flesh, smooth as a pebble.

'Ella… Ella, over here!' Alfie was calling as she bent right over, the cheeks of her bottom on full view to everyone around the pool. He was sitting on Jamie's shoulders, Violet was sitting with Granny and Grandad crayoning and Dan – 'the amazing father' Ella had admired the previous evening – was asleep on a sunlounger.

I tightened my sarong around me and, still holding Freddie, went to sit with Violet and Joy – safety in numbers and all that.

'Hey, Mummy,' Violet shouted, announcing my arrival.

Jamie waved, Ella looked up and gave me her whitest Instagram smile and Joy lowered her sunglasses like she couldn't believe it was me.

'Is Freddie better?' she asked.

'What?'

'Doesn't he have a headache?'

'No, he's fine.' Then I remembered with a thump that she knew what I'd said about her being bossy. 'But thanks for asking, Joy, you're always so thoughtful,' I added. Yes, if pressed, I could admit to her that I'd said she was bossy, but I could also deny it, say Ella lied. Apart from the fact it would let me off the hook, it might make Joy feel better – I didn't want to hurt her and felt so bad about the comment.

'It's just that Violet told me he had a headache.' She put her sunglasses back over her eyes, before adding, 'Like Mummy.' A shady comment needed shade. She was obviously still smarting from what Ella had told her; I didn't blame her, who wouldn't?

'No, Freddie's good, and so am I.' My voice faded; there was no point in trying to defend myself.

'Oh, you're in swimwear,' she said, in a way that one might say, 'Oh, you're in sewerage.'

'Yes… I thought I'd have a swim in the pool today,' I said, feeling even more self-conscious.

'Is everything okay – with you and Dan?' She peered at me over her sunglasses and I just nodded, my cheeks burning.

I always felt Joy knew everything about everyone, sometimes before they knew it themselves. She'd told me I was pregnant with Alfie, who was a surprise, to say the least. I denied it emphatically, insisting privately to Dan that she was losing her marbles. But then, only days later as I vomited into the toilet bowl, I thought of Joy.

'I wonder what to cook tonight,' she half-murmured to herself now as we sat in the sunshine.

'We could make those meatballs?' I suggested, on safe ground, eager to get back to where we were. 'The Elizabeth David recipe?'

She was about to respond when Ella, who'd now finished posing by the pool, started wandering towards us, all golden tan and tight abs. 'Hey girls,' she said in that cutesy voice, waving at us madly like we were miles away.

'We were just wondering what to cook for dinner this evening,' Joy said, taking off her sunglasses, shielding her eyes with her hand and looking up at Ella.

'I think the meatballs,' I said, settling back down like it had already been decided. Me, Joy and the meatballs had history – we made them every year, they were a Taylor signature dish.

Ella had arrived at our sunloungers and now knelt at Joy's feet. As the mother of her only grandchildren, an heir and two spares, I was sitting to her right hand on my sunbed throne. Surely I was allowed to be a little comfortable; even Ella's nasty little leak about what I'd said hadn't damaged mine and Joy's bond.

I'd tried to be friends with this woman, who had criticised the Taylor website I'd worked on, who'd referred to my nursing career as bed-making, badmouthed me to my mother-in-law and then threatened to tell everyone about what she called my 'dirty little secret'. God, I hoped she was bluffing, but clearly she knew *something* or she wouldn't have said it. I didn't trust her, so how could we possibly be friends? Ever since her Louboutins hit the gravel and she gave me that first cutesy little wave with just her fingers, I knew she'd had it in for me. But why? I sat by the pool going over and over this, aware that those bikini bottoms were halfway up her bum and her husband couldn't take his eyes off her.

'Meat... balls?' Ella was saying now in response to my suggestion, like I'd just suggested we go and kill a local dog for supper.

I nodded vaguely and turned to Joy. 'We could make that lovely garlic sauce we made last year, in the South of France?' I said, aware I was excluding Ella, but making it clear that this is what we do, what we've always done and she couldn't just turn up and change things. Joy was about to answer me when Ella butted in, 'The thing is, as I said last night, I don't eat meat.'

'Oh, of course, you mentioned that.' Joy nodded. 'So, what can we make for you?'

'Well, I was thinking… we could *all* eat vegan? It's healthier for the kids too,' she said accusingly, like I'd been feeding them chocolate bars all week.

'The children eat a lot of veggies,' I said, 'but I like them to have a varied diet and iron is very important to growing kids.'

'Yes, and there's plenty of iron in leafy greens, you don't need to give them dead cow,' she said, at which point Violet, who'd been sitting nearby on her tablet announced that she had no intention of eating 'dead cow' ever again and wanted to be,' a veganarian, just like Auntie Ella'.

'That's fine, but let's start when we get back from the holidays,' I said. I was sure Joy was finding all this tiresome, she just wanted to make dinner for everyone. If Ella wanted a bowl of bloody broccoli then so be it, but I wanted meatballs, and so did Joy, who usually didn't trust anything she didn't do herself, including veganism. 'Ella, I respect your choices,' I started, 'but would you mind not talking too much about not eating meat in front of the kids?'

She pulled her head back on her neck with feigned surprise. 'Why on earth…?'

'Sorry, it's just that it's hard enough to get Violet to eat anything, and if she thinks meat's bad for her, then—'

'But, Clare… it IS.'

'That's your opinion… I…'

'No, not *just* mine, it's proven.'

'Okay, well, if you'd just—'

'And it isn't just about diet, it's about the environment. Cutting meat and dairy products from your diet could reduce your carbon footprint by over seventy per cent…'

'I'm sure you're right, but it's a decision Dan and I will make together at some point, and later the kids themselves. It's not something I want to scare my children with on holiday.'

'Wow,' she said. 'Calm down, Clare.'

'I *am* calm,' I said, forcing my voice into calm mode. 'And I get what you're saying. In many ways, I *agree*, Ella, but I don't want my children to stop drinking cow's milk or eating meat – yet. If, when she's older, Violet chooses not to eat meat or dairy, that's her choice, but as a nine-year-old child, I still believe she needs the nutrients and the protein…'

'Oh Clare, you're so wrong…'she said, shaking her head.

'Look, as their mum, I just want for you to you respect what I ASK,' I said, far too sharply, and far too loudly, causing Joy to look up, and Jamie to stare over protectively, clearly concerned for his wife.

I was embarrassed, I shouldn't have been so quick to snap, but I felt under pressure. It was supposed to be a holiday, but there were too many things to worry about, too many people to please, including my kids, one of whom was now battering the other with a plastic bucket over the head. My husband seemed oblivious to this attack because he was far too busy staring at Ella.

'Alfie, stop that NOW!' I yelled, climbing off the sunbed inelegantly, and waving my finger. 'STOP that now!' I repeated angrily, aware that my aggressiveness was subconsciously aimed at Ella and not my little ones, who were really just playing – if a little fiercely.

'What's going on?' Jamie called across the pool. He got up and was now standing at the far end, bronzed, slim, handsome. Ella was walking back to join him, like she was escaping my wrath. Meanwhile, I'd left my sarong on the floor, and my dimpled hips were on full view as I marched across the tiled floor, barefoot and barking like a bloody sergeant major.

When I got to the boys arguing over the bucket, I swooped down and snatched it from both of them, causing Alfie to burst into desperate sobs, shouting, 'Spiderman, Mummy's stolen my bloody Spiderman,' as I walked away clutching it. Dan, along with everyone else around, was now looking at me like I'd stolen a child's toy and made him cry for my own sick pleasure. I shouldn't have responded like that – the mummy bloggers would have reasoned with the children, distracted them, made it all fun, but not me, the frazzled forty-something.

I felt terrible, and as I did the walk of shame back to my sunlounger, I could see Ella and Jamie were now both standing together, watching me, judging me. And even in that moment, when I should have been thinking about Alfie and how I could calm the situation, all I could think was, *What are they saying about me?*

CHAPTER THIRTEEN

'Jesus, it was a bucket – a tough plastic bucket, Dan. He was hitting him hard with it,' I shouted, still angry two hours later when Dan complained about my outburst by the pool.

'But you didn't have to yell at them.'

'All hell was breaking loose,' I said. 'But you weren't even aware of that.'

'I was, and it was nothing, just the usual Alfie and Freddie stuff you deal with every day. It's not *like* you to lose it with the kids,' he said. He was sitting on my bed in the children's room while they'd gone out walking with Granddad, looking for 'Italian insects'.

'I know, but I feel under pressure, after everything.' This was how it was now. However hard I tried for it not to – it all came back to the affair.

'I'm sorry. How many times can I apologise?'

'You and… her… it's affected my confidence, I feel like I'm a bad wife, a bad mother… a bad daughter-in-law. I worry I'm not giving enough to the kids, and at the hospital I just can't concentrate, and it's life and death. I can't afford not to be on top of that.'

'Hey, Clare, stop beating yourself up,' he said gently. 'If it's any consolation, I feel the same sometimes, like I'm not a good enough husband…'

I wanted to say 'You're not,' but resisted.

'And there's the kids,' he said. 'I sometimes feel like I don't spend enough time with them.'

I wanted to say 'You don't,' but once more I kept it in, because we were talking. Me and Dan were actually talking – we weren't shouting, or accusing or blaming, we were just talking to each other and it was good.

'I sometimes feel like I don't deserve this life,' I sighed. 'I have great kids, I have you and the family, lovely holidays like this...' I gestured towards the window; this one looked down onto the car park, but he got the gist. 'Your family are good to me... to us.'

He nodded.

'I used to think I was a good mum,' I continued, 'a good wife, but then... you...'

'Don't, Clare.'

'I'm not saying this to make you feel bad, I just need to be honest about how I feel. I'm coming through the other side now, and it's been painful, but it's made me think – what didn't I do? Where did I fail as your wife that you needed to be with someone else and how can we stop it happening again? I mean it isn't like it was the first... there was the stewardess, she called me at home for heaven's sake, she knew where we lived, Dan. You compromised the safety of our children...'

'Clare, you're being dramatic, she wasn't dangerous,' he said, irritated, perhaps a little embarrassed still. Then he spoke more gently. 'I can't change what happened, but I can't keep apologising either. I just hope that one day you can forgive me.'

I felt the bed creak. He stood up and walked away. I'd lost him again. I could have kicked myself – why didn't I just let the conversation flow, why did we always come back to this, to her, to his infidelity? 'Because for you those two women are always there,' is what my friend Jackie would say. 'For you they sit there like great big gooseberries whenever you're with Dan, and until you can remove them from your head, nothing will change.' And I had removed Carmel, I'd moved on, but this Marylin thing had brought her back.

Joy's way of dealing with it was to sweep her under the carpet, remove her, remove them from our lives and pretend nothing happened. But for me they were like a bloodstain on a white carpet: it didn't matter how hard I scrubbed, I couldn't get rid of them from my marriage. They were always with him, the smell of their perfume lingered in the air.

Dan paused at the door. 'Please try not to… dwell on the bad things,' he said.

I nodded my head slowly, unconvinced I would ever be able to shake them off. I know, I know it takes two, it was his fault as much as theirs, if not more. But I couldn't hate him, because if I did, I'd have to end my marriage, and, after everything, I still loved him.

'I'm going to check on the kids,' he said. 'They will have run Dad ragged by now.'

We both smiled at that. I liked it when Dan smiled.

'Poor Bob, he looks tired to me,' I said. Bob never seemed to have the stamina that Joy did when it came to the children.

'Yeah, you're right, and it is his retirement. Been at it over 50 years. *Left school at fourteen, you know?*' He said this in his father's voice. It was something Bob often said, it was his badge of honour: 'I didn't need no university education.' I could almost hear Joy correcting his grammar in the background, and I laughed. Bob was very proud of his lack of formal education; he was a self-made man. He didn't get the modern world, the internet, the signing of contracts – 'We just shook hands in my day,' he'd say, and Dan would turn pale at the very thought. 'I'm amazed Dad hasn't been fleeced, or bankrupted, the way he does business,' he'd once said to me. 'Taylor's could have been so much bigger if he'd been more open to change.' But Bob wasn't interested in making millions, he just wanted everything to run smoothly and if things weren't right, he'd just fix them. There were lots of staff at Taylor's, but

Bob seemed to operate in his own orbit with his own rules, and Dan just let him get on with it while trying to drag the company into the twenty-first century. There was a lot of potential, and I knew it sometimes got to Dan that it wasn't being realised, but as Bob always said, 'All I ever wanted was to be able to provide for my family – anything else is a bonus.'

Dan was now standing in the bedroom doorway, about to leave. 'What was that with you and Ella earlier?'

'What was what?' I asked, knowing the red leopard-skin patterns that formed on my neck when I didn't tell the truth would soon give me away.

'You know what I'm talking about. When you raised your voice at her, by the pool?'

'Oh that, I just asked her not to go on in front of the kids about eating meat, making it sound like poison.'

'You don't like her, do you?'

'I tried! When they arrived on Wednesday, I thought it might be nice to have another woman around, we could go shopping together and—'

'Ha! I doubt you two would shop at the same places.'

'What do you mean?'

'Well, look at her.'

I was stung. 'You mean young and slim and—?'

'No, there you go again, putting yourself down, comparing yourself. I meant expensive. Ella likes designer stuff. Jamie was complaining last night that she spends a fortune on clothes. He's got his hands full there.'

'Well, it's not up to Jamie to keep her in Gucci. With her modelling and whatever else it is she does, she can probably buy her own, can't she?'

'I suppose so. Modelling can be lucrative, can't it?'

I nodded. 'But working on the social media at Taylor's isn't.' And I should know.

'If she does come on board, she won't be doing that for long. Someone like Ella needs more than Taylor's.'

I tried not to read too much into his words, but the implication was that someone like me didn't need more than Taylor's.

'Does she need more than *Jamie*?' I wondered. 'They're so different. She seems so materialistic, and—'

'They've only just got married, give them a chance!' he laughed. 'Would you be happier if Jamie hadn't brought his new wife on holiday?'

'No.'

'I can see the red patches on your neck.'

Caught. 'Damn you, Daniel Taylor,' I said theatrically. 'I just find her a bit much, with her big-eyed lectures on dead calves, and telling the kids they can't have plastic bottles. I heard her telling Alfie if he didn't flush the toilet, he'd be saving the planet. He didn't know what the hell she was talking about, he just heard, "you don't have to flush the toilet". It's taken me over a year to get him to flush the bloody toilet.'

Dan laughed at this. 'Well, good for her. It's about time our kids understood the meaning of plastic water bottles and waste water – it's their future we're saving.'

'I agree, but I won't be lectured to by Ella. She's a hypocrite, uses wipes to clean off her make-up, and she travels all the time, has a place in America she says she visits regularly – she must jet around on aeroplanes like other people use buses. How dare she dictate to us, like she's some kind of eco warrior, while her make-up wipes are strangling the tuna.'

'Isn't it the fishing nets that are strangling the tuna?' He looked puzzled.

'Yes, but my point is that maybe she's as responsible for the death of the oceans with her fancy wipes as Alfie is with his flushing. And trust me, if I had to choose, I'd want Alfie to flush – for all our sakes,' I added.

'I too have seen the contents of the toilet bowl after Alfie, and I have to agree,' he said with a smile. 'But, Clare… just go gently, they're only just married, don't want to scare her off in the first week.'

'*Scare* her? You must be joking. Don't you worry, our Ella can look after herself.'

'I'm not convinced,' he said. 'She looks pretty fragile to me.'

'You're the male of the species and taken in by a female's faux fragility,' I said, rolling my eyes.

'Yeah, well she's nice enough,' he continued, 'and she'll be good for Jamie, she's just what he needs.'

'Perhaps,' I said, but before we could continue the conversation we heard, 'Daddy!'

'That's Alfie,' Dan said, half in the room, half out. 'He probably wants to go in the pool. I have to go or he'll just jump in without me there.'

'Yes he will, I know from experience. GO!' I laughed.

'Look, all I'm saying is,' he said, 'just be nice to Ella.' He added a wink to soften this, then made a swift exit. Classic Dan. He once told me that if he wanted to contradict Joy as a kid he used to say what he thought, and before she could respond he'd just make a run for it. Like he'd just done with me now. Despite him cutting and running like that, it was the first time we'd talked in a while and it felt like a small step forward. Even if most of it had been about Ella and the environment (that sounded like a reality TV show if ever there was one), we were opening up, being honest and that was all that mattered, because I couldn't cope if he was hiding anything else. Then I checked myself – I was such a hypocrite, because whatever he might be keeping to himself, it couldn't be as bad as the secret that I was hiding.

CHAPTER FOURTEEN

A little later, I headed downstairs to join them at the pool. Ella and Joy were sitting together giggling when I turned up. This was a little disconcerting. Joy wasn't particularly a giggler, but Dan's words were still ringing in my ears and I decided to give Ella the benefit of the doubt, so I smiled openly at them as I approached.

'Ella and Jamie have just come back from the bakery, they brought back some lovely cakes,' Joy said. 'We saved you one. I've been keeping them in the shade.' She brought out a white cardboard box from under her sunlounger and Ella handed me a plate from a pile on a tray. She smiled, and I smiled back and I thought how it couldn't be easy for Ella coming into this family and despite appearances she may have been feeling as insecure about being the new girl as I was about having her here.

'Dolce Alla Napoletana,' Ella said, as I put the cake on the plate.

'Thank you, it looks lovely.' I took a bite; it was delicious. I found it hard to believe it was vegan, and under different circumstances I might have questioned this – but didn't want to rock the boat.

'It's from a super cute little bakery down the road. Me and Jamie bought them when we went for our run. It's a sweet layer cake, eaten to celebrate Ferragosto, the mid-August celebration of the Assumption of the Virgin Mary into heaven,' Ella said, like she was an expert in random Italian religious festivals.

'Wow,' was all I could say.

'Joy and I are on a mission this holiday, Clare,' she called over to me as I ate my cake.

'Oh, that sounds interesting?' I said.

'Yeah, we're going to create some really amazing new vegan recipes and start a joint Insta account.'

'So you've converted Joy?' I said, and my mother-in-law didn't comment, just smiled serenely, which was so out of character.

'Yeah. Joy and I are going to show you meat lovers that there are better options than eating dead bodies,' Ella continued, which didn't really make sense because Joy ate meat. The redder the better.

'Eww, I don't want to eat *dead* people,' Violet squealed. This was chorused by Alfie and Freddie who hadn't a clue what she was talking about but joined in anyway.

'It's not *dead* people… it's food. Auntie Ella's just being silly,' I said, still trying to keep it light.

'I'm sorry, yes, I was just being silly kids. Your mummy's right.' She looked at me with her head to one side, self-pity and hurt on her face. She did *hur*t very well – could conjure it up from nowhere in fact. To everyone else I must have sounded like a bitch, while Ella seemed perfectly reasonable, contrite even – but I heard the sarcasm in her voice.

We continued to sit by the pool, mostly in silence, with Dan throwing me daggers while the layer cake from 'the cute little bakery' sat in my gullet refusing to budge. He'd clearly heard me calling her silly, taken it out of context and was now judging me for it. *Oh go away, Dan*, I thought. Since when did he get to play the sanctimonious husband?

'So, you must tell me where to find your new vegan Instagram,' I said. 'In fact, I don't even follow your main account, what's your name?'

'It's @EverythingElla123.' She smiled proudly.

I picked up my phone and clicked on her profile. She had over twenty-five thousand followers – I'd somehow expected more for an influencer, but what did I know? 'Wow, lovely photos,' I murmured, scrolling through the selfies with sunsets, selfies in wonderful hotels in long-haul destinations, selfies in swimwear/tight dresses/tiny dresses, all relevant companies tagged for maximum marketing.

Only five minutes before, she'd posted a photo of herself in a long grey silk dress, standing in the villa. 'Home at last! #Home #Italy #MyPlace'

'And, Clare, don't take offence, but I don't follow back.'

'No problem.'

'I don't want to fill my timeline with what you had for your dinner, how much weight you've lost that day, you know? Oh, and when I say "you", of course I don't mean "you".'

'No, of course not.' She so did.

I sat up, still scrolling through all the photos, the beautiful clothes, the cars all tagged, and when I moved to the bottom of the page, I realised the account had only been running about six months. She didn't have a lot of followers for an Instagram model, but she had a lot considering she'd only had the account for six months. 'Do you mind me asking,' I said, leaning over in her direction, 'how you got so many followers in such a short time? We've had the Taylor's account for years and I think we've only got about 500 followers.'

'I know how to do it, know what people like…'

'So what did you do before, if you only started this six months ago?'

'The same. I just deleted the old account, wanted something fresh – no one wants stale old news, Clare. Like I said, you have to keep on top of things.'

I kept looking, trying to ignore what she was saying. It was clearly personal.

'And how can you earn a living from this? I don't mean that in a rude way. I genuinely want to know what an Instagram model is, how your career works?'

She shifted slightly. 'Big companies get me involved in their ads…'

'Big? Like who?'

'Just… I mean make-up and beauty companies… and… you wouldn't have heard of them.'

'I might?' I felt like she was avoiding the question, and I couldn't help but think, what was she hiding – and why?

'Too many to name,' she said and, standing up, wandered over to Jamie, who was sunbathing, and curled up next to him like a baby on his towel. Meanwhile I was left trying to work out just who Ella was and wondering why no one else seemed to question her.

After I'd eaten, I felt obliged to take the others' dirty plates from around the pool and wash up. But when Joy offered to help, I said, 'No, you do enough, stay by the pool. Dan will help me.'

'But that doesn't make any sense,' Ella piped up as she stood by her sunlounger, her breasts gently bouncing under a fitted T-shirt as she tied her hair in a messy knot.

'*Why* doesn't it make any sense, Ella?' I asked, trying not to look at her buttocks in the tiny bikini as she now bent over to pick up one of the plates from the ground.

'If you and Dan are in the kitchen, then Joy has to look after the kids… so she won't be able to lie down and relax. Which is the point – isn't it?' she said, a sense of faux confusion on her face. I knew exactly what she was doing.

'Oh okay, so what do you want to do?' I asked, bored of her picking up on everything I said and sniping at me with that sickly smile.

'Look, you and Joy stay by the pool. You look tired, Clare.' I felt a frisson of irritation at this, the implication being that I looked rough, or old. She always tried to take the wind from my sails. Why was she so hell-bent on undermining me, stripping me of what little confidence I had? She took my plate from my hands. 'I'll help Dan with the washing up. We'll soon have this cleared, won't we, Dan the Man?' she called across to him and he stuck his thumb in the air and heaved himself from his lounger. She then took her nearly naked buttocks and stood far too close to my husband and giggled pointlessly for at least forty-five seconds while he balanced a pile of forks and plates. He couldn't exactly refuse to help, but he didn't have to be quite so bloody eager.

I turned away from them and spotted Bob sitting in the shallow end up to his neck in water, holding Freddie, while the other two splashed around. Joy was now engrossed in her Barbara Taylor Bradford and Dan and Ella were disappearing into the villa with a few plates, and I settled myself down in the shallow end with Bob and the kids.

As I was now there, it meant that I could be with Freddie in the shallow end while Bob went a little deeper with the other two, Alfie on his shoulders. I'd been there a few minutes when Jamie suddenly got up from where he was lying and came to join me.

'You having fun?' he said, sitting beside me, letting his feet fall into the water.

'Yes we are.' I smiled, suddenly feeling a little embarrassed, a little flushed. At thirty-five, Jamie was seven years younger than Dan, and he looked even younger, with the tan, the flat stomach, and the short, boyish haircut. Ella was a lucky girl. 'So, how is married life?' I asked. We'd barely spoken since he arrived and now it felt strange, uncomfortable. I was sad that we'd lost the easy friendship we'd previously had, but under the circumstances I suppose it was inevitable.

'Married life is good.' He nodded. We were both watching the kids, especially Freddie who was now holding on to my leg with one hand and pushing his toy yacht through the water with the other. Bob had been commandeered to 'captain' the flamingo and for a moment Jamie and I instinctively looked at each other and almost smiled. In the past we'd have giggled at Bob grappling with the huge floppy pink creature while Violet and Alfie shouted their orders. But it felt odd, like we didn't know each other.

We sat in silence for a few moments and then he took a breath and said, 'She's a good person – Ella.'

'Oh… yes… yes, I'm sure she is.'

More silence as we continued to watch Bob and the kids.

'She thinks you don't like her.'

What could I say to that? 'Oh. Really?'

I took my eye off Freddie for a moment and looked at Jamie.

'Look, she's a gorgeous girl, and I can see she might be a bit… intimidating? You just have to get to know her,' he said. 'She's very down-to-earth.'

'I'm sure she is,' I said, bristling. Did he really think my dislike of her was down to her looks? I wanted to scream; did no one else see what I saw? 'I just don't know her yet,' I said, holding back everything I wanted to say. 'Anyway, it doesn't matter what *I* think about her. I don't *have* to like her, Jamie. You're the one who's married to her.'

'She's right then, you don't like her?' He looked disappointed.

I didn't say anything for a while, then looked over at Joy, now sleeping – the coast was clear, so I said quietly, 'No, I don't like her, but not for the reasons you might *think*.'

Where once we'd been so easy, so comfortable with each other, we were now awkward and inarticulate.

'Jamie – I tried to like her. I would have been her friend, but it's like she doesn't want that. I think she's keeping me at arm's length, scaring me away because she doesn't want me to know who she is. Who is she, Jamie?'

He pulled his head back in a doubting way as if to ask *What the hell are you saying?*

'Because I don't think you know her either – I don't think she's who you *think* she is… she says she's got properties in other parts of the world, her dad's Italian one minute and a New Yorker the next—'

'I can't believe you're saying this.'

'I'm sorry, but how long have you known her?'

He just shook his head. 'Long enough to know how I feel. She's my *wife*, Clare.'

'I understand, Jamie. I know you're probably ready for something more, someone to settle down with. But, Jamie, is she that woman? Is she warm and loving? Ella chooses her books for the colour of the covers that she can photograph – she doesn't even *read* them. Doesn't that say it all?' He didn't look at me, but the hurt on his face told me again how much he thought he loved her. 'Look, I'm just worried you've rushed into this.'

He bristled slightly. 'Now you're just being unfair—'

'No, I'm not. Do you know if you can trust her? Like really trust her?' I asked. And, taking a big gulp of air, knowing this could break his heart, I told him how I'd seen her inside his mother's room, going through her jewellery. 'Jamie, she stole your mum's earrings… after everyone had been so kind and welcomed her. Especially Joy – she *stole* from her.'

He looked shocked, confused. 'No. No.' He was shaking his head. 'She wouldn't,' he said, adamantly. He was rejecting this out of hand. How could he do otherwise? To hear what I was saying was admitting he didn't know his wife.

Before we could continue, Violet called, 'Uncle Jamie, come in and play.'

Unable to face what I was telling him, I think he saw his get-out and slid into the water, swallowed up in the bright blue delight.

'Let's see how fast you can go on that thing,' he said, instinctively lifting Freddie out of the water onto his shoulders, pushing along the blow-up toy with the other two on, while Bob stood by, relieved to be off duty.

Jamie wasn't stupid, what I'd told him about Joy's earrings would have made him question things surely. But Jamie wasn't good at dealing with the truth, especially if it wasn't pretty. If he was in trouble or he didn't like what he saw, he ran away. Or, just like his mother who, if she didn't like something, would pretend it never happened, he'd have it removed – as she had Marilyn.

I watched the children play, taking it in turns to be thrown in the air by Uncle Jamie, screaming with sheer delight as he whizzed Violet round in the water, and more carefully twirled the boys, who couldn't yet swim unaided. But when I joined them all in the pool, he soon retreated to his sunlounger. And I wondered if in telling him, I'd done the right thing. Had I made him question Ella, or simply made him hate me?

I held on to Freddie as he manoeuvred his toy yacht around the blow-up flamingo, commandeered by Violet and Alfie. I had one eye on the flamingo, the other on Freddie. It wasn't exactly relaxing, but it was fun playing with the kids; they could take my mind off the bad stuff and make me laugh even when I was down. Kids have this amazing talent for removing stress and worry, just being with them puts everything into perspective and wipes away whatever is eating us. My kids are awesome, they make me smile, make me proud, they amaze me, and I'm constantly surprised at how this love I have for them isn't just endless, it grows. My concerns about what I'd said to Jamie just disappeared as Alfie turned into 'a water frog' and Freddie repeated everything he said in his lisping baby voice, and Violet and I laughed affectionately at them. And as the sun shone down on the four of us, it was everything. I knew then that whatever happened with me and Dan, I'd never really be alone, because children take up a space in your heart they never leave, even when they aren't with you.

Our time together now was precious. I had to go straight back to work when we returned home, so I had to make the most of this. I'd allowed Ella to get inside my head. The earring theft, the lies, the vicious personal remarks, her whole bloody presence had taken up far too much of my energy and attention. But now the sun was shining, I could feel the warmth on my back, and the still blue pool rippled only by the children splashing, the flamingo bobbing, and this was all that mattered.

Eventually, Dan and Ella returned from washing up. She appeared by the side of the pool, all smiles, with a tray of orange juice in paper cups. 'Guys, guys, come and get it!' she called, and the children scrambled out of the water for a drink.

'Your husband is great around the house, isn't he?' Ella said, as I climbed out of the pool and she handed me a cup of juice.

'Mmmm. He was probably on his best behaviour for you,' I said.

'Oh, he *was*,' she smiled, 'it was *quite* the performance.' She winked at him and I smiled awkwardly and sipped my juice. Was she trying to make me question what exactly had happened during the washing up, or was it just an innocent jokey remark, one sister-in-law to the other? I didn't know, because I still didn't know the real Ella, I wasn't sure any of us did.

I moved away, putting some distance between us and, while she played Domestic Goddess with her tray of drinks, I picked up my phone and scrolled through my photos. I had already taken some lovely ones of the kids and while looking at the blue sky, blue water shots I came across one from before our holiday. It was a lovely photo of me with a patient I'd known a while, Mrs Marsden. She had terminal cancer, and in the few months she'd been coming for treatment, I'd got to know her well. But as I'd left to go on holiday, she was about to be moved to a hospice. 'Have a wonderful holiday,' she'd said. 'My husband and I often holidayed in Italy. We loved Gianduia; it's this chocolate hazelnut spread – like Nutella, but a million times better. That's what's sad about knowing you're going to die, there are things I'll never see, never taste again. Oh what I would give,' she'd sighed. 'I'd eat it straight from the jar, with a big spoon!' She'd laughed. When we said our final goodbyes, I said, 'Hang on in there, and I'll bring you some of that chocolate spread back – with a big spoon of course!' So I was determined to track it down and take it back for her. I googled the stuff, and found a shop in a nearby town that looked like it'd be likely to have it in stock. I thought about Mrs Marsden, the busy life she'd lead, the way she'd loved her husband, was proud of her kids and I hoped she was still there when I got home. But even thinking about Mrs Marsden didn't distract me for long, and I was soon back on Ella's Instagram. It was like a compulsion.

What was I looking for? Ella was hardly going to post anything that gave her away. In fact, it was impossible to see who she really was in the photoshopped selfies, the choreographed sunsets, the close-up bikini shots. I needed to see the real Ella when she thought no one was looking; there'd been glimpses but nothing I could hold on to. I kept on clicking through her impossibly perfect photos until I couldn't bear to look any more.

I told Dan I was going for a shower and to watch the kids. I headed inside and, once upstairs, I checked through the landing window that they were all still in and around the pool, and when I was sure, I went into Jamie and Ella's room. It hadn't been vacated long by us, they'd only moved in that morning but I wanted to see her stuff, see if there were any clues about her – and, most importantly, any sign of Joy's earrings.

Just walking back into that gorgeous room filled me with sadness all over again. I'd had such high hopes for this holiday and it started with the lovely bedroom, and Dan and I rediscovering each other on that first night. For the first time in weeks I'd felt like we really had a chance, and I'd been right to have faith in Dan, and we still had a connection, something to build on. But it was tenuous, so fragile, and being in this sanctuary could have made the difference, it was our chance to be alone, in a new environment, and make a fresh start.

The bedroom I'd first shared with Dan, looked like a completely different room now Ella and Jamie inhabited it. The bed was unmade, a pot of face cream was open on the dressing table, where a powder explosion covered everything like dust. Ella's clothes lay in pools of fabric on the floor, even her worn underwear abandoned in tiny tangles. There was a half-drunk glass of wine on what had to be her bedside table, where coffee-cup stains had already made circles on the white wooden surface. Jamie's side of the bed was neat and tidy.

As I picked my way across the room, I was struck by how far away this was from Ella's perfectly set-up Instagram pics of folded towels piled in shades, dainty sets of lingerie hung on beautiful hangers on the doors of the old Italian wardrobes like paintings. Not to mention the carefully chosen book in the carefully chosen shade on the bedside table, which was now lying on the floor, disposable and 'sooo yesterday'. And standing there surrounded by Ella's discarded stuff, I realised it didn't tie in with the image she was presenting to us, and the rest of the world. I couldn't help but think that if she treated people the way she treated things, we should be worried. But who was the real Ella – and did I really want to meet her? I felt a shiver run up my spine.

CHAPTER FIFTEEN

I didn't find Joy's earrings in Ella's room, but then again it was such a mess, I didn't know where to look. I felt a little uneasy: I shouldn't have been there looking at their stuff, it was private. If Jamie found me, he'd think I was the one who was weird – or worst, so jealous I'd become obsessed with Ella. As I knew there was a chance the kids might soon come looking for me, I went for my shower. I had to take advantage of this precious 'me' time and luxuriated under hot water for at least seven minutes, which felt totally hedonistic.

After I'd freshened up, it was about 4 p.m. – the time when Joy and I would usually meet up in the kitchen to start dinner preparations. I slipped my feet into the flip-flops by the bed. For a moment I wondered if I should wear some make-up, then reminded myself I was on holiday and to stop putting myself under too much pressure. Besides, in that heat, it just ended up sliding off my face, my mascara forming grey rings under my eyes – accentuating the eye bags.

I went downstairs into the kitchen, where I knew I'd find Joy. I could hear her clanking pots – she'd probably already started on the veg. I reached for my apron on the hook in the kitchen doorway. Joy had bought it for me on one of our previous holidays, and I now brought it with me every time – it was a standing joke. But it wasn't on the hook where I'd left it the day before, so I walked into the kitchen. 'Joy, have you seen my…' And there she was – Ella – wearing my lovely lemon-decorated apron.

She and Joy were poring over my Italian cookery book, Ella asking all kinds of questions and laughing at Joy's comments, which of course she was loving.

I feigned surprise. 'Oh, I was going to ask if you'd seen my apron, but you have it on, Ella.' I smiled my sweetest smile.

'Oops, sorry, Clare.' She put her hands round her back to undo it.

'No, it's fine. Keep it on. It suits you.' I turned to Joy. 'So we said meatballs tonight, didn't we?' I went to open the cupboard where the pans lived.

'Actually, Clare, we discussed the new Instagram account – "Green Mother and Daughter"?'

'Oh… you've named it…?' I was surprised. I didn't think they'd follow up the Instagram idea, but it seemed Joy was as invested as Ella.

'Yeah, we are now officially the Green Mother and Daughter – yay!' She clapped her hands together in a deliberately childish way, while Joy just smiled.

'So we're not going near meatballs – we're cooking totally vegan tonight, and posting it on our account,' Ella said, defiance in her voice, like she wanted a fight. I wasn't giving up that easily, she clearly loved goading me, and for some reason was going out of her way to reject everything I suggested.

'Great, we all adore vegetables and… stuff,' I said, smiling, 'but, thing is, everyone's expecting the meatballs. They love them, they'll all be so disappointed. What do you think, Joy?' I was blatantly asking for her support, pleading for it.

'Ooh, that's a shame, because we've already started on the mushroom en croute,' Ella said, reaching for the pepper grinder.

Joy was just going along with it – clearly this was her way of proving to Ella that she wasn't bossy, that she didn't take over, as I'd accused her of. I was shocked though. I really thought Joy would have rejected the vegan idea out of hand and sent Ella and her bloody lentils packing. I remember when Dan and I were first married, we'd invited her and Bob over for dinner. It was my excuse to use the wedding crockery they'd bought for us and show Joy what a wonderful wife I was. I'd made a vegetable boulangere – it took me ages but I really wanted to impress her. I sat there nervously, at my own table, waiting for her approval, but all she said was, 'Is there any meat to go with the vegetables, dear?' From then on, I'd made a mental note to never serve anything to her without meat or fish, so determined was I to be the perfect daughter-in-law. But it seemed that I'd obviously failed and Joy was giving Ella her chance, so what could I do but go along with it?

Ella was now chopping mushrooms finely, and I have to say, like a chef. I was quite mesmerised.

'Can I do anything?' I asked, feeling like a spare part.

Neither of the women responded, both completely embroiled in their rhythmic tasks of chopping and peeling, together yet apart in their own private worlds.

'The sauce smells lovely,' I said, wandering over to the pan, breathing in the warm, garlicky savouriness. 'The mushrooms smell delicious too, but I'm afraid the kids probably won't touch them,' I said to Ella, shaking my head, though wanting to smile triumphantly.

'I promise you, the kids will love them the way I cook them,' she said dismissively, chopping shallots without looking up.

'Alfie says they look like slugs, and Freddie always follows,' I said. 'I'll apologise for their behaviour now.' I tried a little giggle.

'No need. Never apologise for your children, Clare. Just be super proud of them. I mean, you might not live a blameless life, but I'm sure they will. The secret is not to drag your kids down to the parent's level.'

Irritation fizzed in my head, but I held on, I didn't give her the fight she obviously wanted. I was dying to tell her I'd seen her take those earrings, to say it there and then and take the smug look off her face, but I resisted.

'Perhaps we could do a *few* meatballs?' I suggested. 'For the kids.' I was determined to stand my ground, what little there was left of it.

Knowing there was minced beef in the fridge, I opened it while waiting for Joy's chorus of approval, but before she could say anything, Ella started laughing. 'Oh Clare, you crack me up.'

I looked at her from behind the open fridge door with a rictus grin; a quick glance over at Joy told me she wasn't joining in on this. I was alone, abandoned. 'Why do I "crack you up"?' I enquired, a warning note in my voice.

'Meatballs? You're determined to give your kids meatballs, aren't you? I mean, do you know what's even in minced meat – eww. The clue's in the title. Meat. *Balls.*'

So much for Ella's fragility, I thought, bringing out the minced beef and putting it on the kitchen top.

'Please don't say that in front of the kids, they'll never eat meat again,' I said, in a bored voice. God, she was so annoying.

'Ella, I have to say…' Joy started and I felt this rush of relief like a warm wave. My mother-in-law was now coming to my rescue, and she would agree with me that the children should have meatballs. 'You're so right! Meat… balls – they even *sound* disgusting!'

I stood there, bemused, as they both laughed to each other across the kitchen, repeating the words 'meat' and 'balls' like it was hilarious. But as Joy turned to go back to chopping her mushrooms, I caught her glance and for a split second I saw in her eyes that Joy wasn't finding it that funny. Would Joy ever forgive me for saying she was bossy?

'I'll set the table,' I said, gathering the cutlery together and heading for the patio where we were going to eat. Once outside, the sun was still shining and it lifted me slightly. Let Ella compete with me for Joy's favour if she wanted to, I was the older, more mature woman and I would enjoy this meal graciously. Besides, I knew I was right about the menu, I knew my kids – and when Alfie and Freddie refused to eat and chanted 'dirty slugs' at the table, I would just smile benignly.

Eventually, everything came together, and the family assembled for dinner – Ella's en croute made with field mushrooms and her very own puff pastry. 'Made with nut butter,' she announced proudly as she placed it in the middle of the table, golden pastry on a platter of leaves and edible flowers. I had to admit it looked wonderful, but before we were allowed to start, Ella had to take photos of the family and the food, which didn't go down too well with the boys, and when Alfie started pulling faces, Freddie joined him.

'That's enough now, boys, smile for Auntie Ella,' I tried. I just wanted to eat dinner and relax, but the boys were tired and hungry and resented having to smile for the camera.

'Come on, guys, give me a smile,' Ella said through gritted teeth. 'Say cheese.'

'I hope you mean vegan cheese, Ella?' I said, trying to be funny, but no one really laughed except Alfie, who didn't understand the joke, but laughed so hard he almost made himself sick.

Ella eventually cut the pastry like it was her bloody wedding cake, and I waited for the kids to start grumbling when they realised what it was. But Ella's 'vegan feast' was – against all the odds – a triumph.

'Ella, you're amazing,' Joy fawned.

'Lovely,' Bob muttered.

'Ella, this is delicious,' Dan said. 'Congratulations, we're all converted.'

But it was my children, who ate her mushroom en croute like it was candy, that betrayed me the most. 'Auntie Ella, I *love* this dinner,' said Violet, as the boys ate hungrily, all making a liar out of their mother.

I had to smile graciously when Ella triumphantly raised her glass to me across the table. 'I told you, Clare,' she said. And the candlelight caught the glee in her eyes… and something else. 'You don't know your own kids, they love mushrooms,' she said, then leaned close so close I felt her breath on my face, her cloying perfume in my nostrils. 'You don't know your own husband either,' she murmured, 'and he certainly doesn't know you. Let's hope no one tells Dan the truth about his perfect wife.'

I looked at her in disbelief, and she slowly sipped her wine, never taking her eyes from mine. I turned to look at everyone, but thankfully they were all too busy eating to notice or hear her say anything.

Then she laughed and, putting her arm around me, touched my forehead with hers. To everyone else, this probably looked like a sweet gesture, but it wasn't, because her hand was gripping my arm and I felt the pressure on my forehead. But within seconds she was laughing with Dan about something one of the kids had said, leaving me to wonder if what had just happened was real.

Everyone continued to eat and chatter in the twinkle of candlelight, the tinkle of cutlery, crickets chirping all around us, but I couldn't hear anything, just saw mouths moving.

Let's hope no one tells Dan the truth about his perfect wife, she'd said.

There we all were in the beautiful garden, a glittery table full of warmth and life and family. Night was drawing in, and despite the still unbearable heat, I felt suddenly very cold, like someone had walked over my grave.

CHAPTER SIXTEEN

So Ella was now well and truly one of the family, and as I sat at the table, my world crumbling around me at the prospect of her spilling my secret on a whim, she smiled and pouted and flicked her hair over and over. For the rest of the evening, she took lots of photos, insisting on family selfies, and making us all gather around her. As we danced to her tune, getting up from our seats, abandoning our dinner to stand by her and smile on her command, she seemed to grow and grow, becoming stronger and louder with every click of her phone camera. She bathed in the attention, the acceptance, and continued to overuse the word 'super' as an adverb all evening. And later, when everyone was in bed asleep, I checked her Instagram. She'd posted a photo of the meal and the family at the table. It looked perfect: tea lights, fairy lights, a table groaning with food and a happy smiling family – #MyFamily #Italy #VeganDinner. Several lovely family photos beautifully styled, Ella in the middle, all the family around her – except me. She'd managed to cut me out of every photo.

'She's so… self-aware, isn't she?' I murmured the next day to Joy as Ella took yet more selfies by the pool. The sky was French navy, the bluest I'd ever seen, and the sun was turning everything yellow and gold, but the blot on my horizon was getting bigger by the hour. I was desperately trying to find a way to tell Joy about her earrings but couldn't work out how or when to actually say it. Would Ella then expose me if I did, or would she be too mortified trying to lie her way out of the earring theft? I also didn't want to upset the others: the kids adored her, Dan seemed to think she was fragile, and even when I'd remarked to Bob earlier that she was confident for someone so young, he'd smiled and said, 'Yes, she's a lovely girl.'

I was now testing Joy's opinion of her new family member. I was also keen to bond, hoping she'd move on and forget about my 'bossy' comment as reported to her by Ella.

'Self-aware?' Joy asked, eventually. 'What do you mean exactly?'

It looked like Joy was going to be a tough audience, as tough as Violet, who only that morning had declared Ella to be 'a beautiful, cool princess'.

'I just meant well-groomed, attractive but works at it – you know?'

'Mmm, she's a lovely girl,' Joy said, echoing Bob. 'She's given me the name of her hairdresser in London. Those highlights,' she sighed, and raised her eyebrows. 'That colour would take ten years off me.'

'*Balayage*.'

'I'm sorry?'

'That's the technique. The word's French, it means to sweep – the colour's swept on, gives a really natural look.'

'Ah, yes, I love it, and her nails... have you seen her nails?'

I nodded.

'Just gorgeous.'

My heart sank. It didn't matter if Ella was self-obsessed, always trying to push her views down everyone's throats and judging them if they didn't agree – all Joy saw was a pretty, presentable young woman she could introduce as her daughter-in-law. It seemed that Joy – like everyone else – had been seduced by the honeyed caramel hair and cappuccino-coloured nails. Only I could see beyond the gloss, but then Ella only ever seemed to be hostile towards me, she was lovely with everyone else.

As for Jamie, I'd never seen him like this over a woman. He followed his new wife around like a lost puppy. My brother-in-law had always been a lot of fun and the kids adored him, but he seemed somehow quieter in her shadow. He'd usually lift any family gathering with his easy charm and sense of humour, and Joy came alive in his presence – perhaps we all did. But Jamie had changed. You could see her in his eyes, and when Ella spoke, he seemed to grow in stature, like he was bursting with pride.

Later that day, I bumped into him. I'd just come inside from the pool, leaving Dan with the kids and Ella lying nearby rubbing sun oil in every crevice. Once inside the house, I couldn't help it, I turned around and watched through a window, and within seconds of me leaving, she'd said something to Dan. He was sitting a few feet away from her and looked up, put his sunglasses on his head and sat up to chat. I couldn't hear what they were saying, but he seemed more animated than he had all week. It disturbed me, especially after her comment the previous evening, suggesting someone might tell him what I'd been trying to hide.

I stood for a few minutes trying to work out what they were saying, if the body language would give anything away. As they chatted, there was much smiling, lots of positive nodding from Dan – he even laughed at something she'd said. I could see he found her engaging, but luckily it seemed she was keeping my secret safe – for now. She wasn't going to say anything at this juncture, she was just enjoying playing with him – this was a different kind of sport. He stood up and went over to where she was, a smile in his eyes. My heart started thumping, and I wondered if it had been like this for him with Carmel and Marilyn at first. Was this how it started: a flirty exchange, a harmless giggle? Would Dan, or even Ella, jeopardise their relationship, their family for something more than friendship? I didn't trust her, and I realised then that I didn't trust Dan either.

I held my breath as he stood over her and, taking the bottle of sun oil from her hand, poured some into his open palm and rubbed his hands together. I was breathless as she rolled onto her tummy, and he leaned over her, slowly rubbing the sun oil into her back, her shoulders. Both his hands on her golden flesh, I could almost hear the sizzle as he worked the oil into her, taking such care, so involved in the task.

She was leaning on her elbows. I could see her face now: her eyes were closed, her head thrown back as if in ecstasy, while Dan continued to pour more oil on his hand, slathering it across her back, moving down her body, slickly, slowly, savouring every moment as his hands crept towards her hips.

And as he did this, Ella opened her eyes and looked directly at me. She knew I was there, behind the glass – she'd probably known all the time. Then slowly, she opened her mouth like she was climaxing, and closed her eyes. I was filled with fear and disgust but was unable to take my eyes from what was happening. Then someone tweaked the side of my waist with both hands and I jumped.

'Oh God, Jamie, you gave me such a shock,' I said.

He was smiling, beaming actually, like he was enjoying my reaction. It felt, for a moment, like old times. I tried to forget what was happening by the pool, turning away from the window so I could focus on him.

'Hey, I'm sorry if I upset you the other day… about Ella,' I said.

He shrugged, looking slightly uncomfortable.

'It's another perfect day out there,' I sighed, hating the silence between us, but he didn't respond. He'd seen Ella and Dan and was now gazing past me out on to the pool area.

'My big brother playing the lothario again?'

'I… Yes, I think he's helping Ella with her—'

'Mmm, probably laying it on thick… and I *don't* just mean the sun oil,' he said, unsmiling.

I gave an awkward shrug.

'Don't worry, Clare – she's happily married.'

'Dan's happily married too,' I said quickly, before adding, 'Unless you know something I don't?'

He didn't respond. I wasn't sure if Jamie knew about the current state of our marriage, but Joy probably filled him in during one of their Skype sessions.

'Dan's wasting his time,' he said, nodding his head in the direction of the pool. 'She's not interested in old men.' He winked.

'Ouch, you know damn well he's the same age as me.' I gave him a playful nudge.

'Oops, sorry … I'd better go before I dig myself into a hole,' he laughed, and headed out towards the pool, without looking back. Despite his light-hearted banter, it was clear that Dan applying Ella's sun oil bothered him as much as it bothered me.

I stood back slightly so I couldn't be seen at the window but continued to watch as he arrived poolside, and from what I could tell, he was jokingly chastising Dan for his enthusiasm. It turns out there's nothing like watching your brother-in-law tease your husband for touching his beautiful young wife to make you feel like a wallflower.

I was vulnerable that summer for so many reasons; if I'd been stronger, more tolerant, I wouldn't have behaved the way I did. Maybe then we'd all have left the Amalfi Coast refreshed, with a suitcase of memories, ready to get on with our lives. But we didn't, and I have to take some responsibility for what happened.

CHAPTER SEVENTEEN

The next day, I felt like I couldn't sit round the pool watching Ella preen, so suggested Dan and the kids and I go to the beach. Joy wasn't too chuffed, but I wanted some family time, just us, and I thought I'd leave Joy and her new daughter-in-law to it. If they got on that well, then let them spend all day together – Ella could teach Joy some yoga, and they could cook together again. My theory was that after a day of mung beans and downward dogs, Joy might be glad to see me and the kids for some light relief.

It was beautiful on Positano Beach: lines and lines of overpriced parasols stood along the shoreline like vibrant soldiers, the surrounding cliffs stacked with houses and hotels in every shape and pastel hue. The kids were totally engrossed in the creation of a sandcastle close by, not easy with black sand, but Violet as project manager was making it work. 'It's a palace for a princess,' she was insisting, much to Alfie's disgust. Oblivious to his siblings' preferences, Freddie happily staggered around precariously close to the castle, until one or both shouted, 'No, Freddie!'

'It's nice to be on our own without Ella prancing around in her bikini taking selfies,' I said to Dan as we watched them play.

'She's not so bad. Yeah, she prances around a bit, but she's interesting.'

'Really?' I tried to be nice.

'I reckon you don't like her because you feel threatened,' he said, gazing out to sea.

'Wow. Why would you say that, Dan?'

I *did* feel threatened by her, but not in the way he meant.

'Where do I start? She's young, she's got money, she's child-free and her only worry is which pool in which resort does she choose to deepen her tan in a designer bikini?'

'Not that you've paid much attention,' I sighed, watching Alfie push gritty sand into his brother's ear and giving him a warning call. 'Okay, you have a point, I envy the way she does nothing, has no responsibilities, and apparently no job but plenty of money,' I said, wiping the sand from my feet. 'But there's more to her than meets the eye.'

'What do you mean?'

'I just feel like she's not who she says she is.'

'Who *is* she then?' He was being obtuse.

'You know what I mean, she's all out there and posing, but I don't trust her, Dan. I think she's dishonest.'

'In what way?'

I checked the children weren't listening and, leaning towards him, said in a quiet voice, 'I think she's a thief.'

'You can't just say that, Clare! She's Jamie's wife. Ella isn't a *thief.*'

'Shhh… the children.'

Too late.

'Who's a thief?' Violet asked, her worried little brow all rumpled. 'Did you say it's Ella? Should we call the police?'

'Christ.'

'Don't say Christ, Clare, the kids…'

He was worried about me saying that when he'd practically just announced to the kids that Ella was a thief. Violet was tenacious to say the least and if she decided to investigate, it was only a matter of time before all the kids held their own impromptu kangaroo court, probably during Joy's gin hour that evening.

I turned back to Dan to continue talking under our breaths if necessary, but he'd closed his eyes, making it very clear that the conversation was over.

Later, in the car, as the kids slept, I continued the conversation, keen to share this with someone; I'd held it inside too long.

'When I said before that I think Ella's a thief – I wasn't just making wild accusations,' I said quietly. 'I saw her, Dan... she took your mum's earrings from the jewellery roll on her dressing table.'

'You're kidding me?' He kept his eyes on the road, but I could hear the surprise in his voice.

'No, I *saw* her do it.'

'Why didn't you say anything?'

'I didn't know *what* to say. I was going to mention it to your mum but I don't want to cause a big drama and ruin everyone's holiday. If your mum says they're missing, then I'll tell her...'

'So we don't *know* they're missing?'

'I saw her take them, I'm sure of it.'

'Which earrings?' He was beginning to sound sceptical.

'The diamond drops that your dad bought her for their wedding anniversary. Surely she'd notice if they were missing? They're her favourites.'

'Yeah, probably.'

'But even if she does know, I guess she wouldn't want to rock the boat, like you– not on holiday anyway.'

I was relieved that Dan believed me after all. I'd been concerned he thought I was mistaken, or even that I'd exaggerated what I'd seen.

'Thing is, after seeing her do that, I'm not comfortable with Ella being around the kids,' I said.

'Oh don't be silly, they don't have any jewellery,' he joked. 'And she's hardly likely to steal Freddie's Tonka Toy, is she?'

'You know what I mean, she's dishonest and we don't know what she's capable of – and I'm NOT being silly,' I snapped.

'Well, if what you say is true, it's a worry, but I'm sure the kids are quite safe – and there might be a perfectly good explanation. Why don't you suggest Mum wears them one evening, then if Mum finds out they're gone, that will bring everything to a head.'

I agreed, but given the circumstances, I couldn't be the one to call her out, not now. She'd threatened me. Then again, if she retaliated and told them about what I'd been hiding, I'd just say she was lying. I'd point out that she was lashing out, desperately making things up to get back at me. I suddenly felt like I could see the light at the end of the tunnel – first though, I had to find the proof. Where the hell had she put those earrings?

We continued to drive back to the villa, but I wasn't in a rush to return. I'd enjoyed my Ella-free day, so when I saw a small white van by the roadside with a home-made sign saying 'lemon granitas', I insisted we stop and buy some. We were all hot, the kids were thirsty and Dan agreed, pulling over and parking up behind it. It was a shabby old van, the back doors wide open, revealing a plethora of dried chillies in a million shades of red turning to rust, and it was such a wonderful sight I couldn't help but think it would look good on my own Instagram. Contrary to what Ella suggested, my own photos were mostly family times, the children, friends – and not pouting selfies, what I had for dinner or that week's weight loss, and this felt like a moment I wanted to remember. So I got out and started snapping with my phone, when the owner appeared from the front of the vehicle. She'd been sitting under the shade of an old PVC tablecloth like my granny used to have; it triggered memories of childhood, and the only time I was happy – at my grandmother's house.

She stood, by the van doors. 'Senora, senorita?' she enquired, with a toothless smile, her long gnarled fingers gesturing towards the chillies.

'Granitas, please… er two, *grazie*,' Dan tried, holding up two fingers. 'Oh, and three bottles of water? *Agua*?'

She nodded and went back to the front of the van, where she bent down to a cool box and eventually came up with two plastic cups with straws and three bottles of water. While Dan paid, I took the opportunity to gaze at the chillies, wondering if I'd got the sea in the distance in my shot.

'Do you mind?' I held up my phone and she nodded; presumably lots of pretentious tourists asked this of her. She must have thought we were all bonkers, wanting pictures of her old van. But I took a few more shots as Dan wandered back to the car a few feet away.

I was aware of her standing watching me, but when I put the phone down was surprised to see she wasn't smiling any more. In fact, she had this really weird look on her face, and said, '*Pericolo, pericolo…*'

'I'm sorry, I don't understand?'

'*Morte, morte…*' she yelled in my face.

'I'm sorry, I don't speak—' I started, but before I could say anything she'd grabbed me by the wrist.

'*Pericolo! Morte!*' she said, her eyes boring into mine, her toothless mouth a black hole. I wasn't sure why, but she seemed so alarmed, and I instinctively tried to pull away from her, but she held my wrist tight.

'I'm sorry… I have to go…' I said, and with one yank, I pulled hard and walked quickly back to the car, got in and locked my door.

'You okay?' Dan asked.

'Yeah,' I said, aware the woman was still watching me. 'Let's go,' I said, putting my seat belt on.

'But we haven't had our drinks.' He was holding our two granitas with the water bottles on his knees and a surprised look on his face.

'Let's stop further on. We can't see the sea properly from here,' I said, taking them from him.

'Okay, if you say so.' He was looking at me, confused. 'Are you sure you're okay? You look worried.'

I just nodded, desperate to get away. Dan must have seen the fear in my face and, not used to the car, he put his foot too hard on the accelerator and shot out into the road, almost hitting an oncoming Fiat. In an attempt to avoid the other car, he veered out to the edge of the cliff road where we skidded to the edge of a sheer drop.

'Dan!' I screamed, sweat pouring down my face, as I instinctively turned to check the kids. He managed to gain control of the car and manoeuvred away from the edge, and I turned again to the children who were thankfully so exhausted from their day on the beach even my screaming and the skidding tyres on a hot road hadn't woken them.

'I thought that was it then,' I murmured.

'Me too,' he sighed. 'Bloody Italian drivers.'

I almost laughed at this – how typical of Dan to blame anyone else for his mistake.

We drove for about half a mile and as soon as there was a place to park, Dan pulled up on the side of the road, overlooking the sea. Even then, I looked behind in case the old lady had followed us in the van, but there was no sign of her.

'So, Clare, what was all that about before?' Dan said, taking one of the granitas from me.

'I just freaked out… That woman, she grabbed me.'

'The way you were acting, I thought someone was about to grab your purse or something.'

I suddenly felt stupid. 'No, nothing like that, but did you see the way she had hold of my wrist?'

'Not really. I was checking the kids, Freddie's leg was caught up in his car seat… I only turned around when you got back in. I nearly killed us all shooting out like that, some getaway driver,' he added, trying to lighten the situation. But he didn't make me smile. I was still shaken up, it was really creepy.

'I think she was trying to tell me something,' I said. 'She just kept saying something like, "*pericolo*" and "*morte*". Do you know what that means?'

'I think *pericolo* means dangerous, or in danger? *Morte* means death.'

'Oh God.'

'Clare, you're being dramatic. She was probably warning you about the road. The van was parked on a blind bend, stupid place to stop really – as we found out.'

'I'm sorry, I know I overreacted,' I sighed, knowing this whole situation with Ella and Jamie had got to me.

'I'm worried about you,' he said, one hand on my knee.

'I'm fine, I'm being stupid.' I had to get a grip.

I took a sip of my drink; it was icy and citrusy, just what I needed to soothe the prickles on my arms. And when we'd finished, Dan started the car and drove carefully along the spectacular coast and gently around the tight bends.

'The kids had a great time today,' I said, 'and so did I.' It had been so much more relaxed, easy, by ourselves at the beach. Nothing, or rather no one, to ruin things.

'Me too, it's been a good day. I do love you, Clare,' he said.

'I love you too. And I'm sorry if I sometimes come over as jealous. I don't mean to be – it's just that I don't want to lose you. Again.'

'You won't lose me, you're stuck with me.' He smiled and I put my hand on his knee, old feelings thawing, warm memories of *us* flooding back. Having the time to be together, to be alone, was priceless. It was all we needed to get back on track. Other people and lack of time were the problem in our busy lives.

'Perhaps next year we could go on holiday alone? Just the five of us?' I suggested.

Dan nodded slowly. We both knew it wouldn't be an easy conversation to have with his mother – it was her chance to get us all together, keep us close. As a mum, I understood that, but now, with Ella, things were different. While she was around, nothing would ever be the same.

We drove along and I lost myself in my thoughts. My mind went straight back to the granitas woman. I'll never forget the look on her face. I had no idea what she'd said, but it was the urgency in her voice that freaked me out, and, yes, I'm sure she was talking about the dangerous road ahead, but I took it to mean something more. A warning. I'm not a superstitious person, but later, after it happened, it turned out I was right to be scared.

CHAPTER EIGHTEEN

On our return to the villa, we were greeted by a demonstrative Joy, glass of gin in hand, standing on the gravel outside. She was gesticulating at an imaginary watch in a really annoying way, implying we were late, and some of the loveliness of the day was blurred as I clenched my teeth into a smile I didn't mean.

'It's almost six,' she was saying, as we got out of the car. Despite me struggling to get the children from the car, she continued to talk, without helping. 'We thought we'd go out tonight. There's this gorgeous little restaurant just down the road. We've ordered two taxis for eight o'clock, so come on, get a move on. You all need to get showered and ready. I've been trying to get hold of you all afternoon,' she was saying to Dan.

It had been a long day and with the image of the old lady still in my head and fraught from the journey back, I couldn't muster the energy to try and put up with 'the Ella show' tonight. 'Sorry, Joy, but we won't be coming out with you, the kids are tired and—'

'Oh, but you *have* to. The kids will be fine, they're on holiday!' She turned to Violet. 'You want to come out tonight to a lovely restaurant, don't you, sweetie? They have the most amazing gelato – you love gelato, don't you?'

Violet nodded enthusiastically. 'Is Auntie Ella going too?'

'Of course. It was Auntie Ella's idea.' Then she looked up at me and Dan. 'Ella's been before, says they do the best pasta in Amalfi – and it's her treat,' Joy gushed.

Was there no end to Ella's knowledge and talents?

'No, we couldn't let her pay,' Dan started.

'We aren't *going*,' I said insistently.

'She's adamant.' Joy spoke over me. 'She said, "Joy – it's time you had a night off, you've been in that kitchen since we got here!"' She then added pointedly, through a beaming smile, 'So thoughtful.'

I looked away. I wanted to scream. I was tired and sweaty, I needed a shower, the kids needed feeding, then a bath, and I'd really wanted to spend the evening relaxing in the garden. I'd even hoped to go perhaps for a romantic walk alone with Dan, see if we could continue the good vibes from the day, but those good vibes were already beginning to fade and Freddie had now woken up and was crying. Alfie was moaning he was hungry and Violet was jumping up and down saying, 'Mummy, Mummy! Can I go and find Auntie Ella to show her my beach photos on my phone?'

Violet had been given a very basic phone for her birthday, ostensibly to keep in touch with me and Dan, but like all her friends, it had become so much more. 'Darling, just wait until we're all inside, and you can find her then.'

'But, Muuum! She said if I hurry back she'll put my best photos on her Instagram.'

'Did she?' I said doubtfully, trying to undo Freddie's car seat while Joy wittered on to Dan in the background.

'I mean it's not like I'm being bossy, Dan...' Clearly she still hadn't forgiven me for what I'd said to Ella. It might have helped if she'd faced me with it, asked me what I meant, but she liked to work subtly, and I couldn't address it because how did I know Ella had told her? I could hardly explain that I was listening in on their conversation. Anyway, I figured that once I found the earrings and told everyone about Ella, Joy would know which daughter-in-law was really on her side.

'I *have* to find Auntie Ella,' Violet was saying. 'She said I had to show her my photos straight away.'

'I don't think she did,' I said, with a tense smile. Violet often used other people as a technique for getting her own way: 'The teacher says we *mustn't* do homework tonight' and 'Dad said that last bar of chocolate in the cupboard is mine, not Alfie's'.

'Muum, she texted me and asked if I'd send them, but I didn't have enough data, so I have to send them from the villa.'

'She texted you, on the beach?' I wasn't sure why, but I didn't like it that Ella was texting Violet without my knowledge. Private conversations between my nine-year-old and a grown woman we'd known less than a week? It didn't feel right.

'Yes, she texted me on the beach,' Violet said defiantly, brow now furrowed, hand on hip, then both arms thrown in the air. 'Muuum, pleeeeease! She's got twenty-five thousand followers.'

'And I'm sure they've got *plenty* of Auntie Ella's tiny bikini photos to be going on with,' I said under my breath. 'They can wait for your beach photos,' I added, finally lifting Freddie from his car seat and handing Violet the beach bag, which was big and heavy. 'Give it to Dad,' I said, but Dan and his mother were now walking into the villa. Joy was chatting away, their arms linked, the two of them like bloody royalty, while I, the maid, was left to pick up after them. I was furious and yelled at Alfie to get out of the car, which I instantly felt bad about. And just to add to 'the holiday feeling', Freddie's grisliness was now full on tears and snot. 'Great,' I said, on the verge of tears myself.

'It's okay, Mum, I'll help you,' Violet said, picking up on my distress in her own childlike way. As the eldest, Violet was so aware of other people's needs that her own needs and wants were often overlooked. I couldn't help but feel guilty, as her mum it was my job to make sure she was considered, and with two younger children to worry about, that wasn't always easy.

'No, it's fine, sweetie. I'll take the bag, why don't you go and see Auntie Ella?' I said gently.

'But you said—'

'It's fine,' I repeated, and she ran through the house in search of Auntie Ella and the promised fifteen minutes of Instagram fame. God knows where she'd find her, I just hoped she didn't run upstairs, and go into their bedroom without knocking.

As I made my way into the house, holding one crying child and one beach bag, I could see Joy was now in the sitting room with Dan and Bob, pouring gin. She shouted, 'Hurry up and get yourselves ready, Clare. Remember the table's booked for eight.' Apparently my wishes had been ignored. So instead of a nice evening at the villa with Dan and the kids, I was about to be taken on another of Ella's culinary journeys, with Joy riding shotgun.

I trudged upstairs with the boys, aware we were probably leaving trails of sand everywhere but not caring. I undressed them both, stood them under the shower and then, as they got out, a ping on my phone told me that Ella had just posted a photo. I'd set up my phone to give notifications for Ella's profile, I wanted to see if what she posted tied in with reality. I was glad to see Violet's rather blurred picture of Freddie throwing sand and pulling mad faces – Ella had stood by her promise to include Violet's photos. It made me wonder if Ella wasn't the hard, ballsy woman she appeared to be, having kept her promise to a nine-year-old. Perhaps Ella wasn't all bad? I continued to get ready in tandem with the boys, hurrying them along, putting clean T-shirts and jeans on both of them and managing a quick shower myself. While the boys bounced my perfume bottle along the wooden floor, I threw on a loose white linen dress, a pendant and some lipstick.

After confiscating the perfume bottle, I checked myself in the mirror. I looked okay – not Ella, but okay. I grabbed a clutch bag, while preventing the boys from squirting toothpaste all over the bathroom – maternal multitasking at its finest. I then walked them both down the stairs, which with a two- and four-year-old has to be the longest journey known to man. As we got to the sitting room doorway, I saw Dan lounging on the couch next to Ella. Both had glasses in hand. Both very relaxed.

'There's Daddy, guys,' I said. 'Go get him!'

Dan heard me, looked up in dramatic alarm for the boys' benefit and braced himself for the toddler onslaught.

'Where is everyone?' I asked.

'Dad found an injured bird in the garden, and he's taken Mum and Jamie to see it,' Dan said from under the boys, who were now using his head as a climbing apparatus. 'Violet's with them.'

'Oh, she was looking for you, Ella?'

'Yeah, we found each other.' She offered nothing else, didn't say anything about Violet's photos that she was apparently so desperate to see. She just directed her spotlight smile at Dan, eyes never wavering, dropped her flip-flops to the floor, tucked her bare tanned legs underneath her and got cosy on the couch. Next to my husband.

I wandered over to the sideboard where Joy's gin and Bob's port sat side by side and poured myself a small gin, emptying the remainder of a tonic bottle and grabbing some ice from the bucket. 'Anyone want a drink?' I asked.

'We're good thanks. Dan just made us one.' I turned to see Ella's smile, which disappeared very quickly when Freddie nearly knocked her drink from her hand.

'Careful, cutie,' she said, through gritted teeth. There were times when she couldn't hide how she felt, and this was one of them – she wasn't the kind of girl who'd want a wild two-year-old knocking her drink all over her.

I apologised and gave her a tissue to wipe her dress and she was soon back to the Ella we all knew – or didn't?

'Freddie's gonna be gorgeous, just like his dad, isn't he, Clare?' she said, while Dan positively purred next to her.

'Mmm, he's going to be annoying just like his dad too,' I laughed, to break the sexual tension Ella seemed to be trying to create with Dan. In the sitting room. With me and my kids present.

She smiled again at Freddie, but like the first time, the smile never reached her eyes.

It wasn't long before the others were back from the expedition to see the injured bird. Bob was a bit of a twitcher, but it wasn't Joy's scene at all. I reckoned she only went along so she could supervise their return in time for the taxis.

'Mum, it's so sweet, but it's hurt its wing. Granddad put it in a box,' Violet told me.

Pushing his way onto the sofa between Dan and Ella, Jamie immediately lifted her hand and, looking into her eyes, kissed her fingers rather proprietorially. Without looking at him, she gently pulled away and in that second, I saw their story: Jamie was totally smitten, but for Ella this relationship was like her Instagram: pretty pictures, lovely places, sexy clothes. But I didn't see love.

'Yes, we're hoping if we can keep it safe from cats, with a little water it might get better. Poor thing's exhausted,' Bob added, flopping down on an armchair, while Violet sat on the arm.

'You and Violet both need to prepare yourselves for the fact that the bird may die,' Joy announced in her usual rather blustery way. She was trying to protect them from hurt, but in the process managed to dampen their hope.

Bob nodded grudgingly, while Violet looked crushed.

'It may be the kindest thing, Violet,' she added, on seeing her face. 'Sometimes Mother Nature has a plan – and the weak ones don't survive. Now, where's that taxi?' She wandered over to the window. Damn that little bird, she was clearly thinking. She couldn't control it and would probably have been happier if it died – a serious threat to a bird's life was nothing compared to a serious threat to Joy's dinner plans.

I glanced over at Dan, still trying to tame the boys, now hurling themselves at Uncle Jamie, next to him. A wall between Dan and Ella? Or was I just imagining it?

Jamie was laughing loudly and tickling the boys, but when Joy turned away from the window, the pained look on her face told everyone they were making too much noise, and Jamie immediately announced a round of 'The Silent Game'. This basically involved all children being quiet and sitting still, and whoever did this for the longest was the winner. It was a family favourite, for obvious reasons, and had been created by Joy for her own rowdy boys – 'the perfect "game" when we need some immediate peace and quiet'. It was brilliant, but it was also a strong indication of the kind of mother Joy had been.

Unfortunately, at two years old, Freddie was a little young to understand the finer points and complex rules of 'The Silent Game' and after about ten seconds was shouting and doing star jumps. But when Alfie joined him, banging into Joy carrying yet another full glass of gin, she yelped in horror and stood there arms out, mouth open like she'd just been shot. Bob leaped up to get a towel, saying 'It'll be fine,' as she tried to hide her scowl with, 'It's not a problem.' But it clearly was.

'Sorry, Mum,' Dan said, after several unsuccessful attempts to get Alfie to apologise.

'Don't make him apologise, Dan,' she said. 'Only if he wants to. It's meaningless otherwise.' And with that she swept out of the room to change. Her parting comment was lost on Alfie who sat with a scowl and his arms folded.

'He's tired, Dan,' I said.

'Stop making excuses, he's being really naughty and I'm very cross!' Dan yelled at him, and I saw his little face crumble.

Alfie erupted in tears and ran over to me and lay in my lap sobbing. Dan had been too heavy-handed, as I later pointed out in no uncertain terms. He'd given me a hard time for snapping at the kids by the pool when they were fighting over a bucket, but it was okay for him to yell at Alfie just because he'd accidentally banged into Joy?

Alfie's meltdown had now caused Freddie to try out some attention-seeking behaviour by pouring his glass of juice on the floor, so Dan yelled at him too. All this gave Ella the perfect opportunity to console Freddie by lifting him on her knee and stroking his hair, which he was a little unsure about because 'Auntie Ella' hadn't so much as looked at him until now.

'Shall we go for a little walk?' she asked Freddie.

I immediately bristled. 'We don't have time, Ella. The taxi will be here soon,' I said, thinking: *no way are you going wandering around outside with my baby.*

'It's fine, there's plenty of time. It's only half past seven, the taxi isn't due until eight.' She said this like I was being fussy, stupid, so I had to put her in her place.

'He's tired, he won't want to walk now.'

'He'll love a little walkies, won't you, Freddie?' she said.

'He's not a dog,' I snapped.

Her face went quite pink. 'I'm sorry, Clare. If you'd rather I didn't take Freddie for a walk, I understand,' she said. She was playing the victim for the others' benefit. They were all taking in the scene, it was impossible not to.

'It's not that I—'

'I'll come with you, we'll both go,' Jamie said, picking Freddie up, putting him on his shoulders, and putting me in my place. I felt embarrassed. Why had I been so mean to her, in front of everyone too?

'Are you sure you're okay with this, Clare?' she said, making it an even bigger deal.

'Yes, yes, it's fine…' I said.

'Oh Clare, I do wish you wouldn't worry so much, it isn't good for the lymphatic system, you know? It's what causes the bloating,' she said earnestly, like she was addressing Jabba the Hut.

'My lymphatic system is fine, thank you,' I said, unsmiling.

Dan shot me a look, but I ignored him. He had no right to chastise me when he'd just caused the boys to go into total meltdown.

Within minutes, Joy was back and danced into the room, doing a twirl. 'Will I do?' she asked in a really irritating coquettish way. But having offended Ella, and probably pissed off Jamie, tonight I needed Joy's support. So I raved about her dress and told her how young she looked, which went on far too long, but I had some making up to do.

Ten minutes later, Jamie and Ella walked back through the door, having taken Freddie for his walk. She was holding him in her arms; he'd clearly been too tired to walk, as I'd suggested. 'He's just the sweetest little thing. Can Jamie and I have him?' Ella asked, with a giggle.

'No,' I said too quickly.

The others turned to look at me. My face burned.

No one spoke until Jamie piped up. 'Just as well. Freddie weighs a tonne, too heavy for me to carry. I'm glad Ella works out – she can carry our kids,' he said, trying to lift the mood. But I didn't laugh, and he damn well knew why.

CHAPTER NINETEEN

We all sat looking at each other awkwardly until Joy quickly rallied round and, landing on safe ground, asked Violet, 'Do you like my dress, darling?'

'Yes, Granny. It's such a lovely blue,' Violet answered, always the diplomat.

'Violet's right, it's a lovely blue,' I heard myself say. 'And you know what would look gorgeous with it?'

'What?' Joy's head was to one side. She was smiling. If there was one thing Joy loved talking about more than herself, it was talking about what she was wearing.

'Your diamond earrings – the ones Bob bought you for your anniversary – they will be stunning against that blue.'

I flashed a look at Ella, who was staring at the floor.

'I've got some eyeshadow that shade too – come on, I'll do your eyes,' I said excitedly.

'There really isn't time…' Ella started.

'Oh no… the taxis will be here soon,' Joy added.

'There's *plenty* of time,' I said, warming to this. 'Come on, Joy, if we're quick we can turn you into Helen Mirren's younger sister.'

Joy couldn't resist. She loved being made a fuss of and as she was one of Helen Mirren's biggest fans I knew I'd hit a sweet spot. As we left the room, I smiled at Ella, who looked suddenly worried, and, over my shoulder, repeated a similar sentence to one she'd used on me earlier – 'Oh Ella, don't worry so much!

Think of your lymphatic system,' I said and followed Joy up the stairs, two at a time.

I popped into my own room to grab the blue eyeshadow and to give Joy time to discover her earrings weren't in the jewellery roll, and as I headed into her room clutching my make-up bag, it seemed she had indeed failed to find them.

'Oh, they *must* be here, Joy,' I said, gently taking the roll from her hands and looking through it. 'You always bring those earrings on holiday. Only last year you were saying how they go with anything.'

Her fingers were pushing into the silk pockets of the roll. 'I may have left them at home, Clare,' she offered, but I could tell she didn't believe that. I even wondered if she was perhaps telling a white lie to save any embarrassment.

'No, you didn't leave them at home – you had them with you… Don't you remember – you wore them on our first night here?'

'Oh… oh yes, that's right. I probably put them down somewhere.' But Ella was now calling from downstairs to say the taxi had arrived. Unsurprisingly, she seemed to want us distracted from our search.

'It's a mystery,' I said loudly for Ella's benefit as we walked downstairs. 'I mean there's only us. And it's not like anyone *here* would take them.' I let it hang, as Ella muttered in agreement and hurried the others out of the front door.

'It's fine,' said Joy, 'we'll find them, I'm sure.'

The kids piled into the first taxi and I was about to get in with them when Ella gently touched my arm. 'Sorry, Clare, but I need to go in the first one. I booked the table and I want to make sure it's the right one. I want it to be really special for you guys.'

I didn't care, I just didn't want to be in the same one as her, so I started to get the kids out of the taxi so they could come with me and Dan in ours when it arrived.

'No, no, don't move them, the kids can come with me and Jamie,' she said. 'We can get them seated at the restaurant, and give you guys a little break.' This sounded like she was being caring, considerate, but I didn't trust her, and since when has a short taxi ride sans kids been a little break?

'No, really,' I said, still trying to move the children out of the taxi.

'Clare, they're fine,' Jamie said as he joined us. 'We can look after three children, we're not idiots.'

I stood back, and didn't say anything. Jamie had never been rude or cutting like this before. Jamie and I had always had a special friendship: we shared a sense of humour, we had our little in jokes, usually affectionate jibes about Joy or Bob, nothing mean, just smiling at the way Joy took over, or how she bullied poor old Bob. But since he'd arrived there'd been nothing, not a glimmer of recognition in something that happened, something that was said. I'd looked at Jamie, tried to catch his eyes, waiting for that secret smile, the acknowledgement that we both knew what the other was thinking – but nothing. He never met my eyes any more, and only seemed to talk to me when Ella wasn't around. I wondered if, despite her attractiveness and apparent confidence, she was the jealous type? Was Jamie not allowed to chat to any other women, even his sister-in-law?

'What was all that about?' Dan asked as I joined him and his parents waiting for the second taxi, the kids now being driven off with Jamie and Ella.

'Oh, I just wanted the kids with us. But it really doesn't matter as long as we all arrive at the restaurant in one piece,' I said, wondering if Ella had deliberately booked the second taxi later – or not at all. Or was I being paranoid?

'Rather them than me when Freddie realises Mummy isn't with him.' Dan rolled his eyes.

'Jamie and Ella insisted,' I murmured, not wanting to involve Joy in this. I still wasn't sure what her feelings were towards Ella and I was being careful.

I glanced over at Joy and Bob sitting on the steps. Joy looked older somehow, her usually animated face and gossip-laced lips still and quiet for once. It was easy to forget she was seventy, and Bob a couple of years older. They both seemed in their own worlds and I tried to imagine how they felt. The shaky business that had once been Bob's life was being handed over to his sons, the older of whom was recovering from an affair and trying to rebuild his marriage, the younger newly married to someone they didn't even know. They were passing everything they'd worked for over to their sons, and they may have had their doubts. All four of us were on new or shaky foundations, nothing was solid or sure, and nothing was ever written in stone. It's true that no marriage is ever totally secure, but both their children were in the midst of emotional flux, and who knew how that would affect the future of the family, and their happiness, not to mention the livelihoods of everyone involved?

I'd always considered them both to be invincible. Bob, the quiet but solid backbone, and Joy the queen of the family, but here she was, an old lady sitting on the steps, waiting for her lift. It was a shock to see them looking so vulnerable all of a sudden. It made me think about Ella, and if Joy was somehow being taken in by her, manipulated in a way. It was the unknown that bothered me. Ella was a woman who made her living by selling a version of herself; no one really knew her, least of all us, her new family. And if she walked into one of our bedrooms and stole something precious, what might she take from us next?

I thought of Joy and Bob as my parents and I'd do anything for them, and if that meant protecting them from someone like Ella then I would. When Joy supported me through Dan's affair, I realised she'd do anything for me too, and her actions, as unorthodox as they were, made me appreciate how much she cared about me. And despite her criticisms and, yes, the bossiness – we had a respect and a love for each other. My own mum had been short on love and died too young, beaten up by life. It's a cliché, I know, but I was determined my life would be different, that I'd provide a better childhood for my kids. I knew I had to have a secure job, a good marriage, and when I left school, I went straight into nurse training. Funny, I had this naïve dream that working incredibly hard in a skilled and vital job would provide financial rewards, but nurses are paid very little for the work they do. Meeting Dan was the high point of my young life. I loved him, he brought the financial security I needed and was the father I wanted for my children. It might not sound romantic to put it like that, but when you've come from nothing, it's everything. And I wasn't prepared to give up my everything without a fight.

Eventually, the taxi arrived, and we finally reached the restaurant. I ran in, expecting child meltdown and chaos, but it all seemed rather calm.

'Have they been okay?' I asked, arriving at the table and settling in next to Alfie. Freddie was sitting between Jamie and Ella, and Violet was on the other side of the table with Alfie and now me.

'Of *course* they've been okay, Clare,' Ella answered, like she was bored of saying it to me. 'I asked the restaurant to bring them some gelato before the main course so they'd shut up.' She smiled proudly. I looked around to see if anyone else had registered the rather horrible phrase 'so they'd shut up', but everyone was too busy sitting down, scraping their chairs, discussing the décor.

'Oh,' I said, putting out my arms across the table to my littlest one. Obviously I was horrified about this; it was hard enough to get them to eat properly the best of times, let alone after ice cream for starters. But I wasn't going to put up a fight, especially not in front of the children.

'Freddie, do you want to come over here and sit with Mummy, darling?'

He was a mummy's boy and always wanted me, wherever we were, but he looked at me and just shook his head.

'Freddie's fine here with me and Auntie Ella, aren't you, mate?' Jamie said, ruffling his hair.

'Course he is,' she added, putting down her Martini and kissing Freddie on the top of his head, but never taking her eyes from mine. And when she finally stopped kissing his head, she smiled at me, a little too sweetly, before sinking her teeth into the olive from her drink. I wanted the night to be over as quickly as possible. But I did wonder if perhaps in drawing attention to the earrings, I'd drawn the battle lines with my sister-in-law?

A little later, when Ella became bored of playing mother, she started on a story about how she basically saved the world – all from the kitchen of a top hotel in rural France.

'I worked there for a couple of weeks between modelling assignments,' she explained. 'The customers all said my vegan avocado flatbread was delicious, the best ever. I came up with new recipes, a whole new menu – the chef asked me to stay, said business was so much better since I'd arrived, but I had a modelling assignment in Rome and had to leave the next day.'

I listened along with the others, who seemed completely charmed by her, but it didn't sound plausible to me and I wondered just how much of it was real and how much was exaggeration. Unable to take any more, I excused myself and went to the ladies'. And, as I washed my hands in the stained Carrara bowls, with the swish waterfall taps and the heaven-scented soap, I killed at least ten minutes in there, just wanting it to end.

Once home from the restaurant I immediately disappeared with the children. They were tired and needed to go to bed, and I needed time alone to think. And once they were settled, I lay in bed going over the situation again and again, questioning myself and my own reaction to this stranger in our midst. I'd have welcomed another 'me', another daughter-in-law, who would share my perspective, just someone to talk to, like a real sister. I'd always wanted a sister, but from the get-go, Ella didn't want to get close to me, quite the opposite in fact. She seemed to hate me on sight and had since made it her daily goal to offend or threaten me. All the snide remarks, the smug, knowing smiles, the way she told Joy what I'd said about her on the very first night. Why would she do that? The subtle way she even excluded me from conversations with Violet, the way she tried to 'mother' Freddie and the way she flirted with Dan quite obviously in my presence. The way she threatened to tell my 'dirty little secret', the comments that my nursing career was 'bed-making', the way she referred to my weight, 'chunky' and 'bloating'. The list was endless.

If I'd tackled her about any of this, she could say I was paranoid – there was nothing tangible there, no evidence, and she could simply accuse me of being 'touchy' again. But... I had seen her take the earrings. This was tangible, not subject to my sensitivity or paranoia – and throughout all this, the earrings were keeping me sane. They were tangible proof that she wasn't the person everyone thought she was, and if I could just prove she had them, then I could confront her and everyone would see what she was.

The next morning, while they all played around the pool, I went into Ella and Jamie's bedroom. I quickly checked the en suite first, where high-end face creams sat like fat little soldiers in tubs, no doubt waiting to have their photo taken. I checked the cabinet, the side of the bath, to see if there was a detachable panel, all the time aware that I had probably watched too many thrillers and smiling to myself about Dan saying, 'Miss Marple goes to Amalfi'. I also knew (like Miss Marple) that finding stolen earrings in someone's bedroom was like looking for a needle in a haystack, and unlike the crime thrillers, they wouldn't suddenly fall into my hands. Ella could have hidden them anywhere, and having climbed over her clothes on the floor, gone through most of her messy drawers and wardrobes, I was about to leave and give up the whole idea, when I had one last look in the drawer of her bedside table. There were a couple of chargers, a lipstick, some tissues, but when I pushed my hand right to the back of the drawer, I felt something – a box? I had to grab it with both hands; it was quite large – a jewellery box. It would be audacious to say the least for her to steal someone else's earrings and hide them in her own jewellery box, but then that was Ella – audacious. So I opened up the lid, and inside it was as messy as the room. Everything was piled in there, so I rummaged around among the bits of cheap metal, the broken clasps, plastic hoops, nothing of value – until I spotted a glint of diamond, then another. Joy's earrings! I'd know them anywhere – the shape of the diamond was unusual, and so was the tiny drop. I remember Joy saying, 'it's like a tiny tear'.

I couldn't believe my luck. I sat there holding them for a few minutes, dying to rush outside, shouting about what I'd just found. But if I did that, how could I prove that I found them in Ella's jewellery box? She could say I planted them there, and the others might believe that, thinking I'd taken them myself to drop Ella in it. No, I had to leave the earrings where I'd found them and later, when the children were in bed and everyone else was present, I would confront her. She'd probably lie and say it wasn't true but I'd ask one of the others to go upstairs with us as a witness to prove what I was saying was true. I'd be there when she opened the box and she'd have no choice but to own up. Joy would confirm the earrings were hers and Ella would finally be seen for the thief, the fake, that she was. As sad as it would be for Jamie, he would one day thank me for pulling back the curtain on this woman he thought he loved. He'd be fine after a while, probably do what he always does and go off around the world. I was doing this for the family. I was also doing it for my marriage and the business – I had a strong feeling she was a danger to both.

The more I thought about it, the happier everyone would be if she wasn't around, and it looked like I'd just found exactly what I needed to get her out of our lives.

CHAPTER TWENTY

I put the earrings back in the jewellery box and stowed it away in the back of the side table drawer where I'd found it. I discreetly left Ella and Jamie's bedroom, and was just in my room grabbing a spare bottle of sun cream to slather on the kids when I heard voices and a commotion coming from outside.

I immediately thought of the children, so dashed to the landing to look through the window, my mind already tearing downstairs. The thudding in my chest and dry mouth abated slightly when I saw my three standing in the garden with Bob, watching something in the pool. At this point, I allowed myself a few seconds of relief while I tried to work out what was going on. Jamie and Ella were in the pool, and at first I thought she was splashing him, that they were messing about. But from the way Joy was yelling, I could tell something was wrong and it now looked like Jamie was attempting to get hold of Ella. He looked so scared and, watching her erratic movements, I wondered if perhaps she was having a seizure. I immediately ran down the stairs to try and help. If she was having a fit and went under, it could be horrific. From my training, I knew if this was the case, she had to be dragged out of the water and made safe immediately.

It took about twenty seconds for me to get to the poolside, by which time Dan had dived in and was helping Jamie to carry her while she flailed and screamed. They were now dragging her to the side, where Joy waited anxiously with a towel. It was classic Joy – Ella might need lifesaving treatment, but there was Joy with her pale-grey John Lewis beach towel, like being dry was all that mattered.

As I approached, Dan looked at me. 'She fell in, I think she must have had cramp or something—' He turned back to Ella, now sitting on the ground, Jamie's arm around her.

'Ella, let Clare take a look at you. She's a nurse.'

'Can you breathe okay?' I asked her, bending down.

She nodded.

'Cough for me?' I asked.

'I'm… fine,' she said, irritated. She clearly didn't want me anywhere near her, and I looked questioningly at Jamie, who just nodded as if to say, leave it. From what I could see she didn't seem to have any issues or injuries, so perhaps it had just been a touch of cramp?

'Is there *anything* I can do for you Ella?' I asked, standing up.

'You could move your children's toys,' she snapped.

I followed her eyes to a small plastic truck that belonged to Alfie. I looked back at her and my confusion must have shown because Jamie said, 'She fell over it, I think, didn't you?'

She nodded, looking up at him like a child, making him hug her even closer.

'It's a small plastic toy,' I said. 'I don't understand how—'

'So dangerous to leave it there – but don't blame yourself, Clare,' she said in that sickly voice.

'I wasn't,' I snapped, unable to control myself – I'd just run out there to save her life and now she was insinuating it was my fault. 'Kids leave their stuff around. It's annoying, but you just have to be careful,' I said, standing over her.

'She fell over the toy, it was just lying there – she could have really hurt herself,' Jamie said over his shoulder at me as he hugged her.

'This isn't about falling over a plastic truck – it didn't try to *drown* her, there must be another reason,' I said, puzzled as to what exactly had happened. 'Did you get cramp when you fell in, Ella?' I asked.

She muttered something inaudible through her tears into Jamie's shoulder, and he translated, 'She says she needs to go and lie down. She thought she was drowning.'

'She wouldn't have *drowned* – even if she had cramp there are several strong swimmers around – including my nine-year-old,' I said, trying to put this into perspective. 'You and Dan got her out before anything happened, and I was downstairs in seconds.'

'Come on, let's get you upstairs,' Jamie said tenderly, ignoring my comment.

Ella flashed a hateful look at me as he lifted her up. I glanced around; no one had even noticed. They slowly walked away, Jamie with his arm under hers, virtually carrying her.

'If she almost drowned, there's a reason,' I called after them.

Jamie turned, but continued to walk away and, over his shoulder, yelled, 'Clare, there *IS* – she can't SWIM.'

Joy stood with the towel as Jamie guided Ella back to their luxury room with the huge bed, and I stood there feeling like I'd just been accused of something, but wasn't sure what.

'Oh, that poor girl,' Joy said, after they'd gone. She was wringing her hands together, going over the trauma, so I asked her if she was okay.

'I'm okay,' she said. 'But it was such an awful thing to see – she went rigid in the water, ever so frightening.'

Bob was now nodding at her side. 'I didn't know she couldn't swim! Most young people swim these days, don't they?'

'Yes, Violet's a great swimmer, and the other two love the water and I'll make sure they have lessons as soon as they're old enough,' I said, feeling like a good mother. 'I'm amazed, though,' I said, 'Ella's all over Instagram in bikinis, running in and out of oceans all over the world – yet she can't swim!'

Bob didn't seem to hear me and Joy just shrugged, but I was mystified, and wondered what the hell had just happened.

We all spent the rest of the day pottering around and relaxing as we had before Jamie and Ella arrived. It was nice just making lunch, sitting by the pool, and later Dan and I had a wander to the nearby village, where I managed to find a jar of Gianduia for Mrs Marsden.

While we were on our own, we talked about what had happened.

'It was really scary,' Dan said.

'Yes, she seemed absolutely petrified in the water, but as soon as she was on dry land, she seemed to reject any offer of help.'

'Yeah, I thought she'd be glad someone with medical training was around.'

'Well, she thinks I just make beds.' I smiled.

'She really didn't want you anywhere near her, did she?' he confirmed.

'I know. She hates me, Dan.'

He laughed.

'Honestly, I know how it sounds, but it's like she really hates me. She also knows how to grind my gears, the way she's always grabbing you for "a quick chat",' I said, letting him know I was aware of this.

'Oh, she just wants to tell me her latest ideas for the website,' he said.

'Hmm, I think in trying to impress her, Jamie's misled Ella,' I said. 'She seems to be under the impression that we have this huge property company that'll keep her in Prada for the rest of her life.'

'Mmm, you said she also thought we owned the villa, and I've heard the way she talks about "the company". She asked if we had any offices abroad the other day. She does seem to be carried away by it all,' he agreed.

I was relieved, finally someone was seeing the same things I was, and I felt a little closer to Dan as a result. We even walked back to the villa holding hands, something we hadn't done for a while. But when we approached via the garden, I glanced up and saw Ella standing at the landing window looking down on us.

'She's up there at the window watching us,' I said to Dan, trying not to move my lips, looking down, so she'd think I hadn't noticed and would stay. But when he looked up, she'd gone.

It was weird and a bit creepy. I still couldn't really understand what had happened at the pool this afternoon, but the way Ella had looked at me, it felt as if she was blaming me somehow. I'd wanted to help and make sure she was okay but she'd been holed up with Jamie ever since.

Despite my concern, I had to admit I found the atmosphere more pleasant when she wasn't around. No one was walking around with their buttocks hanging out for a start, and she wasn't there lecturing us all on what we should eat and how we should take a run every morning between yoga moves.

'Ella said you and she were planning to cook again tonight,' I said to Joy later that afternoon.

'Yes, she wanted to try out some more new vegan recipes and photograph them for the new Instagram.'

'Yeah… that'll be fun?' I said, looking at her for a reaction. With no Ella around, I wondered if Joy might say how she really felt about Ella taking over the kitchen, getting Joy to do all the real work then claiming it as her own on Instagram.

'Mmm, we may have to start without her,' she murmured, not looking up from her book.

'We might not see her until tomorrow now,' I continued, still keen for a reaction I could read. 'She seemed pretty shaken up, she must be sleeping it off.'

'Mmmm, she probably is.' Joy finally raised her eyes from *A Woman of Substance*, and I thought for one delicious moment she was going to say something outrageous about her new daughter-in-law. I couldn't believe she liked her, and even if she did, the very act of having to tell the ladies who lunch that her new daughter-in-law was an Instagram model would mortify Joy. She looked across at me, and took a breath. I waited with anticipation, but she seemed to think better of it and returned to her book.

I couldn't resist saying something. 'Joy, do you like her?'

'Who, Barbara Taylor Bradford...?'

I knew she was being deliberately obtuse. 'No, Ella.'

She finally put down the book and took off her reading glasses to consider the question for a few seconds, then turned to me and said quietly, 'I don't always approve of my sons' choices, but one has to let them make their own lives. In the meantime, I just wait.'

'You mean wait for the relationship to end?' I asked.

'Perhaps.' Joy seemed overly vague.

'Do you think this will last?'

'Who knows?' she said, putting on her glasses and returning to her book. I felt now that Joy, along with Dan, was beginning to see what I saw. Perhaps when everyone was together it was time to tell them all about the earrings? Once Joy knew this, she'd stop being discreet, and her real feelings would come flooding out. I never thought I'd say it, but I missed the indiscreet, gossipy Joy who said what she thought. That Joy would have banished Ella from her kingdom, but she was just being careful for Jamie. She didn't want to be the one to criticise Ella and lose her son in the process – I understood, I would probably be the same if Alfie or Freddie brought a girl home that I didn't like one day. I wouldn't be able to hide my feelings as well as Joy could hide hers though.

'Shall we start dinner soon?' I asked, feeling like things were returning to normal in Ella's absence.

Joy nodded, and for a moment I was happy, back in my place, the children playing quietly, Dan and Bob watching them – and no drama.

Joy and I changed out of our swimming things, freshened up and met back in the kitchen about forty-five minutes later.

'Ella told everyone we'd be eating about nine, which is a little late for the children, not to mention the rest of us,' I said.

'Well, Ella isn't here, is she?' Joy said mischievously.

'So, seven thirty to eight then?' I suggested.

We both smiled, and I felt that finally I had the real Joy back. I was so relieved to have everything back to normal and so convinced we were singing from the same hymn book, I was dying to tell Joy about her earrings. Several times as we opened cupboards and took out the pots and pans, I almost started to tell her, but something stopped me. I had to reveal this at the right time with everyone there, which wouldn't be easy. I knew Joy would believe me, but there was still the small matter of loyalty to her son. And Jamie didn't want to hear anything negative about Ella, he adored her and resented anyone who said something against her – even if they were right. If Joy sided with me over the accusation, then she would know she might lose Jamie, or at the very least have a big family rift. I needed the earrings to be discovered in Ella's jewellery box, I needed a witness and I then had to step back.

'I wasn't sure about that restaurant last night,' I started.

'Really?' Joy said. 'I liked it.'

'My penne was cold,' I said, 'and it wasn't that tasty. The kids hardly ate anything.'

'The *kids* were too busy climbing over the back of the chairs to eat anything,' Joy said, softening her dig with a laugh.

I bristled slightly, but didn't react – she had a point, the kids were being slightly feral – but they were overtired after a day on the beach.

'Thing is, Joy, I was quite prepared to stay behind at the villa with the children, it just wasn't suitable for them. They didn't want to be strapped to their seats in some fancy restaurant – the food was for adults and the table was booked too late for the little ones.'

'Yes, I know, but it was kind of Ella to take us.'

'It was, but because Ella doesn't have kids,' I continued, 'she doesn't seem to realise that a "chi chi" restaurant isn't somewhere you take children on holiday… bit selfish of her, if you ask me.' I'd barely finished my sentence when I became aware of someone standing in the doorway.

'Oh, I'm sorry, Clare, I thought the way you were scarfing down that penne you enjoyed it. But it sounds like you had a horrible time last night, I wish you'd said,' came Ella's voice, dripping with sarcasm.

Shit! I looked up to see her smile laced with fake hurt. I didn't know what to say.

'No, I'm sorry, Ella, it's my fault. We'd had a lovely day on the beach and we were all tired, I should have stayed here with the children. And, as I said, it wasn't the sort of restaurant for children.' I shrugged awkwardly. I didn't like her, but I didn't want to deliberately hurt her.

'I can see why you might think I'm selfish,' she said, walking in, touching Joy on the shoulder affectionately as she passed, 'but it wasn't about me or the children… or you even. It was about Joy, I wanted to thank her, give her a break from the kitchen.' She moved towards Joy and put her arm around her. 'This woman… she's been so lovely to me, welcoming me into the family and…' Oh God, I could see Ella's eyes welling up, she was turning this into some kind of speech. Joy, of course, was loving it, and it struck me how fickle my mother-in-law could be. 'Look, I just felt you needed a night off from cooking and running around after the children, Joy,' she said, looking around for an audience. 'And if that makes me selfish, then I'm fine with it,' she added, her face a study in sincerity.

Joy smiled, even she was at a loss for words. Was she moved by this? Surely she could see through it?

'Yes, dear, I had a lovely time thank you – I wish you hadn't insisted on paying though.'

'Nonsense, it's the least I can do. Clare told me you pay for the holiday every year – and *I* won't be taking it for granted. *I* like to pay my way, Joy,' she added, with the emphasis on 'I'.

I wanted to say, 'Good God, we get it – you paid for a bloody meal for Joy and Bob, but they and the business my husband runs for them paid for your whole holiday, so I reckon you got a bargain.' But I held my tongue and smiled serenely, not easy under the circumstances, but I managed.

Ella was definitely goading me again, implying I just took the paid-for holidays without showing any kind of appreciation. But Joy knew I was grateful, I'd always told her we wouldn't be able to afford such lovely holidays – still, I'm sure Ella was trying to make me look like a taker. But I wasn't rising to her bait, I didn't want a row now. I had the earrings as my secret weapon, and I wasn't going to spoil that reveal by having a petty squabble.

I think Joy knew what was going on beneath the surface and tried to bring the conversation to a close with a final flourish. 'Well, it was a lovely evening, Ella, thank you.' Then she started muttering about Bob. 'Well, until that silly husband of mine spilt pasta sauce down his shirt. I can't take him anywhere.' She rolled her eyes and shook her head in disbelief. Then she looked at us both, clearly feeling she'd effectively changed the subject. 'Now, are you ladies both okay?'

'Yes, we're fine.' I smiled sweetly. 'And I'm sorry, Ella, I just felt guilty that the children were spoiling Joy's evening, especially as you'd gone to such trouble.' Two could play at that game.

Ella smiled back, a faint nod of acknowledgement, a smugness that she'd won – but this was a small victory compared to what I had in store for her.

'Joy and I had made a start, but you can help us with dinner if you like?' I said, still smiling.

'Clare, have you forgotten I'm cooking a vegan meal for everyone this evening?' She looked at Joy as she said this.

'No, I hadn't *forgotten*,' I said through gritted teeth. 'We just thought as you'd been traumatised and been in your room all afternoon...'

'Because I fell over one of *your* children's toys. I almost drowned...' she said, just in case I'd forgotten it was all *my* fault.

'Are you feeling okay by the way? I could have a look at you if you like?' I said, moving on from children's killer trucks

'No, I'm fine thanks,' she snapped, then Joy cut in.

'Good, I'm so relieved you're okay, you gave us quite a scare, Ella. So, come on then, girls,' she faked brightness, 'I'm looking forward to this. I love working with new recipes. Where shall we start?'

'Let's start with the aubergines,' Ella said, and without taking her eyes from mine, she picked up a sharp kitchen knife and slowly cut into the purple skin and down through the fleshy white pulp.

As I watched, I felt the hairs on my neck stand up.

CHAPTER TWENTY-ONE

The last thing I wanted to do was join in with preparing the meat-free feast with the vegan queen, but if I refused, I was excluding myself – and that's just what Ella wanted. It wasn't the veganism that annoyed me, it was the way she used it like a stick to beat people with – mainly me.

'Have you ever cooked an aubergine, Clare?' she asked, like I was ten years old.

'Of course, I make stuffed aubergines for dinner sometimes. Dan likes them.'

'I bet he'd like mine more,' she murmured.

I looked to Joy to see if she'd heard this. But she had her back to us, her hands in the sink, and even if she did, she wasn't getting involved. I bit my tongue and endured a patronising demo on how to slice and salt aubergines like I'd never seen the vegetable before.

'I'm sorry, Joy, but she's being really annoying,' I said, when Ella popped to the bathroom. Up to this point I'd bitten my tongue, but I'd just had enough. 'Yes, I eat meat, but it doesn't mean I don't eat vegetables. The two aren't mutually exclusive.'

'She means well,' Joy said diplomatically.

'Really?' I wasn't so sure, but clearly Joy wasn't going to agree with me.

'Flatbreads,' Ella said as she re-entered the kitchen, rubbing organic olive oil into her hands. 'I'm going to show you how to make them, it's the easiest thing – and they're the yummiest. Not like the shop-bought rubbish that's filled with baddies, eww,' she said. Did I imagine the overlong glance at the sliced loaf I'd bought the previous day from the supermarket?

She then proceeded to mix flour and water and salt and made a dough and, while I worked on the aubergines, Joy disappeared to 'check on the men', though I think this was just an excuse to escape the atmosphere between me and Ella.

As soon as she'd gone, Ella said, 'I think we'll serve dinner at nine-ish tonight. Okay with you?'

She so knew it wasn't. This was a flash of the toreador's red cape to me, the bull, as I'd criticised her for booking the restaurant so late the previous evening. It would also mean I had to feed the children separately – something I didn't like to do on holiday. It was family time and I liked us to eat together as my nursing shifts at home often meant we couldn't. But I wasn't going to give her the satisfaction of thinking she'd annoyed me, so I said, 'Great, we can eat without the kids,' which took the wind out of her sails.

I continued to chop and salt and fry. All the time building myself up to what was going to happen later. The late dinner would in fact play right into my hands – all the adults, no children, but plenty of witnesses.

'It's more Mediterranean to eat late,' she added. 'After all, it's everyone's holiday, not just the children's.' She really was trying to push me.

'Absolutely.' I nodded vigorously, wanting her to see she wasn't getting to me. Then I turned and said, 'Actually, Ella, I wonder if nine is a little—'

Her eyes lit up; she was itching for a fight. 'Sorry, Clare, we can't do any earlier… it might be even later than nine actually – these aubergines need to be cooked super slowly.'

I laughed. 'Oh, that's perfect – what I was going to say was that nine is a little early as I need to get the children to bed. So, shall we say nine thirty so I can be sure the children are settled and we can enjoy a relaxed evening?' I said, stuffing the final aubergine with gusto.

'Okay… I mean as long as nothing spoils,' she said, but I could see she wasn't happy. I was giving her mixed signals, confusing her, and she suddenly wasn't sure how to play me.

Getting the children settled was a slow process, almost as slow as cooking the stuffed aubergines, which apparently took 'hours and hours'. I'd made them a million times and they cooked within an hour, but I didn't argue – Ella knew best.

I recruited Dan to help with the kids. He always had a calming effect on them and luckily for us they were soon asleep. I went into his single room to change so I didn't disturb them.

'I'm surprised you've agreed to a late dinner tonight,' he said as he zipped up the back of my dress.

'Oh, you know what she's like by now. Ella wants to play hostess, and I couldn't be bothered to argue,' I said. 'She always has to have her own way,' I added. But secretly I knew it was nothing of the sort. Tonight we were dancing to my tune – I was the choreographer, even if it seemed to everyone, including Ella, that she was. 'I've decided to just go along with it all, I don't want to ruin everyone's holiday.'

'Well, I'm glad you're being a bit more chilled about things. She really isn't so bad, and all she wants is to cook for us. She told me she feels so grateful that we've welcomed her into the family.'

'Yes, well, apparently, she has no family, so I imagine she's very grateful,' I said.

'She's had a terrible childhood. Her parents died in a car crash, you know.'

'Oh, I didn't know that,' I said. 'Thing is, she told me the other day that her dad was a New Yorker "born and bred", but I remember her saying her father was Italian – from Sorrento,' I added.

'Perhaps he'd spent time in Italy – or America? Her parents were killed driving home from an evening out. She was really young, left just her and her sister – she told me last night, at the restaurant.'

As my own father was killed in a car accident, this was something I could relate to – if what she said was true.

'Mmm, so you two were talking quite a bit last night,' I said. 'I noticed she'd saved a place for you right next to her.' I smiled at him, letting him know I was watching, but at the same time not overreacting. 'In fact, she sat everyone where she wanted to at the restaurant, didn't she? And what did I hear her saying to you about a private chat… something about the website?'

'Oh, just talk really. Like you said before, she thinks we have this big business, and I don't have the heart to tell her that our Jamie's not a millionaire son of property magnates,' he laughed. 'She's keen to get involved in our Instagram account. Says she'd photograph the buildings and make them look sexy.'

'*Sexy*? Has she seen what kind of property Taylor's manage?'

'Yeah, Dad nearly choked on his linguine,' he laughed.

'I told you, Dan, she's imagining glossy skyscrapers and penthouse apartments with hot tubs on the roof. I don't know how she's going to make a few blocks of flats and warehouses look *sexy*.' I giggled. 'She really has got the wrong idea, and it's not really fair if Jamie's allowing her to think Taylor's is a global property enterprise or something.'

'He does like to impress the ladies, our Jamie, and let's face it – he's never let the truth spoil his chat-up lines.'

'Someone should explain to her,' I said, wondering if that person should have been me.

'To be fair I did try. I wanted to break it to her gently, I said we're a small company doing small projects." But do you know what she said?'

I shook my head, intrigued.

'That Jamie had told her I was too modest! That I put the business down and try to make out it's nothing.'

'Jamie's a bit much sometimes, isn't he?' I smiled. 'He tells these amazing stories about his adventures abroad, and it's great to listen to, he has such an imagination, but I've always wondered if he adds his own colour.'

'Yeah, he's been like that since we were kids,' Dan frowned, 'always wanted the biggest, the best – and if he hasn't got that, he still says he has. But Ella said he'd also told her I had no ambition, which pissed me off.'

There had always been some disconnect between Dan and his brother, which had been kept at bay by Jamie often being on the other side of the world. I wondered how it was going to play out when they started working together.

'Mmm, I'd take what she says with a pinch of salt,' I sighed. 'If you ask me, it's not just Jamie who has an interesting relationship with the truth. I wouldn't be surprised if she told you he'd said something, when in fact he didn't. She was probably trying to cause trouble, she's come between me and Joy, and she tries to come between me and you too.' I gave him a warning look.

'You might be right, but I'm sure she isn't trying to cause any trouble,' he said. Dan just saw what was presented to him, a fragile, innocent rose who was vulnerable and needed protecting. That's why he'd found it so easy to cheat, I reasoned. Because he liked to protect people, and figured Marilyn – and probably the stewardess before her – needed him more than me. 'It wouldn't be in Ella's interests to cause trouble between me and Jamie. We've got to work together,' he said, obviously still considering this.

I just nodded. I wasn't going to get into all that again. Tonight I was going to change their minds. She wasn't the angelic little flower they all thought she was. This was a woman who for some reason seemed hell-bent on tearing us all apart.

'Technically, now she's married to Jamie, they'll have half the business,' Dan suddenly said, like he'd only just realised the implications.

'Yeah, that's why she wants to be involved. I'm worried she wants to take over.' Before Ella, Jamie was planning to be a sleeping partner and leave the decision-making to Dan – but now he was coming in and bringing his wife. 'You won't be able to do anything without her and Jamie's agreement,' I added.

'Yeah, it's going to be tough, especially as neither of them have worked in the property business before.' He pulled his T-shirt over his head as I brushed my hair. 'Then again,' he said, standing next to me, watching me in the mirror, 'perhaps that's not a bad thing – fresh blood and all that. You have to admit, she's full of good ideas.'

I stopped brushing my hair for a moment. 'Dan, someone who thinks cauliflower is a suitable base for a pizza is *not* full of good ideas.' I rolled my eyes.

He laughed. 'Fair point. Now come on, let's get downstairs and see what she's done with a cabbage tonight!'

Ten minutes later, Dan and I arrived at the table in the garden. Vases had been filled with wild flowers, tea lights and candles were dotted all over the table – she'd even put them in jam jars and they glittered from the trees and the garden. It looked lovely, and Joy was complimenting her on 'how magical' it was.

'That's literally money up in smoke,' I murmured to Dan, seeing the Jo Malone tea lights on the table and remembering how much they cost me. I'd bought them for Joy to light in the living room; she loved the 'exotic' Pomegranate Noir, and said it always reminded her of holidays. Ella knew this, as we'd talked briefly about the scent on the first evening. She also knew there were unscented ones specifically for outdoors; we'd used them on her last 'vegan night'. But again, I had to bite my tongue.

We sat down where Ella told us to – she'd made us all little name places with different flowers. I was next to Bob, with a table placing of dying, purple foxglove. 'They're poisonous,' I hissed to Dan, who chose to ignore this as he sat across the table from me, with a tiny clutch of bright blue forget-me-nots on his plate. I wondered if these were as symbolic as my table place flower.

'Finally, you two have arrived!' Ella appeared in the doorway, not sweating (like me) but glowing. She had on a pale blue cotton maxi dress, her long hair in a messy bun, her tan golden even in the candlelight.

She looked beautiful and I complimented her on all her hard work. 'You really have transformed this area, it's magical, Ella,' I said.

She thanked me and walked round the table with a large bread basket, offering it round, and when she came to me, she leaned close with the basket. 'Have you noticed the tea lights, Clare?'

'Yes… they're lovely,' I said, feigning nonchalance, refusing to let her think she'd got to me.

She hesitated slightly, then said, 'They're yours actually… the Jo Malone ones? Such a waste to burn them outside, but I couldn't find the others.'

'It's fine, but, just so you know, the garden ones are on the kitchen table, in a large box. I think I pointed them out to you the other day?' I smiled sweetly.

'So you did, silly me, I forgot!' She put her hand to her mouth, but her eyes said something quite different. God, she was petty – I almost laughed, but rolled my eyes instead.

I turned to Dan across the table, hoping he'd caught some of the conversation, but he was discussing cricket with Jamie.

'It must be nice for you to have a break from the kids, Clare?' Ella said, as she laid down her basket of home-made rolls.

'Yes, nice to be among just grown-ups,' I said brightly, raising my glass.

'Yeah, I know it gets to you being with the kids twenty-four/seven.'

'No… it doesn't… I just meant tonight – it makes a nice change to be just us adults.' I took a sip of my drink. Touché.

She sat down and pushed the large platter into the middle of the table. 'Please start everyone,' she said.

As everyone began to help themselves to the tomato salad with lime and avocado dressing, Ella sat at the head of the table, her chin on both knuckles, and observed in silence. But she wasn't silent for long.

'Yeah, I totally understand why you don't eat without them on holiday. I mean, you want to keep an eye on them, don't you? I read an article about a missing child recently, the parents were only in their garden, kid sleeping upstairs, and someone snuck in. Oh God, makes me go cold just to think about it – poor, innocent little soul just lying there all alone… and they never found who did it, I don't think. More bread, Clare?'

I thanked her and shook my head.

Everyone just murmured agreement and kept on eating, including me. All I could think of was whether the door had been locked and if the windows upstairs were secure. God, she knew how to get under my skin.

'Anyway, don't you worry, Clare, we won't be offended if you feel you have to go and check them. I mean, you'll have to, won't you – any good mother would.'

'And father,' I corrected. 'I'm sure they'll be fine, but me and Dan will take it in turns.' I smiled sweetly.

'Mmm, that's what the parents did in the article I read – but it didn't make any difference. You can't be there with them all the time, can you?' she said.

'Oh dear, I don't think this is very appropriate conversation for the dinner table,' Joy said assertively.

'Hear hear, Joy, to changing the subject,' I said, grateful for Joy stepping in. I lifted my glass, enjoying a minor moment of triumph, while hopefully concealing the fact that I was now fretting about *my* children sleeping upstairs.

Dan and Jamie continued their conversation about cricket, and Joy then offered to help Ella serve the main course, so I was left with Bob, who was lovely but slightly deaf and talking in some detail about the injured bird he'd rescued.

I wondered how Ella had become Joy's favourite in such a short space of time. She'd managed what had taken me years. Then again, I still couldn't work out if Joy really was taken in, or if she was just being nice.

After they'd been gone about ten minutes, poor Bob looked like he was about to pass out with hunger.

'I asked if there were any nibbles to go with the pre-dinner drinks,' he said. 'But Ella said she'd worked very hard and wanted us to save ourselves – which is fair enough… but that starter was only a few little tomatoes.' Always amenable and not willing to enter into confrontation, Bob had been trained by Joy not to answer back, so I assumed he'd just gone along with it, but I had to laugh when he said, 'Good job I found my own nibbles,' nodding his head down to his lap, revealing several digestive biscuits wrapped in his napkin.

'Bob! I didn't have you down as a rebel,' I whispered.

'I know Ella would be very cross, but it's not the war, is it? I feel like I'm on bloody rations,' he whispered back.

I giggled. 'I know what you mean, Bob. I'm starving too – I won't tell her, if you let me have one.' I held out my hand and he smiled and handed me a precious biscuit with a sly wink.

'Don't you get me in trouble with Ella,' he said quietly through crumbs.

I nodded. 'Your secret biscuit stash is safe with me, Bob.'

'Clare,' he muttered, nudging me, 'probably best not mention it to Joy either. You know how she can be.'

'Mum's the word.' I smiled, just as the two other women emerged from inside carrying trays of food.

Dan poured the wine while Ella and Joy took lids off. Then Ella stood there at the head of the table and said, 'Last week, I married my darling Jamie, but I also got an extra special gift on my wedding day, his beautiful family – the Taylors. You've all made me so welcome. I know I only met you all just a few days ago, but it feels much longer.' She smiled, her eyes glistening. She looked over at Jamie, who was sitting there proudly, drinking her in, and she lifted her glass to make a toast. 'As some of you know… I was orphaned as a child.' She paused for effect. 'My sister was my only family, all I had left in the world, and then… then… I lost her too. But now, now, finally, I have a family again.' She stopped for another pause and an additional, stifled sob. 'Here's… to the Taylors!' She sat down, almost collapsing onto Jamie as she did.

We all sat in silence, some of us shocked and sad I'm sure, but some of us wondering just how much of the speech, if any, was true.

Eventually, Dan broke the silence. 'Thank you, Ella,' he said. 'And, as the eldest son, and therefore your big brother, I'd like to say welcome – and let's eat now because I'm famished and Dad might collapse!'

We all laughed at this. Ella's speech had been a surprise, and, if true, quite touching, and it needed someone to break the tension. I could relate to what she'd said. I was also without a family when I met the Taylors and I was grateful to be one of them. I raised my glass to her and she raised hers back in a rare moment of solidarity and I wondered if, another time, in another place, we might have been friends? Even though she'd seemed determined from the first moment for us to be enemies.

I have to say, the food was pretty average, but I complimented Ella on her cooking. 'This is delicious,' I said. Everyone else politely followed suit, and she positively glowed at the compliments, explaining each recipe in detail while we nodded, and Jamie drooled. It was like no one had ever cooked a meal before. And, tellingly, there was no mention of Joy's contribution. At the end of the meal, I was about to remedy this and give Joy a vote of thanks, when Jamie's phone rang.

Ella shot him a look – I doubt he was allowed to bring his phone to dinner.

He shrugged and stood up, saying, 'Sorry, babe, got to take this,' and off he went into the garden.

Ella looked furious, and watched him for a few moments as he disappeared from her view, but I could still see him from where I was. He seemed to be having quite an animated conversation and I couldn't help but wonder who he was talking to.

Ella distracted me though, when she suddenly said out of the blue, 'Dan, did you enjoy the food... Clare says you *love* her aubergines?'

He looked puzzled, like this was a trick question.

'Stuffed aubergines, Dan. I make them at home sometimes,' I reminded him.

'Oh yeah...'

'Do you like *mine* as much as Clare's?' she teased, and she wasn't talking about the aubergines.

'Yeah, great... you can come round to our place anytime and cook dinner,' Dan added. Given our recent troubles, one might have expected him to be a little mindful of my feelings. But, no, there he was, holding up his glass, winking at her like they had this big secret.

'I might take you up on that,' she said, lifting her glass slowly to her lips, never taking her eyes from his. She seemed to positively grow in stature at his attention. And who could blame her? The implication behind Dan's clumsy comment was that she was an amazing cook and I couldn't boil an egg. Why else would you invite someone over to your house to make a meal? She smiled victoriously at me across the table, and I smiled back like none of this mattered. But it did.

'If the rest of your repertoire is anything like this, I'll never eat meat again,' he continued. He really didn't have to keep this going, but he was encouraging her and she was loving it.

'You've clearly been consuming the same old stuff for years. It's boring and unhealthy: time for a *big* change,' she said, taking a slow sip of her wine. 'Sometimes you just need someone to show you that there's another way,' she added, almost breathlessly.

I couldn't stand to watch them any more, so turned to Bob and made small talk about the weather. He was surprisingly receptive, but all the time I was listening to their conversation. I was aware of the meaningful looks, the electricity in the air, and when Jamie arrived back from his phone call and engaged Bob in conversation, I'd never felt so alone. I wanted to cry. I was an outsider at my family's table.

As Ella and Dan's exchange continued, I felt more and more diminished by Dan's lack of tact and Ella's flirty responses. I could almost see how he reeled women in. I thought of Carmel and Marilyn, the 'innocent' remarks, the questions – all with a subtext only they could hear.

Meanwhile, Jamie seemed oblivious; he was doing something on his phone while talking to Bob, apparently unaware that there were fifty shades of flirting going on at the other end of the table.

In retaliation, I leaned forward to speak to Jamie. 'The food was lovely, wasn't it?' I offered lamely. I hoped he'd see my cry for help and rescue me, but he just lifted his head in acknowledgement, nodded and smiled dismissively. I couldn't bear his new indifference towards me – it was strange, and it hurt. But once I'd revealed the earrings waiting in Ella's jewellery box to be discovered, I knew that even Jamie would be grateful to me for revealing his wife's true colours, and we'd be back to how we were before Ella.

She'd come into this family like an earthquake, causing little tremors with each of us – whispering to Joy, meaningful looks at Dan, conspiratorial eyes at Jamie. She'd even had an effect on

Violet, who'd suddenly become obsessed with taking photos of herself. And as for me, Ella had threatened my safety within the family, caused Jamie and my husband to doubt me, to judge me. But now it was time for her to be judged, and as I watched her smiling, and chatting, I waited to drop my bomb.

CHAPTER TWENTY-TWO

After the meal, Ella served vegan brownies with coffee and oat milk. 'Oh, and before you ask, there's no cow's milk, Clare,' she said. 'The clue's in the name – that's just for baby cows.' This with a sanctimonious smile.

I ignored her comment, surprised that Dan hadn't asked for cow's milk, surprised he just poured the oat milk into his coffee. And Joy too. Bob always had his black, so did Jamie, but Joy always had cow's milk – until that night.

I enjoyed the coffee, and was just sampling a second brownie, when Ella said, 'Clare, no offence, but I think it's your turn to do the washing up.' This was delivered in a jokey way, with a sidelong glance at Jamie, and a sly smile.

I would happily have washed up – in fact, I was about to offer and volunteer Dan to do it with me – but it was the way she spoke to me that stung. It was clear she could only function as Queen Bee. And, to do that, she had to diminish the people around her, which seemed to be mostly me.

I just sat there for a few moments, anger pulsating through me, my heart beating so hard, it was competing with the chirp of crickets jangling through the air. I looked around at my so-called family and wondered if anyone would stick up for me, point out that I'd cleaned the villa, taken the bins out, had actually made breakfast and lunch and washed up, most days. I didn't mind, I was happy to do it. After all, much of the work around the villa was created by the kids.

But not one of them – not even Dan – pointed this out, made me feel better, they were all too bothered about being polite, keeping everything nice. Just as Joy liked it. No conflict, no swearing, no problems, just pretty pictures of the family on holiday; let's not talk about the problems, let's just wrap it all up in a nice big bow and keep on smiling. But that wasn't working any more. It was time to shake things up with the Taylors.

'Joy,' I said, 'you know how you couldn't find your earrings last night? I think I know where they are.'

'Do you?' She looked hopeful.

'Yeah. I know *exactly* where they are,' I said, while all the time looking at Ella, but she suddenly seemed very interested in her wedding ring that she was now turning around on her finger and didn't look up. 'Ella, do *you* know where the earrings are?' I asked, forcing her to look at me.

She shrugged. 'No,' she glanced over at Joy, 'of course not.'

'Have you checked your jewellery box, Ella?' I said, and Dan put his head in his hands.

Both Ella and Jamie were now staring at me with such hatred I felt cold, in spite of the heat. No one was moving, it was stalemate, so as I'd set this train running, it was now down to me to see it through.

'Okay,' I said slowly, putting my napkin on the table and grating my chair along the ground. I stood up before anyone could stop me. 'I'll go and look, not that I need to. I know they're there,' I said, turning to my mother-in-law, who looked so embarrassed, I felt quite sorry for her.

'Clare, please…' she started.

I wasn't going to listen to her. No one wanted confrontation, me included, but sometimes there was no choice, we had to face these things head-on.

I stormed upstairs, straight to Ella and Jamie's room, and opened the drawer, where I knew the jewellery box was stashed. Reaching in, I picked it up and sat on the bed, opening the box, savouring the moment when I would show everyone what she was.

I heard footsteps on the stairs, and Jamie walked in, standing inside the room watching me. His arms were folded, his legs apart. He was ready for battle, and as I rummaged in the cheap metal, I looked up at him and said, 'She's not worth fighting for, Jamie.'

I went back to the box, feeling around the chains, the plastic, the bits of detritus she'd just jammed in there, but couldn't find the earrings, so I emptied the box on the bed and continued to sort through the tangled metal and plastic. But there were no diamond earrings.

'They were here,' I said, my hands frantically going through everything, on the bed. 'They were here, Jamie, they were,' I cried.

'What is wrong with you, Clare?' He was shaking his head, looking at me like I was making this up. 'I asked Ella outright. I asked her if she'd stolen Mum's earrings, because you told me she had – but you were wrong. Shit, I almost believed you, Clare. She was so upset, it could have ended my marriage! Any other girl would have told me to get lost, but Ella loves me and trusts me. And I trust her. That's the problem, Clare, you don't trust anyone. Everyone's not like Dan…' He stopped. I don't think he meant to go there. 'I'm sorry, but Ella is genuine and – believe it or not – she cares about you, Clare. She's concerned that you feel the need to tell lies about her. Look at this performance tonight – why, Clare? Are you jealous? Is that what this is all about?' He was still in the same position, his eyes boring into me, disapproving, disappointed, unreachable.

'I… No… I'm *not* making this up, why would I? The earrings… they were here, they were,' I said desperately, my fingers still touching the inside of the box, like they might suddenly appear.

Jamie simply shook his head in disgust, and walked out of the room.

I started to cry. Jamie and my relationship meant a great deal to me, and it hurt that he saw me as this jealous woman telling lies to hurt his new wife. That wasn't who I was, and it saddened me that he didn't realise that. But who could blame him, when I'd just riffled through her belongings and come up empty-handed?

All I could think was, she must have moved them. I didn't follow Jamie out of the room to try to convince him because now finding the earrings was more important than ever. So I just carried on looking.

I abandoned the jewellery box and went back to the drawer – nothing, so I tore around the room, looking everywhere I'd looked before, knowing they'd been here before. I opened a wardrobe, got down on my knees, delving at the back, throwing out shoeboxes, all of Ella's shopping bags. I was being crazy, but I didn't care, I was still convinced I was right and *had* to prove it, in order to not only prove Ella's guilt but to show the Taylors, my family, that I wasn't the nasty, vindictive person they seemed to think I was.

And then I stopped and sat back on the floor to think about it. Of *course* she'd moved the earrings. Jamie had told her that I'd said she stole them, and as soon as she knew I was on to her, she'd reacted. She had all afternoon to move them, while she was in the bedroom 'recovering' from her trauma in the pool. There would have been plenty of opportunity, if Jamie had fallen asleep, or she'd perhaps sent him to the en suite for a glass of water.

At this point, Dan appeared in the doorway, looking furious.

I looked up from what I was doing. 'Don't start, Dan,' I warned.

'Don't start? You've really done it this time, Clare. Poor Ella is sobbing down there and Mum's in tears too!'

I just kept shaking my head through my own tears now pricking my eyes. 'But Dan, I *know*, I *know* I *saw* her – and the earrings were in that box. They were here.' I stopped looking for a moment and stared at the mess on the bed, tears dripping down my face.

'No, they weren't.'

'They were, why does no one ever believe me?' I looked up at him through my tears.

He was holding something in his hand, and as he opened it, I saw a glinting on his palm. Joy's earrings.

'Where did you get them?' I almost couldn't believe what I was seeing.

'They were downstairs, on the shelf in the kitchen. Ella spotted them when she ran inside to get a tissue. Mum remembered right away too. She said they were a little tight the other day, so she'd taken them off. She'd forgotten where she'd put them, that's all, Clare.'

'But that's not true…' I implored.

'How much *proof* do you need? Ella said you'd be like this, insisted I bring them to show you, said you wouldn't believe it unless you saw them. She's a mess thanks to you.'

He was furious, but he was the least of my problems for once.

I continued to sit on the floor, working it out. So Ella took them from her own room, and left them on the shelf in the kitchen – where she'd been cooking all evening. But why had Joy gone along with the lie? Was she saving face? Would she rather join in the lie than upset Jamie? I didn't know anything any more. I thought I knew this family inside out, but Ella had rocked the boat entirely. And what could I do now?

I followed Dan back downstairs like a naughty child, where I was greeted by smiles of pity from Joy and Bob.

Ella stepped forward like Mother Teresa and hugged me. 'It's okay, Clare,' she said, looking into my face, making me part of her drama, using me to show her forgiveness. 'You've had a lot going on. But if you imagine something like this again, just come and talk to me, yeah? I can't be accused of something I didn't do again like that. This is my family now too, Clare.'

What could I say? Any more protesting and blaming would fall on deaf ears.

Joy was sitting on the easy chair, her face tear-stained, while Bob sat on the arm, his hand protectively on her shoulder. 'It's all my fault,' Joy was saying. 'They'd been in the kitchen all the time – I just forgot. And now everyone is so upset. On our lovely retirement holiday.'

'You didn't leave them in the kitchen, Joy. Why are you doubting yourself? You'd never forget something like that.' I heard Dan say my name, but I wasn't going to shut up for him. 'What's wrong with you all?' I said, wanting to say more, but at the same time afraid of what Ella might say about me. *Your dirty little secret, Clare.'* Was she bluffing?

'Stop it,' Dan said angrily, 'that's enough.'

'But she's fake, why can't any of you see that? Look at this afternoon, the way she "fell" in the pool…'

Everyone was just staring at me. Ella started crying, Joy was shaking her head. Jamie was about to say something, but Ella stopped him with a touch on the arm.

'What is *wrong* with you all? So she can't swim,' I said, gesturing towards her. 'Big deal, but all that drama when she supposedly thought she was drowning – which, of course, she wasn't. It was just a performance. Everything she does is a performance.' I was looking from one to the next; no one said a word.

'That "performance" as you call it,' Jamie started, 'is because Ella is petrified of water.'

'Petrified? She doesn't look petrified when she's hanging around the pool in next to nothing for her Instagram snaps.'

He closed his eyes and continued to talk like I hadn't spoken. 'Because her sister drowned.'

CHAPTER TWENTY-THREE

I felt terrible. I tried to apologise to Ella, but she had her face in Jamie's chest sobbing and he shook his head when I touched her shoulder.

Given the story about her sister, I couldn't redeem myself for referring to her accident in the pool as "a performance". There was no point in me trying to speak to her, or to tell the others I was sorry for spoiling the evening, so I just left them all standing around looking at each other. I went straight to bed and just lay there in the kids' room staring at the ceiling. I was frustrated at not being believed, and angry with myself for even mentioning Ella's swimming "incident". In my defence, I had no idea about her sister – but that's not really a defence, I know. If Ella's sister really had drowned then I was a dreadful person for thinking that she'd put on a performance. Yet, in spite of learning about Ella's sister, part of me still felt uncertain. She seemed to have an 'Ella is amazing' story for every occasion. So why not an 'Ella is a victim' story for the times she needed sympathy? I didn't know, but nothing was adding up with Ella.

She'd lived quite a life, if she was to be believed. Her Instagram logged many lovely places, five-star hotels, yachts in the South of France, fairy-tale palaces in the Middle East. She inhabited this wonderful world I could only imagine. I was fascinated, and, yes, a little dubious perhaps. But it wasn't jealousy that caused me to doubt her, it was her – the way things didn't add up regarding her backstory, the way she'd just 'bumped into' Jamie in a bar and married him weeks later – with no family present. And her

Instagram was all quite beautiful – but empty. However prettily you try to dress it up – a life of beautiful interiors and avocado toast soon gets old, and the few friends she tagged were people living in other parts of the world. Which made me wonder where Ella's real friends were, the ones from her home town. And the only sign of family was the photo she'd taken of the Taylors at dinner – which excluded me.

Eventually, I fell asleep, still tossing and turning. I felt ill at ease, like there was something malevolent here, but I couldn't put my finger on what was bothering me. I dreamt of the woman selling the lemon granitas: she was shouting '*pericolo*' and '*morte*' and dragging me by the hand, pulling me away from the villa, but I was screaming for the children.

I awoke to find it was light. Violet was standing over me. 'Mummy, are you okay?' she asked, worriedly.

'Sorry, darling, just a dream,' I said, and suggested we all get up and have a swim before breakfast. The kids loved this idea.

'I love Mummy sleeping in our bedroom,' Alfie said, 'it's fun!'

'I wish you'd stay in our bedrooms at home,' Violet sighed. 'It would be great and you and Daddy wouldn't shout at each other.'

I hugged her. 'Sorry, darling, grown-ups are a pain, aren't they?'

'Some are – but Ella's not. She's not a pain, is she, Mum? She's super cool – and she's a grown-up.'

This was a statement, it didn't require an answer, so I just told them to hurry so we could be first in the pool before everyone else. We all dashed downstairs, and I herded them out into the pool area, where I was surprised to see Dan. He was sitting on a sunlounger by himself. The kids all greeted him with delight, and he reciprocated but didn't look at me.

'You're up early?' I said. 'Not like you.'

He finally looked at me. 'I have a lot on my mind.'

My heart sank. He was pissed off with me from the previous evening – couldn't say I blamed him, but I still stood by what I believed. However many times the others told me Joy had mislaid those earrings, I wasn't convinced. I wanted to talk to Dan, to talk about what had happened the night before. He was obviously still smarting and we had to clear the air. So I suggested the kids play hide-and-seek in the garden, where it was safe and I could keep an eye on them.

'Will you play, Mummy?' said Alfie.

'Of course, darling, just let me have five minutes with Daddy and I'll be with you.'

'What time did you get to bed last night?' I asked, sitting on the edge of the sunlounger next to his, as the children scattered about the garden.

'Oh, two or three, I don't know.'

'Was anything said after I left?'

He looked at me. 'Not really, it was just me and Jamie and... Ella. Everyone kept their thoughts to themselves and didn't start accusing each other of terrible things,' he said pointedly. 'Ella was devastated.'

'I didn't... I still believe she took those—'

'Stop it, Clare, just give it up, will you? Why on earth would Ella steal from her mother-in-law?'

'I don't... She wanted the earrings, she liked them... she might sell them, I don't know.' I tried to keep my voice down so the kids couldn't hear.

'Exactly, you don't know, so why accuse her? And why go on to criticise her for getting upset when she almost drowned, what's wrong with you?' he hissed.

'Nothing... there's nothing wrong with me.' I glanced around to make sure no one else had arrived poolside yet. Any minute now Joy would emerge in a kaftan and matching swimwear and settle down on a nearby sunbed and, while feigning disinterest, would tune in to everything we said. I had to get Dan on side while I could.

'I don't *know* why she took the earrings – and I didn't *know* about her sister,' I said.

'You can see why she'd be so upset though.'

'Yes – of course, and in retrospect I shouldn't have said anything about the pool incident, but I just felt she'd made a drama out of falling in, all the flailing around and—'

'Oh, I didn't realise there was etiquette involved in drowning. If there's a book on "appropriate social responses while your lungs fill with water", I'd love to read it,' he snapped.

'I take it you didn't defend me in my absence last night then?' I said, trying really hard not to cry, because I didn't want to distress the children, and because if I started to cry, I might not be able to stop, I was so overwhelmed.

'*Defend* you? How could I defend what you said? Ella was sobbing and Jamie was so angry, it took me ages to calm them both down.'

'Are Joy and Bob angry with me too?'

'Don't know, they didn't say much. They went to bed soon after you. Mum was upset more than angry, and Dad – well, you know what he's like, just worried about Mum, I suppose.'

It used to be me, Dan and Jamie, but not any more; how quickly everything had changed.

Dan just continued to stare ahead, watching the kids play. 'We only have a few days left – I just wish you'd kept your thoughts to yourself.'

'That's what the Taylors do, isn't it?' I said quietly. 'They keep everything to themselves, brush it under the carpet. Your mum applies another layer of lipstick, your dad ignores it and we all pretend everything in the garden's rosy.'

His jaw tightened. He was a loyal son and brother, the Taylors stuck by each other through thick and thin. 'Sometimes we don't like what we see, and it might not be brave, but it's sometimes *kinder* to pretend it isn't there,' he said.

'Muuuummy, come and find us, ready or not,' Alfie was calling.

'Yeah, Mum, you said you'd play too,' Violet joined in.

'I'll be just a minute,' I said, needing to finish this conversation with Dan. I stood up, tightening my sarong around me. 'I know I probably should have kept quiet, it might have been the kindest – the wisest – thing to do, but I didn't, that was my choice, and as far as the earrings go, I don't regret saying something. Somebody had to and you weren't going to.'

He sat back on the sunlounger and closed his eyes. Just as I was about to walk away, he said, 'You're capable, Clare – you don't know how it feels to be Ella. She doesn't have your confidence, your strength. That comes with time, so cut her some slack.'

'Wow, you've really got to know her, haven't you? So you can be sensitive to someone's feelings! You've never been like that with me.'

'No, because you don't need anything or anyone – sometimes I don't even think you need me.'

I was shocked. 'Is that what you think?'

'Sometimes.' He put his hand on his forehead to shield his eyes, now open. 'Mum's the same, she doesn't need Dad – you both get on with things, you have work and friends and a life and you never ask for help. But Ella… Ella *needs* Jamie, and Jamie likes to be needed. He's never had anyone rely on him before, he enjoys it.'

I'd never seen the dynamic in quite that way before. Dan was right, I was capable, and I'd always seen this as a positive. I was never going to be a clingy, needy person, but perhaps sometimes my strength and desire for independence pushed people away. Even my husband. Had this contributed to Dan's affair? Had Marilyn needed him like Ella needed Jamie? Had Carmel made him feel more like a man because she was so needy? I suddenly had all these questions to ask, but the children were now in full chorus, and demanding we both join them for hide-and-seek.

'You're right, I don't *need* anyone,' I said, walking towards the garden. 'But I can't do this alone – why don't you come and play hide-and-seek with us?'

He smiled at me, a genuine, warm smile, and when he stood up, he walked over and put his arm around me in a loving, almost protective way. 'You and the kids are everything,' he murmured. 'Whatever's happened, and whatever will happen, nothing's gonna change that.'

I put my arm around his waist, hoping he was right. 'It may *seem* like I don't need anyone,' I said, 'but I did *need* to hear that.'

He then announced to the kids that he was going to throw me in the pool, and before I had chance to escape, he lifted me in the air and threw me in. The kids were delighted and came running, all thoughts of hide-and-seek now eclipsed because Mum and Dad were playing in the pool – what fun. I landed with a huge splash to squeals of delight. Laughing, I lifted my head above water, and suddenly I saw her, standing in the bedroom window, just watching. She was staring down at us, unsmiling, her expression something between envy and hate. I looked away for a moment to check the kids standing on the edge, and Dan now splashing me, and by the time I looked back up at the window, she'd gone.

The children joined us in the water and for a while it was just the five of us. There was so much laughter – it was one of those golden times I'll always remember, even when the kids are grown and gone. The pool was the bluest blue, the sun high in the sky; we were all together in this lovely place on a family holiday – and I felt very lucky. But there was a shadow across the sun, and I knew that in the middle of all this lovely yellow light, something dark was waiting for us.

CHAPTER TWENTY-FOUR

Later, Joy and Bob went to Positano for a few hours and we were left behind – the four of us and the children. I'd asked Ella if we could have a quick chat; she'd said there was no need, but I owed her an apology. It stuck in my craw to say it, but I was doing it to keep the peace, so we could all enjoy the remainder of our holiday without an atmosphere.

She was alone, on her phone. I didn't want an audience, I just wanted to get it over with, so I went over to where she was. 'I'm sorry I caused such a scene last night,' I said, kneeling down next to her sunlounger. 'And I'm sorry if I upset you,' I added, careful not to say I was sorry for my accusation of theft. I wasn't.

She stayed gazing into her phone and barely took her eyes from the screen, just nodded slowly and said, 'It's okay, Clare. I guess, at your age, hormones play a big part... you were confused. But I'm afraid now I'm going to have to tell Dan what I know.' Her voice was icy.

'What do you know?' I asked, trying to breathe, the panic rising in my throat, threatening to engulf me.

She glanced lazily over at me, like she couldn't be bothered to even look in my direction. 'Everything,' she said, and then went back to her phone.

'Okay,' I sighed. The threat was real. I couldn't risk it. I wasn't going to fight back. I'd caused enough trouble. I just had to hope that if I stayed away, kept under her radar, she might spare me, at least for the holiday. I'd taken a risk in accusing her of the theft, but I'd been so sure I was right I thought she'd leave in shame, or Joy and Bob would ask her to go. I didn't think anything she said would be believed, but it was me that no one believed – and now I'd made things worse for myself. She was hurt and, after almost ruining everything for her, I had to be ready for her to take her revenge.

I stood up and walked back to my sunlounger. Dan was with the children, so I was free to do whatever I fancied, a luxury, but when almost every waking hour is filled with children or work, it's like you forget how to relax. And given what Ella had just said, how could I ever relax again? I just sat there watching Dan and the children.

'Violet – bring Freddie over here. I've got this hilarious video that will make you guys laugh,' Ella called, and I was immediately on alert.

Dan was relieved of two of his charges as Violet dutifully carried Freddie over to where Jamie had now joined Ella and the four of them sat together laughing at something on her phone. Alfie was more interested in climbing over Dan as a launch pad in the pool, but Violet adored Auntie Ella. She drank her in and, that summer, if you'd asked Violet what she wanted to be when she grew up, I know she'd have said 'Auntie Ella.'

A little later, when I'd put Freddie indoors for an afternoon nap, I waved to Violet getting out of the pool. She waved back and went to lie on her tummy on a nearby sunlounger with her iPad, and, looking at her, I suddenly spotted that she'd hitched up her bikini bottoms. To my horror, her buttocks were on full display and, within a few feet, was Ella, lying on her tummy, on her phone, exactly the same. This wasn't good, my little girl was just nine years old, so I got up from where I was sitting and wandered over to Violet for a little chat.

'Hey, sweetie, do you need some sun cream?' I asked.

She just shook her head slightly and I realised she was pouting into the camera, obsessed with taking selfies ever since Ella had arrived.

'Darling, wearing your bikini bottoms like that must be very uncomfortable,' I said, sitting on the edge of her lounger.

'No, it's super cool,' she answered, not looking up from her screen.

The subtle approach clearly wasn't working, and I didn't want to embarrass her, but worried if she thought it was okay to do it here, she might do the same at swimming lessons, or at school games. 'Sweetie, I think it's a *little* inappropriate for you to be wearing your bikini bottoms like that.'

She whipped her head round, her face completely closed, eyes like Dan's in anger, 'But Auntie Ella does it!'

'Darling, Auntie Ella is a grown-up. You can wear your stuff how you like when you're older, I just don't think—' But before I could finish, she'd turned back to her screen. 'Violet, I will never force you to do anything, but I will make you aware if I think what you're doing is wrong, might harm you or makes you look silly.' With that, I stood up and walked away, aware of Ella following me with her eyes.

'You okay, babe?' she called to Violet, who just nodded without turning round.

I was angry that Ella had tried to push her way in, but that seemed to be her 'brand', as she would probably call it. Still, by the time I sat back down, my daughter had reverted to wearing her bikini bottoms as her mother intended.

I picked up my phone, unable to concentrate on anything, feeling the remnants of Violet's resentment, Ella's eyes watching me, her protective voice to Violet, calling her 'babe', like they were besties – and I looked up to see she was smirking at the other side of the pool.

*

Later that day, I was in the kitchen, making cold drinks for the children, when Ella walked in. She was wearing a small bikini. She seemed so tiny, her body childlike, apart from the full breasts I suspected might not be the ones nature gave her. She took an apple from the fruit bowl. She didn't speak, just stood against the kitchen units, taking aggressive bites from the apple and chewing slowly. She didn't take her eyes off me.

I just tried to pretend she wasn't there and busied myself with the drinks.

'Clare—' she suddenly said, throwing the remainder of her apple at the bin, missing and just leaving it on the floor.

I looked at her and she stared back.

'Are you going to leave that there?' I asked, unsmiling.

'Probably.' A defiant teenager to me as the frazzled mother. She wanted attention and she'd get it any way she could.

'Clare, what is your problem with me?'

'I don't have a problem,' I replied.

She sighed theatrically. 'Yes you do. All that shit last night about the earrings, then coming over to apologise, thinking I'll just say "it's okay, you called me a thief, but I forgive you".'

'Actually, I wasn't apologising for the accusation—' I started, but she talked over me.

'You tried to bad-mouth me to Jamie, you disrespect my sister and I *know* you don't like me being around your kids.'

'I didn't disrespect your sister, I didn't know about her. I just wanted a quiet holiday with my family and I feel like Jamie just introduced you, forced us all together and assumed everyone would get on.' I couldn't say any more. I had to stay on the right side of her – she knew too much.

'Am I so hard to like?' She put her head to one side, and I wondered if she was toying with me.

I didn't answer.

'Look, Clare, we were thrown together, you're right. I didn't choose to spend my holiday – my honeymoon – with you either, but if I want to be with Jamie I have to… It's our *honeymoon*.' She stopped talking. 'I saw you wince at that. Does it hurt, Clare?'

I shook my head. 'Please don't try and deflect from what you did. You took those earrings, I saw you. And you might think you've got away with it, but the truth will out. You're nothing but a thief, and I will prove it… As for what happened at the pool – I just thought it was a little over the top.'

'I didn't realise there was etiquette involved in drowning,' she said, repeating what Dan had said to me earlier. My stomach twisted. Good old Dan, as loyal as ever, he'd obviously made this remark to her. 'This viciousness of yours is just because you're in a stale marriage with a bored man you won't let go,' she sighed.

'He can go any time he likes,' I said, feigning disinterest. She'd really hit a nerve and as much as I tried to ignore what she'd said, it hurt.

'Oh no he can't, because you won't let him. Doesn't matter if he finds someone else who he really loves, you're there with your kids and your handcuffs dragging him back. Women like you make me sick,' she spat.

'You've got it all wrong, you've heard half a story from Jamie via Joy and you think you know my life, my marriage.'

But Ella wasn't interested in my life, she'd rather talk about hers.

'I bet you wish you were on your honeymoon like me, don't you, Clare?'

'No, I don't want your life thank you.'

'Wow. Jealous much?'

'Not at all. I might be in a stale marriage, but your life is non-existent. It's whatever you put on Instagram. It isn't real, Ella.'

'Online or offline, it's better than yours with your flirty husband and flabby thighs.'

Her true colours were really coming to the fore now. Once again she'd worked it so that no one else was around to witness her vitriol, her venom – but I wasn't going to take it.

'You aren't what you pretend to be. The pious little Insta queen who fights the good fight and empowers women body-shaming her sister-in-law. Nice – it shows just who you really are, a lying little thief.'

'Oh, Clare, how many times do I have to tell you,' she sighed, like she was so bored of it all. 'I have my own diamonds, hun, I don't need anyone else's.'

'Doesn't mean you didn't take them.'

'But why would I when I've got my own, way bigger than those weeny things?'

'I've seen your Instagram – I bet those Arab princes pay you for your "talents", in diamonds?'

'Yeah, and wouldn't you like a little taste of that ice, Clare? Something dangerous on a yacht, a sizzle of spice in the Middle East? You're so bored, you'd sell your kids for ten minutes of my life. So you can stop with the sanctimonious shit.'

I couldn't believe the rubbish she was talking; did she really think I'd rather live her empty life than mine, with my lovely kids, my rewarding job?

'I'm *not* judging how you make a living, but I wonder what Jamie would think?'

'Jamie? He doesn't judge what happened before we met, because it did all happen before we met, just to make that clear. And BTW – I don't judge him either.' She was staring at me now. 'In fact, we have no secrets,' she said, without taking her eyes from mine. 'Yeah, babe – we are *super* honest.'

My heart thumped to the floor.

'My husband knows everything. I've had a tough life, and sometimes I've had to make a living and he… well, to be honest,

Clare, Jamie actually likes me to tell him all about it, if you know what I mean.' She smiled knowingly. 'Of course you do. It excites him – and you know all about *that*, don't you?'

'Shut up,' I hissed. 'This is *my* family, and I won't let you wreck my life.'

'Clare, *you* wrecked your own life.' She smiled.

I waited, holding my breath for what she'd say next. She knew, she really knew everything.

'Yeah,' she said, slowly nodding her head – it was as if she'd just read my mind. 'I know – and I'm not bluffing.'

I couldn't speak, this could be the end of everything for me.

'So don't come for me again, big sister-in-law, because any *little* indiscretion I might be guilty of,' she lifted her finger and thumb almost together and reached towards me, 'well, it pales into insignificance next to yours.'

I couldn't take any more, and grabbed the tray with the children's drinks on and hurried out of the kitchen without saying another word. I stayed in control, walking through the house, the big high ceilings and cool marble floors a slight relief from the intense heat. I was hot and itchy, could barely breathe. Ella had the means to blow my life apart at any moment.

CHAPTER TWENTY-FIVE

Devastated, I finally reached the door and went outside. The bright light and searing heat hit me all at once, and wrapped itself around me like a snake as I teetered by the pool. As I walked along the water's edge, Joy lowered her sunglasses, smiled and went back to her book. Bob was snoring by her side. Dan lifted his hand in a waving gesture from the pool with Alfie on his back, Violet swinging from his neck. I looked around for Freddie, my baby – he was asleep, in the shade of a parasol, lying on Uncle Jamie. My family. It took my breath away to see them all like this, the perfect picture of a family on holiday. How different the reality was to the picture we presented – the passions, the guilt and all the hurt simmering just under the surface. *My dirty little secret.*

The children clambered from the pool, rushing towards me for their drinks. I watched them, in awe at their innocence, their purity. No secrets, no guilt – the biggest things in their lives were what was happening now. How I wished I could turn back the clock to a simple time, when I had nothing to hide, and everything to be happy for.

I thought back to that night, the night that changed everything. It was in a villa not unlike this one, Joy's taste ever-present in her choice of our holiday homes. Greece was incredibly hot that summer – almost three years before. It was a difficult time for me. Violet was six, Alfie one, and Dan was there, but he wasn't. He was constantly on his phone, never smiling, everything I said seemed to irritate him beyond words. I kept asking what was wrong, but he wouldn't engage, just kept saying it was nothing, and that I was imagining things.

I was tired from going back to work full-time after maternity leave, and trying to give as much of myself to two young children, but it wasn't enough and I couldn't stretch any further. Dan, like Jamie, was used to being cared for. Joy had treated them both like princes all their lives and Dan was finding it hard not being my number one any more. I was working the night shifts so I could spend the days with the children, and he was working long hours at work, then looking after the kids at night. We literally passed each other in the hall most days, and my priority, like most mums, was our two little children. Dan was a good father, but as he was only home in the evenings, he didn't see much of the children, and he didn't get how exhausting it could be.

Even on our holidays with Joy and Bob and Jamie, I did pretty much everything for the children. I wanted to though, I spent too long away from them at work. But one particular night on that family holiday in Greece, the kids were so exhausted, they just wanted their bath and to go to bed, and, to my surprise, Dan offered – no, he *insisted* on putting them to bed. 'You have a break, it's your holiday too,' he'd said.

'Ooh, take him up on that one,' Joy had laughed. 'Come and have a gin with me and we'll have a gossip.'

I was touched, and hopeful this meant Dan was happier again, back to his old self. So while Dan put the children to bed, I stayed downstairs with the rest of the family. We had a few drinks, played card games and when Dan didn't come down, I assumed he'd fallen asleep. 'He'll be lying on one of the kids' beds, completely gone,' I laughed, when I said good night to everyone a little earlier than usual.

I remember it so clearly, walking up the stairs and hearing his voice. It was tender, gentle, and at first, I assumed he was talking to one of the children, but it was after ten, and too late for one of them to be awake. And when I reached the children's room, I realised his voice was coming from *our* bedroom. At first it didn't make sense, until it dawned on me that he must be on the phone.

Something stopped me from going inside, and I listened to him talking for a few minutes – the odd word, a laugh, the tone he used to use with me. 'What time's your flight?' he asked. Then I heard him say something that broke my heart. 'Yes, yes, of course, darling, I meant every word, but I can't tell her now – we're on holiday. I can't do that to her... or the kids. Trust me, I'll sort it all out when we get home.'

I stood outside the door, trying to work out if any of these words could be misinterpreted. Was it all so obvious? He was my husband, the father of our two children, we were family – we didn't lie or cheat. We loved each other. Didn't we? How naïve I was back then. My instinct at the time was to storm in, confront him, ask what was going on. But I wanted to hear more. I think somewhere deep down I hoped to hear him address one of his friends, or say something that completely reinterpreted what I feared and if I stood there long enough that would make it better. But standing there I was simply exposing myself to real pain, the kind of pain that messes you up for a while. 'Of course I do,' he was saying softly, 'and I *want* us to be together... I know, I know. Darling... listen to me – I need you to be patient. No, I can't! You know I can't – I can't just walk away tonight. These things take time.'

Hearing my husband call someone else 'darling' was the sharpest, most painful slap. I knew then, all the months of feeling unwanted, like he'd disengaged from me and the kids, the late nights, the total lack of interest in me and everything I did, I knew. It all made sense now. But instead of storming in and confronting him, I crumbled, felt my legs buckling under me, and I knew if I went into the bedroom now, it would be over. I had two children, I had a family, it was everything I'd ever wanted; if I confronted him now, that would mean the end of everything. Did I really want that?

I couldn't think straight, I needed time to work out what to do next, so I turned and ran away back down the stairs. I didn't know where I was going but found myself in the downstairs hallway and saw the front door. I opened it and ran outside – I had to get away –and as I ran through the garden, I suddenly banged into someone.

He grabbed me by my elbows, holding me firm, moving his face to mine. 'Clare?' His breath was on me, smoky, dark. After a few seconds, I realised it was Jamie.

'What are you doing?' I gasped.

'I might ask you the same thing,' he said, laughing. 'Are you training for the marathon or something?'

'No... I... wanted some fresh air,' I said, trying to hide my distress with a smile. 'What about you, why are you out here?'

'Promise you won't tell Mum?'

I nodded, vigorously. I didn't really care what Jamie was doing. I was still reeling from what I'd heard Dan saying upstairs.

'Me and Dad.' He nodded over to Bob, a couple of feet away, who suddenly materialised in the darkness and put his hand up in an awkward static wave. I don't know who was more embarrassed, me for running through the garden in tears at night, or these two who were behaving like two guilty children. 'I brought Dad and me a couple of Cuban cigars back from Havana,' Jamie explained. 'But, as you know, Mum doesn't approve of smoking.'

Despite feeling so dreadful, I almost smiled, amused at two grown men skulking in the garden, hiding from their wife and mother respectively.

'Your secret's safe with me,' I said.

'Want to try some?' Jamie was always the little brother proudly showing off how grown-up he was to his older sister-in-law. That's how I saw it then. He was the baby of the family, until our actual babies came along. And even then, as a grown man he was referred to by Joy as 'our late and lovely surprise', because after Dan she didn't think she could have any more children. And ever since I've known him he's played the role of 'cheeky younger brother' to perfection.

I remember him picking up his cigar from where he'd left it on the wall to grab me when I bumped into him, and relit it. Meanwhile, Bob sucked hard on his like a teenager making the most of his weed before 'Mum' discovered what he was up to.

'Try it.' Jamie put the cigar to my lips. I opened them slowly, unsure if smoking a Cuban cigar was the answer to having just overheard my husband telling his lover he'd leave me.

I'd never smoked one before, and I took the cigar in my mouth cautiously, gently pulling in the smoke, the end lighting in the dark as Jamie continued to hold it.

'Tastes like bonfire night, burning wood and treacle toffee,' I said, coming up for air. 'I like it – but there's quite a bitter aftertaste.'

'The finest cigar you'll ever taste,' Bob said, holding his in the air, then bringing it down to his mouth, breathing in, then slowly exuding smoke from his mouth, like a dragon. The two men were experts in their smoking deception, and I doubted it was the first time they'd hidden their vice from Joy. And I remember wondering for the first time what other secrets this family kept from each other.

Suddenly Joy's voice pierced the companionable smoking silence. 'Bob, Bob, where are you?'

Bob almost choked on his cigar, and quickly handed it to Jamie. 'I'd better go,' he said. 'Don't want her coming out here and finding *both* of us. I've got some mints here.' He opened a pack and put a handful in his mouth, giving the rest to Jamie.

Jamie laughed. 'It's okay, Dad, if Mum suspects anything, we'll tell her Clare made us do it.'

Bob rolled his eyes and Jamie just carried on smoking Bob's cigar while his father scuttled off, shouting, 'I'm here Joy, just popped out for a bit of fresh air.'

'He's terrified,' I giggled.

'I don't blame him. My mother's evangelical about not smoking, and, as we all know, her wrath is biblical.' He smiled, taking an elegant toke on Bob's cigar. It seemed I'd inherited Jamie's.

'Your mum wouldn't be cross with you!' I said. '"Our Jamie" never does anything wrong.'

'God bless her, she doesn't have a clue, does she?' He raised his cigar in the air elegantly, and smiled mischievously.

I giggled. Even in my maelstrom of doubt and hurt, Jamie could lift my spirits. I was grateful, I needed this.

'I think I've had enough of this, it's making my throat dry,' he said, dabbing his cigar out on the wall, while I did the same. 'Enough Cuban for one night – let's go inside and get pissed on my mother's gin and blame it all on Dan.'

'Sounds like a plan,' I'd said, following him through the garden, suddenly feeling more light-hearted, more hopeful than I had for months. Jamie wasn't just a brother-in-law, he was more like a good friend. I was incredibly fond of him. I still am.

So we went to the villa, opened the door and I'll never forget it. Everywhere was deathly quiet, all the lights turned off, so Jamie lit a few candles that made our shadows dance around the room. Then he poured two large glasses of gin, and we sat down on the floor by the empty fireplace redundant in a Greek summer. I wrapped myself in one of Joy's expensive pashminas that she'd left on the sofa. It wasn't cold, but I felt so relaxed in the candlelight as he told me about his latest travels.

'Every country I've ever been to has shaped me,' he said. 'I know it's a cheesy thing to say, but the names of those cities are scratched on my heart, like graffiti.'

'Yeah… that is a cheesy thing to say – but it's lovely too.' I smiled, thinking how different he was from Dan. He was younger, easier, lighter somehow, with his easy charm and quick wit.

He told me about his plans to spend the next summer in Penang, and I remember the faraway look in his eyes as he talked of the beaches and the little fishing boats. I knew he'd be off again soon; he always said he couldn't stay in one place for too long. I assumed he'd always be like that, the nomadic brother always moving on. He was like an addict, just one more trip, one more continent to conquer, one more little scratch on his heart. He didn't just bring cigars back with him from his travels, he brought excitement, describing to me those faraway places I'd probably never see, other than through his eyes.

'So why did you really run outside tonight?' he said quietly, as he handed me a second glass of gin and sat back down next to me on the floor. He smelt of bonfires and musk.

I didn't answer straight away, wasn't sure if it was fair to confide in Jamie before confronting Dan. Then again, who was playing fair – Dan certainly wasn't. I took several gulps of gin. Aromatic, citrusy, it burned my throat but also anaesthetised the pain, and I told him what I'd heard Dan saying on the phone about leaving me.

After a while, I looked up at him. 'Don't try and tell me there's a reasonable explanation, Jamie, because there isn't. It's clear what's going on.' My throat was tight with tears and, in the dark, I saw tenderness in his eyes. In that moment, everything changed. He wasn't Dan's little brother who made me laugh, who teased me mercilessly and who I saw like my own little brother. He was Jamie, a good-looking younger man, with a wealth of experience, a weakness for women and a hint, just a hint, of danger.

I didn't know what he was going to do next, but when he leaned in and kissed me, I didn't stop him. Sex with Jamie was like nothing I'd ever experienced – I felt free, and so, driven by gin, hurt and desire, I completely lost myself. That night with Jamie, I wasn't an exhausted mum of two juggling everything and just trying to get through the week. With him, I was gorgeous, sexy – whatever I wanted to be – and most of all I was desired. Jamie desired me and I couldn't fail to respond. I lay back as he took me a million miles away from the night shifts, the baby sick and the unfaithful husband. I tried not to think of Dan while his brother thrust into me, but, in a perverse way, it was delicious; every thrust was a punch to Dan's faithless gut. I hated him, and this hate swirled around with the lust and created an erotic cocktail of feelings that made me cry out in ecstasy. Always aware of the next door neighbours, and later the children, I'd never cried out during sex in our semi-detached with Dan. But there, with Jamie, it was different. I'd felt unloved, vulnerable and lonely in my marriage, and now on the floor, wrapped in nothing but Joy's expensive pashmina, I felt wanted for the first time in a long time.

And at dawn, I lay there, still awake, still wrapped around Jamie, and I *wished* Dan would walk in and find us. I *wanted* to hurt him like he'd hurt me, but most of all I wanted him to know that I was desirable, and if he didn't want me, there would be others.

But the guilt soon stifled any kind of happiness or pleasure.

I remember Jamie stirring next to me and opening his eyes and, realising it was me, he smiled. 'I've always had a bit of a thing for you,' he said. 'Even on your wedding day, I envied Dan taking you back to the hotel bedroom.'

I told Jamie that he mustn't talk like that. 'That can't ever happen again,' I said.

And it never did. But even now, I think about the sexy smiles that start in his eyes, the way he says my name, unfamiliar, yet intimate, and the way he brings the sunshine with him from wherever he's been.

The following day, I felt dreadful, conflicted, guilty, yet over breakfast with the family, no one would have guessed. Jamie was teasing me, throwing the kids in the air, charming his mother, making everyone laugh, and I was joining in. I wonder even now if Jamie did have feelings for me, or if he was just another opportunist, a womaniser like his brother.

And when he left only a couple of days later on another adventure, we all said goodbye to him, as we had many times before. He'd changed me in ways he'd never realise – but I knew I hadn't made a dent on him. Did I have feelings for Jamie, had I fallen a little bit in love? Perhaps, but once he'd left I cleared my head, tried to move on and do the right thing – work on my marriage.

After Jamie had gone, I felt able to confront Dan about what I'd heard. He was contrite, said the woman, Carmel, was a random air stewardess, a silly, stupid girl who'd got obsessed with him. He said he'd just told her he was leaving me to placate her.

I didn't really believe him, but after a while it was too hard not to. If I faced the fact he was a lying cheat, I'd have to do something about it and I didn't have the energy for that. For now I had to stay put. He'd never done anything like this before and swore he never would again and after a while I felt ready to forgive. But I found it harder to forgive myself. My hypocrisy, my own betrayal, tied me in knots. What I did was ignited by Dan's phone call, but that was no justification. But, whatever happened, I knew I had to live with this – I could never tell him, or anyone else. Jamie and I had agreed that. The fallout would have been colossal on so many levels; it would involve the whole family and ultimately my children. My marriage would be over, the Taylors would excommunicate me because they'd see it all as my fault, not Jamie's, or Dan's. In Joy and Bob's eyes, this could never be due to the careless, selfish ways the Taylor boys got their kicks.

So there we were, having returned from Greece, trying to recover from Dan's affair with 'the stewardess', as Joy referred to her. Our marriage was still rocky, and I was secretly recovering from the emotional turmoil of a one-night stand with his brother. I couldn't bear to be near Dan, and he naturally assumed this was my reaction to his betrayal, but actually it was the guilt of my *own* betrayal.

As if that wasn't difficult enough, I was back on the night shifts, juggling two kids, trying to be present for Dan and our marriage. And then I realised my period was late.

CHAPTER TWENTY-SIX

When the pregnancy test was positive, I knew from the date that the baby might not be Dan's. But after many sleepless nights I decided it would cause more harm than good to tell anyone. I had to keep it to myself forever, because the alternative would destroy the family. I would love this baby as much as the other two – and so would Dan.

It was an easy pregnancy, my third, and I knew the ropes. I pushed Jamie to the back of my mind, only ever allowing myself to think of him as Dan's brother, nothing else. Until, not long after Freddie was born, Jamie turned up on my doorstep one afternoon. He'd just returned from his latest travels, Dan was working and Violet was at school, so it was just me and the boys. I'll never forget, he stood in the kitchen while I made coffee and he just said it: 'I know.'

I pretended I didn't have a clue what he was talking about, but he wasn't buying it.

'Clare, Freddie's mine, isn't he?'

I considered a lie in those few moments. I thought about saying I'd done the maths and it was out of the question, after all only I knew the dates. But despite telling myself I could keep this hidden, when confronted I couldn't bring myself to lie about something so big.

'He *could* be yours,' I said slowly. 'I wasn't even sure you'd remember that night, let alone tie it in with the pregnancy.' I added. 'I'm sure there have been hundreds of women since?'

'None of them match up to you,' he'd said. 'You know I've always liked you, from the first time Dan brought you home...'

'Don't,' I said, stopping him from saying any more that couldn't be unsaid. This felt so wrong in the middle of the afternoon, the boys taking their nap, almost time to collect Violet from school. But even so, I felt like we were back on dangerous ground, and if we weren't careful it could happen all over again. So I told him firmly that it was more likely to be Dan's, and he mustn't even allow himself to think it might be his. Since Dan's affair with Carmel the air stewardess, we'd been focussed on making our marriage work. I couldn't let this destroy us.

'Imagine what it would do to you? To Dan, to the family?' I'd said.

He agreed. 'I don't want to hurt anyone, Clare. I guess I just needed to know if I have a child, if he's my boy – you know?'

I'd nodded. 'I understand, but please, for everyone's sake, just try to forget about it.'

'Just so you know, Clare, I'd never say anything. But little Freddie, I mean who wouldn't be proud of him?'

Then he kissed me on the cheek, and thanked me, said I mustn't worry, that he'd never say anything to anyone – 'Our secret,' he'd said. I remember seeing him to the door that day and before he left, he turned to me, touched my face and said, 'He looks just like me, doesn't he?'

'Yes. Though you look a bit like Dan,' I said, which is why no one would ever guess.

So, for almost three years, we kept our secret and the status quo. Jamie continued to turn up at family get-togethers when he wasn't abroad and I was always pleased to see him, not because of any residing feelings but because he was always warm, and easy with me, which was more than could be said for Dan.

'What are you doing with a dork like that?' he'd tease, in front of Dan. 'You could do so much better, Clare, he really is punching…' And Dan would laugh, and say something equally disparaging, and I'd go blotchy on my neck knowing what Dan didn't know. And despite carrying this huge weight around with me, the dynamic between the three of us continued, and I felt like I belonged. Until last summer, with Ella, who wanted to tell everyone and ruin everything.

And yes, now I can admit, when Jamie arrived with his lovely new wife, my first feelings were tinged with jealousy. I'd convinced myself it was nothing, that my feelings for Jamie were sisterly and what happened wouldn't affect anyone if it stayed locked away in its box. Kids looked like their aunts and uncles all the time. No one would question why Freddie looked so much like his Uncle Jamie as long as no one knew what had happened. But when Jamie told Ella, he handed her a little bomb. One that she now held threateningly in her perfectly manicured hands.

Now she knew about me and Jamie, I just wanted the holiday over. So when Ella asked Joy to go into town with her and I wasn't invited – which was clearly deliberate – I spent the afternoon in mild panic. The two of them alone together could spell trouble for me. If Ella was feeling mischievous – or downright vindictive – she was likely to tell Joy everything about me and Jamie… and Freddie. Ella had been building up to something, she had to be after I'd announced her guilt to the family. And now I had nothing – I'd already played the card I was holding over her, but no one seemed to either believe me or care about the theft of the earrings. After all it didn't look like they'd been stolen given they were found in the kitchen – and I was sure everyone thought I was mistaken, or even worse, just nasty.

The children were sitting around with Dan, who was fixing Alfie's toy truck, and Jamie was on the other side of the pool, reading, while Bob snored nearby.

This was my chance to talk to Jamie without Ella around, so I casually walked over, like I was just checking out the pool from all angles.

'Jamie, you told her, didn't you?' I muttered through my teeth, sitting on the end of the sunlounger next to him. I gazed around smiling, pretending to anyone that was interested that this was a friendly chat.

'I didn't exactly *tell* her…'

'She said you told her everything.'

Jamie looked really uncomfortable. He sat up. 'Clare I… I didn't just blurt it out. Me and Ella, we hadn't known each other long when I asked her to marry me—'

'So what has that got to do with anything?'

'She said we had to be able to trust each other, and that meant no secrets. She said if she was going to spend the rest of her life with me, we had to share *everything*.'

'Sshhhh, keep your voice down.'

He looked around shiftily, then continued. 'She's very intuitive, said she knew I was hiding something and if I didn't tell her, she couldn't say yes – she said secrets eat away at people.' He looked at me knowingly.

'Mmm. Or perhaps she just wanted you to tell her stuff so she'd have something over you.'

'Clare,' he said under his breath, 'that isn't true.' He looked out across the pool and I looked out too, making like we were talking about the colour of the water, or the weather. 'I happen to think she's right,' he suddenly said.

'About what?'

'Secrets, they eat away at you. Ella and I don't have secrets. Doesn't it get to you that you're living a lie, Clare?'

'I'm not. We don't know anything for definite,' I said, defensively, and this was true. But if I had to make a guess on dates, colouring, temperament, Freddie was certainly looking more like Jamie's son than Dan's. I had to keep up the pretence though, there was too much to lose.

'You know as well as I do that even if you *could* prove Freddie was yours, it wouldn't be worth the carnage. Dan would divorce me, he'd never speak to you again,' I said, waving to Violet sitting with her dad at the other side of the pool. 'And Joy and Bob… imagine. Then the kids, think of the kids, their world would *end* – especially Freddie's.'

'But like Ella says, this is all about you and Dan and the kids… but have you ever really thought about how *I* feel? What about me, Clare?'

'Of course I've thought about your feelings, but it isn't like we planned any of it. If Freddie *is* yours, then it's just a chance, a weird moment in time and biology that happened,' I said. 'You and I went our separate ways and the fact I was pregnant was *my* issue – mine and Dan's – and, Jamie, it has to stay that way,' I said urgently. 'Please Jamie, for Freddie's sake, if no one else's.'

'What if I don't want it to? What if I *want* to be Freddie's dad?'

I couldn't believe I was hearing this. 'Since when?'

'Since Ella made me realise what I've missed, how I might never have another child.'

I suddenly realised that perhaps it wasn't Ella who was likely to divulge the secret, it might be Jamie. I turned around to face him. I needed to be very clear on this. 'Freddie *has* a dad. You've always known there's a chance you *might* be… but until now you were happy to go on with your life with no responsibilities, no questions to answer. Trust me Jamie, it's best for all of us that we carry on. To say something would mess up all our lives. I don't understand why Ella's encouraging you to dig all this up, she needs to keep out.'

'Ella's "digging all this up" because she cares about *me*. She can see how I am with Freddie, she says he's the spit of me, and we're so happy around each other, and I shouldn't be denied this just because it'll make things difficult for you.'

'It isn't just about *me* – God, I wish it were *only* about me. It's about everyone – imagine how devastated your parents would be?' I hissed under my breath. 'Surely you can see this is just another game to Ella.'

He had this closed look on his face; he didn't want to hear it, like she'd brainwashed him. 'You're wrong. Ella wants this for me because she loves me, and I agree with her. I should be allowed to celebrate being a dad, not deny it, like it's a dirty little secret.'

'Ella's phrase. She uses it a lot about the night we spent together – but it isn't something I view as a dirty secret. And nor is Freddie.'

'So let's bring it out in the open then, let's stop hiding it.'

I was sweating, and it wasn't just from the sun. My heart was thumping, and I could barely breathe. *Please no*, was all that filled my head.

'But we don't *know* he's yours – and it isn't just a case of *paternity*, you slept with your brother's wife, I slept with my husband's brother – so much damage.' I sighed, a big heavy sigh.

The sun had moved around and it felt like the world was sitting on my now-burning shoulders. Ella had now returned and was chatting to Dan. Standing right in front of him, legs apart, caressing her own neck as they talked. He said something and she threw back her head and laughed, then leaned towards him, touching his shoulder. I wasn't sure if she was doing it to wind me up or make Jamie jealous, but either way I didn't care. What she'd said to Jamie about claiming his right as a father was far more damaging to the family than any kind of flirting she could do with Dan.

I stood up. 'I'm sorry – about all this. I hoped we'd be able to be happy, just get on with our lives Jamie,' I said, 'but that's the last thing that Ella seems to want.'

I walked away, knowing this would always haunt us. It was going to be like holding back the tide, and I would only be able to keep this hidden for so long. Now someone else knew our secret, we'd never be free.

I headed along the side of the pool towards Dan, and when Ella saw me, she moved away from him and walked along the other side towards Jamie. My face was burning with anger and shame and guilt and I couldn't even glance at her. I hated this woman for what she was doing to me, to my family. I'd managed to keep a lid on everything until she turned up with her wrecking ball encouraging Jamie to react, and in turn threatening the whole family.

I tightened my sarong, a nervous, self-conscious gesture as I imagined both men watching the two of us walking either side of the pool in opposite directions, and all I could think was how unfavourable the comparison would be. I sat down next to Dan, the kids playing happily in the water. Freddie sat by us in his water wings. I watched Ella from the corner of my eye, as she climbed onto Jamie's sunlounger and snuggled up against him. I had to look away, my eyes stung and I felt this burning jealousy, not just because she had Jamie, but because she had what I'd once fleetingly had with Dan. And however hard I tried, I couldn't seem to get it back. And if Ella had her way, Dan and I would be finished.

'Mummy, Mummy, come in the water with us?' Alfie was saying.

'Ask Daddy please,' I said. I needed to compose myself. I felt nauseous after my conversation with Jamie and couldn't think straight.

Dan reluctantly dragged himself off the lounger muttering something about, 'No holiday with three kids,' and jumped in the pool, where he was soon joined by Jamie, who immediately called for Freddie to jump in and he'd catch him.

'Oh, he's a bit little for that, Jamie,' I said, getting up to stop Freddie just hurling himself in. But just as I reached Freddie, there she was. Ella already had his hand, and was guiding him to the edge.

'Ella, don't let him jump in,' I said, trying not to sound unreasonable.

'He'll be fine, Clare,' she said in a voice that should be accompanied with an eye roll, in fact it probably was – she didn't look at me. She was looking at Jamie in the pool, both arms up like Freddie was a bloody beach ball to catch.

I rushed towards her, to grab Freddie, but before I could, she'd picked Freddie up under the arms and was now swinging him over the water, causing him to squeal with delight and me to shout, 'NOOOO.' But she didn't flinch, just kept on rocking him backwards and forward and just as I reached out to physically stop her from doing this, she threw him to Jamie.

'Ella, I *asked* you not to,' I yelled in her face.

'He's *fine!*' she shouted back. 'Just chill, Clare.'

'Clare, he's *fine*,' Dan called from the pool. Outnumbered by my own husband.

'Unbelievable,' I gasped. It was perilous to dangle a two-year-old over deep water, especially as her own sister had supposedly drowned. But it was about so much more than playing with Freddie. This was Ella making a parenting decision about him that was directly opposed to my wishes. If, further down the line, Jamie insisted on proof that he was Freddie's biological father, who knew where that could lead. I couldn't bear to think of the cosy little weekend visits Ella would insist on, even though she clearly had little regard for Freddie. No, I couldn't let that happen. To her he was just a pretty picture for her Instagram.

Once I saw that Freddie was safely in Jamie's arms, I went back to my sunlounger to try to think. But I continued watching the pool, Ella and my children like a hawk, especially Freddie.

'Me and Freddie could go in the shallow end, you could join us then?' Jamie said to Ella. And I thought, *now* he takes my child into the shallow end.

'No, I don't want to get wet, my hair extensions will be wrecked. I'll come and sit by the side,' Ella called, walking towards the pool. As she approached where I was lying, she bent down and picked up a nearby towel. 'Please don't tell Jamie how to interact with *his* son,' she said, in a voice loud enough for me to hear. It was noisy with the children screaming and splashing, had it not been, someone – Dan – might have heard. Only seconds later, Joy arrived and settled down on a sunlounger not too far from me.

'Did you enjoy your shopping, Joy?' I asked. I wanted to gauge her reaction to me, see if there were any signs that Ella had said anything to her about me and Jamie.

She smiled and nodded. 'Ella and I found some wonderful little boutiques. We'll have go back with you Clare, if we have time.'

Judging by her reaction I doubted Ella had said anything. Yet. She was walking past us and must have caught the conversation.

'I don't think they're Clare's kind of shops,' she said. 'You're not really into fashion, are you?' She glanced over and looked me up and down as she walked by. I looked at Joy to see if she'd noticed, but she was already lying down, reading her book.

My heart sank. All I could think was this could now be my life, the constant remarks, the whisperings, the thinly veiled insults. And Ella wasn't going to directly tell anyone the *real* gossip just yet – she would have her sport first.

She wandered towards the pool, hips swinging, carefully sitting down on the side of the pool. A photo, a selfie, the click, click, clicking of those manicured nails on the screen. She wasn't paying any attention to Freddie, or any of the other kids – she wasn't interested in them, it was clear to see. Then Violet swam over to her and started talking. Ella showed her pictures on her screen and they giggled together. Violet put her hand over mouth and glanced across at me. I could only imagine what Ella was showing her, but I couldn't object. If I made a fuss, it would upset Violet and, in everyone's eyes, I'd be causing another scene.

I was threatened by her around my kids, knowing what she knew and how much she hated me. Might she take it out on them? My insecurity was in overdrive and I suddenly heard myself calling the children. 'Come on now, take some time out of the pool, it's not good for you to be in water all day.' Not surprisingly, they all started whingeing about Mummy's unreasonable request. But I told myself they needed to rest, they needed time out of the sun, but my timing was no coincidence – I also wanted them away from Ella.

I was fully expecting for Ella to fight their corner, and try and overrule me, and I would have fought even harder. But I should have known, Ella was far cleverer. 'Come on, you guys, Mum's right,' she yelled in an unusual show of support for me. 'Jamie, you too,' she said, smiling, and I wondered what she was up to.

Jamie pretended to sulk and threw the pink flamingo at her, which made the kids laugh. 'I'm not getting out,' Jamie yelled in a faux tantrum, which the children loved.

'Uncle Jamie is allowed to stay in, isn't he, Mum?' Violet asked

'No, your mum won't let him stay in either,' Ella sighed, rolling her eyes.

'Muuuum,' Violet was saying from the water, 'but we're having fun.'

'And you can have more fun later, but for now you need to get dried, put some more sun cream on and rest – in the shade.'

'Don't want to *rest*,' she said, folding her arms, her face like thunder.

Dan was ignoring this. He'd taken Freddie from Jamie and was now delivering him at my feet, then collapsing on the sunlounger next to me.

'Oh, I see your shift's over,' I said sarcastically.

'You're the one who wanted them out of the water,' he snapped back and closed his eyes.

'Pleeeeeeease.' Alfie was standing in the shallow end, his hands in a prayer gesture, then Freddie stood up and started to wander back towards the pool on his own.

'Freddie, Freddie,' I called.

'Pleeeease Muuummy,' Alfie was saying on a bloody loop.

'But you promised.' Violet was now at my side, gently kicking my sunlounger. It wasn't aggressive, just a rhythmical thud, thud,

thud, punctuated every second thud by, 'You promised' in her sulky voice. Accompanied by 'Muuummy' from Alfie, and words from the conversation I'd had with Jamie, a cacophony filled my head. Freddie was now walking towards me on wobbly legs, his arms out, crying because I'd asked him to come back, and I wanted to cry too.

'Muummy.' Thud, thud. Freddie now screaming with tiredness and temper. 'You promised.' Violet's foot hitting the wooden leg of the lounger. Thud, thud, thud… going through me like a heartbeat.

'Violet, STOP THAT NOW!' I yelled, surprising them, and myself.

For a moment, we all looked at each other, then Violet's little chin began quivering, and she stormed off. I shouldn't have shouted. They were kids on holiday and they wanted to have fun – they weren't being naughty. I'd just stopped their fun, because I wanted them away from Ella.

'Violet, Violet, come back,' I called, but I couldn't stop her because I couldn't abandon the other two, who were now both sobbing.

'They're tired,' I said to Dan, who had opened his eyes with the specific purpose of looking at me accusingly.

'No, we're not tired, Mummy, you're *mean*!' said my four-year-old.

'Out of the mouths of babes…' Dan murmured, turning around and pretending to sleep.

'Oh fuck off, Dan,' I hissed under my breath, but Alfie must have heard. He dramatically put two pudgy hands to his mouth, his eyes wide. I was horrified. 'Sorry… Alfie, Mummy shouldn't have…'

But my gregarious son needed an audience for this. We'd taught him to disapprove when other children said naughty words, so why not when mummies did too?

'Granny, Granny, Mummy just used a swear,' he yelled across the pool to Joy, who abandoned *A Woman of Substance* to half-heartedly attend to what I'm sure she viewed as this latest Clare-induced crisis.

'Oh Alfie, I'm sure mummy didn't,' she said, smiling, while balancing Barbara Taylor Bradford on her knees.

But my little boy was keen to make sure Granny was furnished with the full facts of Mummy's naughtiness, and he ran over and whispered something in her ear. Which, from the way Joy's face drained of colour, was the f-word. But I didn't have time to deal with her reaction because Violet was now sitting with Jamie and Ella, in tears, Ella's arm around her, comforting her after the vile telling-off she'd just had from her evil mother. I didn't know which way to turn, but just when I thought my children's betrayal was done, I spotted Freddie making his way towards them too, and he was soon enjoying a comforting cuddle from his Uncle Jamie – who might really be his dad.

I felt absolutely wretched – there was only one thing worse than Dan being pissed off with me, and that was my kids being pissed off with me. I looked over at Dan, who was now lying flat out, eyes still closed. He'd obviously decided to step away; he couldn't possibly be asleep with the noise of children sobbing around the pool.

I gazed over at Joy, comforting Alfie, Jamie and Ella trying to console the other two. Even Bob was joining in, getting up from his sunlounger and pretending to trip to make Alfie laugh. The fact was, the whole family were now attempting to repair the damage I'd done, or at least the damage they could *see* I'd done. But they were making things worse, validating the children's sense of injustice. Then I had an idea, and got up from the lounger and called to them all.

'Hey, look, I'm sorry guys, but it was time to come out of the pool, and, Violet, I didn't mean to shout. How about we go to the little shop down the road for ice cream?'

Alfie, who was nearest to me, looked up, and I saw a flurry of activity from Violet and Freddie, who didn't understand the concept of bearing a grudge, and was soon on wobbly feet, ready to join me. But, in the corner of my eye, I saw Ella whisper something to Violet, and Violet nodding vigorously.

'Hey, Clare, why don't me and Jamie take the kids for ice cream?' It was one of Ella's questions that wasn't a question – more a statement of intent.

'Yay!' Violet squealed, like she'd only just been made aware of this, when I was sure Ella had just whispered the suggestion to her. She might only be nine, but it seemed Ella wasn't afraid to use her against me.

'No it's fine, but thanks, Ella,' I called back assertively while forcing a smile. 'I'll take them.'

'Nonsense,' Ella said, getting up from her lounger, taking Violet's hand. 'You're obviously very tired, that's why you lost your temper.' *Bitch.* 'You need some time to yourself without the kids, they were clearly getting on your nerves. Let's be kind to Mum and take the boys so she can have a rest, we don't want her getting upset again, do we?' she said to Violet, who sensed the awkwardness and looked from me to her. I hated to see my little girl in this dilemma and smiled reassuringly. 'Anyway,' she added, as Jamie stood up and lifted Freddie onto his hip, 'me and Jamie would *love* to spend time with them.'

'Yay!' Alfie was now jumping for joy as Jamie, Ella and my children circled around the pool.

Ella took Alfie's hand in her free one, and they all walked past me, waving. I didn't move, just watched them like a family going off for ice cream on holiday.

With the kids gone, it was so quiet. The pool was still, not a ripple. Even the birds had stopped singing; it felt almost eerie. All I could hear in the silence was the imaginary voice of the woman selling drinks on the side of the road, and her warning, '*pericolo*' and '*morte*'.

CHAPTER TWENTY-SEVEN

I spent the next hour on my sunlounger, but couldn't settle. Where were they? How long would they be? Were they okay? I worried because Alfie wasn't good with roads, and despite lots of 'training' from me was easily distracted. Violet would be too busy trying to be like Ella, copying the ice cream she chose, the way she ate it, the things she said. And then there was Freddie…

I couldn't concentrate, and after about half an hour of attempting to read on my Kindle, I had to turn it off. I looked over at Dan, who was absorbed in his book, so I opened Instagram and found Ella's account.

Opening up her page, I was greeted by the usual bikini-baring selfies, and I scrolled through – a photo of Dan, Jamie, tellingly none of me. I looked at her friends, some she'd tagged, and one name led to another, and I looked at the different pages of all the Ella lookalikes and then I spotted @EllaFamily1. It was different from her other friends' accounts, lots of moody black and white shots, and I had to put my reading glasses on to make them out. The photographs had been over exposed and most weren't full face. They were gorgeous photos of a beautiful family – in a restaurant eating pasta, around a swimming pool, a little boy walking through a garden, the sun on his bright blond hair, children laughing with Mum and Dad. Except I realised this wasn't a mum and dad and kids – it was Jamie and Ella, with *my* kids. #Family #Holiday #children

I became more alarmed as I continued to look through swathes of photos of my kids. To anyone who didn't know, this was a family account, and it seemed like the kids belonged to Ella and Jamie. And all the photos gave the same impression – Ella with my children. #FamilyTime. Ella and Violet putting on make-up together at her bedroom mirror. #GrownupGirl. There was even one of them all asleep in bed. #NightNight – she must have sneaked into their room to take that one!

'Have you *bloody* seen this?' I sat up so quickly, I almost fell off the sunlounger.

Dan looked up. 'What now?'

'Don't say "what now?" like that. This is outrageous.'

I was waving my phone screen in his face and he was trying to sit up. 'Clare, calm down, just a minute.'

He peered in reluctantly. 'They're nice photos, I don't see your problem,' he said, like this had nothing to do with him, like it wasn't his family Ella was exploiting.

'My *problem* is that she's implying that the kids are hers… and …' I could barely get the words out. 'She took these photos when we weren't around, without our *permission*, Dan. You can't just photograph other people's kids and put them on the Internet.' He shrugged, and I stopped dead in my tracks. 'Oh. *You* gave her permission, didn't you?' I said.

He looked very uncomfortable. 'No – not exactly, but thinking about it, she was saying something the other day – about becoming a mummy blogger.'

I was furious. 'This gets worse, so she's also exploiting them – getting money and free shit off the back of our kids.'

'She wouldn't do that.'

'She *has*,' I said, prodding my finger on the screen; why couldn't he see what was in front of him? 'I wonder if that's why she was so keen to take them for ice cream…?' I said, refreshing the page. 'Whoa, look at *this*!' Right on cue up popped posed pictures of our children eating ice cream. #FamilyTime #FamilyHoliday. And the most recent was a photo of Jamie with Freddie on his knee, holding a spoon of ice cream to his mouth. #Gelato #Theylookjustthesame. In an instant my mouth went so dry I couldn't swallow. Was she taunting me? What if she'd worked out that through her account, I'd find these snaps and she knew there was nothing I could do about it? This was a warning, Freddie and Jamie together on this account; the hashtags would spill our secret, she wouldn't need to. I couldn't let Dan see it.

Fortunately, he lay back down with his book. 'I don't know what your problem is, they're cute photos of the kids and, okay, I'm sorry. It's my fault, I led her to believe I'd given her permission from both of us. It's not hurting anyone, but if it upsets you, we can ask her to take them down.'

'Yes, will you do that please?' I asked, aware I sounded like Joy talking to Bob. But if Dan asked Ella to take the photos down, then I wouldn't have to tangle with her.

'Yeah.'

'When?' I pressed.

'What do you want me to do, Clare?' he asked, irritated. 'Shall I run into the village now and tear the kids away from the ice cream, make a big scene and drag them back, telling them never to speak to Auntie Ella again?'

'Don't be stupid.'

'No, *you're* being stupid. When they get back, we will just calmly ask her to take down the account – if it's making you so unhappy.'

'Why do you have to add the caveat "if it's making *me* unhappy"?'

'I can't win! Whatever I say is wrong. You do what you want to do, Clare,' he said, and closed his eyes.

I couldn't get through to Dan, so I stood up and wandered over to Joy, who put down her book.

'Are you okay, dear?' she asked.

'You'll never believe this. Ella seems to have a whole Instagram account devoted to the kids!'

I showed her on my phone, and she scrolled through. I was so desperate for her to see what Ella had done now I didn't care what she made of the hashtags, they were open to interpretation and she had no idea, so wouldn't think twice.

'That's a lovely one of all three of them – and that one of Freddie – you should ask her for copies,' she said.

'Don't you think it's a bit creepy?' I asked as she handed me back my phone.

'Why? They're lovely, you can print them and get them framed. They'd look good on your sideboard in the dining room.'

'I didn't even know she was taking them.' What the hell was going on here? Even Joy wasn't understanding the gravitas of this. Another woman was passing someone else's kids off as her own.

'She's been taking pictures all holiday, love,' she said, in the same voice she used to explain to Alfie why he should stop hitting Freddie.

'Yes, but I think it's a bit off to set up a whole account with someone else's kids on and not mention it.'

Joy looked up at me. 'Clare, I'm sure she didn't mean anything. They're beautiful children, she just wanted to photograph them. And I think it's good they've gone for a while today. It's been like a pressure cooker here since Ella and Jamie arrived.'

Finally, she was admitting she felt the same too and I jumped on it, desperate for her to believe me, to be on my team.

'This has made me very uncomfortable. I know you want to believe Jamie's made a good choice, and I don't want to bring up the earrings again, but I'm just not sure Ella's trustworthy, Joy,' I added, not least to pre-empt anything Ella might say to Joy about me and Jamie.

'Oh, she's young, she just wants to impress us all. But you don't see eye to eye with her do you?'

I suddenly felt like Joy was shifting all this on to me. 'No, I don't suppose I do.'

'I really wouldn't take it to heart, Clare. I'm sure she didn't mean anything by the photos, she probably didn't like to ask you because you… well, she's a bit scared of you.'

I almost laughed in her face. 'Is that what she told you?'

'Well, not exactly, she just said she finds Dan easier to get along with. She finds you intimidating – she thinks you don't like her.'

'Intimidating?' I almost laughed at that one, and I was seething that she'd made me out to be the villain. But she'd manipulated the situation and to everyone else that must have seemed plausible. 'She's right, I don't want a relationship with her – she stole your earrings, let's not forget that,' I said, rather lamely throwing the worst thing I could think of at Joy. But what else could I say? There was so much I couldn't talk about, and by skirting around the edges I was aware I was beginning to sound like the jealous older woman in all this. Which I reckoned was exactly what Ella wanted. When Joy didn't respond, I used a risky strategy and pushed her. 'Joy, you *know* she took your earrings, right?'

There was a moment's hesitation before she launched into this weird, accepting version of Joy that had been present ever since Ella had turned up. 'Perhaps she did. But I have them back now, so all's well that—'

It was so unlike her to be passive, and it was all for Jamie, so he'd come back into the fold and stay this time.

'So you admit you think she took them?' I pushed again.

'I don't know, Clare, we'll never know for sure, will we?' She didn't like me questioning her, she seemed flustered, but why?

'Well *I* know for sure, Joy, even if no one else is prepared to say it.'

'Clare, look… I can understand why you might feel a little – *threatened.* Dan obviously… *likes* Ella.'

This comment was loaded, the emphasis and ambiguity placed on '*likes.*' I knew what she was trying to tell me and it hit me right in the solar plexus. So I wasn't the only person who'd noticed Dan paying Ella so much attention? Was Joy trying to tell me something? Was she warning me? Or had this holiday, the intense heat and the tense atmosphere made me so paranoid I'd lost the plot?

Was this true, did my husband have a thing for my new sister-in-law? Or was Joy trying to set me against Ella by *suggesting* Dan liked her? Let's face it, it wouldn't have been in Joy's interests for her daughters-in-law to get too friendly, they might gang up against her. And knowing how she worked I knew it wasn't beyond her to divide and rule, in an attempt to shape the family dynamics in her favour. 'It's about survival,' she'd once said to me when I questioned her spreading a rumour about a friend. 'They're like seals screaming for fish, so I throw them some and let them fight among themselves. It gives me a break, and while they're attacking each other, they aren't watching me,' she said, then must have seen the look on my face and added with a giggle, 'Oh, don't mind me love, I'm only teasing.' But she wasn't.

I didn't get chance to consider Joy's part in the daughters-in-law drama because, to my deep relief, I heard children's voices in the distance – *my* children's voices – and the blood rushed to my chest as I ran through the garden. I probably greeted them like they'd been away forever, but I'd never been so happy to see them.

'God, Clare, we only went to the ice cream shop,' Ella was saying as she sashayed along behind them. She was carrying Freddie, who had his head buried in her neck; the intimacy of this bothered me more than it should, but I was eager to take him off her and reached for him. Instinctively, Freddie would always come to me, and I could see he'd spotted me, because his eyes were open, but he pushed himself back against Ella, like he didn't want to be moved.

'He's certainly bonded with you.' Jamie smiled at her, and she positively glowed, her eyes sparkling back at him.

I couldn't force Freddie to come into my arms. I also didn't want to risk him screaming if I tried, so asked Violet and Alfie about the ice cream they'd had and they described their cones in some detail.

'So, who wants a last swim?' I said, in a blatant bid for The Best Mum award. This was my chance to win back favour with my children. She could buy them all the ice cream they wanted, but at least Auntie Ella was never going to play with them in the water. The older two shouted, 'Yesss!' and immediately began throwing off their T-shirts, but Freddie continued to cling to Ella. 'Freddie, are you coming in the water with Mummy?' I asked gently.

'I think Freddie's too tired for the pool,' Ella said, cradling him.

'Then I'll take him,' I said, unsmiling. 'He can sit with me.'

'But I thought you were going in the water with Violet and Alfie,' she said loud enough for them to hear. 'You just promised them.'

She was right, I had said I would, and I wanted to, but I also wanted Freddie back. I stood there with my arms out for him as the other two called for Mummy to get in the water.

'Go on, Clare, you play with the others. He's fine with us,' Jamie said.

'Yeah… be good for him to get used to Jamie – and me,' Ella added, making it clear exactly what she meant. If I denied them this time with Freddie, would she say something to Dan? I couldn't risk it, so against all my instincts, I went in the water with Violet and Alfie, while keeping an eye on Ella and Jamie who were now playing with Freddie.

Once in the water, I discreetly said to Violet, 'Auntie Ella took lots of photos of you, didn't she?'

'Yeah,' she responded excitedly. 'She always does… Mum, did you know she has twenty-five thousand followers?'

'Mmmm, so I believe.' I looked up and saw them the other side of the pool, Jamie holding Freddie in the air, Ella laughing and tickling his toes. For now I would play with my kids, give them the quality time they deserved. I would deal with @EllaFamily1 later.

CHAPTER TWENTY-EIGHT

Several hours later, I saw Ella go into the villa and followed her. She went into the lounge area, still in her bikini, and closed the door. I wasn't being closed out of a room in my own holiday home, so, after a brief knock, I went in. She was lying on the sofa, scrolling through her phone, doing what made her happiest and probably uploading more photos of *my* kids.

'I can't believe you'd make an account featuring my children without asking me,' I said of the photos.

'What are you going on about now?' she monotoned, without even looking up from her phone. I was gripped by rage, and having been careful with her until now, the time for playing games was over. She'd involved my children, and they were more important to me than anyone or anything else.

'Your stupid bloody Instagram. Photos of my kids like they're yours, what the hell do you think you're doing?'

She finally looked up from her phone, but stayed in the prone position. 'You mean the Ella family account? I thought you'd like their photos,' she said, all innocence. But I saw the gleam in her eye. She was enjoying this. And now I could see how clever she was, always stage-managing the situation, manipulating me so I appeared to be the unreasonable one. It was so frustrating I found it impossible to hide my irritation.

'It isn't my kids' photos I'm objecting to. It's the fact you've posted them without my permission and they're on your Instagram.'

'God, Clare. Get a grip,' she sighed.

'Please take them off NOW,' I said. Loudly.

She finally looked at me through hand-shielded eyes. 'Wow, hun, you need to calm down.'

'No, *hun*. You do!' I spat.

'Anyone would think I'd kidnapped them,' she said calmly, a perfectly posed look of hurt on her face. 'They're my niece and nephews, they're my family too, Clare. I never once said they were my *own* kids. Why are you always looking for ways to get at me? I can't do anything right as far as you're concerned. I even take your kids for ice cream– and you turn that into a drama.'

'That's not true…' I started, trying to compose myself, not show my anger so she could look like the victim. 'I wanted to like you when you first arrived, and you were straight out rude to me. From that first moment, it's like you've had it in for me. But there's no rational reason for that, you didn't even know me – I just think maybe we're very different and find it hard to connect.'

'I could say the same of you, we didn't know each other but you took against me. You told Jamie you didn't like me. So you can't deny it and pretend it's me who's the hater.'

'But that was later, at the beginning I wanted to like you…' I started.

'You don't *have* to like me, Clare,' she said over me, repeating the phrase I'd used to Jamie. The message was loud and clear: everything I'd said to Jamie, he'd shared with her. As he said, she was his wife, they had no secrets. It seemed like everyone was talking about everyone else, repeating each other's words and sharing confidences that were never meant to be shared.

'I don't *like* or dislike you, Ella, because I don't know you,' I said, 'none of us do. We only met a few days ago,' I added. 'I just find it… interesting,' I continued, 'the way you've come into this family and honestly I'm wondering what your deal is. Because within hours of your arrival, you're ripping apart the family business, criticising the website, deciding where everyone should sit, what everyone should eat, implying I'm menopausal, flirting with Dan – and now, now…' I stopped because the look of feigned innocence on her face was making me angry again. I had to compose myself, and tried to continue calmly. 'Now you're posting photos of my kids on Instagram and involving yourself in stuff that doesn't concern you. Stuff between me and Jamie.' At this, I finally made eye contact and she stared back.

'What the actual hell, Clare? It doesn't *concern* me?' She put on her shocked face. 'You think you can just live your life, criticising others from your high horse – blaming everyone else for what's happening to you. I know you disapprove of me, you think I'm not good enough – well, take a look at yourself, the "perfect wife and mother". Screaming at your kids and shagging your husband's brother behind his back. Nice.'

I talked in a calm voice, no swearing, no visible anger. 'I love my kids, they are amazing and sometimes I tell them off because I want them to be amazing adults. You aren't a mother, so please don't you dare criticise my mothering. As for Jamie and me, that happened a long time ago, I was under a lot of stress, Dan had met someone else and I thought he was leaving me—'

'Oh, there you go again,' she interrupted, 'blaming someone else for what *you* did – for the life you're stuck in. I suppose it was her fault, was it… the woman he was seeing? It was her fault you shagged his brother… Yeah, that's it, Clare.'

'That's not what I'm saying, I'm saying things were different then, we were different people, and after it happened, Jamie and I made a decision for it to never be discussed again. Then Freddie came along, and yes, it's possible that Jamie's the father. But it was our secret and Jamie shouldn't have told you.'

'But I'm his wife! We don't have secrets,' she said, repeating the mantra he'd used, that she'd obviously drummed into him. 'Meanwhile, you stick your head in the sand with the rest of the family regarding your own husband's inability to keep his hands to himself.' She paused, to see my reaction, to really hit me with it. 'You blame "the other woman" and you all move on, don't you?' She was reminding me that not only was Dan unfaithful, but she knew about it – she'd made a spot-on assessment of the Taylors too, that's exactly what they did. Obviously, Jamie knew about Dan's first affair because I'd told him the night we slept together, and I assume he knew about Marilyn from Joy. He had clearly told Ella about it, along with absolutely everything about himself and his family. After all, as they both said, they had no secrets. I doubted Jamie had any secrets from Ella, but I was convinced she had quite a few of her own that he wasn't privy to.

I felt like we were on a carousel, going round and round and one of us had to get off. 'Can we not let it go, Ella?' I spoke gently, to appeal to her. 'In the great scheme of things, it doesn't matter, it's the past. You've got your lives before you – I mean you and Jamie, you can travel, see the world, find somewhere to settle—'

'We've found somewhere, a lovely detached in its own grounds, only about two miles from you and Dan. We thought it would be handy for work – oh, and for the kids to visit.' She was looking straight at me, waiting for me to bite. And I couldn't help it.

'Our kids?'

'Who else's? Jamie wants to see more of Freddie.'

My fury rose and I couldn't keep it in any longer. She tried to seem harmless – with her hair extensions and yoga and clean eating and fake lashes. But it was all an image for Instagram, and tomorrow, next week, next year she would shed it like a snake sheds its skin. Only a week before, she was the blushing bride, a few days ago, the girl in a bikini, and now she was playing at being a mummy. It didn't add up, there was no substance behind any of it; she was just trying on other people's lives to see if they fit.

'I don't know what you're playing at Ella,' I said, 'but somehow you've managed to wrap everyone around your little finger, pretending to be Miss Innocent, but it's all fake. Instead of setting up a weird account *pretending* to be a mummy, why not go and *be* one? Have your *own* babies with Jamie, be a mummy blogger, or an Insta-mummy, or whatever the hell they call them! Put your own kids on the Internet. Just stop trying to steal mine!'

She'd sat up on the sofa and was just glaring at me.

'You think you know everything, don't you, Clare? You think you know me, that you know what I'm about – you haven't a clue.'

'Oh, I'm sure I couldn't begin to know everything about you. But one thing I do know is that it's all for show and underneath I bet your life is a mess.'

At this, she gasped and started laughing. 'My life... *my* life?'

'Ella, just do us all a favour and do something real for a change. Have a baby, if you want it that much. Trust me, it'll take your mind off everything else, it'll give you a real life – it might even stop you obsessing over *mine*.'

She looked at me like I was mad. 'Wow.'

'What?'

'You really think I want your life? That I want to go from being me to being a fat, stressed, milk machine? Great idea, Clare. I'll pop out a few kids, get fat, then watch my husband chase other women, but I've got the kids so at least he'll never leave me. I'll show those pretty young things he thinks he's fallen in love with – that's your life, Clare. Yeah, really something to aspire to.'

I couldn't believe the cruelty of what she was saying; it hurt so much to think that was who I might be. I guess the truth always hurts.

She continued, 'I know you hate me, but you hate yourself too for putting up with it. That's why you slept with Jamie, it was your sad little attempt at revenge. But it backfired didn't it?'

'I regret what happened, but I don't regret Freddie,' I said.

'That's exactly what Jamie says, so why don't you let him *be* Freddie's father, acknowledge who he is, tell the family – and, when he's old enough, tell Freddie.'

'No,' I said calmly. 'I don't think you realise the implications, Ella…'

She was still semi-recumbent on the sofa, long brown legs, golden toenails. I envied her physical ease as she slowly crossed those perfect legs. 'Well, I gave you a chance,' she said, threat in her voice, her eyes almost black.

'But I don't have a choice,' I said, panic rising in my throat.

'You *could* have had a choice, if you'd owned up, let Jamie be a dad.'

'Jamie wasn't interested in becoming a father until you came along. You're just here to stir up trouble, and you've really turned his head. You don't want to be a mother yourself, so what exactly do you want money? Is that what it is?'

'Oh, you really haven't a clue, babes,' she said, throwing her head back and laughing, mirthlessly, baring those white teeth.

Everything about Ella, from the rainbow bookshelves to the designer labels, to the clean vegan eating, avocado-with-everything approach to life – it was about image. She was keen for Jamie to spend time with Freddie – but it wasn't because she cared about Jamie. She saw a cute kid with blond hair and she wanted him on her Instagram. Everything in Ella's life was staged: no messy emotions, no flesh and blood, just beautiful selfies, hair extensions and fake lashes. Now she wanted to add one of my kids to her portfolio.

'Clare,' she was saying, 'it's Jamie's right to see his child. He's too weak to fight this alone. He's been stamped into the ground by that awful woman most of his life—'

A flash of insight. Ella had realised how much influence Joy had in Jamie's life and had determined to wheedle her way into Joy's affections so she could position herself front and centre. It was all cooking and gossip at first, but Ella had just been easing herself in.

'Someone has to clean up the mess you made. Might as well be me… After all, you're not going to tell the truth, are you, Clare?' she said knowingly.

'I can't. The kids… what it would do to Dan, to everyone?'

'Dan?' she said, getting up from the sofa, facing me, hands on hips. 'You mean Dan who's cheated on you all your marriage? Because, let's face it, he's never really cared, has he, Clare? Everyone knows he's been trying for years to escape from your clutches, be released from your banal life of domesticity. He only stays for the kids – you'd have to be blind or pathetic not to realise that.'

This felt like a smack in the face, a stinging resounding slap that reverberated through my body.

'Whatever's happened between me and Dan is none of your business,' I said, trying not to cry. Was it true what she said, was Dan really only staying with me for the children? And if so, could everyone see it but me? 'Me and Dan are fine now, it's in the past,' I said, to convince myself as much as her.

She walked towards the door to leave. 'In the past, is it? Okay, so is Dan asking me what I like in bed "in the past"? Is Dan asking if I fancy him more than Jamie "in the past"? Is Dan telling me this morning he would love to kiss me "in the past"?'

This took my breath away. I couldn't speak. Was this true? Had he really said those things, on the holiday that was meant to bring us back together? Or was Ella just lying, lashing out, trying to hurt me?

'And I'm not lying, Clare,' she said, like she'd read my mind. Then she opened the door, and before she left added, 'I've known a lot of men like Dan, and "in the past" I'd have ridden that train, but not this time…' She hesitated. 'When I think about the way… the way… he is – it makes me sick. And a heads up – it *so* isn't "in the past". Ten minutes ago, by the pool, he said he'd love to see me naked.' And with that, she left the room, swinging her hips in her too-small bikini.

CHAPTER TWENTY-NINE

This holiday had been about us healing from Dan's affair, about us finally coming back together, but had Dan had his head turned once more? And if he had, we couldn't come back from this. I couldn't get Ella's words out of my mind: *he said he'd love to see me naked*, and *he only stays for the kids, you'd have to be blind or pathetic not to realise that*. Was that me, blind and pathetic, a stupid wife who'd bought into a big lie? Had I been wrong to forgive him – twice? Or was this just another of Ella's twisted games?

Either way, I was at the mercy of this bloody woman – she knew far too much about me, and she was using it to control me. Perhaps it was time I started getting a grip on things.

I couldn't physically stop her from telling Dan and the rest of the family about me and Jamie, but I could perhaps distract her for now and put her on pause. Thank God for my part-time stint on Taylor's social media, where I'd learned how easy it was to create a whole new world of one's own. So, late afternoon, while the kids played in the garden and Ella and the others lay around the pool, I sent the first message to @EverythingElla123 on Instagram from my newly created account @StarsTV. *Where the Instagram stars of today are the TV stars of tomorrow.*

Heyyy Ella!

I'm just making contact because we TOTALLY love your Insta here at StarsTV! My name's Summer, I'm a talent scout for a brand new, super exciting, but SUPER SECRET, TV show. We're currently slipping into the DMs of our fave Insta crushes to ask if they'd be interested in starring in a BRAND NEW reality show. It's kinda a cross between Love Island and The Bachelor, and that's all I can say just now #supersecret. But there is huge prize money at stake – we're talking SEVEN figures. For now, we're obvs saving all our Insta posts for launch day, and our website is still on lockdown!

All I can say is filming starts in just a couple of weeks, we need you to be single, sizzling hot, with no commitments, and good to leave the UK if needed. If you're feeling this, DM me and I'll get right back to ya with all the deets about channel, prize money and likely exposure for your brand!

Have a great day
Summer xxx

I was wearing my sunglasses and hat, and discreetly glanced over at Ella as she posed around the pool. She might be 'just married' but I'd seen how fickle she could be, moving online from one persona to another – single girl to mummy within a week of being here.

I hoped she'd take the bait, because that would prove everything I thought about Ella, that this was just a bit of fun for the summer. She'd stepped in and caused conflict and upset, and now she'd skip off to what she thought was a moneymaking future filled with red carpets and beautiful people.

I couldn't take the constant threat hanging over me, and this was a last effort to tempt her away – I just hoped she found it irresistible. I pressed send – it felt good to be taking back control.

From my vantage point, I could see her at the other side of the pool. She and Jamie now seemed to sit as far away from me and Dan as they could, but I could tell by the body language that she'd read the message. She seemed more animated, there was much laughter and snuggling into Jamie and I wondered for a moment if she might be conflicted over such an amazing offer.

I kept checking @StarsTV to see if she'd responded, but no luck – mind you, she was now busy applying fresh lipstick, oiling up and taking a stack of selfies. After about 100 clicks, she had to ask Jamie to step in as official photographer – presumably her selfie stick couldn't quite capture every little inch. Next thing, she's standing thigh-deep in the far end of the pool, top off, covering her breasts with both hands. It wasn't really appropriate on a family holiday, but I consoled myself that at least they were keeping it up their end of the pool. No one else would have noticed if she hadn't started shouting, 'Jamie, take it from above', 'Do I look skinny if I stand like this?' and 'Does the water make my eyes bluer?'

'You look great, babe. Yeah, yeah, your eyes are awesome.'

God, I thought, *he's even starting to* sound *like her.*

I kept my sunglasses on and pretended not to notice, but I saw Violet glance over, and the shock on her face was almost comical. It was one thing showing your buttocks, but even my nine-year-old wannabe would draw the line at taking off her top – at least I hoped so.

This awful narcissism continued into the afternoon, and I was beginning to wonder if she'd even read the message when up she popped in my DMs.

Hey Summer,

Wow! I am totally stoked to be in your orbit and would LOVE to be involved in this secret project. It's actually perfect timing cos I'm just wrapping up a big project that I've been working on for months! I am single, sizzling hot, have absolutely NO commitments and I'm good to go. Just tell me where and when you want me!

Ella xxx

Yess! I now had my own little threat to hang over her – in writing. Hopefully this would be enough to shut her up, or send her packing.

A veritable slew of photos followed, so many that I had to turn the volume off on my phone because of the incessant pinging; I didn't want to alert her in any way. These, of course, were all the photos she'd just taken. Even sexier and more out there than usual, they were Ella's desperate bid for TV stardom. I was rather pleased with myself – I'd pitched it just right.

Shame I wasn't going to answer, I could have had more fun, but I now had enough proof that she'd dump Jamie in an instant as soon as that better offer came along. Meanwhile, she'd be so strung out waiting for the response, she might lay off me until I could find the time to chat with her – alone. Yes, I'd let her sweat, make her really want this – after all @StarsTV wouldn't get back straight away. They'd be talking to other Instagrammers about their 'super secret' project too, wouldn't they?

I watched her for the next couple of days. She was happier, her movements quicker, with purpose. I could tell she was mentally preparing to fly away from Jamie and his difficult family. I knew how this felt, because I'd also planned to leave Dan at least twice when he'd cheated. Both times I'd had this crazy idea that we could all go to my cousin in Scotland, then I'd contemplated starting a new life without Dan, by moving to a nursing job in a hospital far away. But for me it had been a daydream; my priority, my real purpose, was to keep my family. I wasn't Ella, wandering the globe, looking for my next hook-up – I had a husband, kids, I had the Taylors. I appreciated what they'd given me. However, Ella was a different woman in a different life and from her swift response to my TV message it was clear that Ella was happy to abandon her husband for the chance to star on a TV show. She was the butterfly flapping its wings – she had no loyalty, no commitment to anyone except herself.

Two nights after she'd received the message about the TV show, we all ate together as usual, but Jamie didn't join us – Ella explained that he had mild sunstroke.

'Oh, I have some skin cream, and some rehydrating tablets if that would help?' I offered.

'Oh, Clare, you're always playing the nurse. No. He'll be fine,' she said, and smirked at me. I felt so trapped, so on edge with her around, but now I had my own weapon, and I admit I was rather looking forward to using it.

So, after dinner, I suggested we both do the washing up together, and no one argued with that, including her. I think the others were a little wary, and didn't want to get caught in any crossfire between us over the Fairy Liquid, so, after helping us clear the table, they happily let us go off to the kitchen to wash up and hopefully work things out. I couldn't wait.

'Are you okay?' I said to Ella, once we'd filled the sink with hot soapy water and immersed the first load of pots.

'I am more than okay, Clare,' she said, and I could just tell she was dying to tell someone her news.

'You seem very happy,' I pushed a little.

'That's because I am.'

As tempting as it was, I couldn't make this go on any longer. I wasn't doing it to get kicks. 'I have something to tell you,' I started. 'It's about the message you received from the TV company the other day.'

She looked at me suspiciously. 'What message?'

'Stars TV… the new "super secret" project? A cross between *Love Island* and *The Bachelor*?'

She turned to look at me. 'How… how do you know about that? Oh. My. God. Clare, have you been reading my messages? Wow, you're even sadder than I thought.' She threw down the tea towel she'd been holding.

I shook my head. 'No, I'm really not that interested in your messages.'

'Liar. How do you know then?'

'Because I sent it.'

'What the hell?' Her mouth fell open, she couldn't take in what I'd said.

'Wow' was all she kept saying over and over. I don't think I'd ever seen anyone so shocked; she hadn't suspected a thing. She was looking at me, just shaking her head. 'How could you, Clare?' She was about to cry.

'Look, Ella, I just… had to do something. You know everything about me, you're constantly threatening to tell – and now I have a hold over you. I just couldn't work out if you'd fallen for Jamie – turns out you hadn't.'

'You bitch.'

She was leaning on the kitchen counter, angry, but most of all devastated that the offer wasn't real.

'You sent me a message stating that you're single, no commitments and ready to go anywhere at any time.'

'Yeah… because I thought it was from…'

'I know, and I shouldn't be meddling in your career, it's none of my business. But you shouldn't be meddling in my life either – and what happened three years ago between me and Jamie is none of your business… Do you see where I'm going here?'

She just stared. I could feel her hate, like a solid block between us.

'So, if you keep what you know to yourself and don't tell Dan – then I'll keep what I know to myself and I won't show Jamie the messages you sent stating how single you are and how you're up for anything, with anyone, for your little slice of fame,' I explained.

She rolled her eyes like a petulant teenager being lectured by her mother – but I saw the pain and disappointment in those eyes. It was so stark, I almost felt sorry for her. 'You've played the bride, the newlywed, you've enjoyed a free holiday and completely beguiled Jamie and his family,' I continued. 'Then, as soon as something better comes along, you're ready to dump him, prepared to end your marriage without a second thought.'

'I *did* give it a second thought, as it happens.'

'I'm sure you did,' I said sarcastically, 'before saying "yes please!" Anyway, my point is, if you don't want Jamie to know that you were about to end the marriage to "star" in a tacky TV show for singletons, then you should keep quiet about me and Jamie.'

She stood for a few seconds, composing herself, all her hurt and disappointment channelling into anger. 'God, what a bitch you are,' she said, like she was talking to herself.

'I'm sorry, Ella, but you drove me to it.'

'No, you're not sorry. You're a smug, jealous cow,' she hissed. 'You've looked down your nose at me all the time I've been here… And thanks to you, me and Jamie are over.'

'You don't have to be *over*,' I said. 'If you don't rock my boat, then I won't rock yours. No one needs ever to know.'

'You've made me look an idiot,' she laughed. 'I've messaged my agent, texted my friends and told them. You've trampled on everything; do you have any idea what you've done?'

'I'm sorry, but I had to…' I had no pity for her. I felt vindicated; she was clearly set on abandoning Jamie and the Taylors at the first sniff of something better.

'Yeah right. You're just nasty. SO jealous because your pervy husband hangs around me all the time. "Let me put your sun oil on, babe",' she said in a whiney voice meant to be Dan's. 'Jamie says he can't keep it in his pants, that Bob told him he worries when Dan does staff interviews because he picks young, pretty women who can't do the job. But that doesn't bother Dan, he soon finds something to keep them busy,' she added with a smirk. 'I see him staring at me– and so do you.'

I didn't want to hear this. 'Ella,' I said, 'I don't know why, but it seems to me all you've ever wanted to do is destroy me, and I don't know why.'

'Me destroy *you*? You told everyone I was a thief, that I stole my mother-in-law's earrings – and then said I was lying about my own sister drowning. Who would lie about something like that?'

'I'm sorry… about your sister. But the earrings, you took them, I saw you.'

'I didn't. Joy told me to get them for her.'

'She said that to help cover it up, that's what Joy *would* do because she doesn't want the embarrassment, the shame…'

'No, she asked me to get them from her dressing table. I took them downstairs to her – she said she wanted me to have them, but I mustn't let you know because you'd be jealous.'

'That's just not true, Joy wouldn't do that. You're lying again, Ella. When will it stop?'

'She said she hadn't bought me a wedding gift,' she pushed on, ignoring me, 'and so I could have them and wear them when I got home, but never in front of you.'

'I don't believe you,' I said. 'I was with Joy when she opened her jewellery roll, she was surprised and upset that they weren't there.'

'She *had* to be surprised, she couldn't tell you that she'd given them to me.'

I rolled my eyes; she really wasn't able to ever take responsibility for her actions. Always the victim, always someone else's fault.

She started to walk towards the kitchen door and I leaned on the counter, surprised at how badly she'd taken it, but at least I'd brought about some kind of ending. Hopefully I'd managed to put a stop to her constant threats. But then she turned around.

'Oh, and by the way, you'll be pleased to know I already told Jamie I was leaving him. Said I had this great offer and had to be single with no commitments – I wanted to be upfront and honest and didn't want to string him along. He didn't have sunstroke, he just couldn't face everyone. So your little plan to blackmail me has backfired spectacularly, babe. Talk away, I've nothing to lose. But you still do.'

CHAPTER THIRTY

The following day, Dan and I were in the garden with the children when I saw Ella slip out through the French windows. I was immediately on alert. In the aftermath of what had happened, I was feeling guilty. I only wanted to do to Ella what she was doing to me, dangle her secret in front of her. It was defensive rather than vindictive. I never expected her to end their marriage within hours of receiving the message and throw herself headlong into a reality-show dream – one that didn't even exist.

I considered explaining it to Jamie, apologising to both of them because it was my fault they were now in the early stages of parting. I consoled myself that if she really loved him, and he her, then this wouldn't have happened – but that would have been a natural break, not something forced upon them by me.

Out of the corner of my eye, I saw she was walking over the grass in our direction. She had this look on her face that made my chest hurt and my heart began pounding as she approached.

I dared to look at her, our eyes met but she didn't flinch, just continued to march our way, hair flying behind her, sunglasses on her head.

'Dan, can I have a word?' She stood over us all, but her eyes were focussed on Dan, she didn't even look at me or the kids.

He looked surprised. 'Yeah, yeah, now?'

'Please.' She turned to look at me. 'I won't keep him for long, Clare, I know it's family time. Just need to discuss something important.' She gave me that fake saccharine smile, and it chilled my bones.

'Ella… please…' I looked into her face, desperate to make some kind of connection.

Dan looked puzzled. 'What's going on with you two?' He was half-smiling, like we were teasing him, but I just kept staring at her, begging her not to say anything.

'Clare, I need to talk to Dan… please don't interfere.' She was adamant. I had only known her for a matter of days, but I'd got to know that determined face.

I briefly looked down at Alfie, who was asking me where the sun slept at night. And when I looked up again, they were walking away. 'In the sky… darling,' I said, glad I was sitting down, because if I'd been standing my legs may have given way.

'But… Mum, does the sun have a bed in the sky?' Alfie was asking.

'Yes… er no.' They were walking quickly. Ella couldn't wait to give him the news. Ella had picked a moment when she knew I couldn't go after them, with only me out there to supervise the children. My 'clever' plan had not only made me the cause of their break-up, but given her even more reason to tell Dan about me.

They stopped when they came to the small garden table and she patted a chair girlishly, clearly asking him to sit down. They were less than 100 feet away from me, but when they started talking I couldn't actually hear what they were saying. My mouth was dry. I looked at my three golden-haired children sitting around me. Violet was playing a game on the iPad, Alfie was lying at my feet, still asking his crazy questions, and Freddie was on my knee. Would this be the last time we'd be like this? Was Ella about to make them children from a broken home?

I discreetly glanced over. She had her hand on Dan's arm, like she was holding him up; he was shaking his head slowly.

I felt tearful. I wanted to run across the grass and scream at her to stop, but it was all my own stupid fault. I wasn't ready to give up on our marriage, our family. Neither of us really wanted anyone else, did we? Were Marilyn and Jamie just our final tests before Dan and I settled into a good, faithful, lifelong marriage?

And as for the Jamie situation – I'd forgiven Dan for sleeping with other women, so he should be able to forgive me.

I looked down at Freddie, sleeping on my knee – a reminder that my betrayal was different, and in the great scheme of things, probably far worse.

I watched them talk; it was quite animated and I couldn't imagine what was being said. I was just aching for the conversation to be over, for Ella to send Dan back to me after she'd told him everything. I'd already started to think about how we'd get through this as a family. If Dan couldn't forgive me, he'd have to move out. Jamie might still try to get visiting rights, or even fight for adoption, but I couldn't worry about that yet. For now, my priority was the kids.

I continued to try to pin down the sun's bedtime routine with Alfie, answer Violet's probing questions about why Auntie Ella was talking to Dad and stroke Freddie's head while he slept, because, in the middle of it all, when life is crashing down around us, it's what we do, us mothers. Walls can be falling down, bombs dropping around us, and throughout the chaos all we care about is that we keep our children safe and happy.

Dan now had his head in his hands and Ella had her hand on his back. She glanced over, victorious, and I was about to ask Violet to keep an eye on the boys so I could go over and take control of my own destiny, instead of leaving it to Ella, when Joy appeared.

'Have you seen Bob?' she asked. 'I don't know where he is.'

'No… He might be asleep by the pool, he often lies under that tree, just to the side.'

'He hides there,' Violet laughed. 'He told me it's his quiet place.'

Joy rolled her eyes. 'I'll check there, thanks, girls.' She set off across the lawn, and stopped dead when she saw the tableau of Dan and Ella. She turned and looked at me questioningly, and in answer I just shrugged, but she kept the same concerned look on her face. Had she heard what they were saying? Was it all too late? I felt awful, she'd be genuinely hurt when she found out about Jamie and me, and I think it would kill Bob, who was such a family man.

I remember asking him once, in a light-hearted way, why he put up with Joy. I'll never forget, he just looked at me and said, 'Because without her I'd be nothing. She's everything to me, Clare, made me what I am, gave me my family.' I'd been rather touched, and hoped that one day Dan might say something like that about me. Right now, I doubted it. He wasn't the devoted type like Bob. And sitting a few hundred yards away from my marriage being destroyed by Hurricane Ella, I knew I never would be 'everything' to my husband.

Whatever happened now was my fault, and I would take full responsibility. If Dan chose to stay or leave, it was up to him. I just had to be strong for the kids while everything fell around me.

I now had to face the consequences of that drunken night three years before…

If the butterfly hadn't flapped its wings, the hurricane wouldn't have happened.

Eventually, Dan stood up. He headed back over the lawn and, in spite of the children being there, I asked quietly if he was okay.

He looked shell-shocked. 'Yes. But we've got a problem.'

CHAPTER THIRTY-ONE

'So Ella told you?' I said.

Dan just nodded, looking past me, like he couldn't even see me any more.

I remained on the grass for a few seconds, the kids chattering, Freddie still sleeping.

'We can work through it, Dan. I know it might not seem like that now, but—'

'So you *know* what she's saying?'

'Yes…'

'She *told* you?'

I nodded, but he couldn't look at me, and I didn't blame him.

'She seems hell-bent on destroying me, Dan… but we have to think about the family and forgive. We *can* move on from this.'

'Do you think so?' He looked hopeful.

He put his head in his hands and I sat there a while, thanking God that Freddie was asleep and Alfie and Violet were distracted by a game of ball. Dan eventually emerged, running his hands through his hair, looking distraught.

'None of it's true, Clare. I never tried to touch her.'

This threw me; what had she said to him?

'What?' I tried to work out how to approach this without giving anything away. 'What exactly did she say?' I asked.

He was slowly shaking his head. 'That I'd tried to kiss her, that I touched her inappropriately, that I'd said…'

'You'd love to see her naked?' I offered. Had she not even mentioned me and Jamie?

He looked up at me. 'God, did she tell you I said that?' He was horrified.

'Yeah.'

'I don't understand,' he said. 'She's invented all this and threatened to tell you... but she'd already told you?'

I nodded. It looked like Ella was playing both of us.

'But, Clare, that isn't all... she's saying it's harassment. She's threatening me with the police!'

'Shit.' She certainly knew how to turn the screws.

Violet and Alfie were wandering back, so Dan gestured for me to stand up so we could talk out of earshot. Freddie was on my knee, so I put him on my shoulder, my heart was racing.

I struggled to get up. Dan didn't help by taking a sleeping Freddie off me, like he usually would. He didn't even seem to register; he was pacing up and down, his hand over his mouth, his eyes darting everywhere.

'She can't call the police for something like that... can she?' I asked. 'And none of it's true so she won't have any proof.'

'God knows what she can do to me, she could tell the police anything. A man can't say or do anything these days without some woman threatening the police.'

'Wow,' I said, sounding like Ella. 'I can't believe you just said that.'

'You know what I mean... and she said she's telling Jamie, and Mum and Dad.' He looked dreadful, pale and fidgety, like he was going to be sick.

I didn't know what to say, what to think. Did I believe Ella or Dan? Let's face it, both had shown they were capable of lying to get what they wanted.

'Tell me the truth?' I asked urgently. 'Is there anything she can get you on... did you ever do or say something that could be misinterpreted?'

He sighed. 'She's an attractive girl. I may have glanced at her, might have given her the odd compliment, but touching her in an *inappropriate way*? God, no!'

'I suppose it's your word against hers, and if you're telling the truth you're okay,' I said bitterly. I was angry at Ella for causing this and angry at myself for not completely trusting my husband, but most of all at Dan who'd been bloody stupid and possibly put himself in the way of trouble with an innocent remark. I'd told him I didn't trust her, but he wouldn't have it and now he could see how manipulative and deceitful she was. But it may already be too late.

'I don't know what to do.' He was panicking. 'What if she dooon't stop, and continues to accuse me when we're back home? Even if I could talk her out of going to the police, she could hold this over me forever…'

Welcome to my world, I thought.

'She's trouble,' I said. 'And it looks like she and Jamie are on the rocks too.' I didn't tell him why.

He didn't ask either. I suppose it was inevitable, a woman like Ella didn't hang around.

'Well, good riddance, it's for the best. Jamie's like her puppy dog. She saw him coming, didn't she?'

'Yes,' I sighed.

He looked at me, hesitated, then went ahead, 'Thing is – she said if I paid her £10k she'd keep quiet, go away, and we'd never hear from her again.'

'You can't let her blackmail us, we can't afford that kind of money,' I gasped, feeling like I was suddenly in a gangster movie. People in my world didn't ask for £10k to keep quiet. That was a hell of a lot of money.

Dan, as always, wasn't listening, he was lost in his own thoughts. 'I wasn't sure whether to believe her – I thought as she was married to Jamie, she'd be with us a while, but if they aren't working out?'

'No, Dan. We don't have the money.'

'But it would be worth it just to get her off my back.'

'But if you're innocent…'

'It doesn't matter. Like you said, it's her word against mine and I don't stand a chance. And she says there's other stuff too – things about other members of the family.'

'That's just more lies,' I said, my heart hammering in my chest.

'I just want rid of her now, Clare – we don't need this. I can get the money through the business. I'll pay it back, just siphon some off – I'm in charge now.'

I was alarmed at how Dan was so quick to try and buy his way out of this. But perhaps having watched his mum remove Carmel and Marilyn from our lives, he figured he could just click his fingers and do the same with Ella.

'No.'

'But we can borrow it.'

'Dan, no. Even if she breaks up with Jamie and they divorce, she'll still be in our lives and back every few months for more money. She could hold this over us for life.'

'But if we do it now, it will buy us time.'

'By paying her you'll make yourself look guilty if she ever went to the police.'

'No. If she went to the police, I'd tell them she blackmailed me – that's illegal, and I'll have proof.'

'Just say no. We don't have the money and—'

'I… I told her I'd pay her.'

'Oh Dan, you idiot.' I wanted to cry. That was almost half my annual salary. We couldn't afford it and what made it even worse was that I'd feel like I was working to keep Ella in manicures and shoes.

'Look, leave it with me, Clare. She wants me to drive her to the airport, doesn't want to say goodbye to Jamie – she's going to an audition. Apparently some TV bigwig saw her on Instagram and they want to make her into a star – sounds a bit far-fetched if you ask me.'

So she was sticking with the story? I'd played a trick on her and she was now even turning that around and making it work for her.

'Dan, you can't take her to the airport.'

'I can – I'll get rid of her, tell her to keep quiet or she won't get anything – then put the money in her bank next week when we're home.'

I wanted her on that plane as much as Dan did. But alone in the car she'd tell him what else she knew about the Taylor family, specifically me – and that couldn't happen. She could have told him about me when she accused him of improper behaviour, but she didn't – she wanted to destroy us individually, then leave. Telling Dan about me and Jamie would be her parting shot. Mission accomplished, we'd all be torn apart.

'I could take her?' I said.

'You aren't insured, and you've never driven abroad. To be honest, I'm not sure she'd want you to take her anyway.'

I went cold. 'Me?' I laughed.

'Yeah. Like *you'd* have something to hide.' He shrugged, not believing for a minute that dependable old Clare had ever done anything he didn't know about.

'Yes, she's quite the drama queen, isn't she?' I said and called the kids for lunch.

'Darling, do you have a minute?' Joy asked, as the children and I ate lunch in the kitchen. My heart sank – what did *she* know?

'Okay,' I said, finishing my sandwich.

'I'll be in the sitting room,' she answered.

I couldn't tell from her demeanour if meeting her in the sitting room was a bad thing, or a gin thing. Either way, I wanted to know what she had to say, so, leaving Violet in charge, I went into the next room, where Joy sat in her 1950s-style beachwear.

'I had to get you on your own, dear,' she said, beckoning me in and making a movement with her hand that told me to shut the door.

'What is it?' I sat down in one of the velvet armchairs.

'It's about Ella. And I don't know… what I mean is, I don't know if this is a thing—' Joy braced herself. 'Look, I don't want you to overreact when I tell you this, I want you to be calm…'

'Okay.' All I could think was, *What the hell is she about to tell me?* Could I take any more?

I was glad I was sitting down because by now my legs would have buckled under me.

'When I saw Ella and Dan talking in the garden, I was confused, and intrigued, as you can imagine,' she started. 'And I overheard them talking. Clare, I think she's accusing Dan of something… not very nice.'

I might have known Joy would pick up on this. What could I say? Probably better to hear it from me than Ella, so I told her what Dan had told me about Ella's accusations of impropriety.

'Oh, Clare, Dan wouldn't… I mean that's not our Dan.'

'No,' I said, 'these things are hard to prove – and disprove. I don't think she'll take it further, she's just trying to scare him.' I wasn't surprised at Joy's inability to see any fault in Dan despite his past record, but surely Joy would now see Ella's true colours?

'Oh dear, it looks like you were right all along about her, Clare.'

'I knew, I knew when I saw her taking your earrings,' I said, feeling stronger now Joy was with me and could see Ella for what she was.

'Yes, she's evil – evil.' Joy was understandably quite distressed by all this. 'What has Jamie got himself into? Blackmail and these terrible accusations!'

'She's just stirring it all up, Joy. It's all lies, don't let it upset you,' I said, putting my arm around her. She felt quite frail and seemed on the verge of tears.

'She's said things to me, Clare, and now they make sense.'

'What things?'

'She said to me a couple of days ago that one of my sons has betrayed the other – in the worst way was what she said.' Joy looked at me. 'I think it's this – all this about Dan touching her – disgusting, how could anyone say that?'

I shook my head and covered up my chest with the cushion.

'She said, "Ask Clare," like you'd know.'

I shook my head again and tried to look puzzled, but I knew my neck was probably turning blotchy and giving me away. I stood up and went to get us both a drink from the sideboard, mainly to give me time to think about my response and hide the redness that was no doubt creeping up my décolletage. 'I… I really don't think – I don't know what she's talking about. You can't trust anything she says, Joy,' I said, and poured us both a very large gin. 'We just have to get through today, I think she's getting a flight home tomorrow,' I said, handing her the drink.

'Ahh, good. I popped upstairs to see Jamie last night, check if he really had sunstroke – he's been all over the world and never had sunstroke. So while she was in the kitchen, I went to see him. He seemed upset, said she was talking about joining a reality show or something?'

The reminder of my own hand in all this felt rather uncomfortable.

'Something like that,' I sighed. 'I think she'd have gone anyway – if it wasn't some vague promise of fame, it would have been something else. Ella thought we were super-rich, she thought you and Bob owned this villa and that the "family business" was just a quaint way of describing some global architectural firm. She fell for Jamie, got caught up in the idea of eloping to Italy and knew it would make a great story for her Instagram. It's what she lives for,' I added. 'You have to ask why someone would spend their life trying to lose themselves in foreign places where no one knows her, where she doesn't have to explain. And, from what she told me, I think she's earned her money the hard way, if you know what I mean.'

'Oh, God, a prostitute and a blackmailer—'

'I don't think she was a prostitute,' I said, 'more a romantic tourist. She just finds someone to be "in love with" for a while, lives off them, gets embroiled in their lives for a season and moves on.'

'But she *married* Jamie, why do that if she only saw him as a summer romance?' She looked horrified, and I felt bad for her.

'Men are a career for someone like Ella,' I said. 'She doesn't need money, they're rich, buy her gifts, feed and clothe her and provide somewhere to stay for a while.'

'Oh dear, I knew she wasn't right for him. I never thought it would last. I never said anything to Jamie, but I wasn't very keen, Clare.' The words tumbled out like she'd been holding them in too long. This was the Joy I knew, gossipy and open – willing to trash anyone just for the fun of it over a glass of gin with ice and a slice. 'I've been nice for Jamie's sake,' she continued, 'but have you seen the way she pulls her bikini bottoms up? Disgusting,' she hissed.

'Yes, it's how they're wearing them these days though, Joy,' I said, bonding afresh. She'd finally realised, and I also felt like I'd finally been forgiven for calling her bossy.

'If the ladies at the golf club ever saw her bottom like that I would *die*.'

In the great scheme of things, Ella's bottom was the least of our problems, and in spite of everything, I almost smiled at this.

CHAPTER THIRTY-TWO

That evening, Jamie and Ella said they wouldn't be joining us for dinner, they were going into the village to dine.

'Ella's flying back tomorrow,' Jamie told us sadly. 'She has a great offer of work and we're just taking a step back, working out if we both want the same thing.'

It was clearly his way of telling everyone they were parting. She'd stuck with the story of the reality show, and he'd believed it. I felt sorry for him, but Ella wasn't who he'd thought she was, and in the long-term, she'd have only brought him more pain. I understood them wanting to spend their last night together without the family, but Ella didn't even come into the sitting room to say goodbye. She waited in the hall, then I saw her fleetingly through the window as she and Jamie got into a taxi. All I felt was relief that we didn't have to all sit round pretending everything was fine, with Joy making small talk and Ella making vicious remarks under her breath.

We spent that evening as we had the first few, Joy and I cooking, and eating outside. We were all so relaxed, chatting, remembering past holidays fondly, laughing with the children, just a family on holiday finally able to breathe – with no shadows.

But not for long.

I woke the following morning remembering immediately that today Ella was leaving. I wanted her to go, it made me happier to think she'd be out of our hair, but I was conflicted and felt on edge, because there was still a chance she might tell Dan everything on the journey there. Perhaps they'd already gone? Or had she and Jamie made up and she was staying – both now ensconced in the big white bed making up for lost time?

As the children were still asleep, I wrapped my cotton dressing gown around me, quietly opened the door and headed for Dan's room.

I stepped out onto the landing. As always, I was drawn to the huge floor-to-ceiling window that looked down onto the pool and garden, the sea misty and glittering beyond. It was so high and full you could even see the winding, treacherous road edging the coastline. I thought of the woman from the granita van again and wondered if she was there now, warning people of trouble ahead.

It was then that I looked down onto the pool, my eyes trying to make sense of what I thought I saw in the water. Long hair billowing out, opening and closing slowly like a golden parachute, her body floating on the bright, bright blue.

It was Ella, swimming in the deep end, and my first thought was: *So she lied about not being able to swim too?*

I stood there just watching, trying to make out what she was doing. Then, to my horror, I realised that she *wasn't* swimming, her face was underwater, her legs limp. I don't remember running, but I must have, because seconds later I was in the pool, trying to haul her out and screaming for help.

I was suddenly aware that I wasn't alone. Someone else was with me, desperately trying to pull her to the side – it was Dan. Where had he come from? And as we dragged her to the side, I was suddenly aware of Joy standing there, holding out her arms and yelling at Bob to hurry up. Then Bob appeared, rushing around the pool with some sort of stick.

Dan was now near the edge, propping himself up with one arm and holding Ella with the other, as I held her legs. That's when Jamie appeared, wailing hysterically as he ran towards us, and hurled himself in like he didn't care how he landed. And when he finally got to her he held her in his arms, refusing to believe she was anything but asleep. It was irrational and terrifying to hear him begging her to wake up. Dan was looking from me to Joy, who was extremely distressed, with both hands over her mouth. She was now kneeling down, asking Dan if Ella was still alive. It was all a blur, like it was taking place in slow motion. I remember the weight of water, the sheer brute strength, and the panic, the utter panic, just hoping there was a chance we might save her.

Eventually, between us, we managed to drag her out, but by the way her body slumped onto the tiles, I knew there was little hope. You could see by her skin, she'd been in the water a while.

Jamie was now on the floor, cradling her head, sobbing, kissing her like he might bring her back to life – a fairy tale turned dark. I had to move him away while I tried to give her mouth to mouth. The others stood over us, deathly silent, as I pushed up and down on her chest, blowing into her mouth. I couldn't stop, just kept giving one more push, one more breath, like that might be the difference between life and death, but in my heart I knew, she was long gone.

It was a while before I finally let her go – I think it was Dan who said, 'Stop now. No more, Clare,' and gently pulled me away.

'Bob, call an ambulance,' Joy said without even turning to look at him.

'It's too late for an ambulance. I think we should call the police,' I said, and Bob did as he was told and headed into the house.

Joy, Dan and I stood in a circle around her body, just looking down at her. 'Mate' was all Dan said to Jamie, his hand on his younger brother's back as Jamie sat on the wet tiles, Ella's head still in his arms. Her eyes were wide open, seeing nothing, and yet I felt uncomfortable, like she was looking straight at me. I leaned over her and, with my fingers, gently closed her eyes.

Bob had called the police, then on Joy's instructions had gone to get the kids up and had taken them into the garden to play. We didn't want them to see or know anything at this stage, and as the garden was framed by trees they were unaware of the horror on the other side. Meanwhile, we waited with Ella by the pool, numb, only saying the odd word, trying to string sentences together to try to make sense of what had happened.

'What was she even *doing* in the water? She can't swim,' Joy said, shaking her head, fear etched on her face. 'It's 7 a.m. in the morning, and she's in the pool – but she can't swim,' Joy repeated.

'Yoga,' I said, and they turned to look at me. 'She always did her yoga out here – every morning about six.' Much later when I scrolled through her Instagram I saw her – as always she hadn't missed an opportunity for a selfie. She was smiling into the camera, wearing the same matching scarlet vest and yoga pants she now lay in, her sunlit hair gathered up in a golden topknot.

'Did you *watch* her doing yoga?' Dan asked in front of everyone, like I was some kind of bloody stalker.

'Not *this* morning, and I never *watched* her,' I said defensively, 'but I've seen her other mornings. Sometimes, if I woke early, I'd take my book… and just sit out there, on the terrace. I didn't want to disturb the children. And she was out there.'

'Yeah… she did do yoga in the morning.' Jamie nodded. 'She wouldn't do it by the pool though, she'd be too… scared in case she fell in…' he said, and at this his face crumpled.

'She *was* in the garden,' I said gently. 'She always did yoga in the garden.'

'So how the hell did she end up in the pool? She wouldn't have gone near the water on her own,' he added through tears.

'Perhaps someone else was there?' Dan said, looking at me. I felt a little uncomfortable.

'Perhaps she just decided to try out a new move by the pool?' I suggested. 'It would look good to have the pool in a photo – on her Instagram?'

'Or perhaps,' said Joy, 'and I hate to say this…. But she was upset about something, and…?'

'She wouldn't.' Jamie shook his head. 'She'd never do anything stupid.'

I found it hard to imagine too. Ella was angry with me, and disappointed about the TV offer that didn't exist, but she wasn't suicidal.

'She was upset about leaving me, but we'd talked. I said I'd go and see her wherever they ended up filming. I was upset, I said some things I regret, but I didn't cause this!' He let go of her head and sat back, his arms outstretched.

'No one's saying you did, my darling.' Joy went to hug him, but he pulled away.

Joy touched her chest, no doubt hurting for her son and hurting because she couldn't console him. 'This is all too much, I need to lie down,' she said, slipping a gold lipstick from the pocket of her kimono and giving her lips a slick of hot pink for the arrival of the carabinieri.

While Jamie and Dan argued about whether they should leave Ella's body for the police or move her out of the sun, I walked over to the garden to see Bob and the children. I felt it would be good to explain to Violet and at least offer some explanation to Alfie as to why uniformed men would be arriving soon. I told them something very sad had happened and Ella had fallen in the water and gone to heaven.

'Was she running, Mummy?' Alfie asked. He'd been warned every day not to run by the pool, and saw this as the cardinal sin.

'We don't know, darling, but this is why you must always be sensible around water and not run or be silly.'

'Was Ella being *silly* by the pool, Mummy?' he asked.

'In a way,' I said, shaken by what had happened and finding comfort in the simplistic way my kids viewed life and death.

Violet was clearly confused and upset, and then Alfie started on the questions about heaven – 'What's it like in heaven, Mummy? Will Ella be able to see Thomas the Tank Engine – is he in heaven?' and so it went on.

I suggested Bob go and comfort Joy while I played with the children for a bit, for myself as much as them. I wanted them round me, my little cocoon. I gathered them up and we went inside, where I made breakfast last longer than usual so we could stay in the kitchen while the police arrived. But after a while they were restless. Whatever had happened it was the last day of their holiday, they wanted to play out, and as I'd made it clear the pool was out of the question, I suggested they play in the garden again. I was trying so hard to make everything seem normal that when the police arrived, I was laughing with the kids – something Dan was only too quick to point out to me later. 'I know you didn't like Ella, but you might have shown some respect,' he'd said.

'And we all know how much *you* liked her,' I'd spat back.

A detective arrived with the police and announced this looked like '*omicidio*'.

Joy had quickly assured him in her Italian voice, 'No, dear – no one killed the girl! It must have been *suicidio*.' She'd obviously been on Google Translate. He asked how Ella had seemed when we last saw her and if anything had happened that was out of the ordinary, but we couldn't really offer him anything.

'I actually think it was an accident,' I said. 'She was probably taking a selfie and fell in. She couldn't swim, you see…'

But, as the detective pointed out, her phone had been found in the garden, and 'If she'd been taking a selfie, wouldn't her phone have gone in the water with her?'

Of course it would; stupidly in all the madness I hadn't thought of that. So what happened?

'She'd had this offer of work in TV,' Jamie said dolefully. At this, I felt my heart pounding through my whole body. No one except Ella and I knew the truth about the TV offer. 'She said it would break her heart not to go… I begged her not to – but this was a huge opportunity.' He added, 'I think she was overwhelmed, it messed with her head, she was very fragile.'

'Yes…' Joy nodded in agreement. 'She wasn't in a good place.'

Each word was like a pin jabbing me, reminding me that if I hadn't goaded Ella with that fake Instagram message we probably wouldn't be here now. What an idiot I was. I might as well have pushed her in myself.

'She only ever sat on the edge of the pool, and the other day she fell in and was so distressed…' I told the police. 'But that's why I don't think she killed herself. If she wanted to end her life, she'd have found another way. I think it was some horrible accident.'

A little later, the detective asked us all separately about a possible motive, family dynamics and why we thought she might have killed herself. It gave everyone a chance to speak honestly, without other family members present, and I desperately hoped Jamie wouldn't tell them anything about him and me; it wasn't relevant to her death. Yes, she wanted Jamie to have recognition for Freddie, but I also knew that wasn't why she'd drowned. She was far too vain to kill herself, and even though the TV offer wasn't real, she was moving on, continuing the life she'd led before Jamie, before the Taylors. As I explained to the police, nothing that happened at the villa had any bearing on her death, because none of us really meant anything to her. It had to be an accident – what else could it be?

As I spoke, the detective wrote everything down, just nodding or asking me to repeat what I'd said. I was as honest as I could be, without spilling my own secrets. 'Ella was happy enough. I'm a nurse, I've worked with psychiatric patients, and Ella didn't seem depressed, and I certainly don't think she was suicidal.'

But why the hell was she close to water with no one else around? Ella was self-preserving; she wouldn't have put herself in danger. But if it wasn't suicide or an accident, then I found myself asking who in the Taylor family had a reason to want Ella dead… but then again, who didn't?

CHAPTER THIRTY-THREE

'Your instinct was right,' Dan admitted once the children had gone to bed and we were alone in the garden. 'Ella... she wasn't trustworthy. I'm not saying it's good she's dead. But she'd have cost us a fortune. Not just her shoddy attempt to blackmail me either. And what if they divorced, which, let's face it, would probably have happened sooner rather than later? Like Mum said, Ella was the kind to demand a huge payoff if there was a divorce.'

'Your mum said that?'

'Yeah, and I knew it was a matter of time before she was filing for divorce – and demanding a big payout. Makes me shudder to think what might have happened to the business if she was still...' He didn't finish the sentence, he didn't need to. But I couldn't help but wonder if Dan had more than one good reason to go down to the pool at dawn and push her in.

The heat and tension continued for forty-eight hours, pulsating through the villa as police wandered the beautiful place in big boots and a forensic team arrived. The children were mesmerised and Alfie kept asking his crazy questions loudly: 'Where is Auntie Ella, is she up in the sky yet? I can't see her,' and 'Who's going to heaven next, Mummy?'

It was extremely difficult, with everyone walking round the villa in shock like zombies, and the carabinieri still swarming. They'd checked the pool thoroughly, talked to each of us in broken English and, between us all, we'd tried to give them as much information as we could to help.

I hadn't slept much. I hadn't told them that the TV offer was fake, and it was me, and I was worried this might come back to bite me. The family still didn't know, and I didn't really want them to, it wouldn't help. So I asked the detective if I could have a word with him on my own.

'But we interview you already,' he said; he was shuffling papers on the table outside.

'Yes I know, but... there's something I didn't mention.'

'Okay,' he sighed, and gestured for me to sit down.

Once seated, I waited for him to put down his papers, and eventually he sat back and gestured for me to speak. I took a deep breath and said, 'The TV offer was something I made up.'

He seemed confused and inclined his head like he was trying to understand.

'It wasn't real... the television offer,' I repeated.

He nodded, but I still wasn't sure he really understood.

'The thing is, Ella bought it... she believed a TV show wanted her, but then I told her it was me and she was upset and said she was going away.'

'Upset?'

'Yes, but I still don't think she killed herself, she just needed to lick her wounds and she'd have been fine.'

'Lick his wounds?'

'*Her* wounds. Like an animal? It's a phrase. I just mean she was upset, but she'd have got over it. I mean, she clearly wasn't committed to Jamie – if she was, she wouldn't have said she was single to the fake TV company, would she?'

'No?' He still looked slightly confused. His English wasn't great and my Italian non-existent, so I wasn't sure if he was understanding me. I was rambling, worried that the police might find the messages on her phone and get the wrong idea. But even to someone who spoke English I wasn't making any sense. Nevertheless, I continued with my story.

'She was angry with me, but I don't think it was relevant to her death. I just thought you should know.'

'Angry, you say?'

'Yeah, she was, but then again, she seemed angry with me most of the holiday. We didn't get on… instantly didn't *like* each other,' I added to try to help him understand.

'Ah. Yes… yes, Signora Taylor, she says—' He looked down at his notes. 'You and the *vittima*… er, the victim? You *hate*…'

'Hate is a strong word,' I said. 'Signora Taylor – Joy said that? To you?' I was surprised that Joy had felt the need to mention this.

'Yes, I made the notes. Not to worry.' He waved his hand at me like it didn't matter, but before I could say anything, one of the officers called him away.

I'd now told the police everything and felt much better. It was all so complicated though.

I joined the others for breakfast straight after my interview. It was the last day of our holiday and we were desperate to leave but had to stay until the police had finished. The atmosphere was heavy and tense, and the heat continued to lie like a thick, airless blanket over us all. We tried to be upbeat for the children, but it was hard, and somehow the conversation always returned to Ella. She'd left but was still with us, and because of what happened she'd always be with us now.

It was a strange time of grief, regret and fear, because we didn't *know* what had happened. But, to Joy's delight, Jamie was back in the fold, his attention had now turned back to her and she seemed strangely happy.

In the middle of the sadness, there were bittersweet moments when we ate together, or one of the children made us laugh with something they said, and though it had been a close call, we'd all – like elastic – bounced back together.

'Oh God, what a tragic death,' Joy was saying over dinner one evening. 'Let's just hope that fragile flower is resting in peace.' She gave a little sigh, and touched her eye with her hankie. Fragile flower is not the term I would use to describe Ella – even in death – but at least this way Joy could paint a favourable and more wholesome picture of her deceased daughter-in-law. 'Such a sad life, she had no family, you know, after her sister died. It just makes me think how lucky we are to have each other – we're so strong together,' she reassured us all repeatedly. 'Detective Bianchi – Roberto – said he thinks it's suicide,' she said over a glass of gin 'for the shock'. 'That poor, poor girl.'

'Trust Joy to be on first-name terms with the detective. I bet she charmed the Italian pants off him,' I'd said to Dan later, when we were on our own.

'Mum seems to cope surprisingly well in difficult times. If something bad happens, she always rallies round.'

'You mean like the way she "rallied round", and removed your lover from the company? That was your mother wasn't it, who sacked her?' I said. It may have seemed callous to bring it up then, but I couldn't help it, the words just came out. I was questioning everything and everyone.

'Yeah,' he said awkwardly. And I glimpsed the child, the mummy's boy who was always protected, never wrong, however naughty he'd been.

'Your mum would do *anything* to keep this family together, especially if she sees an outsider as a threat.' I paused. It was something I'd been going over and over in my mind since Ella's death. 'Do you know where she is now… Marilyn, was it?' I said this as if I couldn't quite remember her name, like I hadn't daydreamed of writing it in her own blood.

'I don't think now is the time to get into…' He shifted uncomfortably.

I'd never really questioned it at the time, just grateful that someone else had done the dirty work and I'd seen the back of Marilyn. But I'd begun to wonder if there was more to Marilyn's 'dismissal' from Taylor's.

'I'm not getting *into* anything Dan, I'm not. It's just that, I wonder what your mum… *did* with her?'

'*Did* with her?' He laughed nervously. 'They found some irregularities with the money… we had to let her go.' He stopped and paused for a moment. 'What are you saying, Clare?'

'I don't know.' All I could think was, *What am I missing here?* I kept thinking, if Ella was going to kill herself, it would have been far more aesthetic. She would have worn something other than her yoga gear. She'd have been in a long white dress, *the drowned bride* – not in scarlet Lycra. As a nurse I knew about the demons people battled, and the mental health struggles that could lead to suicide. I'd sat holding the hands of scared, wide-eyed survivors, and grieving families; I knew the horrors of suicide. But this felt so different. Of course, I couldn't know what was going on in Ella's head, but she'd been happy, looking forward to her next adventure. She was just about to move on like she always did.

'Who knows what happened, and perhaps that's *why* she did it, she'd had enough of the whole Instagram life?' he said.

I reckoned that was way off the mark, she lived for it, Instagram was in her DNA, but I kept my thoughts to myself.

'So. Where *is* Marilyn *now*?' I asked gently.

'She moved to Australia. She had family there. But I haven't made contact… We've not been in touch…'

'And has anyone heard from her since she left?' I asked, ignoring his protestations of innocence.

'How would I know? Clare, can we please move on?' he said, clearly feeling some discomfort.

'I'd love to,' I said, 'I'm just not sure that I can.'

*

Later, when we'd put the kids to bed, Dan, Joy, Bob and I all ate leftovers in the kitchen. No one said very much – we were all suddenly like polite strangers passing the butter, commenting on the weather. What had happened was almost too big to talk about; whether it was suicide or something else, it wasn't something that could easily be traversed. Despite it being late evening, it was hot and stuffy, especially in the kitchen where we all sat round the table, thinking our own thoughts. I could feel knots forming in my head and had to get outside to walk around and think.

'I just need to get some air,' I said, promising I'd be back in a little while. No one seemed to stir; they were so wrapped up in their own thoughts and theories, they didn't have the headspace to even acknowledge my departure. So I left them and, stepping into the slightly cooler night air, I saw Jamie sitting alone in the garden.

I stood a little while and watched him. Was it mine and Jamie's relationship that had bothered Ella more than anything else, and that's why she'd hated me so much? I couldn't help but think about another time when I bumped into Jamie in a garden. I wondered how differently things might have turned out if that night years before Dan hadn't been on the phone to Carmel, his lover, and I hadn't run out into the night and bumped into Jamie. Would Ella have behaved differently towards me? Would she still be here now? Perhaps she'd be out here strolling with me now, laughing about the Taylor boys.

Jamie was sitting at the wrought-iron table where Ella had chatted to Dan only a couple of days before.

'Do you mind if I join you?' I asked, but he didn't even look up.

I stood for a moment, not knowing what to do, then tentatively sat down on the edge of the seat.

'How are you, Jamie?'

He didn't answer, so I touched his arm and he just shrugged.

'Jamie,' I said eventually, having plucked up the courage to say something, 'do *you* think it was an accident… or…?'

He turned to look at me, unsmiling. 'I think it was murder.'

'Oh.' I was shocked, I was expecting him to say he thought it was suicide – an accident even – but not murder.

'Like I told the police, she wouldn't kill herself. And she wouldn't have hung out near the pool alone. I think someone pushed her in.'

I didn't answer him; there was nothing I could offer.

'Ella was braver than me,' he sighed. 'She wasn't prepared to hide in the shadows like us. Even though we were breaking up, she was right when she said I needed to find out once and for all if I'm Freddie's dad and then face it head-on. But that's the last thing *you* wanted, wasn't it? What's happened to Ella has made your life a lot easier. I bet you're *glad* she's dead.' He was looking at me with such hate. The eyes that had only ever shown fondness or desire now stung me.

I wasn't glad she was dead as he suggested, but he was right when he said her not being here made my life easier – of course it did. Jamie was the only other person in the world now who knew how much I might have wanted her dead, and why. I couldn't face any more so I got up slowly and walked away.

CHAPTER THIRTY-FOUR

Detective Bianchi finally left with his team and gave us permission to fly home. He said he'd originally thought it could be murder, but without any evidence, it was impossible to suggest anything other than accidental death. He said we may, at some point in the process, be called back to Italy as witnesses, but until then we were all free to return to the UK.

We were all so relieved, we could finally escape from the heat, from each other, and go home.

The day before we flew back, I played in the garden with the kids. We never used the pool again. I avoided Dan. I still wasn't sure if I knew my husband and more than that, I needed time to think. Weirdly, I felt the need to grieve for Ella, the woman who'd made my life hell, and found myself looking over her Instagram, recalling conversations. I felt like a detective trying to fathom what really happened to her, going through the clues again and again and coming up with nothing. When he did make an appearance, Dan looked haunted and I wondered if he might hold the key to what happened, but perhaps he wondered the same of me? We didn't talk much, just skirted around conversations, and played our parts when expected, when the others were around.

Bob drove Jamie to the mortuary where Ella was; her body was being flown back a couple of days later. That evening, over dinner, he told us all that the police in the UK had tracked down her family.

'I didn't realise she had any family,' Joy said, dabbing her mouth with a napkin.

'Yeah. Apparently, Ella's parents are both still alive,' he said in a shaky voice.

We all looked at each other, stunned.

'What the...?' Dan said.

Jamie was, of course, devastated by this, and was desperately trying to understand for his own sanity, I suppose.

Joy and I both tried to comfort him at the table, while Dan put the kids to bed. Bob was washing up, so it gave Jamie a chance to talk. He was distraught, everything he'd believed about his short marriage was crumbling.

'Why did she say they were dead?' he was asking, his head in his hands.

Joy reached out and held her younger son's hand. 'Perhaps they'd all fallen out?' she offered weakly.

Jamie had eventually managed to speak with her parents on the phone, and they confirmed that Ella suffered from fragile mental health. Which made me feel so terribly guilty. I should have known, but I had no idea. If I had, I would have behaved quite differently towards her. But I'm aware that's no excuse and I couldn't forgive myself for the way our relationship had been.

'She seemed to be so strong, so confident,' Jamie said. 'But when you got to know her, she wasn't at all,' he added. 'Her parents said she never got over her sister, she lived with the grief, and they're convinced that's why she killed herself.'

'It makes sense,' Joy sighed. 'I can't imagine how her parents are coping...'

'I wonder if that's why she told us they were both dead,' he said, lifting his head from his hands, 'because seeing them reminded her of her sister and what happened? I just wish she hadn't lied, that she'd told me the truth.'

'Who knows?' I said. 'Sometimes it isn't about telling a lie – it's simply about not telling the truth to protect others.' I knew how that felt and sadly realised a connection with Ella then that I'd never felt during her life.

'She must have had her reasons,' Joy said. 'It seems like her whole life was a mystery really.'

'Yeah even to me. That's what I found so intriguing about Ella – you couldn't really pin her down.' Jamie smiled to himself at some half-remembered moment.

'I still wonder how she made a living just from posting pictures. Did her parents shed any light on that?' Dan asked, as he arrived back at the table.

For a moment, Jamie hesitated, then said, 'Apparently, Ella lived from one man to the next. They paid for everything and she didn't need a job; she just lived her life… guess I was just another one of those men.' I guess the sadness for Jamie was perhaps that Ella hadn't been so open with him as he had with her.

'Oh my God!' Joy clutched her chest and gasped in horror at this. I'd told her it was what I'd suspected, but still, I don't think she could quite get her head around it.

'I wonder if she ever had any feelings for me,' he sighed.

Joy offered a half-hearted, 'Of course she did.' But I couldn't give him any comfort. I had no proof that she'd loved him, and as much as I wanted to ease his suffering, I couldn't lie to him. The fact Ella was prepared to walk out on Jamie so easily once she got my message suggested she hadn't loved him. I wondered if, after her sister's death, she'd even been capable of loving again?

'Mate, she was definitely on the make.' Dan was saying what no one else could. 'I know now isn't the time to be telling you this – but she tried to blackmail me.'

'What?' Jamie paled. 'I can't believe that,' he said, clearly shocked. He really had no idea who his new wife had been, but then who did know Ella? She probably hadn't even known herself.

'Yeah, she tried to say I'd propositioned her, touched her.'

Jamie shook his head in disbelief, and Bob grunted in agreement as he returned from washing up.

'That's enough of that now,' Joy said; it was all becoming a bit unsavoury for Joy. 'Bob's going to pour us all a nice G and T with ice and lemon now, aren't you Bob, and we're going to have an early night before the flight in the morning.'

That was how it was with the Taylors, Joy always taking charge, sweeping any problems under the carpet, but it had worked until now – but perhaps Joy had realised that Ella wouldn't be so easily cajoled?

On the flight back the next day, we must have seemed like any other family returning from holiday, waiting in departures. The kids were tearing around, Joy was sitting in her eye mask (the stress of the last few days had apparently played havoc with her skin), Bob was doing a crossword and Dan and I were bickering about when was best to feed the kids. Meanwhile, poor Jamie just sat quietly, presumably trying to work out what the hell had happened. He'd arrived only days before as a newlywed, and now he was leaving a widower.

Suddenly Violet was pulling at my arm. 'Mum, Mum, we have an emergency!' she said, and I instinctively looked at the double doors that led from Passport Control – I'd had this feeling that Detective Bianchi hadn't quite finished with us all yet.

'What emergency, darling?' I asked.

'I need the toilet.'

I laughed, relieved there were no carabinieri to see us off or otherwise, so, leaving the boys with Dan, us girls went together. And afterwards, as girls do, we had a little wander around duty-free, where Violet sprayed perfume on us both and we looked at the jewellery. Violet said she would have the big diamond ring in the window, but I said I'd opt for the small diamond earrings.

'You could have Granny's,' she said. 'I'm sure she'd let you. Ella doesn't need them now, does she?'

Violet, at only nine years old, obviously hadn't been privy to what really happened, so was clearly confused at the snatches of conversation she'd overheard.

'I think Granny has them,' I said, knowing Joy had got them back.

'No, no, she gave them to Ella.' Violet was shaking her head vigorously.

'Why do you say that?' I asked, my heart beating like a drum.

'Because I was there, I was playing hide-and-seek with Alfie. I was hiding behind the sofa and they came in and Granny said, "Ella, I want you to have my diamond earrings for your wedding present, but don't tell Clare. Just go and get them and hide them in your jewellery box *darling*,"' she said in Joy's voice. So Ella had told the truth… she hadn't stolen the earrings after all.

CHAPTER THIRTY-FIVE

Now

I remember the details so clearly. The way she smelled of salt and lemons. The way her skin shone gold, and the way she laughed, throwing back her head, white teeth bared, mouth open, lost in the moment. Only now, a year later, can I grieve for the young woman who came into our lives so briefly, and whose truth we tried to grasp like a silver fish, slipping from our hands.

Now, away from that pressure cooker of last summer, I can see that perhaps she wasn't who I'd thought she was. I'd maybe pinned some of my mistrust, my vulnerability, my fears onto this stranger, when really she was just protecting herself, travelling the world alone, lost without her sister. It was other people who lied, who manipulated; they were the ones who wanted to save themselves, and if that meant hurting me, then so be it.

In the year since our ill-fated holiday, I have realised a lot of things. That the Taylors aren't as perfect – or as kind and inclusive – as I'd believed. And Joy isn't the benign dowager that she pretends to be; I should have known when she organised my honeymoon, removed the other woman and convinced me to stay in a marriage that was killing me. I also realised in the heat and secrets that my marriage hadn't withstood the storm of Dan's infidelities, and I was living on the edge, not knowing, not trusting, always looking over my shoulder. I'd known in my heart all along, but recently, it's been staring me in the face, and I can't live the rest of my life feeling like that.

Jamie didn't, in the end, join the business – he did what he always does and took a flight to somewhere far away and hid for a few months. It was understandable really. His new wife had died, he was hardly going to turn up for work on the Monday morning rubbing his hands together and asking 'Where do we start?' But, surprisingly, Bob really did abdicate all responsibility, and Dan was left completely in charge of the business. But it seems that last summer had affected us all, and Dan didn't have the same energy and enthusiasm for work he'd had before. He seemed to take time off, go AWOL for hours in the evenings when he said he was working late – and I wondered if he'd met someone again.

I asked him gently, I asked him angrily, and when that didn't work, I found myself checking his phone, hacking into his emails, becoming someone I never wanted to be. I questioned his keenness to finish work early to pick Violet up from school – something he'd never expressed an interest in before. And when he started quoting Miss Thomas, Violet's teacher, I knew. It was like a half-remembered song. I couldn't recall the words, but I knew the tune and it made me sad, reigniting past hurt. I didn't want to spend the rest of my life feeling this, never being able to rest, threats waiting around every corner. The trust had gone, and when there's no trust, there's really nothing left.

I told Joy, and said I wasn't sticking around this time, I was filing for divorce, but she told me I was making a mistake, offered to go to the headmistress at the school and have Miss Thomas sacked.

'You don't get it, do you, Joy?' I said. 'It isn't about a flight attendant who served him beer, or the pretty accountant at work, or even Miss Thomas – it's *Dan*. Your son isn't who you think he is, who you pretend he is.'

'Darling, I'm not stupid, you're right of course – but boys will be boys,' was all she said, and I knew in that instant that she'd withdrawn her support. I was leaving the Taylors, and so the Taylors were leaving me.

I can see now that Ella and I were both victims, both outsiders in this family who would only ever support each other when it came right down to it. Joy was fine when you were with her, on her side, in her family, but when she saw a threat, she played her hand. In her own, subtle way she came between us. *'Do you like Clare, Ella? I worry she's a little fragile… on the defensive at the moment, especially with someone as attractive as you.'* She was setting the scene, suggesting there may be a problem and giving Ella the diamond earrings I'd always admired, knowing it would hurt me and perhaps even cause some resentment. Joy couldn't know that I'd see Ella 'stealing' them and cause such conflict, such hurt. I realise now that Joy was using me to fire the bullets while appearing to stand back – I was the idiot who made Ella's life hell for two weeks. But Joy was using the two of us like puppets. Ella was no angel, she could be dishonest, mean, self-obsessed, evidently used her lovers' money to survive. God knows what she wanted with Jamie, he wasn't some yacht-owning millionaire with a palace somewhere, so unless she actually loved him, I can't imagine why she married him. I don't suppose I'll ever know what her motives were for coming into his life, but ultimately she was a pawn too.

As for Jamie, he's okay, and we are finally talking again. When he returned last Christmas, he hugged me as usual and it was like nothing had happened – everything just slotted back into place. Jamie's never said anything again about wanting to be Freddie's dad, he's just been happy to see him like he has the others. I want us to be friends. I feel like we all went through such an ordeal last summer. I want to talk about it, and so does Jamie. Both Joy and Dan don't have that need, they've moved on, for them it was in the past and they don't want to go there – 'Don't dwell on it, dear,' is Joy's usual response if I try to talk about it. For Dan, it's probably too painful; after Ella's accusations he was so hurt he never really talked about what happened. But whether his hurt was at being innocent or being robbed of his next fling, I don't know.

Jamie came home from Thailand last week, and he called in to see me, which was nice. I was having a rare morning off and he happened to be passing. I made us coffee and we sat in the living room, chatting, while watching Freddie play with his toys.

'This is nice, just like old times,' I said, and after more talk about where he'd been and where he planned to go next, I went deeper. 'How are you *really*?' I asked. 'Have you been able to move on… a little?'

'Yeah. I guess. I still keep in touch with her parents.' He smiled fondly at this.

'I didn't realise.'

'Well, I haven't mentioned it – don't think Mum would approve, you know how she is.'

'Yes, she wants to forget it all, pretend it never happened.'

'I do too. I went away hoping to forget, but I can't, and her parents are the only link – it's like she never existed.'

'Do you still look at her Instagram?'

'I can't. It would be like looking into the past, when we were happy, the wedding photos – everything.' He shook his head, his eyes red with threatened tears. 'No… perhaps one day?' He tried to smile.

I look sometimes. It's weird that the account still exists and she doesn't; her fantasy life outlived her. I suppose it's like a headstone for the twenty-first century: 'Ella was here'. Our online lives are our immortality. I think she'd like that.

When she died, the *Manchester Evening News* did a big article all about her detailing the sadness of the new bride who couldn't bear to live.

'How are her parents?' I asked.

'Devastated. They still hadn't got over her sister's death.'

I recalled their grey faces at the funeral. We spoke briefly, offered our condolences, but this poor couple who'd lost both their children were inconsolable. 'Losing both daughters…' I shook my head, unable to imagine it.

'They said they couldn't rest when Ella's sister was flying, and with Ella, they worried about her travelling everywhere – they didn't hear from her for months.'

'Flying?'

'Yeah. Carmel was a flight attendant. She sounds just like Ella, a free spirit,' he said wistfully.

I tried to smile in acknowledgement of this, but my mind was only focussing on one piece of information – *Carmel loved being a flight attendant.*

There must be more than one flight attendant called Carmel, from Manchester… mustn't there?

'What happened… to Carmel?' I asked.

'She was depressed, something to do with a man… he was married, said he'd leave his wife, but he didn't and when he finished it, she lost it for a while. Her mum said she couldn't get over it, she kept trying to get in touch with him, but he didn't pick up, changed his number. She became obsessed for a while, even called him at home, but his wife was pregnant, said she knew all about it. She told her he'd never any intention of leaving her for Carmel. She said if Carmel contacted them again they'd call the police. Thing is, he never told Carmel he was married, and that was it for her, she felt like she'd nothing to live for. Imagine feeling like that? God, she must have been so broken. In the end, she took her own life.'

CHAPTER THIRTY-SIX

Hearing about Ella's sister was like a bomb going off in my head. Even though I kept telling myself this had to be a coincidence, I knew it wasn't. In effect, I'd been the one to land the final blow to Carmel. No wonder Ella hated me, she must have known. She was out for revenge. She didn't 'bump into' Jamie in a bar in Manchester, she knew him online, she'd seen his posts, she knew he was Dan's brother and she could get to Dan (and me) through him. Marrying Jamie was extreme, but I think Ella was a woman of extremes; she partied hard, she travelled all over the world and she could do anything she wanted. She wasn't just a free spirit, she was a restless spirit and she had decided to avenge her sister's death, but it had all gone horribly wrong.

For the next couple of days I kept my theories and the information to myself. I didn't even tell Dan at first, I just wanted time to work it out. I also wondered at the implications – did Dan know that Carmel was Ella's sister?

Over the past year, I've felt the fabric of our marriage tearing further apart, and this recent affair with Miss Thomas has ripped the last few threads. But every cloud and all that – because in a way it's also completely freed me – I don't rely on Dan for my sunshine, or my shadows, any more. We live in the same house, we share our children while we're waiting for the divorce to be finalised. And I'm fine, looking forward to a new adventure having extricated Dan from my heart and my head.

On the evening after Jamie's visit last week, Dan and I sat down to a last supper together to discuss finances now the house has been sold. We talked about the new, smaller house I'll share with the kids, while Dan will be renting a flat nearby so he can see them.

'Are you sure this is what you want?' he said. I assured him for the hundredth time it was.

'It was never the same for us after last summer,' he sighed, pouring himself a glass of wine.

'It was way before that, Dan.' I looked at him doubtfully.

'Oh, they meant nothing, you knew that.'

'No I didn't, and they may not have meant anything to you, but they meant a lot to me. They broke up my marriage – well you did.'

'You really won't take any responsibility, will you?' he said, slowly shaking his head and looking at me. It was moments like this that made me strong, and reminded me why I was uprooting the kids, breaking up the home.

'Do I take responsibility? Do *you*?' I paused for a moment. 'Do you ever feel any guilt about her death… Ella I mean?'

His forehead creased and he looked angry. 'No. And why should I? She could have ruined me.'

'Yeah, but I still wonder why she made those accusations.'

'Because she was toxic,' he sighed.

'Or wanted to hurt you, hurt us?'

'Look, Clare, I'm tired. Now, you might enjoy going over this, but I don't. Working out the psyche of a madwoman isn't on my to-do list, so let's leave it, eh?' His anger was still fresh, alive, it hadn't subsided. He stabbed at the broccoli spears on his plate, then looked up, saw me watching him. 'What? I just want to forget she ever existed.'

'Like Carmel?'

He threw down his fork. 'Who? Oh God, her? We're getting divorced Clare, why are you still clinging to this? You still can't let it go, can you?'

'Unlike you,' I said. 'You can walk away from anything, anyone, and leave them behind. You're all the same, you Taylors, you move on when you don't like the view.'

'Well it's a good job we're parting and you don't have to put up with us any more. You won't be a Taylor either – bet you're glad about that.'

'Did you know that Carmel took her own life?' I said, ignoring his childish comments.

'I heard… something,' he muttered, going back to his broccoli. 'You never mentioned it.'

'Why would I? It was years ago, why would I bring it up?'

'How did you hear…. that she died?'

'I don't know – someone called me, found my name and number in her phone.'

'Who?'

'God, Clare!' His face was red with anger or something.

'Please, it's important. Was it her sister who called you?'

'It might have been… yes, yes, I think it probably was.'

'Ella?'

'What the hell are you going on about?'

'Did her sister say it was your fault?'

He shrugged. 'Her sister screamed down the phone at me, called me a murderer – I just turned off the phone, you can't deal with people like that.'

'Well, you can, if you have any compassion, or any sense of responsibility – but you don't, do you?'

'It was nothing to do with me!' he said, his voice raised, anger bubbling just under the surface.

'It had everything to do with you,' I said.

Abandoning his supper, he stood up and walked to the other side of the kitchen and leaned on the countertop, as far away from me as possible. 'I told you, it wasn't my fault. You know what she was like, stalking me, calling at all hours, she drove me to distraction!'

'Then she called you at home and I answered. We never heard from her again.'

'Good.'

'No, not "good". She was devastated. A young woman you'd promised everything to killed herself because of you – because of us. And it's about time you knew this. Ella was her sister.'

He seemed genuinely shocked; he walked back to the table and plonked himself down on the chair. 'Carmel and Ella – sisters?'

I nodded. 'You really didn't know?'

'I swear I didn't.'

I wasn't sure I believed him. Wasn't sure I could ever believe anything he said ever again.

CHAPTER THIRTY-SEVEN

Over the next couple of days I kept thinking about Ella and Carmel, and felt the need to reach out to their parents. I wanted to acknowledge their daughter's death and recognise that a year had now passed since they lost her. Now time had moved on, I hoped it might help them to talk to someone who was there during her last few days.

I got their number from Jamie. I didn't think it was worth telling him everything just yet; he'd already had his heart broken and was doubting she had loved him at all. This information about her sister that Dan and I had buried would confirm all his fears, that Ella was with him for reasons other than love.

So I called Mrs Bailey, who seemed almost pleased to hear from me. 'Call me Sheila,' she said, and asked so many questions about what happened on the day.

'Jamie told us you tried really hard to bring her back, love – me and Robert are very grateful,' she said.

I felt like a fraud; we'd been enemies in life, and yet Ella's death changed all that for me. It had taken me a year to come to terms with what happened, to understand why she did what she did – and how she was a victim too.

Sheila went on to talk me through both her daughters' lives, and I listened, then asked all the relevant questions gently. This was definitely the same Carmel who Dan promised everything to; she was young, fragile and her heart and mind was broken.

'Our Ella never got over losing her sister,' Sheila sighed. 'She threatened to go round to his house and kill him. Me and Robert managed to convince her that wasn't the way. But she lived with all that grief and anger inside her, and it was inevitable, I suppose.'

'Do you know the man, the name of the man that Carmel was with?' I asked, holding my breath.

'No, she never told us. I think Ella knew, but we never asked. I think it best we don't know.'

I did too. What I'd said to Carmel when she called our home was from Joy's script, but I take full responsibility. I told her I was pregnant and we were happy – when in truth, I'd never been so unhappy, and the baby probably wasn't even Dan's. What lies I told her that day, setting off a chain reaction that had led to the death of two sisters. Sisters who would have had their whole lives ahead of them if it wasn't for the Taylors – and me.

*

Yesterday, I was invited to an afternoon tea at Joy's. She's keen to keep me on side, and insists that we must stay friends even though I'm divorcing her son.

'It doesn't affect our relationship,' she said, and I'm grateful. It's important that the children have access to their grandparents, and anyway I want to be able to call her up if I need help with childcare, or advice.

The afternoon would no doubt involve tiny amounts of food, and huge portions of gossip, and though it wasn't my scene I know she wanted me there to keep up appearances. She wanted her friends to see how civilised her family was – even in the throes of divorce we could take tea together.

I arrived early with home-made chocolate cake; the kids had had a hand in it and I wasn't convinced that the explosion of smarties and handprints on the top would earn it a spot on Joy's table. But

I'd tell the kids it had pride of place and any uneaten cake would be sent home for them anyway, along with all other leftovers. Joy had to keep an eye on her weight – God forbid she ever rose above a size ten.

'Joy, I came early because I wanted a quick chat,' I said, as she busied herself with the best china on the dining room table which she'd had Bob move into the conservatory.

'Lovely, dear,' she said, with barely concealed disgust as I handed her the messy cake.

'So, can we talk?'

'Of course,' she said. Clearly whatever I had to say couldn't possibly be as important as her afternoon tea, so she continued to faff.

'It's about Ella.'

She almost dropped a teacup and, holding it to her chest, turned quickly to me. 'What *about* her?'

'Do you know anything about her family?' I asked.

'No, only that one minute she didn't have parents, the next she did,' she said spikily, wiping a cream jug with a tea cloth. 'Bob really doesn't know how to wash up,' she muttered.

'Do you remember Ella mentioning her sister?' I pressed.

'Oh, the one who walked into the sea? Yes, I remember, but, mind you, we never knew what was real with Ella, did we?'

I didn't respond. Joy was trying to get me on side and suddenly happy to gossip about Ella, but in Amalfi she'd sided with her, and put obstacles in the way of any friendship we may have had.

'Remember Carmel, the first girl that Dan had the affair with?' I continued.

'Oh darling, you're not going over all that again, are you?' She stopped what she was doing to look at me with a pained expression.

'No,' I said assertively, 'I found out that Carmel was Ella's sister.'

'No!' she said, then stood a moment, fork in hand. She seemed flustered, but continued to lay her cake forks in a neat line on the napkins. 'Are you sure?'

I explained that Ella and Carmel's mother had confirmed they were sisters and also said that Ella was filled with anger.

'She wanted revenge,' I said. 'She hated Dan – and me of course, and wanted us to pay for what happened. It's a shame that Jamie was a casualty – and you too, but she hated the Taylors.'

'Revenge and hate are very strong words, dear. I think she must have just resented how close we are, what a happy family unit we've created. She could never have come between us though. That's probably why she gave up,' she said, continuing to bustle at the table.

'No, it wasn't that, Joy,' I said. 'Apparently she resented the fact Dan still had a family, a sibling and a happy marriage, when, because of him, she'd lost hers.'

'I sensed the anger. She was a very dangerous girl, leading our Jamie up the garden path, saying those things about our Dan.' She went pink with anger, just like Dan had when I told him. She hadn't really heard what I'd said, wasn't prepared to take on anyone else's pain, just hers and Jamie's and Dan's. And it struck me – Dan's actions and then Joy's need to protect him had caused this.

But she hadn't even acknowledged what I'd said regarding the two dead women – all she cared about was herself and her precious family.

CHAPTER THIRTY-EIGHT

I couldn't believe Joy wasn't moved by the news that Carmel took her life because of Dan. I even went on to describe Ella's mother's faltering voice on the phone. I asked her to imagine how it must feel for a mother to lose two children.

'Oh I know. Terrible business,' she sighed. 'Darling, could you just pass me the sugar spoons, the tiny ones over there, so much nicer than big teaspoons, don't you think?'

The ladies arrived, and Joy greeted them like she was the queen. They were all like her – silk scarves, fake smiles. I don't know why, but I sat through an hour of tittle-tattle and macarons until I couldn't take any more and offered to clear the table.

I smiled calmly, gathered some of the lipstick-marked teacups and took them into the kitchen, where I plonked them down, leaned against the kitchen oasis and took a big, deep breath.

'Oh, so you've escaped?' a voice said in the corner.

I jumped, but it was only Bob, calmly stacking plates into the dishwasher.

'Oh, it's all too much,' I said, glad to have someone, anyone to talk to.

'How about a nice mug of tea?' he said, and I wanted to hug him.

'That would be lovely. I've had enough fine china this afternoon to last a lifetime!'

He laughed. 'Joy loves her fancy crockery – that china was a wedding present from an aunt of mine, cost an arm and a leg. "We can't ask for that," I said, "it's too much money," but you know Joy, she put it on the gift list and she got it.'

'Mmm, Joy always gets just what she wants,' I said, with a smile.

'Yes, she can be quite… strong-willed, our Joy.'

I smiled in acknowledgement of this.

'I know she can be a bit prickly sometimes,' he said, like an apology. 'But it's been a difficult year for her – since Jamie and Ella… and everything. She's worried about you and Dan now – thinks you might take the children and live somewhere else and we won't see them.'

'I would never do that, Bob.'

He looked down at me kindly. 'That's good news.' 'I know our Dan, he's got a roving eye, but none of them mean anything – you were always his real love, wife, the mother of his children.'

A roving eye? So that's how Joy and Bob were packaging their son's infidelity now?

'And that awful stuff with Ella. It really upset Joy to hear she'd said those things about Dan touching her. Like he said to me, "Dad, I only put my arm around her waist, might have accidentally touched her bum," and off she goes saying all kinds of things. The world's gone mad, Clare – and our Dan said she'd been giving him the come-on all holiday, then got all funny and said she was going to the police. It's all that '*me too*,' stuff it's turned women's heads. Political correctness gone mad, Clare.'

I couldn't even find the words to respond to what he'd just said This was the other side of Bob I'd only glimpsed before, the part of him that smoked cigars round the back of the house, and ruined his appetite with contraband biscuits before a meal. This Bob was only unleashed when Joy wasn't around to reprimand, or correct him.

Then he said, 'But seriously, love, at the end of the day, even if you two aren't together it still has to be about family. No one else matters – as long as the family are okay, that's what Joy always says – and she's right.'

'Family *is* important,' I conceded. 'I just think that she might take it too far sometimes, protecting the family at all costs,' I added, thinking of Dan and the way she dismissed the women he'd hurt like it was their own fault and none of the responsibility was his.

'But at the end it's all we've got, isn't it, Clare, our family? Joy once told me that if anything happened to our boys, her life would be over. "We have to keep them safe, Bob," she said. "Whatever it takes…"'

I felt the hair on my arms prickle and suddenly reality hit. I watched him pottering around the beautiful kitchen built on his sweat and Joy's specifications.

'Ella didn't commit suicide, did she?' I heard myself say into the silence.

He looked at me as he closed a cupboard door, folded a tea towel and eventually Bob shook his head, very slowly. 'Ella was causing problems for our Dan,' he said, taking a breath. 'She wasn't right for our Jamie, for the family.' He refolded the tea towel a second time slowly so he didn't have to look me in the eye. 'I tried to reason with her, Clare, but she wouldn't listen, said she'd ruin us all; well, we couldn't have that, it's not fair on Joy, the boys, you must understand. You won't tell anyone, will you? Joy, she'd be so upset if she thought I'd—' he started, and I saw tears in his eyes.

I couldn't get my breath. After a year of wondering what happened, of trying to work out Ella's death, this had never been a scenario I'd ever considered. Bob, the quiet one, the ineffectual washer upper in the background who lived to please Joy and keep her happy.

'Bob, you can't ask that of me. This is a woman's life we're talking about, not some slight misdemeanour…'

'But Joy – she'd never forgive me.'

'You can't hide this forever.'

'I have to. If she found out she'd leave me, and I couldn't bear that, Clare, please. My job is to protect Joy and the boys. "Keep them safe, Bob," she says… "We have to keep them safe." That's why I had to deal with Ella, she was dangerous, not just to our boys – to all of us. She was messing our Jamie around, saying Dan touched her *and* she was going to tell everyone about you and Jamie and—'

'You know about me and Jamie?'

He nodded. 'Oh yes. I've known for a long time. Our Jamie always had a soft spot for you – oh, it would never have come to anything, he just wanted what Dan had, always did. That night when you two… we were having our crafty cigars and I saw the way he looked at you in the garden. I blame Joy, she used to buy them the same toys when they were kids—' He chuckled to himself. 'Anyway, I went to bed, left you and Jamie in the garden, then later, much later, Joy sent me downstairs for a glass to put her water in, you know she'll only drink from certain glasses?'

'Yes,' I said, feeling sick.

'I heard you both in the living room, it didn't take Columbo to work out what you two were up to.' He laughed at his own rather lame joke.

'Does Joy know… about me and Jamie?'

'No. It would break her bloody heart, she adores our boys and the idea that one of them… with the other one's wife… And, like me, it won't take her long to do the maths. To think that one of Dan's children could be Jamie's! Imagine?' He leaned on the kitchen counter, turning pale at the prospect. 'I thought we'd managed to avoid the truth coming out but then Ella turned up in Italy. We were sitting by the pool one day,' he continued, 'and I heard Jamie telling you that he and Ella wanted custody of Freddie, that she was going to tell everyone. Then there was the stuff she was saying about Dan – Joy told me… and I couldn't bear it. All that upset, Clare. It was too much. Joy's heart couldn't take it.'

'So you…?'

'She was just there, in the garden, doing her yoga. I called her over to the pool. I just did what I *had* to, Clare – I kept us all safe.' He was putting two teabags into fresh mugs and he looked at me. For a moment, he had that vague look on his face that he often had when he was confused, or appearing to be confused. Then he gave me a little smile. 'Now, you and I both know each other's secrets. If you don't tell mine, then I won't tell yours.' He gave me a wink as he put a mug of tea down in front of me.

EPILOGUE

I'm standing in the sitting room waiting for Dan to come home. The big window is filled with the golden autumn. Frilly leaves of every hue fill the frame like a giant painting. I'll be sad to leave here.

I pull my cardigan around my shoulders in the chill; like the summer heat happened to someone else, the pressure cooker of last summer is so far away. And tonight I'm going to push it even further.

I've asked Joy to look after the children because it's time Dan and I talked.

'Ooh, date night?' she asked, eager eyes, those hot pink lips pursed with hope. 'Are you two having second thoughts about the divorce? I hope so. I'm so glad you've seen sense, darling.'

'Well, I've come to my senses at last,' I'd said, smiling.

Her delight was clear to see. 'Good girl,' she said, like I was five years old. This was the Clare she knew and loved. I was sticking it out, ignoring the 'dalliance' and standing by my man. Joy thought she had us all back under her control and, most importantly, next summer's family holiday could now be booked.

How could his mother even think I would contemplate staying with Dan? As if I needed any more encouragement to continue with this divorce, I hear that Marilyn's back from Australia and she and Dan are back in touch. A friend of mine saw them in a restaurant in Manchester, and apparently they are still 'very close'. I wasn't remotely affected by this news, not a twinge of jealousy or regret – all I thought was, 'at least she's alive'. I just hope she stays that way, because we don't all survive the Taylors.

So tonight, on what Joy assumes is 'date night', over a candlelit supper in a nearby restaurant, I am going to tell my soon-to-be-divorced husband about me and his brother. I'll point out that our youngest child might not be his and also tell him that his own father is trying to blackmail me into keeping his own secret. Then I'll tell him how Ella died, and that I'm going to call the police.

I have no idea how Dan will take all this, and I'm not sure I care, I just want the lies to stop. His mother filled his head with too much stardust, too much self-esteem, and allowed her sons to live without consequences. She was always there to chopper them out of difficult situations, and remove people who caused problems. Only, this time, without her knowledge, Bob had gone one step further.

And now, I'm glad to escape from this toxic life of lies and secrets and selfish people who don't really care about anyone but themselves. Perhaps they aren't even capable of love. We'll see when the truth comes out and Joy's love for Bob is tested.

The Taylors seemed to want me never to trust anyone but them. But I am learning the only person I can trust is myself, and I know I can teach my children to trust and be trusted – and to never keep secrets from the people they love. My family are Violet, Alfie and Freddie and I intend to keep them very safe, and very close.

Last summer my sister-in-law turned up and my life changed. Then I saw Ella as the enemy, when, in truth, she could have been an ally. But, although she's not around to see it, I will help her achieve what she wanted. I will bring down the Taylors and get her and Carmel the justice they deserve. In another time, another place, we could have been sisters-in-law but also friends; sadly the Taylors ruined that, as they'd ruined so much, but not any more. I let Ella down badly but I won't let her down again. In the end we can't rely on anyone but ourselves, Ella knew that, but in the end she couldn't help herself. So now it's up to me to do it for all of us: me, Carmel, Marilyn and Ella – my sister-in-law, who *always* finds me. No matter how far I run, I know she will always be there. With the flap of a butterfly's wing, she invited the hurricane, stirring up the sediment at the bottom of the stagnant pool, ripping open the secrets that held us all together. But in doing that she showed me what I must do to live the life I deserve.

After tonight there will be no more hiding, no more secrets, and no more lies. If there's a hurricane building, I'm ready to face that storm.

A LETTER FROM SUE

I do hope you've enjoyed reading *The Sister-in-Law*. If you did enjoy it, and want to keep up-to-date with all my latest releases, just sign up at the following link. Your email address will never be shared and you can unsubscribe at any time.

www.bookouture.com/sue-watson

These are uncertain times, and when you read this, who knows what will be happening in the world? I just hope that this story can take you away just for a little while, to another time and another place where we could meet with friends, hug our ageing parents and enjoy a family holiday. We may not have realised how lucky we were to have those simple pleasures, and my guess is we'll never take them for granted ever again. Let's look forward to their return, and in the meantime, stay safe.

This novel was partly inspired by the recent real-life drama in the British Royal Family when Meghan Markle arrived – and left! It made me wonder about what happens when a stranger suddenly becomes a relative, and how one person can impact on a once tight family circle. While researching this book I talked to lots of different people with varying family perspectives, and discovered that the closest families can still be fragile, vulnerable. And introduce someone new into the unit and dynamics change, allegiances break, secrets are spilled – and people get hurt.

I've really enjoyed writing this book, and hope you enjoyed reading it. If you did, I would be very grateful if you could write a review. I'd love to hear what you think, and it makes such a difference helping new readers to discover one of my books for the first time.

I also love hearing from my readers, so do get in touch. I'd love to see you on Facebook become a friend, like my page or come for a chat on Twitter.

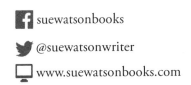

suewatsonbooks

@suewatsonwriter

www.suewatsonbooks.com

ACKNOWLEDGEMENTS

As always, my thanks to the wonderful team at Bookouture, who give so much to each and every book.

Thanks to my editor Isobel Akenhead, for coming up with the killer while sorting through my forest of words, seeing the wood for the trees, smoothing the knots in the plot – and banning my mixed metaphors! And to copyeditor Jade Craddock for providing that extra polish.

Thanks to Kim Nash and Noelle Holten for their hard work in getting my books out there and to Sarah Hardy for reading this at an early stage, and providing invaluable insight.

Thanks to my family and friends for their continued love and support, and for always telling me 'you've got this' even when I haven't!